AMERICAN VALUES

A Novel by

JIM WILLIAMS

Also by Jim Williams

Irina's Story

The Sadness of Angels

The Demented Lady Detectives' Club

The English Lady Murderers' Society

Tango in Madeira

The Argentinian Virgin

The Strange Death of a Romantic

Recherché

Scherzo

Anti-Soviet Activities

Farewell to Russia

The Hitler Diaries

Print edition 2017

Licensed by Marble City Publishing

Copyright © 2017 Jim Williams

ISBN-10 1-908943-85-8

ISBN-13 978-1-908943-85-9

Praise for Jim Williams' books

Farewell to Russia

"There are going to be very few novels of any kind that are as well written. Totally authentic. Totally readable. Far too good to miss." *Ted Allbeury*

The Hitler Diaries

"…steadily builds up an impressive atmosphere of menace." *Times Literary Supplement*

"…well written and full of suspense." *Glasgow Herald*

Last Judgement

"…the author journalists read for their next scoop." *Sunday Telegraph*

Scherzo

"Sparkling and utterly charming. Devilishly clever plot and deceitful finale." *Frances Fyfield – Mail on Sunday*

Recherché

"A skilful exercise, bizarre and dangerous in a lineage that includes Fowles' *The Magus*." *Guardian*

The Strange Death of a Romantic

"This is an extraordinarily witty and assured novel." *T J Binyon – Evening Standard*

"…seriously good…technically brilliant…constantly suggestive… dreamy but sinister glamour." *Times Literary Supplement*

ARROYO SECO

1

Everyone knows there are no blacks in Washington. Yet there he was in Pennsylvania Avenue no less, on the corner of Ninth opposite the Department of Justice that everyone called the Hoover Building, except the Attorney General, who had his office there and liked to think of himself as Hoover's boss but was mistaken. As proud as Lucifer he looked in his dove grey roll brim hat, green and purple check jacket, painted tie, crimson vest spread across a paunch festooned with a gold fob, pleated pants the color of fresh peas, and tan and white two-tones. I see him now, shining with the sparkle of someone who knows he has style even if the ensemble has been put together from ready-to-wear and thrift stores. He carries the thing with the dignity of a man in Papal robes, with the touched by God assurance of someone who knows he is going to Heaven. Not the smooth arrogance of the tele-evangelist but the gravitas of a man who has contemplated crucifixion and decided he can bear it even if it's the last thing he seeks.

I admired him. Or, at least, I admired the man who presented himself to my imagination. The reality was some other place beyond my vision, with the people who exist behind the surface of Renaissance portraits that show us the divine spark within the humble tailor painted by Moroni or the whores who stand in for the Virgin because they are available and cheap. The real person – if we assume such a creature exists – was, I would guess, the same moral mediocrity as the rest of us, but today, for some reason I would never know, the old black man had decided to show himself on the corner of Ninth and Pennsylvania and invite Pilate and the High Priest to take him if they chose.

'Would ya look at that!' said a voice. A regular blue cop, standing with his partner, doing nothing in particular except keeping an eye out for Mexicans without even knowing he was doing it because it was part of his reflexes.

'Don't get excited,' Jeb Lyman said calmly to the cop. 'Look at the medal,' and, when the cop did, said, 'What did you think? That he could walk on water?'

Like me he'd seen the National Medal of Merit pinned discreetly to the lapel of the old guy's check jacket. He probably carried the citation folded inside his pocket. So not entirely a mediocrity. Rather a once in a lifetime hero, who in a moment of thoughtlessness had saved a child from a fire or helped his neighbor during a flood. Or – and I didn't care to think this because I liked him – he was someone who'd sold out his own at the time of the Resettlements when his brothers and sisters went South, and so earned himself the right to stay behind for a season. Except that most of those who'd taken that option had been pulled out of the Potomac over the years and these days were even rarer than genuine heroes.

The cop spotted the medal and it annoyed him, so he turned on Jeb and snapped, 'Who the hell are you to be telling me my business?' This to a well-made man in a hat and a sharp suit standing on the sidewalk outside the Hoover Building. His friend nudged him, but Jeb flipped his badge anyway and said nothing because silent politeness is the best way of dealing with morons.

'Why did you want to see me?' Jeb asked, taking up the conversation from before we were distracted.

'A story I heard, that's all.'

'Who are you?' the cop asked me, going for broke. 'You're not an American.'

'He's with me,' Jeb said.

'I'm English,' I said and reached for my journalist's credentials but Jeb stayed my hand.

The cop had the guts of the truly insane to whom pride is everything even though it leaks into the air with every word he speaks. He was still game to roust me for something and even fight his friend if he tried to stop the action. But he also had the attention span of a gnat and his eye was caught by the sight of a truck of indentured Mexican workers. I guessed they were construction crew repairing the Triumphal Arch that had been built a couple of years before to celebrate Victory on the occasion of the President's seventy-first birthday and seventh term of office but like everything else in this country was falling apart because of the war shortages. The truck was stuck in traffic and the Mexicans were shouting abuse in Spanish and rattling their chains. The guard bulls were chambering a round in their rifles in case they needed to keep order.

When I looked again, the old man was just a shadow turning a corner at the edge of sight and he no longer figures in this story. Except that apparently he does because his image continues to haunt me, though later when I mentioned him to Jeb he'd forgotten the whole incident; so it seems we saw different things.

Was the old man a sign? We see such markers everywhere though as often as not they are no more than the stray branch of a tree standing at a crossroads that points the way to nowhere. Yet, in my heart I believe the old man did serve as a sign because I saw him and I made my choices and I took the path I took.

2

At the time of my Washington posting I was forty years old and freighted with no more than the usual disappointments that are uninteresting except to strangers met on trains or in bars when both parties are drunk enough to suppose they are wise.

It was the summer of 1960 and America was full of the ballyhoo that passes for an election campaign. It was difficult to say why we – the British and to some extent the rest of the world – were interested when the outcome was known in advance, but the fierce optimism of the American psyche still fascinated us: the ability of its people to act as if Jesus was about to return every four years, and yet recover and carry on when He didn't.

This time around the Republican candidate was Richard Nixon, who had made his name in the late forties as an ambitious young congressman, persecuting blacks and homosexuals through the House Committee for the Moral and Racial Purity of America. The Democrats fielded Joe Kennedy, former bootlegger, friend of gangsters and ambassador to Great Britain, whose main aim was the creation of a political dynasty. In the end the outcome would be the same as it had been on every occasion since 1932, when Big A – as the President was known – had beaten Roosevelt in the Democratic primaries and then carried the election with a promise to deliver American Values and a New Deal that would end the Great Depression.

Three decades on, we read about this event in the history books. His supporters liked to refer to it as 'the Second American Revolution', though it was carried off without a civil war or much violence in the streets. Soon after his victory, the President forged an alliance between the Southern wing of his party and the conservative Republicans, who were too surprised at being let in on a game they thought they'd lost to be overly critical. Together they packed the Supreme Court with his supporters and passed the Defense of American Values Act which allowed him to do pretty much what he wanted provided he kept to the outward forms of the Constitution.

Since Big A's first victory the result of every election was that the candidates of the main parties sooner or later agreed to sink their differences and rally behind a national unity figure – the Man himself – who would be elected unopposed behind his front organization, the National States Democratic American Party. Strictly speaking, other candidates were allowed to stand – and some heroes or madmen invariably did – but they were usually arrested on morals or corruption charges before their campaigns made headway.

Much of this was in the future when my plane landed at Lindbergh Airport that summer of sixty, but something like it was inevitable if the system ran true to form. This makes it difficult to say now why the election still held the excitement of uncertainty so that I was looking forward to my posting. Perhaps it was that the country itself was novel to me in small ways and large. Perhaps, too, it was that engaging American optimism I've spoken of, that allowed them always to think the future would be different from and better than the past, though nothing had changed to give any reasonable foundation to this belief. It was difficult to convey to European readers how pervasive it was: from the tone of the TV shows to the stray remarks of friends and strangers. Even the most miserable losers seemed to buy into the idea that they had a great inheritance they'd squandered through their own fault. Confronted with the world's shortcomings, Europeans have Marx, class solidarity and revolution. Americans have the Bible, Christian charity and self-help books.

Whatever the case, people in both places manage as best they can, and wonder why life isn't all they'd hoped for.

I cleared Customs and spent an hour being quizzed in Immigration. My papers were in order – I was a fully accredited correspondent of *The Manchester Guardian* – but I'd forgotten how isolated Americans were despite inhabiting a great empire. The name of my newspaper meant nothing to them except that it would be full of opinions that weren't theirs. They knew foreigners were often critical of their country and they resented it in a way the English, for example, didn't when their own was disparaged. Not that the English liked criticism, but they treated it as a case of ignorance not a challenge to a deep religious value. In the end, however, U.S. Immigration let me through.

I was met in the arrivals hall by Perry Cawthorne, long-time Washington hand who showed his face at head office every once in a while. I imagined that, to an American, he looked a quintessential English gent in his bow tie, Harris Tweed suit and brogues, his face round and florid and his fair hair still full and wavy despite his sixty-plus years. To me he looked like someone who would steal your wallet on a race track, but the reality was that he was just a professional journalist, admired by his peers and more outgoing and cynical than was fit for human company. I was replacing him for unstated reasons, but I noticed the whites of his eyes were yellow and the rumor at home was he had pancreatic cancer, which turned out to be true. He was dead three months later, and Jeb Lyman and I got drunk to his memory – at least I did, since Jeb didn't touch alcohol.

I spotted Perry easily because he was a still figure among the crush of people. I'd forgotten how crowded American airports and railroad stations were. I wasn't used to the mill of young men in uniform on furlough. They filled the hall with their families and girlfriends and reminded me of the time when I'd done the same stuff in the last European war. The Americans had an attitude towards them as if the fact of military service conveyed a sort of holiness. I didn't think we were holy but it was one of the country's illusions that I liked. It spoke of people with good hearts.

'Harry my old son, my cock sparrow, the love of my life!' boomed Perry, spotting me and pushing forward with his arms out as though to hug me. 'How are you, dear boy? Still blooming? Still dipping the wick as necessary? Still pissing off the Powers that Be in whatever circle of Hell our lords and masters are living' – crossing himself – 'may God save their souls?'

'Hullo, Perry.'

Close by stood another man, motionless among the throng. My age, handsome in the unlikely way of a comic book hero or Hollywood star that Englishmen rarely match, dressed in a tailored blue two-piece, starched button-down shirt and black Oxfords. He wore a narrow brimmed fedora, the kind Sinatra sported that had never caught on at home, and a narrow tie that was a lighter blue than his suit. The clothes suggested someone dressing to a regulation requiring modesty but with style. The expression on his face was relaxed, even friendly.

'Let me make the introductions,' Perry said. 'Harry – Jeb. Jeb – Harry. Jeb is one of Hoover's Finest. Forget any stories you heard – God forfend that they were derogatory. Jeb is, if not exactly on the side of the Angels, at least inclined that way. Isn't that so, my old son? On the other hand, Harry here is on the side of the Powers of Darkness like Yours Truly.'

'I'm pleased to meet you, Harry,' said Jeb with a grin that seemed to come from natural warmth. He extended a hand and we did the standard firm shake and engaging of the eyes. His build was trim rather than gym-fit and he had the loose movements of someone who knew how to dance.

It wasn't a place to talk, so we made our way through the crowd. Draftees, waiting for an army bus, queued in the hall behind a bellowing sergeant. Kids in the pale khaki shirt and shorts of the American Youth were already collecting for Winter Relief. They stood below the portrait of the President in the Oval Office. It was framed either side by the national flag and showed Big A smiling genially. His toothbrush moustache had been a fashion statement among his generation since Errol Flynn, the movie star, had taken it up. It appeared in old newsreels and on the upper lip of bureaucrats of a certain age, but Jeb Lyman was comparatively young and I noticed he didn't wear one.

Once we were outside the building, he gave me a card. It read

Jubal Nephi Lyman
Special Agent
Federal Bureau of Investigation Division
General State Police

The address was the Department of Justice Building and the contact number was handwritten, meaning I was privileged to have it. I'd expected that the GeStaPo would assign one of their people to me and had the natural reservation of journalists towards policemen. What I didn't expect was someone who might become a friend, and I'm not sure even now that anyone else did. Friendship is an unreliable tool of manipulation and it takes a certain blindness and arrogance to suppose it will always work out one way.

We cleared the airport hall and Jeb called a taxi. No official limo for us. He joked that Hoover kept his boys on short rations, which I think was a point of pride not a complaint. Even so, for this getting to know you session, we merited lunch at *L'Escargot sans Toit*, a good French place along the street from Harvey's, which was a no-go area because the Director ate there with his boyfriend

Clyde Tolson.

During lunch, my new acquaintance chatted in a relaxed way about the Agency, though, when it came down to it, he said nothing you couldn't pick up in other places. People joked that Hoover was the one person in the Administration who'd been in post even longer than the President, though it wasn't true. What was true was that he'd stood by the future President's side during the abortive coup in 1923 that gave rise to American Patriots Day, for which he'd been rewarded. Previously, the FBI had been essentially an intelligence gathering operation run by a small elite. The General State Police, on the other hand, covered the entire field of law and order except for the highway patrols and specialists like the Coastguard. Or that was the theory.

Jeb said, 'The truth is that the members of the Cabinet have packed the Administration with their own people, and the chiefs hate each other and loathe Hoover. Every one of them has created his own intelligence organization under the cover that they're only conducting research or providing security for their own buildings. It suits the President if they fight among themselves and nobody knows exactly where he stands.'

We turned from Hoover to the subject of the election, which after all was the reason I was in town, and I asked Lyman what would be in it for the losing candidates. It was understood that they would get something out of the deal that kept Big A in power.

He said, 'Joe Kennedy is too old to stand next time and is just keeping the seat warm for his kids. My guess is he'd like to be Vice President with no responsibilities beyond fundraisers. The thing to look out for is what his boys get. The story is that Joe Junior is looking to be Attorney General, which would make him well-placed to do his brother Jack a favor if the Director ever retires. President and Director of the GeStaPo in sixty-four: it's quite something to aim for, always assuming…'

'…that Big A doesn't stand again or that Nixon doesn't take over?'

Jeb gave me a wry smile. But he was only playing at sharing secrets. This one was somewhere between a statement of the obvious and the gossip you could pick up at any bar inside the Beltway.

The more interesting question – which I didn't ask – was whether Joseph Kennedy Junior was the liberal that rumor had him. After twenty years of phony victories in a war that never ended, there were some people – and maybe Joe Junior was one – who thought it was time to draw the whole South American adventure to a close. He had the profile to pull it off, since he was a decorated war hero who came close to being killed during the 1944 campaign in Brazil. But whatever his intentions, it couldn't be done as long as the Old Man was alive. The creation of a self-sufficient empire in the Western hemisphere was the cornerstone of his foreign and economic policy, ever since he set it down in his book, *My Struggle*. If he gave it up, what had all the expenditure of blood and treasure been for?

The other interesting question was where Hoover stood on this matter. But neither of us raised it.

'So…' breathed Perry, loosening his belt after the meal, 'we come to the point of this lovefest. D'you want to explain how things work between us, Jeb, or shall I?'

'There's not much to explain,' Lyman said. 'You clear your stories with the Agency before you file them back home. Perry can explain the details, but we pride ourselves on processing them within twenty-four hours.'

'You read them?' I asked.

'Personally? Hardly. We have guys who do that sort of thing: the Federal News Bureau. If they raise a serious issue, I talk it over with Perry – and now with you. Call it "liaison". You want to know if we take the scissors to your copy? Not so as you'd notice, which Perry will confirm. If national security is involved, we might ask you to take a story out, but we still have the First Amendment.'

Which was true so far as the First Amendment was concerned; it had never been repealed. On the other hand the TV, radio and press had toed the line since Father Coghlin's morality drives in the thirties and Nixon's committee finally nailed Ed Morrow and the CBC Ten in forty-eight. Foreign correspondents could file whatever copy they pleased, but they risked losing their accreditation. Press freedom requires the courage to publish and not just the right. I didn't know whether I had it or not.

Perhaps I waited too long before agreeing. Perry changed the subject. 'Don't think it's all take and no give. It's a two-way street – one thingy scratches the other whatsit and all that. Jeb can be very helpful when it comes to a steer on who's who in the Washington *beau monde* – and the *monde* that isn't so *beau* as well. If you need a ticket of entry to pretty much any social gathering, he can get it for you.'

'And the White House?'

Lyman said, 'You'll be among the first to get the official press releases and you'll be on the list of permitted invitees. If you don't receive an invitation, then you contact me and I'll arrange if I can. Don't waste your time harassing the White House Press Office because they'll simply pass the request to me for approval. Same deal if you're looking for an official comment on a story: the White House staffers won't say a word without the Federal News Bureau approves.'

He meant that I could do nothing in Washington without the GeStaPo being agreeable, but that perhaps we could reach an accommodation. I was to sup with the Devil and this was the aperitif.

Messages delivered, Jeb called for the bill and carefully

put away the receipt after engaging the *maître d'* in conversation in well-accented French. His mix of suavity and bureaucratic detail when it came to the receipt interested me. Instinctively I associated culture with liberal values, but rationally I knew it wasn't so and that cruel men can have the most refined artistic sensibilities.

'I expect you fellows have things to talk about,' he said tactfully as he pushed back his chair and made to leave. 'I need to get back to the office. Once you have your feet under the desk, give me a call, Harry; I'll arrange to make a few introductions to people you may want to know, and then I'll leave you to get on with your job.'

It was nicely done. I said I was happy to have met him and confirmed I'd make the call in a few days. Since Perry was returning to England, Lyman gave him the football buddies' farewell and then headed for the door. Once he was gone, Perry sat down. He said nothing. I waited. He still said nothing. Then I realized he meant that we were still being watched or the table was bugged; so I made a comment that Jeb Lyman seemed like a good guy who could be useful and we fell to talking about practical matters. Although I was booked into a hotel, the plan was that I would take over Perry's apartment at least until the lease ran out. We also talked automobiles. Perry didn't have one and recommended I use cabs or hire if needed. With most of Detroit's production going to the Army, even used cars had become expensive. Taking the bus or the train meant one learned what ordinary people thought and talked about.

'And that's it for now, dear boy,' he concluded. The jovial expression was gone and he looked weary and ill, so it seemed an afterthought when he said, 'I still haven't packed my doings, so it'll be a couple of days before I can let you into the family mansion. I suggest you do a bit of sightseeing to find your way around.'

Something needed to be said and so, expecting a banal

response, I asked, 'Have you enjoyed your stay in Washington?'

He glanced at me sharply. 'Let's say it's been interesting to stay in a city where one's friends and acquaintances occasionally disappear.'

I suppose I shouldn't have been shocked but I was. I said, 'Disappear?'

'Or have accidents. You'll find that hospitals are a great source of information.'

Already he was on his feet, a fat man with a friendly face and the manner of a fictional uncle. Later – when the news of his death came through – I wished I'd known him better and we'd talked more, though I think it an illusion to suppose we might have become pals. He extended a hand and, when I took it, I found something pressed into my palm.

'Don't look so surprised,' he murmured; then more loudly said that he looked forward to seeing me at his place in a few days when I could help him move his luggage out of the door. He turned and I watched him leave. I picked up my hat and told a waiter to fetch my suitcase from the cloakroom, and as an aside asked for the men's room. I went there and locked myself in a cubicle.

I looked at the object Perry had forced into my hand. It was a key with a manila tag attached and writing on it. I read the words and numbers and memorized them carefully, then ripped up the piece of card and flushed it down the toilet bowl. I returned to the restaurant, where the waiter gave me my case.

It seemed I was ready to take up my post.

3

Three years on I was still in Washington, comfortable with the city and its people. I fell into the routine of work: attending the daily briefings of the Office for the Dissemination of American Truth and submitting my copy to the Federal News Bureau for approval. I saw Jeb Lyman socially and now and then professionally if I wanted access to the White House or a cabinet member. Foreigners of a certain kind carry an immunity and I went about my business without worrying that I was going to be picked up and given the third degree by the GeStaPo, or found some day in a ditch along a quiet back road in rural Virginia. I lived on warm terms among the city's political and cultural elite, who had accommodated to the regime. I studied them and in the normality of their behavior I struggled to remind myself that they saw the world differently than I did. For them the American Dream was still going forward and the purposes of God were still being realized. Where I saw a sham of democracy, they did not. Where I saw arbitrariness and brutality, they saw the actions of straightforward clear-thinking men confronted with the problem of making America great again, words that were everywhere repeated like an anthem. I no longer tried to persuade them out of their opinions because it was like trying to argue a man out of his religion and the effort made me angry.

Unsurprisingly the 1960 election had turned out as Jeb Lyman foretold. Big A was still President, Nixon got the Defense portfolio, and Joe Kennedy was Vice President. In the nature of things there were some minor wrinkles which interested political journalists if not the world at large. In December sixty-two, old Joe had a stroke which made him unable to perform even the nominal duties of his office.

17

His eldest son, Joe Junior, took these over alongside his post as US Attorney General and was most often to be seen at Big A's side at public events, which must have put Nixon's nose out of joint. Of the two contenders for the succession, I thought Nixon was probably the more able, but he had the appearance of a lizard on a bad diet and I didn't blame Big A for favoring Joe Junior.

As for John F. Kennedy, who had aspirations to take over from Hoover, he was thwarted because the Director showed no signs of retiring. According to insiders, JFK had counted on his brother, as Hoover's nominal superior, to force him out, but the same insiders also told me that Hoover had the goods on Joe Junior, and so the latter left him alone. JFK's own reputation, behind his glamorous wife Jackie, was none too savory if the rumors about his womanizing were true. These days he was Deputy US Attorney General.

There was another America outside the Beltway, of course, but as a political correspondent I didn't see it, though it sent messages by way of rumor and a largely self-censored press. I recall someone on my own paper's foreign desk remarking that no news had come lately out of the Northwest states – not that much news ever had. I checked in an idle moment and he was right. Since 1960 the number of stories had halved compared with the previous three years but the significance was hard to interpret. The sample size was so small it might be natural variation, but it was equally possible that something was happening out there that the Administration didn't want to reveal. I became attuned to these dark spots. Even in a place as staid as Oklahoma, Tulsa fell quiet for a week in October the previous year and something similar happened in Portland, Maine. One rumor – never verified – was that there had been draft riots in both places. After twenty years of 'victories' in Central and South American it was entirely possible.

Occasionally the Administration would signal that there had been a problem. Usually it involved a city like Chicago where, on account of its size, news had to be managed not suppressed. Typically it would report a bomb outrage. The perpetrators were described as Hispanics or mixed race degenerates who wanted to bring back people of color from their resettlement camps and introduce communism, miscegenation and homosexuality. The terrorist cell was always small and unrepresentative and the authorities always acted with prompt justice in restoring normality.

I wondered if these were signs that things would have to change, now that the Old Man's grip on power was starting to slip. It was a stupid question because, if I had thought more deeply, I would have realized change was inevitable and there were only two directions in which it might go: towards greater oppression or a loosening of the reins. What I could not have foreseen was that my own future would be bound up with the outcome of the struggle between these alternatives. I saw only the events unfolding immediately before me, and most of the time they seemed to be about other matters entirely. Yet, at one level, the end of Big A's rule and a vision of the America that would follow are what this story is all about.

Meanwhile, in those three years since my arrival, there were changes too in my personal situation. I've already said that my failings are of an uninteresting kind, but you still need to know something of them even though I despise the efforts of writers who treat miserable alcoholics as though they are honorable casualties in the war to extract significance from Life. Back in England I'd failed at two marriages. The fault was mine because my wives were good women and I was a neglectful husband and a bad parent to my two sons. The immediate cause was one of the curses of journalism: irregular hours and easy access to booze, but a truer explanation may be that in those early years I lacked a real sense of my identity and values and I was seduced by the role of journalist, a sort of glamour that existed only in my head. The fact is I was not a wise man and did not realize that the only remedy for the condition was a prudent humility in relationships as well as everything else.

I was told back in London and in my early days in Washington that in no time I could fix myself up with a beautiful twenty-year-old Latina mistress, or younger if that was my inclination. I noted the point for what it said about the people who made it, but I stayed away from the bars and hotel lobbies where undocumented Mexican girls hung out, and when my American acquaintances offered to introduce me to the friends of their girlfriends I gave a polite refusal.

The fact is I'm attracted to women old enough to be my wife, and they get older as I do. I need the feel of a real person, who has traveled at least part of the road I've traveled and with whom I can talk about the journey and its destination. I love women for themselves and not just for the sex. I suspect this makes me a pervert.

I met Maria because I was helping the New York bureau on a piece that had nothing to do with politics. It was a magazine-type article on American health care, a subject about which the British felt superior. Manchester thought that any criticism would have more impact if it could be prefaced with the headline 'EVEN IN THE NATION'S CAPITAL…' whatever we considered shocking was happening. More mundanely, if I had nothing better to do in the political slack season, I could save New York a train fare and hotel bill, and instead hire a cameraman and arrange to spend a day or two hanging around one of the hospitals, under whatever cover of lies I could dream up.

For no other reason than it was the only place that extended an invitation, I completed my piece by visiting the Freedmen's Hospital. Its address was a building fifty or so years old, located at Bryant and 6th, a section of the city I didn't know well. As the name suggested, it had been founded to serve the black population way back at the end of slavery, but that purpose had vanished in the last decade with the final Resettlements. These days it was looking for a new role and source of prestige, but, in the climate of Big A's America, its history told against it and now it mainly served poor whites and Hispanics. Not that I knew any of this. They probably invited me to gain some favorable press coverage for their good work. I had no intention of disparaging the dedication of the staff, but my job was to look for angles that would confirm our readers' prejudices.

I first saw Maria talking to a colleague about whatever colleagues talk about in corridors. I was being escorted by one of the hospital manager's clerks, the Freedmen's having little notion of how to organize public relations. The clerk, a woman, called out Maria's name and she turned and gave a look of frank curiosity in my direction. Yet it was only momentary; she had a strong sense of priorities and knew she must deal first with her colleague and so she turned away and continued her conversation, and the person she was talking to smiled and went away content. There was a strength of understanding and sensitivity in the small decision made in this situation and I liked it.

The clerk introduced us. Maria was a senior nurse and could explain much of her department's work to me. I was appropriately grateful. The clerk begged to be excused.

There are some women – and they have to be encountered in the flesh – who make an impression so intense and overwhelming for as long as one is in their presence that one wants to flee them in order to restore a sense of calm. Merely beautiful women do not have this effect though what else is necessary I am not sure.

21

Certainly there has to be a sense of a person behind the beauty and a feeling that that person is full and complete, womanly and owning herself, and capable of loving or rejecting you entirely as she decides. There is probably still more, I can't say. All I can say is that whatever creates it, the impact is immediate and with Maria I felt it.

So, at this first encounter, we stood and talked a while in the corridor with ward staff and patients passing either side of us, me and this woman I wanted to look at forever yet run away from. I saw immediately that she wasn't young – forty perhaps – and from her figure I knew she had had children at some time and made an effort to look good afterwards. Twenty years before, she would have been a lovely girl among so many lovely girls. Now she was a beautiful woman whose beauty had lasted with a few characterful lines here and there but in a face charged with intelligence and seriousness imposed by life, and an astonishing pair of brown eyes that always fixed me questioningly. I don't know why I felt she had experienced great sadness, but I thought so, and yet she wasn't soured by it, merely touched with the degree of wariness of a person who has been hurt.

Now that we spoke, she faced me directly, engaging my eyes and without distraction, expecting in return that I would pay her my attention. Her conversation both now and when we talked with patients was to the point but touched with little grace notes of care as to how the other person might take what she was saying. For all my indifference to this particular project, in her company I found myself becoming interested in the problems of providing hospital services to disadvantaged people.

So I did the tour and took what notes I could while distracted by the glow of the woman at my side and the feeling that I was with someone of compassion and integrity. All the time I wanted to get away from her because the thought of having a relationship with a person who, without meaning to, so imposed herself on my thoughts and senses made me dizzy. Yet, equally, I wanted to see her again and find out who she was, this stranger. And so, as we finished and she was asking me whether there was anything else I wanted to see or any question I wanted to put so that she could satisfy herself that she had done a good professional job, I answered:

'No, thank you, you've told me everything I needed to know. But I was wondering…'

'Yes?'

'Would you like to have dinner with me?'

Immediately I thought it was a selfish invitation. I hadn't asked and she hadn't revealed whether she had a partner or children at home, though I'd deduced that she'd had at least one child sometime in the past. I'd supposed she was free because I needed her to be free even though part of me wanted her to say no. She gave me a frank, puzzled stare. She was clearly surprised to receive the invitation.

'Would I…?'

While I waited, she seemed to be mentally going over her calendar or perhaps considering whether she should leave a precautionary message for a friend saying where she was going and who she was with. I wasn't used to having my invitations met with such a reaction.

'OK, my shift is nearly finished,' she said – I hadn't even thought about her working hours – 'so, if you could wait say half an hour, we could do dinner. But locally because I need to be home to do cleaning and stuff that I'd planned.'

And that is what we did. Her shift finished and she changed into her neat chain store street clothes and we went to a nearby Italian restaurant. The food was unpretentious and the price modest, and at this hour the place was mostly empty and the atmosphere unromantic. Maria ate heartily because she was hungry at the end of a

23

working day. I ate with relief that the heat of her presence was beginning to wear off and that I could begin to have some perspective on this woman who had so attracted me.

We chatted. I was curious about her but cautious about enquiring too closely into her situation because I was aware that someone of Hispanic origins in Big A's America lived subject to a complex and ambiguous system of gradations under the racial regulations introduce by the Defense of American Values Act, according to the extent of their provable European descent. She was less constrained in asking about how it was to be English and a journalist and working in this country. I think she was simply curious; it wasn't a dating ploy.

She didn't ask about the more personal aspects of my life. Men of my age and type, if single, bear the fact of our past failed relationships on our persons and everything else is detail. The only immediate question is whether the man is truly single, or two-timing is to be added to his sins. The fact of availability once established, only then do the reasons for those earlier failures become relevant. I am not implying cynicism on the part of women. They risk their lives on their decisions, and I think that many of them are insufficiently calculating.

As for this evening, such a calculation was unnecessary. Maria didn't invite me to her place and we didn't have sex; indeed not then nor for a while as she decided whether I was someone she wanted to know. However, we did agree to take in a show together on another occasion, and she did let me take her to the bus.

Two years later we were sharing our lives. Maria continued as a nurse and I was still a foreign correspondent. It was understood between us that things might come to an end, not that we would wish to separate but that circumstances might force a separation. This cool recognition of reality characterized whatever it was that we had and made it poignant – precious even.

As to the causes of our uncertain future, on Maria's side there was the equivocality of her residency status. Lowest among Hispanics were the pureblood indigenous Mexicans, who at their worst could be found working as indentured field hands or on chain gangs. Above them were various classes of free persons, the highest of whom were called 'Privileged Hispanics' and entitled to a Certificate of Moral and Racial Purity. Most of the latter were Argentinians of recent Italian extraction, but there were old Creole families from the colonial Spanish elite who could also demonstrate their European bloodline. Or so the theory went. The fact was that anyone of pale-enough complexion could come by a forged Certificate for a thousand dollars, and the risks were moderate at this juncture while America was still adjusting to the resettlement of the blacks. But Hispanics of all types and grades knew that sooner or later the GeStaPo and the House Committee would get around to them and there would be a great reckoning. I didn't know and didn't care if Maria's Certificate was genuine, but any attempt to marry would cause it to be examined and the penalty of failure would be immediate.

Yet the risks of separation did not lie wholly on her side. There were others on mine and they were less excusable because they stemmed from who I was: the man with two failed marriages behind him. Women take on such men in the belief that they can change them. They rarely succeed. I don't mean that the men are incapable of change, but the process is slow, the failure rate is high, and the causes of change are not so simplistic as the proverbial 'love of a good woman'. If there is hope – if there is hope for me – it lies in the slow working of time, the healing of old bruises and scarring of old wounds, and a deep weariness of being the man I once was. I think that Maria thought I had brought myself to this pitch and that I was worth a chance. But she made it clear that hers was a mature, intelligent love that came with conditions attached for her own self-preservation. I accepted her conditions because I knew she was right. But it meant that our love came with danger as well as passion.

That was how things stood as we entered the Year of Our Lord 1963. I was well-placed in my job. I had a relationship with a woman I loved. I had a friend who was a secret policeman.

I was living in a small rent-controlled apartment a short bus ride from where Maria worked: the same in which she had lived these past five years. I gave up Perry's place when the lease expired. It was more spacious and more luxurious and in a tonier neighborhood, but it was more expensive and, if I were re-posted to England and for whatever reason the separation came, Maria could not have kept it up. Also, no one in Washington in these times gave up a rent-controlled apartment.

I was there one evening, working at a story on the kitchen table with the radio on low and playing a Dean Martin number, when Maria came home at the end of her shift. She had a tale to tell.

It was this tale that took me next day to speak with Jeb Lyman. It was the same day that I saw the black man in his finery walking down Pennsylvania Avenue.

4

I was sitting at the kitchen table, punching out a story on my old Remington, when Maria brought home those things a nurse brings home: the reality of her presence and her tired feet. Outside, the traffic was making its way to the suburbs and kids were playing ball in the street; inside, the evening light was fading and the room was dimly lit by a low bulb in a parchment shade that cast a shadow over a cheap framed picture of the Blessed Virgin that Maria had brought from wherever she came from. On the radio Deano sang *Ain't That a Kick in the Head* and, between profound journalistic thoughts, I was doing my world-famous crooner impression with a spoon as a microphone. When Maria came through the door and had taken off her coat and put down the bag of groceries she bought on the way from work, I grabbed her and we did a couple of turns about the room, dodging the furniture, until we collapsed amid a pile of magazines on the armchair.

I suppose all couples have their fantasies and this was mine because in my imagination – and I hope in truth – as we circled the kitchen, Maria in my arms laughing and complaining that I was a fool, I was living the romance that people convinced of love can live in ordinary life. And in her imagination? She never said in words, but her smile and the softening in her eyes spoke of some relief from the silent sadness I had noticed even on that first date, and, if I could give her this small gift, I was grateful.

Then, as she cleared the magazines and kicked off her shoes, and as I washed her feet in warm water and massaged them, she told me of her day and of the strange situation that had arisen and the mysterious patient who had appeared at the hospital. I listened and, as I did so, realized that I would have to speak to Jeb Lyman. Maria would not like that.

There are things in the life of every journalist from which we shelter our families. They may be our knowledge of and silent complicity in great crimes, or simply the petty shabbiness of smoke-filled bars where we exchange drunken stories with men we despise and who despise us. Whatever these things may be, we know that they will diminish us if they become known.

I kept Maria away from Jeb Lyman because I was frightened of her secret history and that, if pressed, because of her awesome courage she would tell it for the sake of truth. I was frightened too of Jeb Lyman because he was a man with whom I was a friend against my better judgment, and I knew that at some time he would make a demand of me which I would agree to and it would hurt me in ways from which I would not recover.

Yet it was impossible to avoid ordinary sociability, and it seemed important to Jeb that Maria and I should get to know his family at a Thanksgiving dinner that first year after we met. Aware that I was English and Maria was a Catholic in the Spanish tradition, he knew that we did not celebrate the holiday and I think he wanted us to experience it both to deepen our friendship and to help us understand America and what the President was trying to achieve to make his country great again. At all events, we appeared at his home in Garrison Street NW, a detached house on a modest lot with a maple in the yard showing the colors of autumn. We did what couples do who are comfortable with living together, and speculated how much this place would cost and whether we could ever afford it and laughed over our guesses. Then we rang the bell and were welcomed in.

There were eight of us for dinner in a room that, in its perfections, seemed to have been furnished in Colonial style from an interior decorator's pattern book. The others were Jeb and his wife Laura Beth, her parents Ben and Catherine who had come for the occasion all the way from Provo where Ben taught Nordic Literature at BYU until he retired, and Jeb and Laura Beth's kids, Chet and Donald, who were a year or two shy of going to college. I noticed that Jeb's parents were absent and recalled that he had never mentioned them in our conversations. From that fact and other small indications such as Jeb's slightly over-groomed appearance and obvious sense of pride in his home and his wife's family, I had a notion that he had been brought up in poor circumstances and had arrived at his station by his own effort of will.

So we said the Thanksgiving prayers and ate the turkey and none of us drank alcohol. Ben talked a great deal and stopped only when, from time to time, his wife touched him on the forearm.

He said, 'A man who is not a Christian is not fit to be an American.'

He said, 'Your Mexican is of a higher racial type than your common Negro, but his laziness means he'll never amount to anything unless directed by the Anglo-Saxon.'

Maria was a certified European and so it was obvious none of this touched her.

Ben was one of those men who have an opinion about everything and confuse rigidity with principles, and their own thoughts with the common sense of all right-thinking people. He stood for a way of looking at things that I held in contempt, yet he had a warm folksy manner and in this intimate family atmosphere in a room decorated with embroidered samplers and the portrait of Big A that hung in every patriot household, God help me but I liked him. Catherine had a kindly nature and talked about charity drives of various kinds that she organised with her friends. The two boys grunted and asked if they could be excused to watch *The Lucy-Desi Comedy Hour*.

It was Laura Beth who interested me most, both for

herself and for what she told me indirectly about Jeb. Also I could not help comparing her with Maria: not in a competitive sense but because I still wanted to understand what had happened to my life and why I was loved by this woman who was sitting next to me, quietly smiling and trying not to put a foot wrong. Laura Beth was lovely, as might have been expected for the wife of a man as handsome as Jeb, and intelligent too. She had studied liberal arts at Radcliffe and worked in one of the Washington galleries, and she had a slender, white-blonde beauty and a manner that managed to be both cool and light. I couldn't help thinking that she was some sort of prize that Jeb had awarded himself, not because he wanted her but because she was the sort of person he was supposed to want and it hadn't occurred to him that he might not. I tried to envisage passion between them but could only imagine polite exchanges between two people who wanted to behave well and probably would. Yet, when Jeb was with me and we talked about the ordinary stuff of life, he always spoke of himself as a lucky man in his family life, and I think he was sincere.

We did not repeat this experience. I believe Jeb and I both detected its subtle wrongness and relegated it to the ranks of those things 'we must do again sometime', while knowing we never will. On the night itself, the dinner party broke up amid expressions of goodwill and Maria and I took a cab home. There was a chill in the air and we had brought coats and Jeb helped us into them. It was then, as we were all exchanging farewells and any particular remark could be lost in the general hubbub, that Jeb said the only other memorable thing I recall from the evening.

He said, 'You do understand that I would never do anything to harm you or Maria, don't you?'

I hadn't supposed that he would. But he had supposed that he might.

'That's a promise,' he said.

30

*

When it came to the tale of the mysterious patient, Maria wasn't a natural story-teller; few people are. She began by describing in detail the layout of the hospital, which she thought was important when it wasn't. She talked about her shift pattern, which apparently explained why she hadn't seen what she had seen a couple of days earlier, though I don't know it would have made a difference. Then she came to the point.

'We have a patient who seems to be off the books.'

'Off the books?'

'There's no record of an admission. I checked in case the patient became my problem and there was something I was missing.'

'And you were curious.'

'Right – OK – I was curious.'

The patient arrived late at night, brought to the Freedmen's no one knew how, passed through admissions like a rumor, and was housed in a private room with his or her own nurse (the sex being unknown).

'They're running some sort of isolation protocol, but I don't recognize it.'

'You mean there's an infection?'

Maria shook her head. 'It's kind of like infection control but not. They're not going through the disinfection routines you would get with a contagion; nor are they masking-up the way you would with an airborne disease. There's a – I don't know how to describe it – a lack of consistency, as if they know they should be doing something but don't know quite what it should be.'

'They're improvising?'

'Could be – though I don't see how that should be so. I mean we have protocols for everything.'

I couldn't comment. I didn't know if it was true.

Then she came to the point that rang my bell.

She said, 'There's security.'

This took me by surprise because my recollection of the Freedmen's was of an easy-going place staffed by people who joked with their patients even though they were overworked and underfunded.

'Hospital security?' I imagined a retired cop with a big gut and bad veins, whose notion of the job was to say 'hello' to whoever came his way.

'Twenty-four hours. Never fewer than two men.'

'Uniforms?'

She shook her head. 'Dark suits and ties. White shirts.'

'Young? Old?'

'Twenties. Their hair…' Maria ran a hand over hers.

'A buzz cut?'

'I don't know the word. Short. Flat.'

They sounded like military, but that didn't make sense of the civilian clothes, which were more suggestive of the Agency. I had no theory that explained all the data.

I said, 'Presumably someone knows what this is about – the doctors – some of the nurses?'

'The patient came with a nurse. She rotates with someone else I haven't seen. A doctor looks in but I don't recognize him. The hospital administration must know something but no one is talking.'

I had no answer to any of this, but I knew I had to speak to Jeb about it.

In Pennsylvania Avenue the old black man went about his business and the two beat cops went about theirs while Jeb Lyman and I talked.

Jeb said, 'You want lunch?' He checked his watch. 'I have a half hour.'

We went to a nearby diner that catered for office workers on a budget. We had the counter service: always the same: burger, fries and a cola. Jeb looked at me as he always did: like a kid playing hooky. Laura Beth had him on a diet of lean steaks and salads with low fat dressing, milk to drink.

'So…' he sighed after savoring the first mouthful. 'You start, since you called this meeting. What is it that won't wait?'

What was it that wouldn't wait? I didn't know except there was in Maria's story something fluid. An anonymous patient who suddenly appeared could with equal suddenness disappear.

I told him that this was something I'd gotten from Maria. 'But I don't want her name appearing,' I said. 'I owe her that.'

'All right,' he said. 'No names – not even yours if that's the way you want it. What is it that Maria has to say that she's reluctant for me to hear about?'

So I told him, giving all the details as best I could recall them, and Jeb listened mostly in silence. When I'd finished he called for my coffee and the tab and we moved to an empty table by the window.

He seemed disinclined to offer anything by way of explanation though I wasn't surprised. I asked, 'Is this patient one of yours – the Agency's?'

Jeb shrugged. 'I haven't heard. But that means nothing. There are thousands of cases. I'll check.' He looked for my angle. 'Are you expecting a piece for your paper out of this?'

'Not if it touches on national security.'

'But?'

'People sometimes use the Agency's resources for private purposes – repaying favors: that sort of thing. Also, this may not be an Agency case.'

'The buzz cuts?'

I nodded. I'd never thought about it before, but Agency personnel almost always wore their hair like a Hollywood matinée idol, trimmed neatly with a side parting and a touch of brilliantine. I said, 'I thought military.'

'The lack of uniforms says not.'

'Maybe they don't want to advertise. Maybe they want people to think GeStaPo.'

'It's an appealing idea. You're thinking that if this is some sort of ploy by Nixon's people to push any blame onto us, then the Director might release the story to embarrass Dicky and put him in his place. You have a theory?'

'Not really. It occurred to me we're dealing with someone Nixon owes – a VIP. I don't say it explains all the facts.'

'A VIP lodged in the Freedmen's with white trash and Hispanics? Is that really your take? I think they'd prefer a country club atmosphere.'

'Too much chance of being recognized? Maybe the illness is something shameful. Alcoholism?'

Jeb laughed. 'Alcoholism is shameful in Washington? Who knew?'

'Venereal disease?'

'OK, venereal disease might be a problem but people usually lie about it: give it another name. Then again, have you thought that maybe it isn't the VIP himself but someone he knows? There's a senior senator on Nixon's former House Committee, the one he chaired before his Cabinet appointment. The rumor is the old boy recently mislaid a mistress, a twenty-year-old porn star, following a lively party at his place on Long Island. The betting is he shot her or she overdosed or he pimped her to someone who does those things. Either way, if she's still alive, she would fit the profile of someone you might want to hide away at the Freedmen's.'

'And Hoover would allow such a story to be released?'

'Maybe. It would depend on the politics, and I'm not up to date. I'll check and let you know. I'm guessing you don't want to waste your time if this is going nowhere.'

I didn't want to waste my time.

5

I received a call the next night, but neither the timing nor the subject was what I was expecting. The clock showed close to midnight. I was sleeping and Maria was tossing restlessly as she did before a change in her shift pattern. I heard Jeb's voice on the line.

He said, 'I hope I'm not waking you.'

'At midnight? How could that be?'

He chuckled in that easy way that made me forget who he was and what he did.

'I have a scoop for you.'

'Really?'

If I sounded skeptical it was because the Agency was more in the habit of delaying stories than handing them out. Jeb picked up on this and sounded almost apologetic.

'Call it a thank-you for the information you gave me.'

That woke me up. I reached for a cigarette.

'You have more on that story?'

'In good time. This is something else. Find yourself a photographer and get your hide to the Arc of Hope. Say forty-five minutes? You'll be expected.'

The Arc of Hope was part of the President's legend that he gave up the chance of becoming a great architect in order to dedicate his life to the American People. The truth was more mundane. He was raised in Brooklyn, son of a customs official who emigrated from Austria back in the eighties of the last century. Father and son didn't get along and Big A found himself bumming around New York, boarding in low rooming houses and scratching a living selling watercolors of the skyscrapers that were just then going up. This was before the Great War, when he made the rank of corporal and caught a whiff of gas. Afterwards he was involved with veterans' organizations and worked them into his own brand of politics that in 1932 took over a country sickened by the Depression. Other than the watercolors, he had no training in architecture. Still, it was an obsession.

The Stadium of the Americas was one of the grandiose projects that seemed to feed this inner need. It was built for the 1936 Olympics on a tract north of the Arlington National Cemetery so there would be a view over the river towards the White House and the Capitol. Its capacity was a quarter of a million for no other reason than that there was nothing bigger, and even during the original games it came nowhere close to being filled. The theory was that afterwards it would be taken over by the Redskins or the Senators, but its empty vastness even with a good home crowd made both teams and spectators feel like losers and these days it was used only occasionally for military parades and rallies of the Klan and the President's party organization, the NSDAP. The nearest it came to serving a significant purpose was in the fifties when it was used as a holding pen for blacks in their tens of thousands on their way to being resettled in Brazil and other points south. Most of the year it stood vacant and crumbling and at night it looked like an ancient monument eerily lit by the fires of homeless men and women seeking refuge.

The Arc of Hope was part of this folly. Conceived as a rainbow modelled in reinforced concrete, it symbolized the aspirations of Americans as embodied in the President's vision. More practically, in the spirit that built the unfinished Beltway, it showed the government's commitment to modernity and the Age of the Automobile. It was designed to drive a highway in a great arch over the middle of the stadium before dividing at the eastern end to cross the Potomac bridges. However, ambition could not suppress the rumors that the engineers had been browbeaten and thought the inclines too steep, the spans too wide and the pylons too weak to support the weight and stress of heavy traffic. Drivers stayed away and it carried only a thin stream of vehicles even at the busiest times, and at night it was mostly deserted except for repair crews proving the engineers right

After Jeb's call, I phoned Dave Kowalczyk, who was my photographer when need arose. We agreed to meet at the Potomac side of the Arc and play it from there. We arrived by separate cabs to find that even at this hour whatever was going on had attracted a crowd of night owls and journalists and the city cops had erected rail and sawhorse barriers. Too far away for me to see any detail, an array of lights framed a clutch of vague shapes like a theatre set, and in the depths of the stadium there was a glow, but the distance and the angle made it impossible to say what it meant.

I saw no sign of Jeb, but I took him at his word and Dave and I forced our way to the barrier, where we were blocked by one of the uniforms. I showed my press card, dropped Jeb's name, produced his card with its FBI and GeStaPo logos, and said that he was here and expecting me. The cop called his sergeant over and the latter looked at my credentials sourly and nodded me through.

'What's going on?' I asked.

'You're the one with the fancy friend,' said the sergeant. 'Ask him.'

'How does it go – *To Serve and Protect*?' I said.

The motto seemed only to rile him. 'Wrong city,' he said. 'Go fuck yourself.'

I didn't stay to push my luck. The accident – or whatever it was that had happened – seemed to be just the further side of the crest, which was one reason we couldn't make it out. Dave took a couple of speculative shots of the police and fire service milling about on the carriageway; then went to the side-wall and took some aerial snaps of the depths of the stadium.

'There's a big fire down there,' he said.

I looked over with a feeling of vertigo. I saw a circle filled with flames and a few satellite blazes, and the tableau was surrounded by a jam of people and vehicles but I couldn't get my head around the scale. There was nothing I could think of in that enormous grass and concrete concourse that was likely to burn and I supposed that a truck or car must have crashed through the side-wall of the Arc and plummeted into the stadium. Spectacular enough, but, as scoops go, this one did not seem to amount to much.

'There's nothing more to see here,' Dave said. 'We've got to get closer to the action.' He set off at a trot toward the lights and the crowd at the crest of the overpass. I followed him, yelling 'Press' at anyone who seemed interested, which was no one much. The area around the crest was circled by the spotlights I'd noticed earlier and a line of uniforms was conducting a fingertip search of the blacktop, which showed signs of burning. Two photographers in civilian overcoats and fedoras were taking pictures of each find in situ before it was moved to a small pile composed mostly of painted sheet metal except for a tire that, so far as I could tell, came from a sedan. Outside the circle of lights, on the western side of the crest were a couple of black-and-whites, a police department truck and an unmarked limousine. Beyond them another barrier and another crowd of onlookers.

'So?' asked Dave, skeptically. 'Why are we here at' – checking his watch –'fuck, it's one-thirty! For a highway accident, already?'

I shrugged. I didn't know. I glanced at the side-wall again, which was more by way of a fence. To reduce the weight on the bridge it was constructed of concrete posts and metal rails, designed to resist a swipe from a careless driver not a square-on collision. At this point a section was broken and there were more burn marks on the uprights.

As far as I could judge, a car had breached it and shed some bodywork and a wheel in the process. If there were casualties, they were probably somewhere in the blaze below.

'I have all the shots I can use,' Dave said. 'You gonna talk to anyone – get the story?' He sounded doubtful. We both knew that wasn't how it worked in Big A's America. In the ordinary way, I'd have to wait for the press release – unless I found Jeb Lyman and he explained what this was about and why I was here. I guessed he was below in the stadium, and that was where I should be. From memory, the main entrances were on the western side and I was about to set off in that direction when I felt something beneath my shoe and looked down to kick it aside.

What I saw was a spent bullet, and it told me part of what I needed to know.

This wasn't a regular highway accident. It was a cops and robbers' chase that the cops had won.

So Dave and I crossed the Arc to the further side and made our way to the main entrance to the Stadium of the Americas: a line of gates that opened into a gigantic marble ticketing hall with statues of naked over-muscled athletes in niches around the walls and here and there the ashes of small fires and other signs that homeless people had been camping where there was cover against the weather. I imagined they were still somewhere about: lurking in the miles of seating around the stadium, waiting to repossess their shelter. Meantime it was taken over by police, fire crew and G-men. One of them asked me for ID and I went through the same routine as before, but this time the agent seemed to expect me, and Dave and I were let through.

Ignoring the stairs and exits that led to the spectator areas, we emerged from a long tunnel on to a security strip and a cinder track that circled the main field. The further side of the stadium was invisible except as a distant blackness against the urban glow. In the middle ground burned the fires we'd seen from the Arc, whose crest was dotted with stars from the spotlights while the dramatic sweep of the underside flickered with a pearlescent grey from the play of firelight on concrete. For a moment, it was beautiful and I had a glimpse of Big A's vision, and also of its failure. He had taken no account of the human beings who would come to inhabit the product of his dreams though they could not live up to his aspirations.

We crossed the field in the direction of the flames, Dave taking pictures as we went. Once or twice we were stopped, but Jeb's name worked its wonder each time. The main fire was still blazing and it was easy to imagine it as a car but the truth was that the source had burned to a shapeless core. In the surrounding nimbus of light, I noted more automobile parts and what looked like an intact body that had probably been thrown out by the original blast. Some fire crew had armed themselves with a grapple and were trying to drag it away but the hooks ripped through the charred shreds of clothing. I looked around and spotted Jeb standing among a group of other G-men. He saw me and waved me over. Though maintaining his trademark stillness, I sensed his excitement: that of a kid playing by a bonfire and, now I thought of it, I felt the same.

'So how do you like it?' he said.

'Colorful,' I said, which disappointed him. 'Am I missing something? It's a car smash.'

'You think so?'

'I'm guessing there was a chase. I found a spent bullet on the roadway.'

'Good catch. The police were set to stop them but they got away and there was a pursuit.'

The answer suggested the police had been forewarned, but this came to me only later. For now, I asked – still looking for the angle that had brought me here – 'Who did they rob?'

'Not robbers.'

'Don't tell me they overstayed their parking?'

Jeb grinned and said, 'Terrorists.'

Which brought me up short. In a country as full of small arms as America and as anarchic in its concept of masculinity, it wasn't that the fact of terrorism was a surprise but that a terrorist act was being admitted as soon as it occurred. As a foreign correspondent, I knew the authorities always reviewed the possibility of hiding such incidents or passing them off as something else, and only as a last resort or to make some political point did they admit that their perfect society contained dissidents. Yet here was Jeb telling me what had happened even as the terrorists' getaway car was burning behind him.

He anticipated my question. 'The story is going to be released. I'm just doing you a favor by letting you in first. Get your copy to the FNB overnight and it'll be approved for immediate wire transmission. In addition, you should get syndication rights for the photographs.'

'Why?'

'Why make it public? There was a bomb in the car. It went off and blew the damn thing off the overpass. The signs are all over the road and too many people saw the explosion.'

'You know who these characters were?' It had crossed my mind that this might be a set-up for a show trial of someone who had fallen out of favor, though nothing came to mind except the Nixon-Kennedy thing, and I had no sense that events had got that far.

'Nobodies – mulattos passing as white to avoid Resettlement; undocumented Hispanics; college kids who've been brainwashed by Marxist professors. You're wondering if it's going to go anywhere? Maybe Joe

Kennedy Junior is a commie or Dicky is a pansy? Forget it. It's nothing more than a nice story I thought you'd like to have.'

I stared at Jeb for as long as I could and he returned his usual frank, open gaze and smiled. I noticed that the fire crew had snagged the body and dragged it clear. The underside was still unburnt and something had fallen out of the corpse's pocket. I stooped and picked it up. A driving license in the name Charlie-Joe Svensen, scorched but still legible. I passed it to Jeb who was about to slip it into his pocket when I asked, 'Do you know who he is?'

Jeb looked at the name. 'Probably some guy on an assembly line in Detroit. This is a cheap fake. Some of the people working the bottom end of that business take genuine ID and knock off a hundred lookalikes. The world is full of Charlie-Joe Svensens on the lam but in a country this size the chance of running into two of them is effectively zero, so the faker figures why bother to be original?'

This made sense. Then, before I could put any more questions, Dave called over, 'I'm finished. Out of film.'

I asked how much I owed him and paid him cash against his receipt. I told him to work overnight to develop what he had and get the results to the FNB for approval to transmit. He said, 'Nice doing business with you,' and sloped off to find a cab.

I looked about, wondering if this was finished or there was more to it. Jeb made small talk.

'D'you know why we let the fire burn itself out? No one wanted to get too close in case there was more unexploded ordinance – though how that could be escapes me. Also – and this takes some believing – whoever designed this place decided that its construction made it fireproof; so they didn't run any water supply outside the perimeter buildings. How far is that? Half a mile? A mile? My sense of distance goes when I'm here.'

'I should phone Maria,' I said. I was debating whether to write up the story at home or find a coffee shop that was still open, where I could work while I still had the buzz.

'I'm hungry,' Jeb said. 'Let's go eat.'

We found an all-night diner where beat cops took their breaks and illegal bookies ran their business from a payphone. A couple of cops were eating pie at the counter and the bookies had other things to do. The only other people were a man and woman arguing about the affair they were having. I ordered coffee and a pastrami sandwich on rye, and Jeb ordered milk, eggs and pancakes. Because I knew she would be awake and worrying, I called Maria from the payphone and told her I was fine and would be home in an hour or so. She said that she loved me and I said I loved her, both of us in the tired voices that sound insincere but are not.

I didn't suppose that Jeb's invitation was as casual as he pretended, so I asked, 'Do you have any more information on the patient at the Freedmen's?'

'What made me think you would ask that – though, as it happens, it's a convenient question. Your gut feeling was right. The guys guarding whoever it is aren't Agency.'

'Nixon's people?'

'It's only guesswork that Dicky knows about this, but they do seem to be from the Defense Security Detail.'

'I thought DSD only handled Defense Department internal affairs?'

'Sure they do – all ten thousand of them at the last count.'

The DSD operated as an addition to the military police and reported directly to the Secretary of Defense. I had only a vague idea what they did and hadn't realized there were so many of them, but the disclosure was of a piece with the competition between the chiefs in the Administration to control their own sources of intelligence.

I said, 'So what are they doing? Don't tell me Hoover doesn't know.'

'Who knows what Hoover knows? Mystery is his stock in trade; he turns even ignorance to his advantage.'

I wondered where the conversation was going. Jeb was evidently willing to talk about the subject. I asked, 'What's the Agency's theory?'

'Officially we don't have one – unless Edgar knows but isn't telling. Your guess that Nixon may be covering up a scandal in order to repay a favor to one of his backers has a lot of appeal – in fact some of the boys are running a book on who it might be.'

'Any other ideas?'

'You can get good odds that it's connected with an accident on the Freedom Through Strength program.'

'There's been an accident?'

'Not that I heard of. That's the point.'

I considered this but it made little sense. 'Freedom Through Strength' was one of the fancy names politicians give to their schemes to suggest firmness and nobility of purpose instead of grubby deal-making to help their friends or vacuous plans to fool the public. The object of this particular program was to develop long-range rocket technology and it was based somewhere in Florida. The general idea had been around since the forties, but the military had never got behind it because bombers were an adequate means of demonstrating American power to the Mexicans, Brazilians and their kin. The Army's problems lay in holding territory not flattening cities. Then, shortly after he became Secretary of Defense, Nixon took up the program with the fervor of a convert. Probably his motives were political: to align himself with Youth and the Future. There was talk of getting a man to the moon in the next twenty or thirty years. If the rockets had any other use, the Great American Public hadn't been told.

'I don't see it,' I said. 'Accidents happen all the time,

but they're no more than a minor embarrassment. And why the Freedmen's? Any casualties the Army couldn't handle on site would be shipped to Miami not to a poor people's hospital in Washington.'

'Like I said, you can get good odds.'

Asking for favors is like comedy: it all depends on the timing. The man and woman who were having the affair got up from their table, gathered their hats and coats and left. From their body language, I didn't think their relationship was going to make it. The two cops slapped cash on the counter and followed the lovers. I turned to Jeb.

I said, 'So, are you going to tell me why we're here?' I tried not to sound suspicious or annoyed. Jeb looked sympathetic as a friend might.

'I know: you're tired and you still have a story to write. And there's Maria to think about,' he added – meaning that he thought about her too.

'Then say whatever you have to say and we'll wrap up.'

'That sounds reasonable.'

'So?'

Jeb leaned forward. His smile was slightly goofy as if he knew he was about to say something he shouldn't say, but – shucks – let's say it anyway.

'I was just wondering if you could help me with something.'

6

I said, 'You want me to help you?'

I couldn't interpret Jeb's voice. He had a way of apologizing that could make me feel guilty. He said, 'It isn't something you have to do. I can't make you – I wouldn't want to.' He made no reference to the scoop he'd just given me.

'But?'

'But wouldn't you like to know the name of the guy the DSD are protecting?'

'I take it that's a rhetorical question – but, in case it isn't, the answer is I would like to. Except there's a problem.'

'And what's that?'

'If the answer is interesting, I won't be allowed to print it.'

Jeb laughed in his easy way. 'Well, you got me there. You may be right. But we'll never know until we find out the guy's identity. Then – if you can't print – we'll owe you one. Either way you can't lose.'

Something about this conversation was off and I realized what it was. 'Why are you asking me?'

'It's more that we'd like Maria's help.'

'Don't split hairs. All the Agency needs to do is ask the administration at the Freedmen's. If you don't want to, then plant someone or do a black bag job on the files. Whatever – the last thing you need is help from me or Maria.'

The door of the diner opened. A man in a loud check suit came in, sat at the counter and started to hold one of those conversations with the short order cook that seem to make sense but don't because they come from a different story. I had one of those late-night thoughts – not profound

47

enough to qualify as an insight – that whatever Jeb and I were doing probably didn't matter to anyone else.

Jeb checked his watch. He said, 'It's two-thirty. You have a story to write. I don't expect you to understand everything.'

'Humor me.'

'It's politics. Jack Kennedy has the knife out for Hoover and Hoover needs an ally. His problem is that Nixon doesn't give a shit except that JFK hates Nixon as well. Hoover would like Nixon's friendship, but he'd rather have his balls, because it's no secret that he doesn't do "friendship" except for Clyde Tolson.'

'Nixon's balls being the mystery man in the Freedmen's?'

'Maybe. Who knows? Hoover would like to know, but he's in a bind. If he sets the Agency on Nixon and the man finds out he's being investigated before Hoover has the goods, it could backfire. He might ally with JFK to the extent of forcing Edgar out.'

'Hoover must have enough on both Kennedy and Nixon already.'

'You don't understand. There's no such thing as "enough". You don't get the way Edgar thinks. The truth is – though he doesn't know it – he would *never* betray either Kennedy or Nixon because he would lose his job in the same instant out of revenge. Instead he's looking for the Holy Grail: the piece of dirt so toxic it makes him immortal because Nixon couldn't allow it to come out even with the consolation of having Edgar's head on a pole.'

'And that's what he thinks this is?'

'What am I: a mind reader? There could be a hundred stories like this one and Edgar could be chasing every one of them. Where we came in is: why am I asking you and Maria to help? And the answer is that you're a correspondent for an overseas newspaper. You're deniable.'

'You should be a salesman,' I said.

Jeb knew I would agree to his offer. No, that isn't true. Rather he knew he ran no risk in making it and that, even if I refused, there was nothing I would or could do to hurt him or the GeStaPo. He didn't threaten me, not even by implication – he would never do that. I was his friend and he had confidence in me and his own powers of persuasion and the rightness of his cause. If I had refused and if something bad happened to me or to Maria, it would not have been ordered by him and he would have been genuinely sorry.

He said, 'Look, Harry, I do understand but truly there is no downside. So the DSD catches you while you're looking around? You're a foreign correspondent and it's what you do. DSD has no say as to your posting; that's the Agency's business. We slap your wrist and you carry on. And as for Maria, the worst is she loses her job and we find her a better one, still in Washington.' Then he made his pitch. 'Harry, I'm not going to say that this is some earth-shattering story you're going to be allowed to publish. If it's what Edgar is hoping for he'll bury it in his secret files to use behind the scenes and you won't get anywhere near, though more likely is it's something for a gossip column and means nothing at all. The point is that this is how you make your mark as someone we can trust. Don't get me wrong. We won't ask you to be a stooge, spouting propaganda – that sort of stuff you'll be able to take or leave. But you'll be an insider that people can talk to and know that you treat them seriously.'

He looked at me. And to understand that look you have to understand also that Jeb was not a bad man – or, at least, he was not a man with a bad heart. I can say no more than that he was an American doing what he thought was the best an American can do by his god and his country, and even I, who am neither an American nor a religious person, can recognize that there was a nobility in this. Did I believe him – that he had my interests in mind? I did and I didn't. It depends on what level you probe and the time of day and the mood in which you find me. It depends on whether I have a reliable memory of my own history, knowing what I know now and after my attempts to explain and excuse everything that happened.

I said, 'You're trying to convince the wrong person. I don't have entry to the Freedmen's. You know that. You want me to ask Maria.'

'If you ask her, I think she'll agree – I mean agree to try. She may not succeed; I recognize that. I'm not unreasonable.'

I said, 'I promise to try'– and, now I think of it, that was the worst of answers because it committed me to Jeb's cause while trying to shift the responsibility for the decision onto Maria. Afterwards, when he'd left, I stayed in the diner, writing my story at the plain wooden table with its coffee stains and cigarette burns, while a new shift of cops came in for a break and workers from a wholesale vegetable market argued about football plays. As I sat there I wrestled with the feeling that I'd been a coward but the clues were so subtle that at the time I did not know if I was or not.

With writing my story, clearing it through the system and getting it wired, it was ten in the morning before I was finished and I went home instead of going to the office. On the occasions when her shift changed, Maria had a day off work. By the time I reached the apartment, she'd cleaned the place and gone for lunch with one of her friends. I crashed on the couch and slept. She returned at four bringing food for dinner and a blouse she'd picked up from the sale rack at J C Penney that she wanted to try on and show me. While she changed, we kept up the conversation between rooms. She asked how I was and why I didn't come home last night, and she paid attention when I told her about the incident on the Arc.

'They actually admit it was terrorists?' she said. She was as surprised as I'd been and I explained it in the same terms Jeb had used.

So we talked on: me describing my evening, the crash, the suspected bomb, the fire, and Maria enthusing about the cheap blouse in which she looked beautiful. In a balanced life, I think these two strands were of a piece, each worth its weight, and Maria wasn't ignoring me: just making me share the space with the other things that are important. She proved it by asking questions whenever my narrative flagged – which it did because I was distracted trying to work out how to raise the matter of the patient at the Freedmen's Hospital and 'oh, by the way, would you mind risking your job for me?'

Then she took the subject out of my hands.

I'd fallen silent. Maria had put the blouse away and begun to cook an early supper before she started her late shift. There was news on the television: flickering black and white images of the anchor man and some stills lifted from Dave Kowalczk's shots. The news reader was giving out details of the terrorists: two Mexican names, an Anglo and someone called Blessed Salvation Jones, who was a mixed-race woman pale enough to pass. There was no mention of Charlie Joe Svensen, but that didn't surprise me if the ID I'd seen was a fake. A couple of talking heads from both Republican and Democratic parties nodded themselves stupid as they praised the President's firmness towards these 'godless scum'.

Meantime Maria changed the subject and talked about her lunch date with Linda, who also worked at the Freedmen's but wasn't on the same shift at present, which was why they'd met outside work to catch up. They'd chatted about mutual friends.

'You remember Alice Seebold? We were close for years but she moved to Chicago twelve months ago because of her husband's job. I used to tell you about her and you met her once.'

I probably had met her but the description meant nothing. I used to fake familiarity because relationships were important to Maria and it offended her to think I didn't care that much, but the fact was I knew hundreds of people through my work and had become immune even to their evident sorrows. I didn't know why I was supposed to be interested in either Linda or Alice.

'You're not listening,' Maria said.

'I am,' I said. 'But I'm not following.'

'You should, because it matters.'

'How so?'

'Because Alice works at Mercy Hospital. She nurses trauma patients.'

Now I was interested. 'You've spoken with her?'

'Linda has. She took over Alice's apartment when they moved, and there are still landlord issues and old bills to sort even a year on. They talk now and again. Linda called her two days ago.'

'And?'

'Alice says that Mercy has a high security isolation case just like ours.'

There is something in human psychology that looks for patterns and connections, and that relates other people's stories to our personal lives in surprising ways. Every journalist knows that if he publishes an article about a UFO sighting, there'll be reports of a hundred sightings and all of them will be fraudulent or deluded, a joining of the dots that shouldn't be joined. I had no doubt that, if I wrote a piece about the patient at the Freedmen's Hospital, it would generate more of the same and most of the stories would turn out to be grandma in a coma or a child with meningitis; the doctors insensitive and the relatives panicking and accusing them of hiding something.

I wasn't surprised when Maria said, 'According to Alice, there are rumors of more – dozens, maybe. They're scattered through the system, so no one knows the exact number.

If this was true then the only half-plausible theory we had was false. The patient at the Freedmen's was not an alcoholic politician or his lover put away to hide his shame. He was... I didn't have the slightest idea.

I said, 'And how would Alice know? Sorry – I'm not questioning what you were told. But how would she know?'

Maria shook her head, disappointed. 'I thought you'd be interested.'

'I am – Jeb is.'

'Jeb? Then why doesn't he find out? He's with the GeStaPo; all he needs to do is ask.'

I told her as Jeb had told me: about Hoover, Nixon and both Kennedy brothers; the politics of the thing.

She was scornful. 'We live in a dictatorship and the secret police can't find stuff out? Is this what we pay our taxes for?'

We thought this over and began to laugh with the laughter that always stopped our exchanges from becoming angry when otherwise they might. She came over to me and laid her head on my shoulder and I kissed her hair. I eased the tension by saying something about her work: that after being out and about all day she would be tired on her shift. And it was then that I decided to take the plunge. I told her that Jeb wanted her to discover the identity of the unknown patient and find out what was wrong with him.

She wasn't angry and she wasn't frightened. She said,

'Only Jeb could ask for such a favor.' She looked at her cooking: something with chilies and refried beans. 'This is ready. We should eat.'

I said, 'If what Alice told Linda is true, don't you think it may be important to learn what it means?'

'Yes, I do. That's why I told you; not just to make small talk about my day.' She laid out salads and a plate of tortillas and opened a bottle of beer to share. I took a seat and waited while she looked around the kitchen like an old person who has forgotten something. She was upset but not with me. 'I can try,' she said. 'Take some food. I can try, but I don't see what I can do. The guards have the room tightly buttoned up.'

'Maybe you should take a look in the records office,' I suggested. 'At night it may not be manned.'

She nodded. 'If I can get into it – and if there are records.'

'You don't believe there are?'

'Think of the efforts they've gone to: their own security; their own nurses; a doctor from outside. I don't think they want to leave traces.'

'But you can check the place out?'

'Yes – you can tell Jeb that I've tried.'

I didn't respond to this, but we each looked into each other's eyes and I thought she was telling me that I'd sold a little piece of her but she would forgive me.

We ate our meal and I volunteered to clear and wash the dishes. Maria retired to the bedroom to sleep for an hour and change into her nurse's uniform before leaving to take the bus. Having finished the dishes, I sat in the comfortable chair and read the local newspapers in the half-darkness by the light of the parchment-shaded lamp. The accident on the Arc had made the late editions and I studied the various accounts, which were all the same account, for what they could tell me. If you were to succeed as a foreign correspondent in Big A's America, you had to interpret the unintended code in which everything was written. In this case, there seemed no more to the business than a story they couldn't suppress and so they'd decided to use it for some bombast about defending American Values and the purity of the white race against degenerates, subversives and sexual deviants. I wondered if I was trying to join the dots that should not be joined.

I was dozing when Maria touched me on the shoulder and leaned over to kiss me on my closed eyelids. I woke and saw her in her topcoat, hat and low-heeled shoes. She smiled and whispered, 'I'll try,' in a way that confirmed I was forgiven for my small treason. I had a notion that a large part of love was the giving and receiving of acts of forgiveness and I was almost glad I'd given her cause because it had made us think about the depth of our relationship and the boundaries of the permissible. She left and I returned to dreaming about her, about Jeb, the accident at the Arc and the mysterious patient.

I was still dozing in the chair at midnight when the telephone rang. I wasn't the sort of reporter whose work meant calls at any hour. Offhand I couldn't think of anyone who would want to get in touch with me.

'Bennet,' I said.

'Maria,' she said. Her voice sounded muffled.

'Are you calling from the hospital?' It was something she never did except once in a while at the end of a shift, if she was going to be late or wanted me to do something before she got home.

'Yes.'

I thought the line had gone dead; it sometimes happened if the GeStaPo were over-zealous in monitoring my contacts. It reminded me to say, 'You recall our conversations about phoning me at home?'

Breathing then more silence.

'Maria?'

'I'm still here. I'm a little upset is all. I was wondering if you could come to the hospital to pick me up as soon as possible?'

Pick me up? I didn't have a car. Maria could have called a cab instead of me. And why would she break her shift?

'OK, sure,' I said, and, as casually as I could, 'Has something happened to make you feel unwell?'

'Uh huh.'

'Do you feel you can tell me?'

'I'll explain when you arrive.'

'Just a clue in case I need to bring anything with me – or anyone?' I was thinking of Jeb.

'I have to ring off,' Maria said. And this time I thought she was frightened. I waited, listening to her breathing and suddenly aware that I'd put her in danger. She seemed to collect herself and her final words were calmer.

She said, 'I have to get back on duty. One of our patients has died.'

7

It took me half an hour to get my act together, call a cab and drive to Bryant and 6th. It was heading for one in the morning and the streets were empty except for trucks making night deliveries or collecting garbage. Without the distractions of daytime, I noticed the flags flying limply on public buildings; the billboards with Big A's portrait: relics of a rally, a week or so ago, to celebrate one of the regime's new festivals, Patriotic Americans' Renewal Day. Now they had the irrelevance that night and silence lend to everything except the small details that relieve the stillness: a light over a flophouse doorway; a derelict moving between trash cans.

Maria had done the math and was standing just inside the main door of the Freedmen's, wrapped in a short navy cloak over her nurse's uniform. I paid off the cab but she didn't wait for me; instead turned into the main corridor and walked to shelter at the angle of one of the side columns that divided its length. I followed.

We hugged for maybe ten seconds: the wordless clinging that relieves distress and loneliness. When we pulled apart, her face showed a fierce vulnerability that looked like anger but was not. I felt not only love but pride in her because she was running the greater risk. To tell her so, I said something forgettable, as most expressions of love are.

Nurses and orderlies passed us but paid no attention. I wanted to talk about her: was she OK? But she had screwed up her courage to stay focused on the matter in hand. She put two fingers to seal my lips and said, 'He died about an hour and a half ago. I heard his nurse talking to one of the guards – not everything but enough to get the sense. You understand? It's difficult for me to leave the ward. Difficult to explain why I'm near a private room where I'm not working. I was there only a minute.'

'That's all right,' I said; then asked, 'So what happens next?'

'It depends. If they follow the standard protocol, the nurse will wash and dress the body. There are procedures to follow to close the eyes and deal with wounds or burns or if there are fluids, and she will follow them. I think this will happen with this patient and it's taking some time. Then an orderly will take the body to the morgue.'

'Where is it?'

'On the ground level in a small building across a court.'

I thought about this. I still could not see how there would be opportunity to view the corpse – still less to photograph it with the ancient Leica I'd brought with me.

I asked, 'Is the morgue manned at night?'

Maria shook her head. 'The technician only works in the day. The orderlies hold a key in their room. They let themselves into the morgue and either put the body in one of the coolers or leave it on a gurney for the technician to find in the morning, along with the notes.'

'Are you sure about this?'

'Yes. Sometimes a nurse will go along. It happens: a patient is too fat and there's a problem in steering the gurney or the arms keep flopping off; or it takes two people to lift from the gurney to the cooler, and there's only one orderly available. I've done it.'

Which meant there was likely to be no one in the morgue, if I could get into it before they got around to moving the body from the deathbed. And in turn that meant I had to lay hand on the orderlies' key, a problem to which I had no immediate solution.

'How long do bodies remain in the morgue?'

'Normally the families take them next day; two days maybe. If there's to be an autopsy the medical examiner may step in and move the body to the DC morgue. But in this case – if the Defense Department is involved – they may take it to Walter Reed.'

I checked my watch. It was still not long after one. I tried to calculate how long I had before the body was out of my reach, but I had neither a plan nor enough data. I tried to imagine the scenario from the point of view of whoever was directing this operation. Given the strangeness of whatever the patient had died from, they would probably want an autopsy. Given the secrecy, the DC medical examiner would be out of the picture. As a military hospital, Walter Reed was a possibility but there'd be other Army facilities I'd never heard of. Yet did it matter? Once the body was shipped from the Freedmen's, I was never going to see it again.

The other consideration was speed. Whoever was directing this would want to move the body and cover the tracks as quickly as possible. If the patient wasn't even in the hospital's records, they had no reason to wait for the morgue technician to arrive in the morning. My best guess was they would shift the body within the next hour or two. Which meant...

'Where is the orderlies' room?'

'Ground level – at the back. What do you intend to do?'

I had an idea which I couldn't grace with the title of a 'plan'. It felt more like jumping off a cliff in the hope of getting smarter on the way down. It meant relying on the orderlies being intimidated by the presence of the mystery patient and the authority of the DSD. And it would help if they were stupid.

I asked Maria to show me the way. She did so and we threaded our way through the night-time corridors. I was surprised at the number of staff still at their jobs, having never thought much about the subject before. The difference from daytime was fewer people out of uniform and a change in the quality of sound, the faintest of echoes. It wasn't an enormous place and in a minute or so we were at a door with a plastic sign that read 'Orderlies Room', scratched paintwork, and a tarnished brass kick-plate. I advised Maria to stand where she wouldn't be seen and turned the handle.

No surprises. A plain room except for a girly calendar and a Monroe pin-up. A desk with a phone and the usual stuff. Lockers. A table with a set of mixed chairs in stained pinewood that had rubbed pale where these things do. Pressed aluminum ash trays with brewery logos, filled with butts that accounted for the fug and the smell. Two men in grey hospital coveralls smoking and playing cards.

I looked nothing like the DSD guards described by Maria: too old, wrong haircut, and lacking the sullen look of men who would rather be killing people than watching over them. But, in my overcoat and hat I might pass for the guy who gave orders to such types.

I flashed my press card to men who'd never seen one and said, 'Schroder – DSD. The patient on floor three has died and we want to move the body. Give me the key to the morgue.'

I held out my hand while they looked at each other.

The slow one asked, 'You want us to take a stiff to the morgue?'

'Did I say that?'

'It's the system. We're the guys who move the patients.'

I stared him down. 'What patient? You've never heard of this patient. He was never here, never died and no one took him to the morgue. And my name isn't Schroder. Now give me the key!'

This was B movie dialogue, but scenes for which life provides no experience have to be improvised from material both sides will understand. I needed to prime expectations so they knew I would slap them around and if necessary shoot them with the gun I didn't have, because that's the way things were supposed to happen.

'Hold your horses,' said the not-so-slow one, 'I'll get the key.' He rose from his chair, easy and heavy, went to the desk and pulled a key with a tag from the right-hand drawer. 'Here it is, pal. All I ask is you bring it back when you're finished – you not being here and all.'

I spared him a thin smile and tipped my hat. 'The American tax payer thanks you.'

Maria was staring at the wall, looking blindly at a fire emergency poster. She fell into step and we walked to the exit to the courtyard and crossed to the low unlit brick building with the 'Morgue' sign. The lock turned easily and we went inside. I wasn't bothered about switching on the light. Any passer-by would assume an orderly was in.

Pale strip lighting gave everything a greyish tone. A bank of coolers along one wall. A sink and preparation surfaces along another beneath a grilled window. A chemicals cabinet with a refrigerator below it occupied the third; both opening only to a key. The fourth wall was fitted with general shelving and cupboards, a clock and a locker for the technician's stuff. The shelves held beakers, vessels and other equipment that meant nothing to me. I recognized only forceps and what I thought was a Stryker saw.

In the middle of the room was an autopsy or preparation table – I didn't know if there was a difference. Next to it an orderly had parked a gurney with a body on it. Maria stepped over to the gurney and coolly folded back the sheet from over the dead person. He looked to be a working man in his fifties: the visible edges of his teeth showed some missing and the others were smoke stained; the skin was wrinkled and jaundiced, the hair thin and worn in a comb-over. Maria glanced at the notes. She said, 'Giuseppe Malatesta – died of pancreatic cancer. I don't think he is our patient.' I didn't think he would be.

I gave Maria the door key. 'Take this back to the

orderlies' room. Tell them some guy you don't know asked you to do it. Then go back to your ward and work to the end of your shift. I'll see you at home.'

'You are going to stay?'

'My only chance is that they bring the body here and feel they can leave it unguarded because the building is secure.'

'Do you think that will happen?'

'I've no idea, but it's the only game.'

'You'll have to hide.'

I pointed to the technician's locker. It was made of painted sheet metal, tall and broad enough to hold a man. The door had a cheap lock and the key was in it. I figured to hide there.

Maria looked distressed – not losing it; that was never the case. I told her I'd be all right though neither of us knew if it would be so. We kissed and she left and I had one of those feelings that come at stray moments – some important and some seemingly random – that we might never see each other again, though Jeb had assured us that we were running no serious risk.

I opened the locker door. The overall size was tall enough, but at a glance I saw that a foot or so of space was taken by a shelf for small possessions; in this case, a fishing magazine and a pack of Chesterfields. The shelf was riveted to the shell, so I was stuck with it. Below was a hang rail and the technician's coveralls. The effective space was less than five feet. I was going to be cramped.

I couldn't risk more time to reconnoiter. I returned to the outside door and switched off the light. A weak glare from the courtyard filtered through the window and I was able to make my way back to the locker without colliding with anything. Once inside I tried out various positions to find the most comfortable, but I suspected that, whatever I settled on, it wouldn't stay comfortable for long. If a DSD guard and not an orderly delivered the body and stayed any time, I wasn't sure how I would manage.

My other problem was keeping the locker closed once I was inside. Unless the key was turned, the resting position of the door was an inch or so ajar: enough to be obvious. The key worked only from the outside – after all who would want to shut themselves in? The door was made from a single mild steel sheet, folded to turn the rough edges inside and reinforced midway down by a soldered metal bar. By pinching on the bar and using finger pressure on the folded edge nearest the lock I could pull the door enough to give the appearance of being closed and locked with the key; and if someone tested it from outside, it would even offer a little resistance. But it would be illusory. One tug and the door would open.

My hope was that tug would never come.

I folded myself into the locker space and did my trick with the closing door and waited what I took to be five minutes. My bent back and neck ached and my knees burned with lactic acid. I knew I couldn't keep this up. I got out of the locker and stretched and exercised to relieve the aches. I practiced getting back in the safe position and calculated that, as a minimum, I needed five seconds. If I listened intently I thought I would probably get those five seconds, but it was too close to call.

I considered the alternative. I could wait at the door and waylay whoever brought the body. There were plenty of heavy objects in the morgue to let me cold cock whoever it was. Or so the theory said, and maybe it's true for specialists in close combat. Amateurs, however, are more likely to miss, or use insufficient force, or kill the victim. I wasn't in the game of murdering innocent orderlies doing their jobs, and if one of the DSD guards brought the body and my first blow missed, I wasn't going to get a second. If there were two of them, they would probably kill me. Knocking people out is for Hollywood and cheap thrillers.

I was just a middle-aged journalist looking for a story and it wasn't my business to risk life and limb or start an international incident. The locker was the only option.

The matter was taken out of my hands by a noise outside the door. I was back in hiding before I heard the door open and the click of a switch. Noises were fairly clear, but I could see nothing, not even a trace of light.

There were two voices, which had to be the DSD agents.

First Voice said, 'Did you get that name Schroder? Who do we know that's a Schroder?'

Second Voice said, 'I thought maybe the body wagon had arrived – that would explain – but I checked and they're still gassing up.'

'It still bugs me. Maybe those bozos in the orderly room misheard the name? You don't suppose Doc Vipic is here?'

'Nuh. Last I heard he was still in Chicago. I put a call through to pass the message the patient had died, but there's no way he gets here so quick.'

There is a boundary between puzzlement and suspicion and I wasn't yet sure which side this exchange fell on. The conversation broke off and was followed by other noises I supposed had something to do with moving the gurney. If the wagon was on its way, I thought the chances were they would wait with the body, in which case my efforts were a waste of time.

Then First Voice took up his theme again. He had what I thought was a high Appalachian whine. He said, 'Let's think this thing through, Jerry.'

'What thing?'

'The Schroder thing, what else? '

'You think it through.'

'I am doing – that's my point. This Schroder gets the key to the morgue in order to bring down the body.'

' 'Cept he doesn't bring down the body because we've

just brought it down.'

'Except – as you say – he doesn't bring down the body. In fact he doesn't even go to the room where the body is. Instead, a few minutes later he returns the key.'

'A nurse returns the key.'

'You're right.' – a pause – 'So why doesn't Schroder do it in person? And what has he done in the few minutes he has the key?'

'He steals something?'

'Like what? All there is here is standard hospital stuff. Nothing connects to the patient. But Schroder – he knows about the patient.'

Another pause and Second Voice said wearily, 'Shit, you think he's still here?'

No reply.

One – two – three. The silence became noises I took to be footfalls. Then a cupboard door opened and closed. A metal object was knocked in passing. Ten seconds of uncertainty, followed by a slight feel of tension on the door.

Second Voice said, 'This is locked. The tech must have the key.'

There is a law in these things: the rhythm of human action. Try once – try twice. You never try just once. I waited for that next pull on the handle.

But, before it came, First Voice said something I'd never thought of, and the surprise of it almost made me want to laugh. He said, 'Schroder isn't here.'

'He's not?'

The tension on the door eased.

'He's not.'

'OK. You want to enlighten me?'

'He's planted a bug. I should have realized before now. This has all the marks of a GeStaPo black bag job: it has FBI written all over it.'

Second Voice groaned, 'Christ, but I think you're right.

So what do we do?'

'I think we go get coffee some place where we can talk freely. When the wagon arrives, we'll tell them to watch their tongues. Then, once the body has gone, we'll get our boys to do a sweep, and, whatever equipment they find, the Boss can decide whether to stick it to Hoover.'

8

Life can change in an instant and afterwards there is no going back to the person we once were or the easy courses of our previous existence. The only question is whether we recognize the moment when it happens so that we can adjust to the new reality and, if it is a tragic one, try to mitigate its effects. My moment happened when I opened the locker door and the light in the morgue was still on and a single DSD agent was standing not six feet from me, bored and fingering the objects on the shelves to my right.

I didn't know why he was still there, though now I have to suppose the two men had second thoughts and decided one of them should stay to keep watch over the body while the other had coffee. Whatever the case, he spotted the movement and turned towards me and reflexively reached for the gun that was under his jacket. I had no training for this eventuality. I just reached for the nearest object – the Stryker saw – and swung it in his direction. It caught him full on the side of the head and pole-axed him so that he keeled over and banged into one of the gurneys, sending it skittering across the floor. In less than five seconds from opening the locker door, I was looking at a dead DSD agent stretched out in front of me, with the left side of his skull caved in at the temple from the weight of the Stryker saw and the force of my blow. As I've said, amateurs are in no position to anticipate the effects of their actions.

I now knew this from experience, and also, as soon as it happened, that my life was irrevocably changed. I'd become a killer – some might say a murderer – and there would be no way back from this fact. What faced me with overwhelming urgency was whether I had the nerve to deal with it. I began by checking for a pulse on the fallen man in case my immediate feeling was wrong. But, of course, there was no pulse.

I had to decide my priorities. Above all what I needed was time. The only thing that suggested my presence in the morgue was the corpse of the DSD agent. There was no spare gurney on which to place and cover it – and I doubted it would stay unnoticed for long – but there was the bank of coolers that would provide an even better hiding place. None of them was occupied and there was a key in the door of each. It wasn't difficult to haul the dead man and lift him into a box on the lowest row. The morgue technician might notice in the morning, but I fancied he would be occupied first thing with drinking coffee, reading the newspaper and doing the other things that people do who work alone, and then he would attend to the corpse of his only customer, the Italian who had died of pancreatic cancer. Once he did figure out that someone had been in his sanctum during the night and left him a present, he would need to open the cooler, and for that he would need the key, which I proposed to take – though I recognized there might be a spare to hand.

This scenario might gain me until noon before the discovery was made and acted on. What it didn't take account of was the second agent who would notice his friend was missing as soon as the wagon arrived to take the mystery patient, which I expected at any time. I guessed his first reaction would be puzzlement and annoyance, but he would put these feelings aside while he saw to removal of the body. In the best case, he would have to go with it and only later would he file a report when his partner failed to appear. In the worst case, he would go looking for his friend and begin interrogating the orderlies and hospital security, if there were any. It would take a stretch of imagination on his part to leap from 'missing' to 'murdered' and still more to work out where the corpse was. The enigmatic 'Schroder' would be on his mind but this would hinder rather than help rapid action. If

– as he supposed – Schroder was with the Agency, then the problem was above his pay grade and he would lay it off on his superiors, who would have to come up to speed and plan a course of action and mobilize resources.

However the matter played out, I was fairly confident of being safe until midday: time for Maria to meet me at the apartment after work and for us to decide what we would do next. In fact, since discovery of the body didn't directly and immediately lead to me, I might easily have a day or two before the pieces were put together, but I could use that margin of safety.

Now I think of it, the brutality of these events wasn't in the killing, but in the searching of the body. The killing was an accident without thought and over in an instant. The search was a deliberate violation, an unholy intimacy that brought home to me that I'd reduced another human being to a powerless object, even though the dead man would have had no compunction in killing me. I retrieved his wallet with ID and fifty dollars in cash, both of which might be useful. He also had the morgue key, which gave me some protection against being suddenly interrupted. And there was a gun, which I pocketed. It was an automatic, but beyond that I knew nothing about small handguns. I also took the spare magazine.

Finished with the body, I looked for signs of blood but found none beyond a slight smear on the floor. I moved the gurney with the dead Italian back into place and set about wiping surfaces and the locker in the hope of erasing my prints which were on file with the GeStaPo. Only when this was done did I turn to the matter that had brought me here: the mystery patient.

At which point the door rattled.

'Jack? This is Lewis, let me in. There's still no sign of the wagon. You want coffee?' The voice was unconcerned. Why should it have been otherwise?

I froze. I reminded myself that I had the morgue key.

Unless I gave him cause, Lewis-whoever wasn't about to pull out his piece and break down the door. He was going to curse and then go to the orderly room to hunt out a spare, or maybe just look for his partner.

'Damn it, Jack' – still calm – 'am I standing here talking to myself?' More rattling of the door. 'Jack?'

I pulled the automatic out of my pocket and studied it. These things came with a safety catch, didn't they? And it would be on. If I could find it, I would be ready for Lewis-whoever as he came through the door, and putting one or several bullets through him at this range wasn't beyond even my abilities. Neither was it beyond my moral capacity – or at least it wasn't beyond the capacity of the stranger who had come into being five minutes before.

But that dumb bastard was fumbling and couldn't find the safety catch.

And the other man didn't break down the door. Instead I heard a muttered sigh and then he walked away, his steel heel-tips clicking on the paving of the courtyard.

I pulled back the cover from the mystery patient. He lay on a gurney parked next to that of the dead Italian but, unlike the dead Italian, he was in some sort of sealed body bag with an unfamiliar hazard marking. If I broke the seal, it would be noticed but in the first instance the men who moved the body would not be suspicious and their immediate concern would be to get it away from the Freedmen's to – wherever. The broken seal would most likely be discovered later rather than sooner and it would take time before they worked out that it had happened at the morgue. I didn't think that breaking into the bag reduced my margin of safety. In any case, why stop? They couldn't execute me twice.

So I broke the seal without thinking that maybe it was there for my protection. I unzipped the body bag and took half a dozen shots of the occupant, hoping my antique

Leica was good for the conditions and the light settings were right. The corpse was that of a human being not an alien monster or a member of the Legion of the Undead, and my mind, concerned with the task of photography, registered only the bare fact that there were a lot of burn dressings that made it difficult to get a clear picture. In other respects, there was an ordinariness about this dead person, that made the incident less interesting than if I'd been taking snaps of my children. The mystery, the danger, the whatever-it-was lay in the context of who this person was and how they died and I had no grip on that. I zipped up the body bag, did my best to cover the broken seal, and moved the gurney back to its place. Then I turned off the light and slipped out of the morgue, and no one stopped me.

The courtyard had its own access onto the street. I caught a night bus going my way. It was sparsely filled with cleaners, workers at the end of their shifts, and a couple of young GIs sleeping after partying all night. The passengers were mostly Mexicans – pure-blood natives working as indentured labor, not Creoles to judge from their features. American friends sometimes told me of a time when there were few Mexicans in Washington but lots of blacks. The Hispanic migration had replaced the previous African one, and my friends – liberals talking to other liberals over drinks and canapés in some official reception or other – would ask slyly: given the goal of purifying the bloodline and values of the American people, what had been achieved by substituting one inferior race for another?

Then again, what was the point of any of it, except to ease the anxieties of frightened limited white men by soothing them with fierce certainties?

I reached our apartment and let myself in and no one jumped out of the shadows to arrest me. It was still two hours short of dawn. I fixed myself a drink and sat down to work through the calculation of my position that until now I had felt only instinctively. Jeb Lyman would still be at home but I wasn't going to call him except maybe to judge if he would stand by his earlier assurances now there was a dead DSD agent to account for. My invention of the mysterious 'Schroder' had been useful at the time, but I was conscious that I'd unintentionally drawn the Agency to the Defense Department's attention – precisely what my involvement was supposed to avoid. The only consolation was that there was no hard evidence of the connection, and a G-man would have had no reason to lift the cash, ID and gun of the dead man. Hoover would be able to talk himself out of any responsibility.

I was packing a suitcase when Maria arrived home. She knew immediately that something was wrong. I asked her to take off her street clothes and sit down in her usual seat, and I removed her shoes and began to massage her feet as I did every day out of love. She sat there tensely, watching me do it, and gradually I told her the story of what had happened at the morgue and how I'd become a killer in the time it takes to swat a fly and with even less premeditation. I told her I had photographs of the mystery patient, but for the moment they seemed unimportant to both of us.

At the end she said, 'They'll trace us here those – people. They don't know you, but they know that a nurse returned the key of the morgue and someone inside the hospital leaked the news that the patient had died. My time missing from the ward will be noticed, and the other nurses won't protect me – I wouldn't expect them to. If I go back to work I'll be arrested – today or tomorrow.'

There was no answer to this, and she wasn't angry. She had a quick intelligence and had worked out even those things I hadn't said. She had accepted the risks, but whether she would have accepted them without her love for me remains unanswerable. The journalist inside me

72

tries to recreate this scene so that I can interpret it, but all I see is two undistinguished people in their ordinary clothes, quietly discussing their future in a cheap apartment. There should be drama, but there isn't.

Maria asked, 'Will Jeb Lyman stand by his promises?' I knew she'd always been skeptical of those promises.

'I can't say. When we thought this through, neither of us had in mind that I was going to kill a DSD agent. Without that, I could be left free under the Agency's unspoken protection. But now we're talking about one of their own, and the DSD will come after me unless Hoover openly intervenes.'

'So Jeb can't help us?'

'He can – but only if the GeStaPo stashes us where the DSD can't find us.'

'You mean a GeStaPo prison.'

'You'll be safe with Jeb,' Maria said. 'I can take care of myself – we have ways of going underground. I mean people of my background.'

That last part might be true, but Maria couldn't know how safe that would be. There's a world of difference between being one person in a sea of undocumented immigrant workers and the object of a GeStaPo or DSD manhunt. If she was caught by either of them, we both knew she would not survive their attentions. Her offer was to save me by cutting loose, and on this day, when I had just discovered myself as a killer, the thought of being the man who would sacrifice her to save himself was one I could not bear.

I broke down and began to cry.

We went to bed and lay down in our clothes and held each other and I slept for an hour until I woke to a grey dawn and the sound of Maria making coffee. She brought it to me and sat on the edge of the bed and we resumed our conversation.

'Where would we go?' she asked.

I'd thought about this but hadn't come to any final conclusion. The newspaper had a plan for getting its people out in case of emergency, but it didn't provide for passengers. I said, 'The main thing is to get out of Washington. I was thinking of Chicago.'

'I thought you didn't believe the story Linda got from Alice – about the second patient?'

I told her what I remembered of the conversation between the two DSD agents. 'The doctor who saw to the Freedmen's patient is called Vipic. He seems to be based in Chicago – or maybe has another patient in Chicago; it wasn't clear. It may be coincidence, but what they said seems to corroborate Alice's story. I'd like to talk with her.'

We both knew this wasn't a solution to our problem, merely a deferment, but for the moment it was the best I could do. Maria nodded. She said, 'I packed a valise while you were sleeping. We're going right away?'

'Not right away. I have things to do. I want to get the film developed and I need cash. But we should get out of this place.'

'What do you intend to do with the photographs?'

'I'm going to send a set to Jeb. Since the DSD doesn't want the Agency to know what they're doing, I figure it can only help us if they do. Also, I don't want to burn my bridges. If I send in the pictures, it'll be a mark of good faith.'

There wasn't much else to say. The apartment had been the base for our life together, the place where the small gestures that sustain the daily routine of a relationship are carried out. And in the space of a couple of hours we abandoned it as if it had never meant anything. There were a couple of cheap hotels in the neighborhood and I booked us a room for a day in Maria's name. She was supposed to deposit her papers for inspection by the police and return the next day, but this wasn't a fastidious place and ten dollars solved their problem. I left her to sleep and went about my necessary business.

I took a cross town bus to visit a shop off 28th Street SE which serviced cameras and processed Dave Kowalczyk's films when he lacked time to do it himself. It was run by a Japanese-American who answered to Ito, though I don't know if that was his name. I sometimes wondered what he thought of Big A's America and his place in it – whatever that was – but it wasn't something we ever talked about. I asked him if he could develop the film in an hour and make me two sets of prints. I also asked for a couple of passport-sized photographs and the gum used for mounting. He didn't question my reasons but said he could do what I wanted. We went into a small upstairs studio for the passport shot; then I left him to it and went to find a diner and get breakfast. I also took the opportunity to go to a branch of my bank and draw five hundred dollars from my checking account, which raised some eyebrows and a request for identification, but they paid out.

I returned to Ito's, asked for my prints and settled with him.

'There's something else,' I said.

He cast a glance at the prints he'd just rushed through and said, 'I thought there might be.' He looked at me calmly and neutrally, like a floorwalker in a high-class store.

I pulled out the key Perry Cawthorne had given me on the day of my arrival at Lindbergh Airport way back three years ago and passed it across the counter. I said, 'I want the box that this fits.'

Ito nodded and went into the back of the shop. He returned with a small metal case that a construction worker might use to carry a few hand tools. He went to the front of the shop, turned the door sign to 'closed' and disappeared into the back again. I opened the box and took out two envelopes: one thin and one fat, but both of a size to slip in my overcoat pockets. I wiped my prints and left the open box on the counter. I quit the shop before Ito re-appeared.

I took another cross-town bus and returned to the hotel. I found Maria in our room, and this time she threw herself into my arms and cried. In a strange and probably selfish way I was glad because something in me – my wounded masculinity perhaps – needed her to reflect my own fear. I calmed her and asked a few regular questions: had she eaten? Could she use more clothes? None of them mattered; they were only noise to distract both of us. What we wanted was to make love – for the reassurance not the pleasure of the thing. And so we did it now, still in our clothes, on the bed with its broken mattress and the window letting in daylight and the stares of anyone who cared to stare from the high building opposite – once, then a second time, intensely and selfishly. Afterwards we didn't talk. There was no bathroom, and Maria washed herself down at the basin like one of the women in a painting by Dégas, women whose actions seem gentle and self-absorbed and who are unaware of the man in the room, watching them and trying to understand who they are.

We re-ordered our clothes and Maria asked how I'd managed my errands. I said I'd done OK.

She asked, 'Can I see the photographs?'

I said, 'Sure,' and laid them out on the dressing table.

Maria looked at them and gave a pained sigh.

'Do you know what they mean?' I asked.

She shook her head.

The pictures were of a young black woman. She was extensively burned, to judge from the dressings. Her hair had fallen out or was shaved. And she appeared to be pregnant.

9

Everyone knows there are no blacks in Washington. Yet a young black woman whom someone loved had died in pain at the Freedmen's Hospital when she should not have been there at all. There was a tragedy and a mystery in it, and Maria and I did not know what it meant.

I thought back to the favored theory: that Secretary of Defense Nixon was covering for one of his political cronies. It was perfectly plausible that a white congressman or senator who hated people of color nonetheless kept a pregnant black mistress. The boundaries between the things we hate and the things for which we lust are confused, and consistency has never been a prominent characteristic of human beings though hypocrisy has. So it was a believable theory except for two things. It didn't account for the burns the poor woman had suffered, and it didn't explain the second patient at the Mercy Hospital in Chicago.

I remembered that Jeb had told me of an alternative: the longshot that would get me good odds with the GeStaPo in-house betting syndicate. The military were running a rocket program somewhere in Florida and had suffered a major disaster which Dick Nixon wanted to cover-up in order to preserve his credit as a worthy successor to Big A. Granted there was no evidence that such a disaster had occurred, but that is the beauty of conspiracy theories. This one accounted for the burns on the corpse and the possibility of multiple victims squirrelled away in the hospital system to keep the incident under wraps. It didn't explain how a young, pregnant black woman could be among the dead. She wasn't supposed to be in Florida – or anywhere else in the United States.

I didn't believe either theory, but I didn't have another.

I notice how, so often, the things that affect us profoundly cause us to fall into silence. To say anything to the point means we must search our memory for appropriate dialogue – a role to play – and hence the words may signify nothing, though they disguise this fact even from ourselves.

Maria placed the photographs back carefully on top of the dressing table and said only that she needed to sleep. I checked my watch but did nothing to dissuade her. My plan was that we would hole up for the day and catch an evening train to Chicago and then… My thoughts didn't stretch much further.

I checked the contents of the 'scoot box' I'd picked up from Ito. The thin envelope contained an American passport and a domestic identity card in names that weren't mine. The thicker envelope held a thousand dollars in mixed small bills.

The scoot box is a fantasy – more for reassurance than use, though we don't tell ourselves this. The truth is that foreign correspondents, for the most part, are failed thriller writers not heroes and the fake identity in the envelope is of a piece with the fake identity we imagine to be ourselves. In reality, when we are arrested, it usually happens without notice. There is a knock on the door or we are picked up in the street or caught by a police sweep at a forbidden demonstration. If by chance we get wind of what is coming, the protocol is to take our own passport and head for the airport or, in my case, the train to Canada and hope we are ahead of the security services. Once arrested, we stay put, don't try to escape, and wait for the British Foreign Office to work its diplomatic magic. Which inspires us with confidence.

Attempting to flee the country with a forged American passport is a sure-fire way to get shot as a spy. It is suited only to those who have killed a DSD agent and for whom the alternative is to go to the chair or die in a torture cellar.

I pocketed the papers and the money and turned to examine the ID I'd taken from the dead agent. His name was John – alias 'Jack' – Ephraim Wagner and he was a captain in the U.S. Army. The picture showed a handsome man in his thirties with a buzz cut and a serious expression. I found it difficult to relate it to the man I'd killed, and that was probably as well. I wondered if at some point I would be overwhelmed by guilt and horror at what I'd done, but I had a strange feeling this would not happen – that I had truly crossed a threshold of experience. But it was possible that this was just part of the process.

Wagner's photograph was fixed to his ID and wasn't to be removed without damaging the rest. I considered the alternatives but decided I couldn't pass as him even if I changed my haircut. I applied gum to one of the shots taken by Ito and positioned it to cover the original. The result was okay at ordinary speaking distance but wouldn't get by if examined. The question was: who would have the guts to demand a close check of a DSD agent's ID other than another agent or the GeStaPo? Put like that, the risk of using it seemed reasonable unless I ran into an obsessive clerk who saw himself as dictator within his own small world.

Maria woke as the long rays of late afternoon sunlight were casting the shadows of the window blinds across the room. She freshened up and put on her regular clothes. We spoke little and what we did say had the brevity and purposefulness of street signage. Nothing was broken in our relationship, but we both sensed that it might be if we moved from the task in hand to an exploration of how we had got where we were and our fears for the future.

We checked out of the hotel and took a couple of buses to Union Station, avoiding the attentions of any cabbie who might remember us.

Twenty years before, there had been talk of the death of

the railroad under competition from a long-distance airline network, but it had never happened. The war had taken most airplane production, and what was left was mostly used by politicians, rich people and the military. The rest of us were confined to overcrowded dilapidated rolling stock and an infrastructure that needed repair and investment, both of which were promised after the latest drive for victory succeeded, and had been for twenty years.

In its heyday fifty years before, Union Station had reflected the country's aspirations to imperial grandeur with its great barrel-vaulted ceiling and the marble and white granite hall, overlooked by statuary that paid homage to the Greeks and Romans. The reality of empire had blackened this glory with grime and smoke; rain and snow had entered by the broken skylights and weather-streaked the walls; birds nested among the stone centurions and fouled them with their droppings. Above the general gloom of the huge noisy concourse the flags and slogans of the regime hung or fluttered, proclaiming the moral righteousness of the American People in the cause of Humanity, but they failed in their effect like the tokens of a parade that has already passed by.

I scanned the crowd. Military police were moving among the mass of young conscripts as they flowed to and from the former Presidential Suite that these days served as a forces' canteen. The boys joshed with them or ignored them and continued dozing on their kitbags, playing cards or strumming on guitars. GeStaPo agents lounged in pairs by the exits, conspicuously unable to look either relaxed or harassed and hence visible to anyone with an eye. I noted them but had no reason to think they were expecting me. The moment of truth – if there were one – would come at the ticket counter when a clerk, alerted to look for a man of my age and appearance with an implausible American accent, would call to one of the watchers and ask him to examine my papers. I approached that clerk now.

I said, 'Two for the next Chicago train.'

My accent didn't register with him and he didn't look up. He said, 'Train's full,' and signaled for the next in line.

I tapped on the glass and badged him with agent Wagner's ID. 'This says it isn't.'

He looked up, bored. 'Uh huh. You got a travel warrant?'

My mistake – soldiers and agents of the government don't pay cash.

'Last minute thing. I'll pay and claim back.'

He thought about this, and then issued the tickets. I paid him. He would or he would not remember me, and any hesitation on my part would only reinforce his memory. I ushered Maria away and we joined the press of passengers waiting on the platform for a B&O train signed Pittsburgh and Cleveland with an extension to Chicago.

But first I dropped an envelope containing a set of photographs into the mailbox. I didn't know if this was wise or not.

We found a carriage with the seats taken mostly by soldiers on furlough or between postings: young men in their late teens and twenties. Now I thought of it, it was unusual to see males of that age out of uniform, which even disabled veterans wore from a sense of pride. I'd got used to old men performing the work of the young that they wouldn't do in England: pump jockeys at filling stations; short order cooks; traveling salesmen carrying sample cases like the fellow sitting opposite me. Young women, too, journeying alone for a brief tryst with a fiancé or trailing children on the way to a parent's home, their faces anxious and hopeful. On the railroad, I sensed a people uprooted by an unending war and waiting edgily for the future they were promised. I wondered how long they would wait, but history teaches that there is a lot of patience in a nation.

The soldiers were good-natured. They accepted with grace when I bumped them out of a couple of seats, using my DSD badge again. Or perhaps it was the sight of Maria, her face relaxed into beauty by her tiredness. They doubled-up in the other seats and indulged in horseplay until the night wore on and they went to sleep or drifted down the train to find a quiet spot to smoke.

Maria and I were still saying little beyond the immediately necessary. I wondered how I could change this and whether it lay with me to try or if to do so would be an intrusion. I closed my eyes and dozed a while. Outside, the night fell as we traced the valley of the Potomac. I remember slowing as we passed Harper's Ferry, where old mad John Brown had fought for the freedom of the blacks who no longer lived in this country but someplace else where we were assured they were happy. Looking through the window I saw a glimmer of moonlight on the river mingled with my own reflection. Then we were swinging through curves as we scaled the eastern escarpment of the Alleghenies where the lower crests were silhouetted here and there with the ragged shapes of hemlock and maple, black against the star field.

I slept some more and woke to daylight, feeling hungry and remembering we'd made no provision for food. Maria smiled and told me we'd passed several cities during the night. Cumberland and Wheeling, she thought – which was what the soldiers had told her though they may have been joking. I detected sulfur in the air and thought we might be close to Pittsburgh. A stop was scheduled there and the train would be re-configured – some coaches decoupled and others joining – before the next leg to Cleveland. I could pick up something to eat.

So Pittsburgh, where things went as anticipated. Some of the soldiers left and others joined and began playing a harmonica and singing jazz songs fresh from Europe where the music was the fashion. The traveling salesman shouted, 'Will y'all hold it with that coon music!' and said to Maria, 'Those boys should know better than to offend a lady's ear. The problem is that this music is so seductive – yes, it surely is.'

The conductor came along the carriage and clipped the tickets of the new joiners. Two agents in hats and suits followed, randomly checking papers, mostly to make sure there were no deserters among the GIs. I showed my American civilian ID. They left Maria alone. The harmonica player struck up a country number about a woman's love for that no-good man, and the old traveling salesman tapped his foot and took a slug of whiskey from a bottle kept in a paper sack in his sample case, the same he'd been sipping at all night. He winked at me but didn't offer any.

We reached Cleveland sometime in the afternoon, after much shunting and a change of engines so we could use the Union Terminal. For me it might have been Pittsburgh except for the canals and the lake to the north and a river, the Cuyahoga, that I'd never heard of. I felt disoriented, unable to remember whether I was supposed to make a time shift or had already done so or it wasn't due yet but only as we got deeper into Ohio. The soldiers switched again – some leaving, some joining – and the traveling salesman said that this was his stop and thanked me for our conversation, though we'd scarcely spoken a word. A young woman took his place and sat silently gnawing her lip and looking every few minutes at a watch with a thin white strap.

There is a difference between the sudden shock of terror and the grinding boredom of fear. For good or bad, terror provokes action. Fear depresses the spirits so there seems no way to escape it, and it is probably in this low state that people confess to crimes they may or may not have committed. Once we left Cleveland, the conductor did his round and the two GeStaPo agents repeated their routine of rousting the soldiers. I had a feeling that, if they asked me for my papers, I would fold and tell them the whole sorry business – though in truth I don't think I would have acted on this impulse. In the event, it didn't come to that. The G-men yanked one of the soldiers out of his seat and hauled him off to the baggage van and manacled him to a rail until he would be offloaded in Chicago and sent to the stockade.

Outside the window the flat farmlands of Ohio and Indiana laid themselves out under a clear, seemingly infinite sky, with little evidence of people except the orderly fields, the occasional dirt road leading to a lonely farmstead, and the small towns with their grain silos and harvester repair shops at which our train did not stop. Mile after mile of this scene, with nowhere to go to escape or relieve it, added to my mood of fearful serenity. From time to time I checked with Maria to see if I could read her. Always she gave me a gentle smile, but we continued to say little. There was nothing to talk about that would not break us apart or send the young woman with the cheap watch running in horror to fetch the G-men. So we found ourselves in the crowded carriage with the person we most loved in the world, and yet the feeling was of loneliness bordering on despair.

And then it was night-time and we were in Chicago. I had been there once before at a celebration of the thirtieth anniversary of one of the milestones in Big A's 'Second American Revolution', when the Mid-West moved decisively into his camp. On that occasion, I'd persuaded the newspaper to spring for a night at the Waldorf Astoria in order to be close to the politicians. This time I found us a place in Lincoln Park, with a door squeezed between store fronts and signs in Spanish as well as English. I gave my ID to the desk clerk who put it in a drawer with others for collection by the police and return sometime the next day. At Maria's suggestion, I told him she was a lady friend I'd picked up in a bar and she wouldn't be staying the night, so papers were unnecessary. Five dollars settled the matter.

'A lady friend, huh? You sure know how to spoil a girl,' she said, when she saw the room.

Throwing my hat on the bed I said, 'Well, nothing's too good for you, doll.'

'James Cagney?'

'Humphrey Bogart.'

'Nothing like.'

She stepped towards me and let me take her in my arms. She asked, 'Where have we been these last two days?'

I shook my head. I said something about the loneliness of trains, but the words aren't memorable to me now, only the feeling that we had taken a brief journey away from each other and then discovered that we were bound together. I by the attraction to her that I had felt with almost unbearable intensity from the time I first saw her. She by whatever qualities I have, which she never named. Except she said that at times I made her laugh. Thin stuff but enough.

We went to bed and slept out of exhaustion. Our plan – though not much of one – was to phone Alice's apartment in the morning. Then, if as was likely she happened to be at the hospital, we'd go there and try to find opportunity to speak with her. I did not know what we would learn, or what we would do with the knowledge, or where we would go next. I did not know whether Jeb was my friend or my enemy because the accident of another man's death had moved us into territory that friendship never contemplated.

In the morning, we made the call from a payphone in a bar, Maria doing the talking because Alice didn't know me. I kept my head close to the earpiece in order to follow.

A man's voice said, 'Warner Seebold here. Who's speaking please?'

Maria mouthed, 'Husband.' She said, 'Oh, you won't know my name. I'm just a friend of Alice from Washington that happens to find herself in Chicago. Is she there? Or maybe she's gone to work?'

For a moment Seebold didn't answer, but I could catch his breathing.

He said cautiously, 'What hospital would it be – the one in Washington?'

Maria glanced at me. I nodded. She said, 'The Freedmen's. Why do you want to know?'

Another pause, then, 'I'm sorry – I was just checking – I'm probably being silly. What did you say your name was?'

I shook my head. Maria said, 'You won't know it. We never met, though one time we were supposed to go out on a foursome. What's wrong? Is Alice there?'

'Alice.' One word, sighed and signifying nothing.

'Yes, Alice.'

'Yes – Alice. She isn't at work and she didn't come home last night. I'm worried about her.'

10

Maria had known Alice Jurgens, as she was called before her marriage, for four years before her friend decamped to Chicago in pursuit of Warner Seebold. It was one of those things that surprised, then didn't surprise at all once you knew Alice. At that date she and Warner weren't hitched.

There are people – and Alice was one – who form new friendships quickly and enthusiastically, and the person on the other end is delighted though puzzled to have acquired a new best buddy from nowhere. This state lasts a few months or maybe a year, and then it seems a mistake has been made and you, the new friend, are not the best buddy after all because someone else is. There's no quarrel; in fact everything continues quite amicably. However, there is a drawing back from that initial intensity and an undertone of embarrassment at the revelations and promises made and at your naivety.

Alice and Warner moved to Chicago and married. Then Alice discovered that the nice Jewish doctor was not the love of her life but only an understanding person with more integrity than most of the people she knew. She began to look elsewhere, still convinced that this feeling she had for other people was authentic and someone would fully reciprocate. Warner gave the short version of this over the phone, skipping the psychology which was beyond him. He and Alice were living separately but they often went for a meal or to see a movie together because he was still in love with her and couldn't figure out why he was living alone. He had gone to her apartment to pick her up and drifted off to sleep while waiting for her. The night had passed and Alice had not come home. He said he didn't know why, but something in his voice told me he wasn't telling the whole truth and that he was a very frightened man.

I prompted Maria to arrange a meeting. 'Not at Alice's apartment. Somewhere public – a place where we can have coffee and doughnuts.' If Alice had been arrested, it was possible her apartment was being watched and even that this call was bugged.

'How will we recognize each other?' Seebold asked.

'What will you be wearing?'

'It's a sort of Scottish tweed jacket with elbow patches.'

'I'll recognize you,' Maria said. In fact, out of caution, she'd lied earlier about not knowing him – it was impossible to be Alice's friend and not to have seen him. During love's springtime Alice had paraded the diffident doctor in front of everyone she knew.

'And you?'

Maria rang off without giving her name or any description.

Alice lived in a small loft apartment not far from South Michigan Avenue and the hospital. There was a coffee shop a block away. It was the lull between early and lunchtime trade, which allowed Seebold to find a table by the window so we could see him from the street. Before we went in, I went through a routine of checking the parked cars and any loitering pedestrians in case the Agency or DSD had put a tail on him, and saw none. Then again, how would I know?

Chicago this time of year with Thanksgiving still a way off was cool, but the doctor had taken off his topcoat so we could see the tweed jacket. He was a slender man of thirty-five or so with dark, wavy hair and a thin, melancholy face, not unattractive and without the look of people whose sadness is at have been beaten down by life. He had instead the air of a man who made a habit of thinking seriously about things, and this quality and his apparent stability was what had attracted Alice. In addition to the tweed jacket he wore a check shirt, knitted tie, mid-brown cardigan, twill trousers and brogues. The effect was Central Casting's notion of a boho intellectual, but Warner Seebold carried it naturally because it was who he was. Maria told me that when he wasn't doctoring he hung around clubs where black music disguised its origins and was played by white musicians. He had read Kerouac's banned novel about life on the road free of American Values and everything else the President was trying to achieve.

We went into the coffee shop and joined him at the table. His expression said he recognized Maria but couldn't place or name her. When he opened his mouth, I shook my head and he knew better than to press the point.

As an ice breaker I asked, 'You were in the Army?' Most men of his age had been.

'Uh huh.'

'Where?'

'Colombia.'

I nodded. Colombia had been conquered in forty-two or forty-three, but, after a honeymoon period, like every other place it had degenerated into a guerrilla war. There had been a bad flare-up of violence some ten years ago and I guessed Seebold had seen service then.

'I escaped the worst. I was in the Medical Corps. And you?'

'I saw service,' I said. It established the connection we did not need to speak about, though I meant on a different continent in a different campaign. Europeans of my age had fought in the Russian war. I spent the bulk of my time as a clerk at divisional HQ and escaped most of the killing stuff. I say this because it is important to me not to seem a hero when other people are. The flaws in my behavior are due to ordinary selfishness and poor judgment and not the demons inflicted on men by experiences they should not

91

be asked to have.

I came down to business. I said, 'You're worried about Alice but you haven't called the police.'

'I was thinking about it when you called. Then I wondered…'

'You wondered whether it was safe. I'm guessing she had something on her mind – something going on at her work.' It was fair to assume that if Alice had talked about her concerns to her friend Linda she would have done the same with Warner Seebold. 'Did you know about it? We're speaking about the patient who was kept in isolation and guarded.'

'I'm a pediatrician. I never had cause to be in that part of the hospital.'

'What are we talking about?'

'Burns – tropical diseases – trauma – whatever it was the patient had.'

'Alice knew?'

'Nobody knew – none of the regular staff. Not really. But Alice had a habit of taking up interests or causes or hobbies… or whatever grabbed her attention' – he meant people. He looked to Maria for confirmation. 'It got to her – the patient no one knew anything about: the whole set-up with the secrecy and the precautions and the personal medical staff brought in from Christ knew where. She set out to get answers.'

'And got them?'

He shook his head, thought a moment; then said, 'Well, maybe a couple. She phoned other friends who were nurses. Two said there was something going on where they worked. No, let me re-phrase that. They wouldn't give straight answers; so Alice decided they were covering for similar cases. Then she did the math and thought there had to be a hundred patients – perhaps more. She could easily have been wrong.'

Except that she had vanished. I didn't say it. Instead I

asked, 'Did she see the patient or talk to anyone who saw the patient?'

Seebold nodded. 'Just the once. They were moving him for some reason to do with the room. Alice said he was covered head to toe in a sheet like a corpse, but the sheet slipped and she caught a glimpse – just a glimpse – before they put it back in place. Then someone noticed her and she was bawled out.'

'And?'

'It was a black man.'

'A man?'

'Yes. No age – no sign of what was wrong with him – just a glimpse. A black man. That's all she said.'

Everyone knows there are no blacks in Washington – and the same goes for Chicago. But the significance was still beyond me and I wasn't sure what I'd learned except an indication of the possible number of patients and the fact that the sex didn't seem to be material to whatever was going on. Had we come so far to learn only this?

I asked, 'Have you heard of a doctor by the name of Vipic?'

Seebold looked startled. I suspected I'd touched on something he knew but Alice didn't.

He said, 'Major Luther Vipic. I caught the name because one time a car came to collect him and the driver gave his name at the desk. The hospital doesn't have a Doctor Vipic – Major or otherwise – so I figured it was the mystery man's medic.'

That fit with what I'd overheard in the morgue of the Freedmen's but added nothing beyond confirmation.

Seebold fell silent for a moment. I guessed he was wondering how he'd come to be talking to strangers about these things and in the process gained a small insight into his own neediness. He realized too that the fact that we already knew about the mystery patient meant he was compromised if we chose to betray him. He said, 'You can have this for free. Although Vipic is military, the car was civilian and had Nevada plates. When I was in the Army there was talk of a hush-hush facility they ran somewhere in the desert a half-day drive from Las Vegas. Camp MacArthur – you won't find it on any map. Nobody I met ever claimed to have been there and nobody knew what they did beyond soldier's gossip. And maybe it doesn't exist.' He smiled with the weak smile frightened men give to persuade themselves they still have courage. He said, 'I liked the idea that the Pentagon was working on a race of world-dominating female sex-robots.'

'That would be neat,' I agreed.

I tried to remember what I knew about Las Vegas. As far as I could recall, it was a no-account place in the middle of the desert that didn't figure much in the news. I had an idea that back in the thirties the Mob had tried to turn it into a resort for gamblers and party girls, but that was before the GeStaPo broke the Mob's power. Although the Mob still operated where it made an accommodation with the local politicians, the Las Vegas project never happened, and the city lived off the Army and passing traffic on the way to California.

As for Camp MacArthur, it meant nothing to me; but that didn't signify. I don't make a point of remembering the names of army camps.

'So what are you going to do?' I asked. It occurred to me that he hadn't put any questions to us, and I think it was because he didn't care about the answers.

He looked at me as if this wasn't important. He said, 'I'm torn between going home to change and freshen up, or hanging on until Alice shows – which she has to do some time, yes?'

'Why didn't you phone the hospital last night and ask?'

'She has to show sometime.'

'No, she doesn't. Alice has been arrested. In your heart you know that, and that's why you haven't called to find out. So what are you going to do?'

He didn't contradict me. He said, 'I'll pay the bill.' Then, sadly, 'I guess I'll go home.' He made to put on his topcoat.

'They'll be waiting for you there. By now Alice will have given up your name.'

'If they wanted to, they could have arrested me last night.'

I shook my head. 'They didn't know you'd be at her apartment, but at some point they'll send some guys to toss the place for any notes Alice made. Go or stay, you'll be arrested.' I don't know why I was pressing him on this. I had no help to offer or any practical suggestions. If I read him right, he was even less equipped to run than Maria and I. And running would almost certainly be fatal. Maybe keeping his nerve and denying everything was his best strategy after all.

He said, 'You were right not to give me your names. But' – he looked at Maria – 'my first impression was right: I've definitely seen you before. I'm sorry about that. I may remember it – your name – that's all. You understand?'

'We'll have to hope not,' said Maria.

Seebold nodded; then seemed to have a thought. He said, 'This' – he waved his arms – 'is still a free country. It's just that we exercised our freedom to become paranoid. Do you think that's true?'

'Maybe,' I said. People make irrational choices, so it was possible. I checked my watch. 'I suggest you leave first.'

'OK.' Seebold got up and finished putting on his topcoat. He didn't offer his hand or any farewell words, but took the tab to the counter and paid. He went into the street and turned right, and Maria and I sat, seeming to hold our breath for a minute.

'Well?' she said.

'I want to follow him a while. Didn't he say Alice's

95

apartment was just a couple of blocks away?'

'I think so.'

We put on our own coats and left the coffee shop. I looked right and saw Warner Seebold making his way slowly through a thin stream of pedestrians. We followed at a distance and it didn't seem that anyone else was tailing him, and the cars parked along the sidewalk were empty. After two blocks, he started feeling in his pockets – for a key, I guessed. He was outside what looked like an old commercial building that had been cheaply renovated for apartments: a double doorway and a row of ground level windows behind rusted bars; a date – 1890 – and some carved scrolling on the stone pediment above the door. A car was at the kerb directly outside. Two men in the car.

There was shock but no surprise in what happened next. As Seebold pulled out his key, the front doors of the car opened and the men got out. They called something and he turned in time to be grabbed by both arms and pinioned against the wall. As these things go, there wasn't much violence. Seebold, in his prissy way, looked like an offended maiden aunt, and his two captors didn't seem disposed to rough him up unless he fought back. They bundled him into the rear seat and the second man got in next to him. The driver made for the car door but, as he did so, the wind blew his hat on to the sidewalk and he had to stoop to pick it up.

I saw that he had the face of a clean-cut young man and that he sported a buzz cut and not the slick trim of a Hollywood actor.

Maria and I turned on our heels as nonchalantly as we could and set off in the opposite direction at a regular pace, and no one would have suspected anything except that we held hands tightly, the way people of our age walking a Chicago street at eleven in the morning do not. To find a chance to talk about what had just happened we went into a tavern where I ordered drinks and took them to a booth. It was still early, towels were draped over the beer taps and the place was empty except for the career drunks, who ignored us.

Maria asked, 'What did we just see?' I could sense the tension that held her voice steady.

'The good news is that was DSD not the Agency. Either the Agency doesn't know where we are or Jeb is cutting us some slack. Either could be true, but I don't think anyone as yet knows we're in Chicago.'

'I haven't showed for work and the DSD will have realized that the nurse who returned the morgue key to the orderly room was me.'

'No one knows you planned to come to Chicago. Not even Alice. When they interrogate Seebold, they'll concentrate first on finding out what she told him. Only then will they get around to who he's been talking to. He doesn't know our names and the odds are he won't remember yours unless it's put to him. Alice spoke with Linda not you and has no notion of your involvement, so they won't pull it out of her. The agents working on her case will be running behind events in Washington, relying on briefings once maybe twice a day. If I had to guess, I'd say there was no way they can put all the facts together until tomorrow.'

Some of this was true and some probably not. But Maria believed I knew more of the world than she did, and I owed it to her to pretend it was so. I put a hand on hers and said, 'What I mean is that we can stay calm because for the moment we're safe.'

We sipped at our drinks, searching for ways of speaking that would make sense. I wanted to tell Maria that what was important to me was that here and now she was with me, but I didn't know how to say this and sound as sincere as I felt. A uniform cop came in. He exchanged a few words with the bartender and cast a relaxed eye over us, seeing whatever he was primed to see. Adulterous lovers making final farewells before going home to their families with smiles and explanations of where they had spent the previous night – who knows? The bartender slipped him an envelope and he gave a cheery farewell to all and left.

Maria turned from the cop to me. She asked, 'What do we do? Where do we go?'

Well that was easy – as long as I left the 'we' out of the calculation. According to the book, I should run for Canada, confident that I would make it before my part in the killing at the Freedmen's became clear. And in any case I had my shiny new ID and passport. There was no question that this was my safest option.

But I also had Maria, whom I had selfishly compromised because I wanted to do Jeb Lyman a favor.

And so, as had happened that night at the Freedmen's, my life became something different from one moment to the next because of what I would say now.

'We'll go to Las Vegas,' I told her.

11

Las Vegas. If I was mistaken, I was heading away from safety, but I could see no alternative. I considered staying in Chicago and working some of my contacts, thinking I could maybe make a connection with someone who would provide Maria with a set of ID and travel papers. But the appeal of this solution was only superficial. In addition to the silent censorship, the news industry had long been penetrated by regime toadies and informers. The men who complained about the government in bars, at race tracks and private briefings, and whom in the ordinary way I would have considered my friends, would swallow their regrets and give me up to the authorities for the sake of their families, their careers and their lives. I knew this because my own lack of courage meant I feared I would do the same even at the cost of despising myself.

Maria asked, 'How does going to Las Vegas help?'

'Vipic is almost certainly based there or at Camp MacArthur. He's our only link to solving the mystery of the patients.'

'But why would a black man or a pregnant black woman be at an army base?'

She meant that everyone knows there are no black people in America.

'I don't know. Maybe that's the point. They shouldn't have been there – but they were.'

Maria had raised a good question. Where should all the black people be? The Resettlements had started in the forties after the wars in Central and South America really got into their stride. Large numbers had been rounded up and shipped to the conquered territories, but their role in the labor market prevented further deportations until it was accepted that they would have to be replaced by Hispanics.

99

Then in the fifties two things happened. The first was the Brazilian campaign, which brought a huge territory already populated by blacks into Big A's empire. Surely they would accept their brothers from the North even if they spoke English not Portuguese? The second was a show trial of a preacher called Martin Luther King. He was placed at the center of a terrorist conspiracy, which may or may not have existed, and sent to the electric chair. The resulting panic was whipped up by the Administration into grounds for a general clear-out of African Americans from the territory of the United States. The official story was they were living the carefree life of happy coons somewhere in the jungle. There was newsreel footage to prove it, but no one had ever been there to find out and talk about it.

I looked at my glass and wondered whether to buy another drink but thought better of it. Meantime the unspoken question remained between us: *how does this get us off the hook?*

I said, 'I don't think Jeb or the Agency care that a guy from DSD got killed.' I didn't know if this was true but it was plausible. 'We need something to trade for their support. If we follow through on the deal to find out what the Department of Defense is up to, we may learn information we can use.'

And then the GeStaPo will kill us. But I didn't say that.

'Do you think Jeb will live up to his promise?'

'I think so,' I said. But did I? It was the promise of a secret policeman, yet for some reason I believed him. *You do understand that I would never do anything to harm you or Maria, don't you?* His words not mine.

'Have you had any contact with your office?'

'No.' Under the pressure of events I hadn't thought about them. They would miss my dispatches soon enough, but their ability to help was limited to the scoot box and appeals through the embassy once it was known I was in the hands of the authorities. They weren't going to solve my immediate problems. I told Maria this, more or less.

'So what do we do – I mean this minute?'

'I don't want to leave a trail. We should go by bus – buy a ticket to one of the intermediate stops so that Las Vegas doesn't figure on anyone's radar. There's a Greyhound bus station on West Harrison Street.' I reached for my wallet, which I'd never got into the habit of calling a 'billfold'. I peeled off some money and gave it to Maria. 'Go to Marshall Fields or one of the other department stores. Buy a basic change of clothes for both of us because I don't think laundry is going to be high on our list of priorities. Then meet me at the bus station in, say, two hours.'

'And what are you going to do?'

'Return to the hotel to pick up the bags and get my papers from the desk.'

'What if those people are there?' Maria didn't name them.

'They won't be,' I said. 'My new ID isn't on anybody's list. That's why I need to go back and get it.'

She tried to appear calm because that was who she was, but I reassured her all the same. I took her hands in mine across the table, the way that lovers do. But instead of whispered endearments I said, 'My papers go to the local police and are checked against the GeStaPo grab-sheet. The people who are after us are DSD and they don't have access. Trust me on this. So far we are safe.'

'And if I don't see you?'

And if you are under arrest or being tortured or dead?

'Head for Seattle – as far from Washington as you can – and try to cross the Canadian border. There are people who run contraband blacks across the line. They may help, but I can't tell you how to find them.'

There was nothing else to say but, like other people in emotionally heightened moments, we parted as though there should be, because we were frightened that this was all there would ever be and it would end in banalities. We kissed and I left the bar first so that Maria could see if anything happened to me when I stepped outside. I chanced a final glance at her and with the love I felt came the hollowness that haunted me in all my relationships.

I may love you, but in the end you are on your own. You always knew that, didn't you?

I took the bus back to the hotel. The street looked clear; the parked cars empty; the pedestrians going about their business. The only odd note was a stationary truck blazoned with American Youth banners and swarming with kids in uniform. They were collecting old tires; part of the drive for scrap materials – the resource problem the war was supposed to solve. I didn't know why there was a rubber shortage. The Administration boasted of Fordlandia, a vast complex of plantations in Brazil that was supposed to deliver all the rubber America needed. Apparently it didn't.

I lounged in a doorway and watched the truck to see if it moved. After a minute or so, two boys emerged from an alley leading to the rear of the block. They were rolling a couple of tires and whooping like it was a game. They loaded the truck and it crawled along the street to the next collection point. I slipped through the door into the hotel. A cop was standing at the desk, talking with the clerk.

'Mr. Johnson,' said the clerk. I was Mr. Johnson on the theory that I might get overlooked among all the other Mr. Johnsons in any grab-sheet. 'You're in luck. Joe just brought yesterday's batch of papers back.'

I nodded at Joe the Cop and murmured, 'Officer.' The clerk thumbed through the bundle and came up with my ID. I said, 'You have my bags. Two.'

'So I do.' The clerk opened the door behind the front desk that led to a small baggage room where he'd dumped them when I checked out earlier.

The cop said, 'You here on business, Mr. Johnson?'

'Uh huh.'

'You got a sample case?'

'I'm not in sales,' I said. I didn't want him looking inside to find the clothes of a female who was not in the hotel register.

'First time in the Windy City?'

'Second.'

'And where to next?'

'Detroit.'

Joe the Cop nodded and I felt my pulse slow. This was small talk. The clerk pulled the bags and asked me to confirm they were mine.

'That's what it says on the tags,' I said and tried out a smile.

So we did the civilities and I left the hotel and took the first bus I could see only to get off after two stops and find the right connection to take me to West Harrison Street.

I set down this scene in which nothing much happened, because at the time I was wondering: Is this how it's going to be and nothing that used to pass for normal will ever be the same and fear is going to be what gets me up in the morning and accompanies me to bed at night? If that was the case, I wasn't sure I could take it.

I reached the Greyhound bus station towards one. It was crowded with the usual mob: draftees, wives and girlfriends, the cheap end of traveling salesmen and a few moms and pops from small town Illinois who'd been to see the kids in the big city. A couple of cops in plain clothes were turning people over for their papers but they didn't have the tense look of men on a mission and I was pretty sure they were looking only for the usual deserters and undocumented Hispanics. I saw Maria sitting on a bench with her back against a building wall-papered with advertisements for War Bonds and Quaker State Oil and the one that urged Mothers to stay home and raise babies for the White American Race, which everyone ignored on account of the labor shortage. Maria saw me but waited for me to make a move.

I found a ticket office with people milling around, and a set of posters with bus times and destinations. I checked out Las Vegas. The distance, mostly by Route 66, was a little shy of two thousand miles but that didn't matter since I wasn't proposing to do it in one hop. Springfield, Illinois was closer at something over two hundred and took about eight hours with stops. I booked two tickets and deposited the bags. I returned to the main area where Maria was still waiting. She followed when I stepped out into the street.

'You OK?' she asked before I could put the same question.

I shook out a smile and said, 'I'm fine. We're going to Las Vegas by the scenic route; first stop Springfield. The bad news is the early buses are full, but I have two seats on one that leaves at six. Until then I propose we eat and go see a movie.'

'You're just an old romantic, aren't you?' she said, but her voice couldn't sustain the humor of the words. Her eyes were bright with moisture and I kissed the space between them.

I suggested the film because we needed to get off the street. I remembered a cinema a few blocks away and once we'd got some food inside us at a family-run Italian place, we went there. At this time of day it was a thin house but warm and dark and smelling of stale tobacco smoke. The main feature was something by Hitchcock, *The Birds*, but I dozed through most of it. The program was continuous and the next show began with a Daffy Duck cartoon followed by a Movietone newsreel that woke me because I was always interested in what the regime thought of itself. It had nothing to say about the incident at the Arc of Hope, which didn't surprise me since I'd seen no movie-cameramen there. But thcrc was an inspirational piece about the rocket program at Cape Canaveral with Dick Nixon spouting guff about 'the future of Humanity among the stars'. I waited to see if there was a similar piece boosting the Kennedys, but there wasn't. The omission made me wonder if their stock was falling.

We quit the cinema in time to catch the bus without waiting around and drawing attention. There was nothing to do but hunker down in our seats for the long haul, most of it by night, across the flat prairie of central Illinois. As usual, the young soldiers provided the only entertainment: country songs to a harmonica accompaniment that became slow and melancholy as the night wore on; that and a child mewling from time to time and a woman sobbing hardly loud enough to be heard. We halted a while at Joliet and Pontiac and maybe other places I slept through. Between stops the night was black except that now and again a gas station, a motel or a country store would emerge from the darkness like a brightly lit tableau in a theatre or a nativity scene, with an old man in a felt hat and coveralls and a worn-looking woman in a woolen dress standing by a pick-up loaded with their furniture.

So we arrived in Springfield, with the morning some hours away. We needed to wash and to get some sleep after the restless dozing on the bus. I checked the times and fares for the next leg of our journey and bought tickets; then we found a low-rent hotel squeezed between a record store and a shop-front church, the Baptist kind with a grandiose name and nothing much else. The room comprised a bed, a chair and a closet, and the bathroom was down the hall. We made love in the bed, not for the pleasure of the thing but by way of affirmation, and then we bathed together and laughed because it was new for us. The clerk didn't require identification, so I supposed he had a deal with the local cops. In addition to stopovers like us, he hired out hot beds by the hour, which would explain it.

There is a romance in American place names that often belies the reality of forgettable cities with smokestack industries, used car dealerships and trailer parks. In our imagination, we follow a parallel geography that allows us to flee from our sorrows towards our hopes, guided by the words of songs that play on this magic of names. I had no particular reason for setting Galena, Kansas as our next destination beyond a desire to make time by resting less frequently. But behind the decision lay a vague memory that the word 'galena' was a metallic ore, and somewhere in my mind it conjured up a picture of alchemy and the possibility of transformation.

We grabbed a few hours' sleep and rose at noon to catch the bus. Our goal was upwards of five hundred miles away across the whole of Missouri and we would arrive sometime around dawn next day.

Long journeys distort our feeling for the flow of time; detach it from familiar reality so it ceases to be intuitive and has to be calculated. We say to ourselves, 'It must be Friday' – yet it doesn't feel like Friday. We check our watch and see it's six o'clock. But is it morning or evening? A glance out of the window reveals only the scenery we have looked at for miles, and the light is equivocal. Suspended like this, we lose connection with both the good and bad of life, and, despite the dreariness, a part of us is lulled and never wants to arrive at our destination.

We reached St. Louis – not a town I knew, except it was a hub for marshalling boys conscripted from the Mid-West and sending them to points South. A crowd of GIs was gathered around the troop movement office, bullied by their sergeants into some sort of order. In an out of the way corner a dozen indentured Mexican field hands were held in the pen reserved for them. They were loosely chained to a rail running the length of a wall, but free enough to help themselves from a pot of rice and beans. They ate their food, talked, cracked jokes, and sometimes pissed against the wall; and generally they looked as happy as men in their situation might hope to be.

I got off the bus and bought snacks and drinks at a kiosk. The bus driver had gone for dinner and a chat with his buddies and was in no rush to return. I offered some of the snacks to Maria but she showed no interest. She was looking at the Mexicans.

'Those men are slaves,' she said.

'The Supreme Court says they're not. It would be against the Constitution.'

A case whose name I forget had decided the point. A slave works for no reward and under compulsion. An indentured field hand has put his name to a labor contract and earns a nominal dollar a year. To a lawyer, it makes all the difference.

I said, 'In any case, slaves are black and Mexicans aren't.'

'It isn't a joke!'

I grabbed Maria's hand which she had raised as if to strike me. I put her fingers to my lips and said, 'I'm sorry. I forgot you don't really get English flippancy. It's just something we do when the subject is too serious to talk about.'

She took her hand back; owning herself once more in her entirety; not needing my comfort or explanations; preferring to nurse her anger. But she understood that this was not the time or place to draw attention to either of us. In any case what was the point of displaying her sorrow? For the most part no one gave a shit about Mexicans. It was a commonplace that here at least they got a bed and three squares, which was better than back home. The rest of us working stiffs should be slaves already.

She asked, 'Where's the driver?'

'He's coming,' I said. I saw him crossing the tarmac from the cabin where bus crew holed up. He was carrying an unfinished sandwich and he took a detour to throw it into the labor pen: a small act of charity for which there was no figuring. He clambered into his seat.

'All aboard that's coming aboard!' he chanted and started up the engine.

He was about to close the door and put the motor into gear, when a figure broke from the crowd and swung a canvas kit bag through the gap.

'The hell!'

'I beg your forgiveness, sir,' said the newcomer, heaving himself into the space after the bag.

'You got a warrant, soldier boy?'

'I don't have no warrant, but I do have a ticket, sir.'

The boy – I guessed he was a year or two turned twenty – reached into his pocket and produced the ticket. Now I could get a good look I understood the driver's request for a travel warrant. The stranger was of the age when most young men were in the services and probably he had been. His haircut had once been military and he was wearing an Army blouse under a worn Air Force leather jacket, both shorn of insignia. The giveaway was his pants, which were blue jeans; and his feet were in ordinary work boots. He was slender and lithe and had dark, youthful good looks – or what might have passed for good looks if they had not been so changeable in a way that was disconcerting.

When I got to know him, I understood that this was because he was unsure who he was or wanted to be. The only certainty in his sense of identity was that he was someone tremendous.

12

The bus driver said, 'That bag's too big to take inside.'

The young man looked at it as if its size was a surprise to him and he had started with something smaller. He said, 'Well, I sure would not want to incommode anyone' – pronouncing each syllable of 'in-com-mode' straight out of the dictionary – 'not anyone, sir. No, I would not. But this bag contains all the possessions I have in the world, and, though they ain't worth nothing, I surely would not like to lose them.'

The driver didn't want to get out of his seat and open the baggage locker. He bawled down the bus, 'Anyone got a problem with this feller's kitbag?' And when no one had, he said, 'OK, stick it in the aisle and we'll look at it again at the next stop.'

The young man smiled and flipped a salute. He hauled his bag down the bus, muttering 'sirs' and 'ma'ams' until he reached the last free seat, across the aisle from my own. He took it and let out a stagey sigh; then closed his eyes, still smiling as though he could see something the rest of us could not see and it amused him. The bus set off.

I didn't know the boy or whether I liked him. He was one of those people whose behavior seems at a tangent to what is happening; not exactly detached or fantastic but based upon an interpretation of a situation that I didn't share. There didn't seem enough in what had happened to account for the smile, but for a while at least he stuck with it. I tried to place his accent, but knew little of the subject beyond that he came from the South. The slow pace and polite phrasing were something I'd noted on the occasions I'd encountered Southerners, but I'd never known what to make of these traits of speech. They seemed to stem from a wariness of others or perhaps of the speaker's own nature, as if they were a spell to ward off a violence that was always just beneath the surface. But, as I say, this was something I'd never understood.

I glanced at Maria but already her eyes were closed.

We crossed Missouri mostly at night. I abandoned the plan to head for Galena after learning it was a largely abandoned mining town with nothing much to it except a Kan-O-Tex service station. Instead we aimed at Joplin, which was just this side of Galena on the Kansas border, though I was tired and had lost any real sense of place.

I dozed and remember little of the darkling landscape beyond the dim shape of the Ozarks and a comfort break at a no-name road-stop where some of us took a quick coffee and slice of pie at a diner near an abandoned drive-in whose screen still glimmered in reflected moonlight. We smoked cigarettes and ate or drank in silence except for the server taking orders in a low mutter between talking to a woman with copper hair, a bruised cheek and defiant eyes; that and the sound of night creatures rooting in the trash cans. The truth is I was awake only part of the time and the rest was no more than a semblance of sleep; but since the intervals were irregular, I couldn't say to myself, 'I'm another fifty miles on,' or 'another hundred.' Instead from time to time I would look at Maria when the headlights of a passing car gave a fugitive illumination. Sometimes she gave the appearance of sleep and sometimes she would acknowledge me and smile.

I remembered that we were here because I'd decided that to cross the Canadian border wasn't safe for her – and yet I'd told her she should try to cross the Canadian border if we got separated. The contradiction made me suspect I was being dishonest in the low way men are with women when they lie about how many drinks they've taken or the money they've lost to the bookies, because lying is easier than taking a knock to their self-esteem. Was the truth that I was here because I'd made a promise to Jeb Lyman, or because I was a journalist and wanted to get to the bottom of a story? In short were there more important things for me than love and respect for a woman? When she smiled, I had a feeling Maria knew the answer but was sparing me because, however I felt, she loved me.

Sometime during the night a voice not much above a whisper said, 'Are you awake, sir?'

It was my neighbor across the aisle. I saw only his shape blocked out against the window but there was no mistaking the even tone of his Southern drawl.

He seemed to know I was listening even without a reply, because he said, 'Traveling is a lonesome thing to do, would you not say so, sir?' And then, 'I can tell that you agree. I have traveled a lot, yes sir. There are few of these United States and countries within our greater territories – meaning Mexico and so forth – that I have not visited while performing my duty.' He left that 'duty' dangling, expecting a question perhaps.

After an interval he said 'I was a US Marine,' and waited to judge the effect. When I didn't answer, he said, 'Not many men of my age have the qualities to be a US Marine, but I was one and I have testimonials and certificates that will prove this if needed.'

'Yet you're not one now,' I said.

He chuckled. 'I knew you was awake. No, you are right, sir. I was honorably discharged.'

'Why?'

'I can't say – I mean I know but I can't tell you for reasons of national security. Still, you may be assured that the reasons were good because that is the meaning of "honorable". It is a point I particularly want to make so there is no mistake. There are people who look at me and ask why I am not in the Army and so I have to insist that the reasons are honorable, d'you follow me?'

'Yes,' I said.

'Thank you, sir, for being so understanding.' He leaned

over and extended a hand to me. I couldn't see it, but found his ghost fingers scrabbling at the sleeve of my jacket. 'Allow me to introduce myself,' he said. 'My name is Charlie Joe Svensen.'

We were silent a while and the only noise was the hum of bus wheels on the blacktop and the horns of passing trucks. Then, perhaps because the loneliness he'd spoken of had got to him, my new acquaintance spoke up in the same even tone.

'I have the advantage of a poor education,' he said, then paused, fishing for a response. Getting none, he continued, 'You heard me right – the advantage. The teachers in your regular schools are sad specimens of human beings, who teach things only by rote and lack any true spark of creativity. They are unable to recognize a student who has anything in the way of original thought, and, if they see it at all, they treat it as a spirit of rebellion and try to crush it. And sorry though I am to say it, some of them have undesirable morals when around children – I'll say no more.'

The matter of education seemed to be a thing with him.

'I was forced to teach myself: reading books and watching the better sort of program on television; that and talking to people I respect, though there are sadly few who deserve it. I am what is called an "autodidact", which is a word you probably don't know. It comes from the Roman and means I am a person that has taught hisself. I've heard it called "learning at the School of Life", and there is something to that. Life is a finer college than you will find in your Ivy League. Your Harvard and your Princeton stultify the mind because they aim to produce members of the elite like Ford automobiles coming off the assembly line. And the elite – I'll tell you this and some day you may thank me for it – they don't want to know or let anyone else know how things really are. They want to be comfortable with the same thoughts as their daddies and they want the rest of the people to think they are worthy of all the good things that have come their way through the accident of birth.'

The next remark may have been a continuation of the same theme; it's difficult to say. Charlie Joe Svensen's thoughts were like an index ordered in a way unique to him, and the real subject was something else that was hinted at but never voiced. I think I must have dozed briefly.

'… P'tit Antoine Molineaux. Not a famous name because he chooses to hide his light under a barrel, but one of the wisest men I ever met. That is God's truth, sir.'

I didn't recognize the reference and thought it was maybe to some Appalachian hellfire preacher Svensen had seen on television, except the name sounded Cajun.

He said, 'There are deep, dark currents beneath the surface of things. That is a fact which nobody can deny, though it is given to few people to fathom these mysteries. And why is that, do you think, sir?'

'I don't know.'

'Because the Truth is deliberately kept from us. Yes sir, de-lib-er-ate-ly! And who by? Why, by those same elites whose daddies sent them to the Babylon of Harvard and Princeton! This is the secret that is being hidden from the American People. There is a conspiracy and it has a name: "the New World Order".'

The expression was unfamiliar but it sounded like one of the slogans put out by Big A and the NSDAP to promulgate 'The American Millennium – a Thousand Years of Democracy and Prosperity!' Yet the way Svensen spoke, it implied subversion.

He seemed concerned about what other people thought of him, as though he could hear unspoken criticisms and they were unbearable.

He said, 'You should understand that I am traveling with a particular purpose.'

I'd asked nothing on the subject.

'My goal is Las Vegas.'

I didn't comment.

He repeated, 'Las Vegas – yes sir. And I imagine you want to know why.'

'Tell me,' I said, but he became evasive, not so much because he was frightened of revealing too much but that he wanted only to tantalize while keeping his secret. Or so I concluded.

'These are things known only to certain people – I name P'tit Antoine Molineaux for one. It is enough that I am going there – I mean to Las Vegas – as part of my education in those things that the Illuminati wish to keep to theirselves. Things are happening in Las Vegas, make no mistake. And people who are true patriots and those who know the true nature of things need to find out about them, yes.'

He asked me where I was going, but, when I didn't answer, he seemed to forget his own question. It was the same when he asked my name and I didn't give it.

Late that night we made a stop at Springfield, Missouri, which for all I knew could have been Springfield, Illinois where Maria and I had passed the previous night. I remember nothing except the bus station and a few low rise downtown businesses, and the bus station was like the others that marked our journey, though dimly lit and quiet. The passengers piled out of our vehicle to stretch their legs and use the rest rooms. There was no food to be had and nothing to do except move about like restless cattle. Maria took me aside to a sheltered corner near the ticket office.

'Who is that man?' she asked. Her voice was urgent and distressed; more than I could account for. But in my business I was used to strangeness in other people and it didn't disturb me and quite likely made me insensitive to the reactions of others.

I told her, 'His name is Charlie Joe Svensen.'

I didn't mention it was a name I knew from the incident at the Arc of Hope when it had figured in a set of faked ID. I wasn't sure whether that meant something or not.

'Who is he, Harry?'

'He says he's an ex-Marine, which may be true, but I think he's a deserter.'

I'd noticed that at the earlier road-stop and now at Springfield, Svensen had taken his kitbag with him when he got down from the bus, as if he wasn't sure of getting on again, and at both St. Louis and wherever, he'd boarded at the last minute and I thought he would do the same now. My guess was he was trying to avoid anyone checking his papers, but it may have been part of the drama he was playing out in his head.

I asked, 'Were you listening to our conversation? I thought you were asleep.'

'I couldn't help it. I didn't hear everything. What is he doing? Why is he on the bus?'

'I think he's just a drifter. You know how things are. The country is full of young men who've been damaged by the war.'

From my investigations for the newspaper I knew there was a big homelessness problem among vets and a lot of mental illness. On our journey we'd seen derelicts hanging about the bus stations, bumming dimes from GIs who believed they would never end up like the men they were helping but gave money anyway out of pity mixed with contempt and the American instinct for charity that is authentic and virtuous. In the end I hadn't written up the story because I knew it would never get passed. It was a case of self-censorship, but I lived with the shame because I told myself I had other more important stories to tell.

'He frightens me,' said Maria.

'There's no reason why he should.'

'Where did you say he was going?'

'Las Vegas.'

Maria shuddered. We'd talked about making up time by staying on the bus and buying an onward ticket to Vegas once we reached Joplin instead of switching to a later ride. Now it no longer seemed such a good idea.

I said, 'We'll change buses at Joplin like we originally planned.'

'I think we should.'

We re-joined the bus. I looked for Svensen. He'd got off at Springfield but I hadn't noticed him among the other passengers, which figured if he was keeping away from prying cops. I gave no thought to where he'd been. As we took our seats, he pulled his trick of coming on board last, toting his kitbag and making a quiet fuss with that same slyly peaceful smile on his face. The driver had changed over but the new one made no comment about the bag.

The passengers settled in for the next stage. The newcomers tried to strike up conversations with those who had long distances already under their belt, but made no headway against the torpor of the latter and soon gave up. The bus resumed its general silence broken only by occasional muttering.

I dozed again but was woken by a low voice. It was Charlie Joe Svensen and he spoke with the slow earnestness of an evangelist asking if I wanted to be saved.

He said, 'I wish to tell you something important. I have said the same thing to many people but they mock my words. Believe me when I say: *Conspiracies are not meant to be understood!* No sir, they are not. And this is something we forget at our peril when we try to pit our puny minds against the greatest and most cunning intellects in the modern world.'

I said, 'You mean the Illuminati?'

116

'Why, thank you sir. I'm gratified that you have been paying me some attention. Yes sir, I do mean the Illuminati – though that is the name we apply to them; they have secret names among themselves.'

'I see. And you've been trying to unravel their conspiracies?'

'I have been making researches; traveling the country; speaking to many people and piecing together their stories. I think I may fairly claim to be the most fully-informed person in these United States on this matter, excepting, perhaps, P'tit Antoine Molineaux. And even in his case there are things I know that he does not.'

'OK. And what have you discovered?'

Svensen didn't answer immediately; nor when I put the question again, thinking he hadn't heard me. A half hour went by before he next spoke.

'You shouldn't pay me no mind. Sometimes I just say things come into my head.' He leaned across the aisle and whispered, 'There are spies aboard these buses, which I was forgetting. There are things I know, and when I get to Las Vegas, it shall be proved that I am right.'

The sun came up and we traversed a landscape marked by the tailings of abandoned mine-workings. And in due course we arrived at Joplin. The passengers got off to eat and use the rest rooms while the bus was taken away to gas up. Those of us who were leaving collected our bags. Tired from the journey, my plan was to get tickets for the final leg to Las Vegas, buy another change of clothes, then find a room where we could hole up for the day. I bade my farewells to Charlie Joe Svensen and tried to sound pleased to have met him.

'We're leaving here, but I hope you find what you're looking for in Vegas.'

'Thank you, sir.'

He held out a hand and I took it, though I'd come to the

conclusion that I didn't like him and thought there were times and places where he might be dangerous. I could account for his behavior only by picturing him as someone who approached strangers expectantly, in the hope of making friends, only to find they would always disappoint him because they would not recognize the specialness he saw in himself.

He said, 'Hold on to that thought I gave you. You remember that?'

'Conspiracies aren't meant to be understood.'

'You have it right on the money. I can see you are an educated man, but I knowed that from your accent – somewhere back East, I think?'

'Good luck.'

'Yes – and you too, sir. And to your lady wife, though we haven't spoke.'

He turned his back on me and I left to find Maria among the other women queuing for the rest room the way women have to. I wanted to quit the bus station and proposed she get something to eat at the lunch counter of a nearby diner and keep an eye on the bags, while I bought tickets for the next day's ride. I went back to the bus station and the ticket office. I noticed a crowd gathered round a newsstand but had other things on my mind.

So I bought the tickets. Meantime the bus had returned to the pick-up and the passengers were re-boarding. I didn't see Svensen among them but he no longer interested me and it took a moment before anything in the scene struck me as odd. Then I noticed that, as well as the usual bored cop checking papers, standing next to him were two young men in suits and topcoats and they had the trademark buzz cut I was getting to recognize. DSD agents – but how had they found me? I did a quick look-away before they could see my face, and headed for the station exit, and in my hurry stumbled into the people by the newsstand, which was selling *The Joplin Globe*.

Only then did I see what had attracted their attention. It was there in the headline and in large letters on the stand.

JAPAN EXPLODES URANIUM BOMB !!!

13

I stepped into the street. The two DSD agents didn't follow. As I walked to the diner where I'd left Maria, I tried to figure out how they knew to look for me in Joplin. The immediate answer was that Warner Seebold had given me up. I remembered his lack of faith in his own courage in a situation that was none of his making. I didn't resent his betrayal, but the important question was: how much could he tell them?

I went over our meeting in Chicago. Seebold had pointed me at Las Vegas, but he couldn't know for certain that we would head there or by what means, and still less that Maria and I would cover our tracks by making stops on the way. He didn't know my real name or about the 'Johnson' ID I was using. On the other hand, it was reasonable to suppose that by now the DSD had matched me to the killer of their man in Washington and also identified Maria. Still, I didn't see how they could connect me to 'Johnson'. They weren't the GeStaPo and I didn't think their resources ran to a search of hotel registers and, even if they did, they would have to check thousands of registrations for the single night we spent in Chicago. They would look for couples but I'd made a point of checking in alone. Even if they got that far, they would have to run mugshots past the hotel desk clerks to get a confirmation. However I played this scenario, I thought my identity as 'Johnson' was still safe.

So what did they have? Photographs from my press credentials and Maria's file at the Freedman Hospital. A possible destination: Las Vegas. A more probable destination: Canada. They knew nothing for certain and were spreading their resources thinly, covering their bases, checking all routes to Las Vegas and the Canadian border, using only their own people because they didn't dare approach Hoover's Finest. Well good luck with that. It explained why I'd had no sight of them at any of the stops before Joplin and it was probably only chance that brought them there. They had to assume I was ahead of them, and this was the first opportunity to get their men in place.

I held that thought. These people – as Maria called them – pictured us as fugitives, traveling by the quickest route. Joplin meant nothing to them; they had no reason to expect us either to join or leave the bus there. The purpose of the check at the bus station was simply to see whether we were among the existing passengers going on to Las Vegas. And if they didn't see us? What reason did they have to interrogate the driver or other passengers and what chance anyone would remember two strangers seen in the dark or care to get involved?

My analysis wasn't watertight, but my best guess was that Maria and I were still running free. Our only immediate problem was that Nixon's boys would be staking out the Greyhound stop in Vegas and the tickets I'd just bought were useless. A day's rest and maybe I could come up with a solution.

Joplin's economy had taken a dive after the local mines gave up and it derived little benefit from war industries. The diner was in a row of failing businesses and thrift stores along a street of broken sidewalks and automobiles with rusted bodywork and sun-bleached paint jobs. The décor was repair shop calendars and football pennants. Maria was sitting at the lunch counter on a high stool with our bags at her feet.

Next to her was Charlie Joe Svensen with his kitbag.

He gave me his I-know-something-you-don't smile and said, 'I'm glad to see you weren't picked up back at the station, Harry.'

I hadn't given him my name and didn't know how he'd got it.

I said, 'I thought you were going on to Vegas.'

He grinned as though he'd put one over me, which I suppose he had.

'I thought *you* were going on to Vegas.'

I hadn't mentioned Vegas when we bade our farewells not half an hour before. I glanced at Maria and she gave a slight shake of her head. There were other people in the diner and as far as I could tell, Svensen had done nothing to her beyond confront her with his spooky mannerisms. These didn't amount to threats, but in some ways they were more frightening because they were unintelligible, like those of a madman who yells curses in the street but never approaches passers-by.

He reverted to his soft Southern politeness. 'Do you want to take a seat, sir, so that we can talk?' He tapped the one next to him so that he sat between me and Maria. No doubt in his eyes it demonstrated that he controlled the situation. 'You can order coffee and a sandwich; there's no rush.'

I ordered coffee. I left him to speak because it seemed to me that he hated silence, perhaps because his own existence became uncertain if he couldn't generate reactions from other people.

'Y'all are wondering how I know the things that I know,' he said at last.

'I imagine you'll tell me.'

'Wouldn't y'all care to guess?'

'I'm fresh out of guesses.'

The response disappointed him.

'Well, maybe this isn't the time for games. The fact is I was listening when you and your lady wife were conversing during our stop in Springfield. That's how I know your name and intentions.'

I hadn't seen him. I called up a mental picture of the spot where I'd taken Maria aside and he didn't fit in it.

'You were spying on us?'

'That's an ugly word, sir.'

I think he was genuinely hurt – that he truly hadn't seen things that way. In his eye, he was only trying to establish a connection with another person, and some gap in his make-up left him ignorant as to how to do it.

He sighed or pretended to sigh. 'Well, I'm not a man to hold a grudge over a mistake. Let's put that one behind us and come down to the facts of our situation. Y'all were heading for' – he cast an eye over the other customers – 'a certain place in Nevada but changed your plans when you saw…' grinning, 'I don't know what to call them.'

'I know who you mean.' Though as it happened he was mistaken. It was Svensen himself that had caused us to change our plans. 'That doesn't explain why you got off the bus.'

'You think those men were looking for y'all?' He almost laughed in the stagey way that marked many of his gestures. He leaned forward and whispered, 'They were after me! Yes, sir!'

'And why is that?'

'Because I am one of the ten most wanted men in these United States!'

Was this kid real? I didn't know what to make of his youth or his mix of slyness and goofy innocence. I had him down as a loser, drifting in search of the undefinable something that makes existence meaningful, which most of us find in our day to day lives without really trying. But it was possible I was wrong. I admit I was thrown. I'd already concluded that the two DSD agents hadn't known I was in Joplin. Was it really possible they weren't on my tail but on Svensen's?

Maria said, 'I think we should talk outside.'

It was a good suggestion if we wanted to avoid the attentions of casual snitches.

'That's fine by me.'

Svensen shrugged.

We grabbed our bags and stepped into the street. It was clear we couldn't just stand there, so I began to walk. For the moment, my only plan was to find a motel and I decided to stick with it until I came up with a better idea.

I'd never been to Joplin; neither had Maria or Charlie Joe Svensen.

He asked, 'Where're we heading?'

'Nowhere, but we can't stay put. Come on, we can talk as we go.'

The walk unsettled him because he hadn't proposed it. I hoped to use this advantage to get some truth out of him. I was regretting not telling Maria everything about that night at the Arc of Hope. It had been an oversight but it meant she wasn't alert to the mystery of Svensen's identity. Had he been part of the terrorist gang cornered by the GeStaPo on the bridge and somehow escaped? Or was he just the holder of some cheap forged papers like a hundred other Charlie Joe Svensens? It is in our nature as human beings to fix on coincidences and see them as indicators of deep patterns in reality that will reveal its meaning; and even though that meaning remains beyond our understanding, the coincidences comfort us with the illusion that it is there. I didn't know what I'd got myself into and I wanted signs and wonders that would explain it to me.

Conspiracies aren't meant to be understood.

Jeb Lyman had involved me in this one because of the politics of a contested succession to an aging president: the struggle between Nixon and the Kennedys and the role of Hoover and his GeStaPo in the new regime. But what did I really know of Jeb's agenda? And how did the unexplained deaths of two black people fit with it?

I thought of calling him to explain where I was and how things stood and to ask him about Charlie Joe Svensen. But I didn't know if he would come to my aid or it would be the last thing I would ever do.

While I chewed this over we walked, carrying the bags. Joplin was a small city and the suburbs were no more than a couple of miles from the downtown area. Still, it took time and Charlie Joe was an impatient man. He turned sullen – perhaps because I hadn't risen to his claim to be on the Ten Most Wanted List. He asked, 'You ever been to Oregon, sir?' in a superior way as if Oregon were Tibet and only intrepid types and spiritual heroes had ever been there.

'Is that where you've come from?'

St Louis, where he'd joined the bus, wasn't on any route from Oregon to Vegas that I knew of.

'I been there and other places in the course of my researches.'

'Your researches – of course.'

'I think you are mocking me, sir. You have no reason to.'

'I'm not mocking you. It's just I have no idea what you're talking about.'

The justice of this remark seemed to strike him and I could feel him torn between reluctance to give up the power of his secret and the desire to impress me with its importance. He showed no interest in why Maria and I might be avoiding the DSD, but the fact that we were seemed to give him some confidence in us.

He said, 'The Illuminati are cunning in the way they hide among us – the way they borrow our most sacred values and play them back to us as if they share them.'

'But they don't?'

'No, sir. The slogans of our government – *Make America Great!* – *The American Way is the Only Way!* – and the other words that are holy for faithful Americans,

126

are for the Illuminati nothing but a pretense and a mockery to cover the machinations of the New World Order and destroy everything that is true in this country and the white race.'

'I see.'

'But some of us see through this fraud and are organized against it.'

'Yes, I imagine you would be.'

'Some of us are not fooled.'

I wasn't sure how to read this. Of course, there were opponents of the President's vision of the world and some, like the Catholic Church, could only be subdued, not destroyed. But I didn't see Svensen in this light. The political left had been wiped out as an effective force in a series of show trials and emergency detentions under the Defense of American Values Act way back in the thirties. As far as I knew, the right, except for some religious fundamentalists, had bought into the whole racial mythology. Who did that leave still standing?

We reached a tract of low-cost housing. Blue collar patriots lived here. National flags hung in their front yards and their mantelshelves held photos of the President draped in the party colors of the NSDAP. For the most part they were decent, hard-working people and decade after decade they waited patiently for the end of the South American wars and the start of the white man's paradise. They reminded me how much I hated the deception practiced on them by Big A and those around him.

Beyond the houses the buildings thinned to a couple of cocktail bars with exotic names belied by the faded reality, and a black church abandoned when its congregation vanished as suddenly as at the Rapture. In the parking lot in front of the wrecked church a crowd of Hispanics mobbed a guy in work boots, jeans and a flying jacket, who was picking out men and loading them into an open truck. It was a hiring place for Mexican illegals. Most cities had at least one and they were tolerated because of the labor shortage and their contributions to police welfare.

Without mentioning it, we had reached a motel: no more than a line of cabins and a neon sign by the highway. A few old cars parked by the cabins said that business was poor and the guests on a tight budget. I didn't know what Charlie Joe expected to happen next. As we walked he looked increasingly lost: draped in a loneliness that never left him.

Maria tried a smile and said, 'Well, this is it. It's been nice talking to you, Charlie Joe. We wish you well on your journey.'

I held a hand out to him.

He said, 'Y'all staying here?' He looked round forlornly.

'It's as good as anywhere.'

'And how are y'all getting to Vegas?'

'We haven't talked about it. Hire a car maybe.'

'I guess that'd do if the G-men don't have your number.'

'I think you've misunderstood us, Charlie Joe, if you think the authorities are after us.'

'I don't think I have, sir. And I'd like it if you didn't disrespect me by pretending otherwise.'

I thought then that Svensen was going to make some sort of threat. He didn't need to go to the police: a call might do it. Instead he looked distressed.

He said, 'Those people expect me to be traveling alone, and they think y'all are just the two. They ain't looking for three of us traveling together, y'all follow?'

There was a sort of sense in this. I glanced at Maria.

Svensen said, 'I ain't saying y'all got to share a cabin with me, but if we all in the same automobile? Leave it to me and I can fix us with some wheels. What do you say?'

'I think that would be a great idea,' Maria said before I could respond.

'Yeah, that's right. It would be great.' He smiled again but this time with a childish foolishness. I remembered how young he was; not much older than a college kid; and that, even if he was deserter, it was likely he had seen some terrible things in the war. I still didn't like him but I felt a compassion for him.

I still do, despite what was to happen.

The motel wasn't choosy about its customers and happy to give me a cabin on the back of my papers without enquiring about Maria. There is an illusion about police states that confuses brutality with efficiency, but the reality is they breed corruption and evasion. I rarely had problems suborning the systems they create.

Charlie Joe waited outside. He said he didn't have the price of a room but he wasn't no beggar and would find some sheltered place to sleep. He said he would take it as a kindness if he could use our bathroom to shower and freshen up. I could hardly say no, and I offered to stand him a meal.

He took his shower while singing country and western songs. Maria and I sat on the bed, paired like strangers in one of life's many waiting rooms and, in the same way, cautious of each other's strangeness, as if we feared intimacy and our shared past was a mistake we could not understand. I felt that I was losing her; that I had carelessly allowed Jeb Lyman and now Charlie Joe Svensen to intrude, and that in some way I had valued them more than her. I wanted to speak: to explain that it was not so. But I felt that somehow it was so, and I did not want to voice the words that would say otherwise and, on top of my other sins, make me a liar. Meanwhile Charlie Joe sang about loss and longing and the time we waste on people we cannot let go. The words were meant to be sung by a woman with a broken heart but he delivered them in a high twang as a singer might in one of the roadside bars we had passed, where partners shuffle on a small dance floor with heads lying on each other's shoulders, dreaming.

Charlie Joe came out of the shower and Maria and I took turns to wash. When we were done, we went to the desk and the motel clerk directed us to a Mexican restaurant where we ate alone to a juke box that played mariachi music. In the rest room a poster advised Mexican workers to regularize their status or face penalties. Someone had written on it in Spanish but the meaning was clear. *Fuck you, gringo!*

I wondered what to talk about and remembered that Svensen had mentioned Oregon.

I asked, 'What were you doing there?'

'I was researching the... you know what I was researching.'

'The New World Order?'

'Philosophers have jawed about the world, but real men do something about it. Karl Marx said something like that.'

'That's what they do in Oregon?'

'In Wyoming, Montana and the Dakotas too. The Government don't talk about it, because they like to pretend they run stuff. But there in the mountains and the woods, if you look hard, you'll find the real patriots who've seen through everything.'

I tried to make sense of this. There were persistent rumors and the occasional public trial of armed militias holed up in the wildernesses of the Northwest states. As far as I knew, they were racist anarchists who opposed the authorities out of cussedness and paranoia.

'Why did you leave?'

'Because there's a war going on up there. Those army boys you see everywhere ain't all going to fight in Brazil. There's a mess of them not a million miles from Seattle killing their own kind, except the Government don't say nothing about it. I left because things were getting too hot, and I don't think that bushwhacking poor kids just 'cause they are wearing their country's uniform is the way to go. If things were properly explained, they'd probably join our side.'

Maria asked softly, as a mother might, 'So what is the way to go?'

Charlie Joe seemed shocked that she had taken notice of him. He said, 'I don't know – yet. But I'm traveling and thinking, and when I know the answer I'm going to act on it like Marx said. Though I'm no Marxist,' he added quickly.

Other customers came into the restaurant. The men stood at the bar drinking beer from the bottle. The women sat in pairs, and this early in the evening had a primness about them. Their hands flattened their skirts to cover their knees and their fingers played with the trimmings of their blouses above the cleavage.

I paid the bill and we stepped out into the darkness under the neon glow of the signs. I was still curious to know about Charlie Joe Svensen while he was in the mood to talk, and I pursued the question that had puzzled me.

I said, 'You told me you were one of the most wanted men in America. That's a big claim for someone who's done no more than fight with some guys up in Oregon.'

'Oh, that ain't nothing,' Charlie Joe said. 'There's a lot more fighting going on than folks know about. But what really spooks Big A and his servants is knowledge.'

'Knowledge?'

'Of what's really happening.'

'That so?'

'That is truly so. And I have the knowledge that I've pieced together from what I was told by P'tit Antoine Molineaux and others and which I aim to verify by going to Las Vegas.'

'I see. And what is that knowledge?'

Charlie Joe hesitated. He said, 'Y'all have been kind to

me and for that reason I really don't think I should tell y'all.' But I could see he wanted to tell me.

'I'll take the risk,' I said.

I waited a moment, then turned to Maria and suggested we go back to the motel.

'OK – OK,' Charlie Joe said. 'I'll tell you. But you remember that y'all heard it here first.'

'All right, I'll do that. What is it you have to tell me?'

'Well, OK, I'll tell. This is what I know' – he breathed in – 'I know what has happened to all the Negros.'

14

Charlie Joe Svensen didn't tell me what had happened to the Negros. Not then. He knew he had me, even if he didn't know why, and he was determined we were going to stick with each other all the way to Las Vegas. I doubt his reasons were clear even to him. When I was with him I had a sense of an emptiness that sucked things in so that it might be filled and it seemed to me that Maria and I had simply fallen within his orbit. But I admit this was only an impression.

We returned to the motel and he bade us goodnight. He seemed cheerful. He always was when he felt himself on top. He said, 'I'm going to find a place to put my head and maybe look for some wheels. I'll see you folks in the morning.' He laughed and wagged a finger. 'Don't y'all go running away now.'

'We won't,' said Maria. She smiled but I saw tears sparkle in her eyes.

We watched him walk off into the darkness and neon glimmer, jauntily kicking the roadside trash and whistling. Earlier we'd noticed a gas station on the point of closing and he'd said something about breaking into the rest room and laying up there. Another time he said he might boost a car at one of the cocktail bars and sleep in it. Maria and I didn't care what he did. We had things to talk about. We needed to find once more the core of what we were to each other, and I wasn't sure this was possible.

So we returned to the cabin. Maria undressed and took a shower, and I sat on the only chair, wrapped in my silence like a prostitute's john who has no idea of the person he is or why he is there even though both these things should be clear to him.

Finally I asked, 'Why did you agree that we all go to

Vegas together?'

She came out of the bathroom and glared at me.

'Because he's terrifying and dangerous. For God's sake, he *stalked* us when we got off the bus in Springfield! We're safe only because he thinks we're his friends. What on earth made you talk to him in the first place?'

I told her then about everything that had happened at the Arc of Hope and that someone called Charlie Jo Svensen had been there, and maybe this was the same person and maybe it wasn't because he was supposed to have been killed.

'And what does it mean if it is the same person?'

'I don't know.'

'How could he have found us?'

'I don't know.' I shook my head. 'I don't think it's the same person.'

'But you don't know.'

'No.'

I undressed and showered in turn, and when I was finished Maria had already slipped into bed and closed her eyes. I turned off the light and got in beside her. I put my arm around her and she turned and kissed me warmly. But when I tried to touch her more closely she pushed my hand aside.

We woke to Charlie Joe banging on the door and shouting, 'Come on, folks: y'all wake up now!'

I let him in and he made himself at home, straight away going to the bathroom for a shower and a shave. I looked outside and saw a Chevy Styleline parked there, a pale blue four door model maybe ten years old with some dings and rust but overall not too bad.

'You came in this car? Where did you get it from?'

'You seen the time? It's nine o'clock already.' He laughed in an excited way I didn't care for. 'Don't you worry none. I went to that Prairie Paradise Lounge – the cocktail bar? – and won me this little beauty in a card game. There won't be no police looking for it, trust me.'

I didn't trust him and I didn't buy his story, but neither did I believe he'd done something so stupid as to steal a car people would look for. I considered asking for the vehicle's papers, which the owner should have given him, but decided not to. The car was a fact, and how Charlie Joe came by it was a problem for another time.

'Wait outside,' I said. 'We need to wash and dress.'

When he was gone Maria asked, 'Where do you think the automobile came from?'

'I'm guessing he found a vacant house – the owners on holiday or something.'

'Then why didn't he say so? He lies about everything.'

'I don't think he knows the difference.'

Maria nodded. There was no point speculating. She said, 'We need more clothes.'

'We'll drive into town; get breakfast; pick up whatever.' I looked at her, hoping for forgiveness. 'If the police know about the car, it all ends there.'

'Yes it does,' she said.

I paid the bill and loaded the Chevy. I decided it was safer not to return to the motel once we were done in town. I explained to Charlie Joe about the things we needed and it didn't seem to worry him that we would be seen around and could be linked to the car. I said the plan was to set off and head for Las Vegas.

He said, 'That is OK with me, sir. I been looking on a map and reckon the distance is about thirteen hundred miles. If we spell each other, I think we can do it in four days easy.'

In town we bought a basic change of clothes and I added jeans and a plaid work shirt because my suit was looking tired after all the travel and sitting around. Maria bought a dress and fixed her hair. I was still good for cash but conscious that we needed to be careful. It gave me the idea that we could cut our costs if we bought two small tents and camped at sites along the route. I also thought there was less chance that anyone would look for us there.

Charlie Joe picked up on my money concerns and surprised me by pulling out his wallet and waving it at me. He said, 'I told y'all I had a good night at the cards. Before I took his old Chevy, I won a coupla hundred cash from the guy, and I don't mind contributing to expenses. I don't want no one saying Charlie Joe Svensen don't pay his way none.'

The cash worried me more than the car, which could have been easily stolen. I tried to imagine Svensen playing poker and winning, but I couldn't make it credible. All the same, I said thanks. We bought the camping gear and loaded it in the trunk of the car. I also bought a newspaper, which was full of the Japanese bomb story.

Noon came and we got on our way to Vegas.

Charlie Joe took the first spell of driving. It excited him and I suspected he'd never had a car of his own but had learned to drive in the Army. Beyond warning him to drive within the limit, I was content to give him his head. Maria and I sat in the back but spoke very little. Instead, for a long time we held hands, which is something that people who are comfortable in such a situation rarely do, so that it seemed to me impossibly sad. How had we got here? By decisions and gestures that at the time seemed directed at something else and whose motives were never fully examined.

As a distraction, the journalist in me turned to the story of the Japanese uranium bomb. Only a few days before, I would have been the go-to guy to report the American reaction to the English public. Instead I was cut off from my contacts and trying to make sense of the thing.

The idea of a bomb using the power of the atom had been around since the thirties, when physicists suggested it might be possible. But given the cost, nobody much had been interested. The U.S. Navy wanted ships, and the Army's problem was to hold down vast swathes of territory against an active insurgency, not flatten cities. Only the Air Force had any enthusiasm on the general principle that bombing stuff was a fine way to conduct a war. But they were removed from the issues on the ground in places like Venezuela and Brazil. Similar considerations must have affected the other Great Powers because nobody had pursued the technology until now.

I could only guess what had motivated the Japanese. In a mirror of American policy, they had got themselves locked in a decades-long war to conquer China and take its resources. I could see that the huge Chinese cities might be plausible targets for the new weapon. But if that was the case, I thought the Japanese would fail; the Chinese would take their knocks and fight on, and all that would be served would be a ratcheting up of the hatred and the horror.

Whatever the case, I didn't see the Japanese move as directed at the United States. Relations between the two countries weren't good and there were tensions in the Pacific, but the reality was that each was fully absorbed in the unending follies of their Chinese and South American empires and neither could afford hostilities against the other. The newspaper was full of hysteria about the threat posed by 'the slavish hordes of the Orient', but this was standard garbage for internal consumption: part of the President's tactic of mobilizing the population by exaggerating external dangers and playing to its prejudices. I was more interested in how this development would affect the politics between the Kennedy and Nixon factions, but the paper didn't say and I didn't expect it to.

As journeys go, the long stretch from Joplin to Las Vegas was a tedious one. In the miles since Chicago, I had burned out the romance of great distances across the seemingly endless American landscape. We stuck with Route 66 through Oklahoma, picking up food supplies at a roadside store outside Tulsa, and for a while crawled behind a military convoy.

That night we camped among pine woods at a place named after one of the Indian tribes. This late in the season – after Labor Day – there were few vacationers but adjacent to the lot where we set up our tents, a party from the League of American Girls had made camp and they kept us entertained with patriotic songs in the evening and calisthenics in the morning.

I caught Charlie Joe watching the girls in the same intent way he seemed to watch everything, as though a barrier of incomprehension stood between him and whatever he observed.

Noticing me, he gave the goofy smile of someone caught out. 'Pretty girls,' he said.

I expected him to add something salacious but he didn't, which may have been part of his prudishness. Instead he said in a melancholy way, 'I got a wife. I ain't seen her in a while, but we ain't separated or anything. It's just I had important things to do.'

'In Oregon?'

'And the Dakotas. My researches.'

'Yes – I can understand they were important.'

He must have picked up something in my voice because he flinched. He said, 'There is no need to humor me, sir.'

'I apologize.'

'I accept your apology. My wife is in Texas. I'm a New Orleans boy, myself' – he pronounced it 'N'awleans' – 'but she is presently in Texas. I'm fixing to go there sometime.'

'I don't know either place well.'

'No? Well, I count myself a well-traveled person. It's necessary if you're of a mind to educate yourself, which is the autodidact way of doing things.'

'I didn't know you were married.'

He smiled. 'Well, we all have our secrets, don't we?'

We left the campsite in the morning. To make up time we took turns and drove twelve solid hours with little on the road except rural traffic, the occasional soldier thumbing a lift, and Highway Patrol cars that ignored us.

After the revelation about a wife, Charlie Joe was more comfortable with abstract subjects and knew a little about photography. Where he claimed to have made a study of the matter, he would state a firm opinion that didn't invite a reply. I didn't care for his monologues but they passed the hours through the endless miles of the Texas Panhandle and New Mexico, which is where we camped the second night in cool clear weather under a starry sky.

During all this time, Charlie Joe didn't revert to the subject of what had happened to the blacks. When I tried to raise it, he parried my question as if I'd asked a different one, turning it into an occasion to tell more of his personal history.

'The Negros was mostly gone when I was growing up,' he said. 'I remember some when I was real small. You'd see them – you know? – all loaded in trucks and going someplace or other no one ever talked about and such a wailing as you never heard. My ma said that, when she was young, there was plenty of colored folk around. This would be in the thirties, I guess. They was being moved on, she said, because they was all stupid and criminals; and if they was left, then there would be miscegenation because white boys couldn't keep their hands off Negro women, and some white women of the low trashy kind had a liking for jazz and colored men, same as they do now except that these days it's for your Mexicans. I don't remember many Mexicans from my childhood. Most of them came later, when the Negros was already gone.'

As far as I could gather, Charlie Joe's father had died or disappeared and his mother was a self-absorbed and disappointed woman, though he may have been projecting his own feelings onto her. They had moved around a lot and she was presently living in the Dallas area. There was mention, too, of a couple of brothers, but I had no sense they were close.

On the third day, we passed through Flagstaff Arizona and camped in a ponderosa pine forest on the slopes of a mountain beyond the city. We shared the ground with Vernon and Evelyn, an affable retired couple from Newark. Vernon was block warden for the apartments where they lived, and cheerfully reported on his neighbors to the police, which he considered a civic duty.

Evelyn told me proudly, 'Vernon has been a Party member almost from the beginning, when that awful communist Roosevelt nearly stole the Presidency.'

A lot of older people still blamed Franklin Roosevelt for destroying American Values and excused the excesses of Big A by talking about the worse things that would have happened if FDR had got his way. His exile and assassination hadn't ended the bitterness his memory caused in certain circles.

That night we shared a barbecue with our new friends because to do otherwise would excite suspicion. As it was I caught them glancing at Maria's dark beauty and their looks of distrust whenever Charlie Joe attempted to be sociable. He told them that he was a soldier on his way to Tucson and Maria and I had kindly given him a lift.

'That was a very patriotic thing to do,' said Vernon solemnly. 'Supporting our boys and all.'

But I don't know he believed us.

We left early next morning. Las Vegas was almost two hundred and fifty miles away but we calculated we could do the distance in a day. Once there I proposed we find motel rooms so we could rest and freshen up. And then we would go our separate ways.

I still hadn't told Charlie Joe of our intentions and he hadn't told us his except that he was 'researching' the things he had learned from his time with the militias and his guru, the mysterious P'tit Antoine Molineaux. Yet I sensed there was a connection: that both of us, from different directions, were looking for an answer to the same question.

Everyone knew there were no blacks in America.

What had happened to them?

The official story was that they had been re-settled in the conquered territories – mostly Brazil, in places like the rubber plantations of Fordlandia – and in the early years the Administration released documentaries showing these new Brazilians whooping it up in the way everyone knew Negros behaved, and pleased with their lot. Then the general population lost interest and latterly the only news out of Brazil concerned unending guerrilla warfare.

I'm not sure I ever believed this account. But I don't know that I cared to ask if there was another story.

I discovered Charlie Joe Svensen's version of the truth, when our car got a puncture and we had to change the wheel. We were somewhere in the Mojave, a couple of hours out of Las Vegas, driving under a relentless sun across a desert marked with Joshua trees. We didn't hear the tire go, but felt the vehicle cant to one side and the steering jerk and we heard the flap of rubber ripping itself to pieces.

'God damn it!' Charlie Joe said.

'Calm down,' I said. 'It's just a tire. You've changed a wheel before, haven't you?'

So we got out of the car and set about jacking it up and making the swap. There were no particular problems but we were tired with the journey and of each other's company and looking forward to a bed and maybe a beer or two. It was probably this that made Charlie Joe let down his guard and tell us what he'd learned. That and his sense of self-importance, because in the end his secret did not mark him out as a superior man unless he shared it and won our admiration at his profundity.

'I know y'all want to know what it is *I* know concerning the fate of our Negro brethren,' he said as he sweated over the jack. 'Well, I guess there's no reason not to tell you, because it's just the facts of the case and the Truth that the Illuminati have been hiding from us. And sooner or later the Truth will out, right?'

'That's what they say,' I agreed, and I passed him some of our water, which he drank and splashed a little on his face. I looked at Maria, who was sitting in the shade of the car, her eyes closed but her mouth tense. She was listening.

'All right then,' Charlie Joe said. 'It's like this. Y'all can forget all that hogwash about settlements in Brazil and happy jigaboos tapping rubber somewhere out in the jungle, because that ain't what happened.'

'No?'

'*No*. And the reason is this. The problem for our so-called President and his fellow-conspirators in the New World Order has *never* been how to control twenty million raggedy-assed Negros – not when you got two hundred million whites ready, willing and able to do the job. No sir! *The problem* is with the whites.'

'The whites?'

'The very same. Because what are you going to do when all those fine Americans that you been lying to and robbing in order to make yourself rich with all the good things of the earth discover what you been doing, as they surely will? Because they ain't going to take it lying down, no. They are going to feel a righteous anger and rise and overthrow your New World Order and all its devilish works, unless you can find some way of stopping them. Unless you can find a way of controlling *the whites!*'

'I see,' I said, though I didn't know where this argument was going. Or perhaps I did but chose not to accept that people can believe such things despite the evidence that no idea is so stupid that a charlatan cannot find followers who will give their lives and treasure in its defense.

'*That* is where you'll find your missing Negros,' Charlie Joe said with complete assurance. 'Scattered across this nation in small and secret groups and maybe also in the territories: an army of black men that has been recruited, armed and trained by our own government for the express purpose of dominating the white race. For the moment, we don't see them because they are held in reserve. But some day we *shall* see them because the scales will fall from our eyes and we shall behold the wickedness of our rulers. And on that day, this great Negro army will come forth, ready to wage a race war against us – perhaps to win that war because we have become weak and effeminate and distracted by our own pleasures. Because that is the purpose of the fighting in Venezuela and Brazil and other places. To destroy the lives and vigor of American youth, so that there will be no one left to defend the white race except the feeble and the degenerate. *That* is what my researches indicate, and that is what I intend to prove by finding one of their bases and getting the evidence.'

'Camp MacArthur?'

'Yes. That is where I intend to go.'

Charlie Joe Svensen beamed at me and wiped his hands on a rag found in the trunk.

'I think we are ready to rip and roar,' he said, and let out a yell of triumph, '*Hi, ho, Silver!*' across the desolation of barren earth and Joshua trees, as if for the present, he owned the world and all that was in it.

15

There was a time in the late twenties when the good citizens of Nevada wondered how to make a decent living out of a desert. They came up with gambling, prostitution and easy divorce. Their target market was construction crew on the Boulder Dam.

The Northern Club, the Las Vegas Club and the Apache Hotel dated from this period and there were plans for expansion, which maybe would have happened if Big A and the whole American Values movement hadn't got into its stride and seen off the Mob's interest. The existing casinos survived the general puritanism because they were owned behind the scenes by chiefs in the NSDAP, the President's national unity party, but no more were built. More than thirty years later, they looked tired and dusty and competed to provide downmarket entertainment for forces personnel on weekend leave and stopovers on their way to California.

As for those personnel, most were crew from the gunnery school at Nellis Airbase; but there was also an army base at Camp MacArthur a couple of hours away. The soldier boys rarely surfaced in the city. When they did, they kept themselves to themselves and hinted with a swagger that they were where 'it' – the war and everything – was 'at'. According to the sign at the city boundary, the population of Las Vegas was about thirty thousand.

And those were the facts, as far as I knew.

We found an out of town motel on the interstate that was happy to accept my 'Johnson' papers and that Maria was my wife without checking hers. Charlie Joe said he would make his own arrangements but didn't say what they were. We agreed to eat together first.

We drove into town in the Styleline and passed a

couple of police cruisers without attracting interest. Some way off Fremont, where the buildings thinned to a string of budget wedding chapels run by grinning pastors in black toupees and pink suits, we found a restaurant with a neon sign topped by a pair of glass fiber bull's horns and behind the sign a parking lot of bare tamped earth and a single storey Quonset hut painted a faded blue. It offered the biggest steaks this side of somewhere, and in truth they were big enough.

We sat around the table, our nerves strung out but our faces composed like three strangers in a high stakes card game. It was clear that the moment had come to answer the question we had avoided: what were we going to do next? Charlie Joe had said in general terms that he planned to investigate what was happening at Camp MacArthur, but how he was going to do it was known only to him and I doubt even that was true. Maria and I had told him nothing after we first denied any interest in Las Vegas and were exposed as liars. There was a logic in pooling our forces, but that meant taking on an ally I disliked and distrusted. Yet the alternative held its own risks. On his own, Charlie Joe might easily be caught, and I took it for granted that in such an eventuality he would give us up. He had no reason not to.

It happened that it was Charlie Joe who opened the bidding. He said, 'Although you ain't said so, Mr Johnson, sir, I know you are interested in Camp MacArthur and the things that are going on there. Ain't no use denying it because there's nothing else hereabouts 'ceptin' the gunnery school that might be of interest to someone who wasn't a gambling man. Now, I've been plain with you, and I think it would be gentlemanly of you to be the same with me and tell me your business so's we can see how we can maybe help each other.'

At that moment, while another lie was on my lips, I had an insight. The DSD already knew I was investigating the mystery patients and that I'd killed one of their own. It made no difference if I told these things to Charlie Joe Svensen. The only secret not known to my enemies was my whereabouts, and Charlie Joe knew that without any further telling.

'He has a point,' I said to Maria. I looked to her in case she had some wisdom that had passed me by, but she had got to the same place before me and nodded.

I checked the restaurant for anyone who might be listening, but the only other customers were a mom and pop at the other end of the room eating from plates piled high with steak and fries, and the busboy was standing outside, smoking in the parking lot. So then and there I told Charlie Joe what we knew and what we had done, holding back nothing except the killing of the DSD agent – and my fear that I was on a tenuous string with the GeStaPo holding the other end. He was impressed.

'God damn!' he said in a soft voice. His eyes sparkled and he wiped his hand across his mouth. I realized then that he was astonished to have his beliefs confirmed, in the way that born-again Christians will probably be as shocked as the rest of us if Jesus finally returns.

'Keep it down.'

'But God damn if it don't go to prove I'm right about what happened to the Negros!'

'How so?'

'How so? Why it's as plain as the plainest thing you ever saw. Your man Doctor Vipic, who's taking care of those black folks, is a soldier – which means he *has* to come from Camp MacArthur. And where else could them Negros be hiding? They ain't walking about the city or dying of thirst in the desert. There just ain't no other place hereabouts for them to be doing whatever they're doing 'cept Camp MacArthur. It near enough proves what I been saying!'

'Two people don't make an army,' I reminded him.

147

'And one of them is a pregnant woman.'

'So? Everyone knows that Negros are full of libidinosity. They got to get their ashes hauled somehow, and it follows that some of their womenfolk will get in the family way. If they ain't part of the army I spoke of, what are they then?'

What indeed? Conspiracies are not meant to be understood. But sometimes they are explained with a mad passion and a logic that defies you to find its flaws. Was it remotely plausible that a bunch of armed misfits holed up in the mountains waiting for the Apocalypse could be right and that the New World Order, the Illuminati and their evil army actually existed outside their delusions? I was shaken, not because I believed but because I was bereft of an answer.

I said, 'I don't know what they are. The point is to find out, and for that we need a plan. We're here in Vegas, and Camp MacArthur is in a military zone sixty or seventy miles away, and I don't see how we get from here to there and live.'

This was the time for Charlie Joe to tell me how he had got all of this figured out. But, as I expected, he had nothing to contribute. His grand plan to expose the secrets of the world was just a cover for his self-deception that he was a person of significance and that his journeys were something more than aimless drifting.

Finally he said, 'We got to reconnoiter. When I was in the U.S. Marines we was taught to scout the enemy's position before we took any action. I don't see no difference in this situation. We got to get the lie of the land, a handle on the size and disposition of the enemy's forces. Y'all get me?'

I didn't know what this meant in practical terms, but Maria said, 'I can check the local hospitals – pretend I'm looking for work. Nurses talk to nurses. Someone may have heard of Vipic even if he works at Camp MacArthur.

I find it difficult to believe that the mystery patients – or at least some of them – didn't pass through a hospital here before they fetched up in places like Chicago and Washington.'

'Your ID is compromised,' I said.

'It doesn't matter. I may have to show it, but no one will check against a GeStaPo or DSD wanted list unless they offer me a job.'

'If we're expected in Vegas, your name and picture will be on everybody's desk.'

'If we're expected in Vegas, we're not going to last twenty-four hours. I don't see I'm risking much.'

We don't think of women as brave: not in the way of the physical courage that is taken for granted in men, though the latter often do not possess it and when they do display its signs the truth is that it is no more than reckless anger or stupidity devoid of any virtue. I am not speaking of truly brave men, but those like myself. Women on the other hand are capable of a quiet, measured bravery in the way they handle situations that require thought and sticking power. Maria had this sort of bravery and I loved and admired her for it.

I mentioned then a thought that had passed through my mind as I wrestled with our problems. 'Something happened here that caused the injuries to the patients. It will have left traces. I'm guessing there's a library and it should have copies of local papers. Maybe there are clues there. I can check'

I looked to Charlie Joe for his contribution. He hummed and hahed, then said, 'When we was coming here I noticed there was a trailer park off the interstate maybe five miles back. Folks live there, the sort no one pays attention to. Cleaners, guys who haul the trash. They see things and they ain't afraid to talk 'cause they got nothing much to lose that y'all can't get out of them for a few dollars. I could look-see.'

149

I nodded in agreement and he nodded back. I think he was surprised and pleased that we took him seriously.

Slight though it was, we had a plan.

The library in Oakley Boulevard had been built in the twenties as a small hotel. It went bust when the Mob failed to deliver on its promise of a booming casino industry and had been taken by the city to cover back-taxes. This was set out in a framed history of the place that hung in the main hall where the books were.

The citizens of Las Vegas were not great readers and I was the only person there except a small neat elderly woman with lacquered hair and a gold cross, dressed as though for church. A fancy enamel badge informed anyone who cared that she had given five or maybe ten children to the Nation for the continuance of the white race. She sat behind the desk beneath the portrait of Big A with the usual brace of flags either side. On the wall were a couple of prints: scenes of streets and buildings dating from the period before the Great War when the President had been a homeless artist in Brooklyn. The pictures were devoid of people, which may have reflected Big A's psychology or his incompetence. In England we speculated about this, but the answers were as likely to describe us as him.

I asked whether the library kept back numbers of the local newspaper. The elderly lady purred flirtatiously and I thought I had just made her day.

She asked, '*The Las Vegas Sun*?'

'If you say so.'

'For what period?'

'The last two months?'

'All right then. But you'll have to be careful because we don't bind our journals until the end of the year; so they're loose and a bit difficult to handle.'

She disappeared somewhere in back and returned five minutes later with a bundle of papers in a cardboard cover tied with ribbon.

'I've sorted them so's there's only the two months,' she said, laying the folder on a table with a sweet smile. I thanked her and she said with sincere enthusiasm that she was glad to have been of service. The medal she wore so proudly told me she had bought heart and soul into the President's vision and that if she were to explain her opinions I should hate her. Yet, in her day to day dealings and the love she lavished on her family, I could see she was a good person. Always I struggled to reconcile this contradiction in the American psyche and I despised those who had turned the propensity for goodness into evil.

So I started to read. I began my search two months back because I reasoned that whatever disease or injury had affected the mystery patients could not have occurred earlier, and my best guess at the likely horizon was four to six weeks. As expected, *The Las Vegas Sun* was mostly concerned with local events, sports news and classified advertisements. The national and international news and the opinion pieces gave me a feeling of déja vu because I had read them elsewhere, often in the same words.

The problem was I didn't know what to look for because I had no theory as to the origins of whatever afflicted the two hospital cases we knew of, nor the total number of persons involved. In short, was I looking for a motor vehicle accident or a catastrophe? And always the same question: why blacks?

Although it was generally accurate to say there were no people of color in the United States, it wasn't absolutely true. Occasionally some poor creature would emerge blinking into sunlight from the attic or cellar of a Christian pastor or a bleeding-heart liberal after denunciation by a vindictive neighbor; or a gang smuggling fugitive blacks to Canada would be broken up. And, too, there were stories of people whose race had been reclassified because grandpa was too accomplished a dancer for his own good

151

and appeared with his tap shoes and banjo in an old family album. What these small tragedies had in common was that the race of the participants was invariably stated in the reports. After all, that was the point of the story.

Nevada, however, had never known slavery and there had been negligible migration from the South before the President's Second Revolution put a halt to it. I wasn't surprised that none of these stock items appeared in the newspaper. In fact there was scarcely a mention of blacks at all.

Yet were they lurking, hidden beneath the surface of a report about something that had no obvious connection?

I did a second trawl, setting different parameters; this time looking for anything that had a potential for large scale casualties even if none were mentioned.

And I found it. A short easy to miss piece on the inside page of an edition published four weeks before.

It read:

'Earth Tremor at Arroyo Seco

Federal authorities have reported a minor earth tremor at Arroyo Seco on Tuesday last. People are advised to stay away from the area because of the risk of landslips, aftershocks and the possibility that this is the precursor to a major earthquake. A spokesman stated that there is no cause for general concern.'

That was it. No mention of casualties.

I had no idea where Arroyo Seco was. I went to the shelves and looked out a gazetteer and map of Nevada and spent half an hour studying them because, apparently, there was no settlement there nor any feature of note and so it wasn't listed in any index. I found it only by passing my finger inch by inch over the map. It was located about sixty-five miles north and a little west of Las Vegas. When I checked for Camp MacArthur it wasn't shown, but neither was Nellis Airbase. I wasn't surprised because the location of military and security installations had been removed from maps decades before. It was one of the pieces of purposeless secrecy that affected this country, that matters of common knowledge were denied and language itself became distorted as people struggled to cope with their acquired amnesia.

I returned the folder to the librarian. I took the opportunity to compliment her on her badge, and from politeness asked about her children. She had seven and they were doing fine, except it was clear that the middle one had unspoken problems but that was children: what can you expect? She asked me what a visitor from the East was doing in her city and I said I was thinking of investing, though I can't have looked much like an investor in my jeans and plaid shirt.

'Business or real estate?' she asked.

'Real estate. But I'm concerned about the earthquake risk. It affects construction costs.'

'Well I don't know what to say.' She giggled. 'I mean Nevada is like California; we get earthquakes just all the time. But mostly they're out in the desert or they don't amount to much. I can't remember one that ever gave me much cause to worry.'

'I read that there was one at Arroyo Seco a month ago.'

Her voice dropped and she said slowly and dismissively, 'Oh, Arroyo Seco is no place at all and miles away. We don't pay no attention to it.'

'You didn't feel the tremor here?'

I detected a hesitation before she said, 'I read it was a minor one. We didn't feel a thing and wouldn't have known about it if it hadn't appeared in the newspaper. Now, excuse me please.' She looked at her empty desk. 'I have things to do.'

16

In the heat of Nevada even at this season, we could not park up and discuss things in the car and there was always the risk of attracting attention. We agreed to meet some place other than the motel or the restaurant on the theory that we were less likely to be spotted if we kept on the move. It was an amateur's notion of security that probably owed more to films than reality, but measures like this calmed our fears. For the same reason, I carried the gun I'd lifted from the dead DSD agent. It was in a paper sack ready to be used by Quick Draw Harry Bennet – if he figured out how it worked.

The wedding chapel was a flat-roofed cinder block building painted to look like adobe. The sign said it was the Rodeo Church of God and that it would not be beaten on price anywhere in Las Vegas.

We parked on the sunbaked lot and went inside. The interior was saloon style with the bar serving as altar and a cross made of cow horns standing between a pair of candles in whiskey bottles. Portraits of cowboy movie stars hung on the walls, and the price included a photograph of the happy couple with a life-size cut-out of Tom Mix. A framed copy of the Wallace-Thurmond Act set out who was permitted to marry whom under the 22nd Amendment on maintaining racial purity.

The pastor came hurrying out of a back room. He was a short fellow in a pale blue Western-cut suit with fringes on the sleeves and pockets. His high-heeled boots sported pointed toes and stitched medallions, and his manner was avuncular, reminding me of Lionel Barrymore, the actor with the warm folksy voice, who played Big A's father in the Oscar-winning film about his life. The pastor was the

President's age, and sported the same toothbrush moustache.

'Reverend Eliah Judkin,' said the pastor with a smile of sparkling insincerity. 'Welcome to God's house.'

'My girlfriend and I are thinking of getting married,' I told him, which seemed obvious but had to be said.

He glanced at Charlie Joe Svensen.

'My son by my first marriage,' I said, which caused Charlie Joe to grin.

Judkin said to him, 'Your daddy must have been young, or maybe it's just clean living' – and to me, 'Either way you're welcome, Mister…'

'Huxley – Aldous P Huxley.'

Maria and I had rehearsed the next part and agreed it was best coming from her – the little woman and all that.

She said with a hint of shy simper, 'I want this wedding to be absolutely perfect, and it's so important to get the right setting and atmosphere, don't you think?'

'I couldn't agree more.'

'So I was wondering if you could leave us alone for a few minutes to just kind of soak it in. And, of course, you must give us your brochure – you do have a brochure with all your wedding plans, and all?'

'Well, yes, we do,' said the reverend. His voice was a little guarded and I guessed he had picked up Maria's slight accent because he added, 'While you're at that and thinking about dates, I hope you've given some thought to complying with the Act?' – nodding at the copy over the bar. 'We can do these things quick in Nevada, but the paperwork is the paperwork, if you follow me.'

'Oh, you needn't worry about that,' Maria reassured him.

The pastor returned to his office and came back with a folder of glossies setting out the options and the prices. I noted the chapel was non-denominational and a rabbi or a

Mormon bishop could be supplied at a small charge. Our new friend seemed disposed to take us through the details but Maria said she'd feel less embarrassed if she and I talked it over between ourselves – 'what with money being a consideration and all.' He left us and we took seats at one of the saloon tables. To get us in the mood, the sound system played songs by Patsy Kline and Skeeter Davis.

I didn't want to stay too long with Judkin haunting in the shadows in the hope of a quick sale. I asked Charlie Joe to get to the point and tell us what he had learned.

He seemed sparked up, as I supposed someone of his disposition might be because, in a sense, his world-view was being validated by the secrets and conspiracies around us. He said, 'Well, I guess I've learned a lot, though I'm damned if I know what to make of it. Have y'all noticed that there ain't many soldiers around the town?'

I hadn't thought about the matter. Then again, how many should there be?

'The story I got,' said Charlie Joe, 'is that the Army has pretty well abandoned Camp MacArthur.'

'Are you sure about that?'

'That's what they tell me. About a month ago some convoys came through town, spread over two nights: truck after truck filled with men from the camp. And get this: they was escorted by military police like they was all prisoners. That's the words as they was told to me: *like they was all prisoners*.'

This made no sense but I let Charlie Joe go on. 'Anything else?'

'Sure. The people under guard was not all soldiers. There was civilians as well. Not many, but some.'

'What kind of civilians? Blacks? Mexican workers?'

'White men and a few women. Respectable people in suits who might work in an office or laboratory maybe.'

'But no blacks?'

'Not one – and believe me, I asked.' Charlie Joe shook his head. 'It don't do much for either of our theories, does it?'

No, it didn't. I asked if that was all.

'I don't know – I mean I don't know what's important and what ain't.'

'What about injured people? Ambulances?' said Maria.

'No one mentioned any. But y'all got to understand that there was a lot of trucks – with canvas siding, you know? They could've been filled with injured people, and Negros for that matter, and no one been any the wiser. One thing, though…'

'What?'

'A day or so after the Army cleared out of the base, they was going back. Exceptin' this time they was driving construction equipment. Diggers, big earth movers and such – John Deere's finest. No one could tell me what they're doing up there, and there weren't many of them: just a few drivers and supervisors. I figure they're clearing the site now everyone's gone. Though why they should be doing that beats me.'

I had some thoughts. They didn't explain everything but made a partial sense. After my visit to the library I'd bought a road map of Nevada at a gas station and I laid it on the table now.

'What are we looking at?' Maria asked.

'This road here.' I pointed at a route heading north-west from Las Vegas for about twenty miles into the desert. It didn't carry a State or Federal designation, which meant it was to all appearances a country road leading to a small community, maybe a single ranch, but nothing was named.

Charlie Joe peered over my shoulder. 'I don't see what you're getting at. This road don't go nowhere.'

'That's my point. It should, but it doesn't.' I traced a rough line with my finger, and, allowing for the vagaries of terrain, the road, if it continued, would reach Arroyo Seco.

'So? What's at Arroyo Seco? And why isn't the road shown as going there, if that's what it does?'

'Arroyo Seco is Camp MacArthur. The map doesn't show it in order to discourage people who have no legitimate interest, but it's an open secret hereabouts because of all the military traffic.'

'OK. And…?'

'According to the newspaper, a month ago there was an earthquake at Arroyo Seco. The report plays it down as a minor tremor, but I think it was something major. It would explain why the base was abandoned and the earth movers were sent in to level the site. It also gives us some sort of explanation for the mystery patients: they were casualties.'

'But why only blacks?' asked Maria.

'We don't know that the casualties were only blacks. There could be hundreds of whites, but if they're scattered through the hospital system no one is likely to pay much attention. Your friend Alice mentioned she'd heard of a lot of other possible cases. My guess is that most of those are whites. The blacks are an anomaly. They aren't supposed to exist, and so they have to be hidden.'

And that was it. Neat, as far as it went. But it didn't go far enough.

Charlie Joe said, 'I hand it to you, sir. What you say sounds about right, but it don't explain what Negros were doing at Camp MacArthur. Hispanics I can just about understand: cooking, cleaning and all the dirty work, though in my experience it's the ordinary grunts usually do that stuff. But Negros? Who needs them?'

There was no answer to that on the information we had. Nor to the identity of the civilians Charlie Joe's informants had seen, though this didn't seem to me of great importance. I could imagine the Army using civilian specialists for any number of purposes. Nor did the general secrecy in which everything was shrouded trouble me. The whole country had embraced a paranoid fantasy and most of the day-to-day security measures were against a non-existent threat. Maybe Charlie Joe was wrong and the dead and injured blacks were no more than cooks and cleaners the Army was embarrassed to admit to. Organizations overreact in defense of their reputations and hide their sins rather than repent them.

So far Maria had said nothing beyond putting a couple of questions. I asked her if she had learned anything at the hospitals.

'There is only one hospital,' she said. 'Clark County General. They're short staffed. You never saw folk so pleased as when they thought I might join them.' She smiled but it seemed to me she was tired and trying hard.

'I'm sorry,' I said, not sure what I was apologizing for.

'That's all right.' A pause. Then wearily, 'That's all right. OK, what did I learn? Well, it seems to fit with what you two have found out. Clark County is a small city hospital. Normally it has nothing to do with Camp MacArthur – I mean nothing. The Army has its own facility on the base, and any cases they can't handle they ship out to Walter Reed or one of their other places. Until a month ago.'

'And?'

'I was told about "a natural disaster" that no one put a name to or where it had happened. I wasn't given the casualty numbers, but it was clear there were a lot – I'm not sure anyone outside the administration would know, and maybe not even them. The story is that there were two days of chaos when patients were brought in by Army truck – not ambulances but anything that was to hand. They used Clark County as a clearing station. It did little more than first aid and triage before moving the casualties on to no-one-knows-where. Someone said it was like a storm blowing through. They'd had no training in disaster management and my impression is they found the experience harrowing. Army all over the place, panicking and shouting. Hospital managers running for cover and whining. Men in suits making threats – men who don't give their names.'

'All the same, people talked to you.'

'Nurses talk to nurses. They resent what happened, the way they were treated – the threats. They thought it was safe to talk because it's impossible to keep secret the fact that there's been an incident of some kind. Too many people saw.'

'And Vipic? Has anyone heard of him?'

'Better than that.'

Maria seemed to hesitate, and I wonder now if it wasn't because once she spoke, she would unleash a course of action that might otherwise have been different.

She said, 'I've seen him.'

I wasn't too surprised that Vipic was in Las Vegas; only that Maria had chanced to see him. As far as I could gather from what I'd overheard at the Freedmen's and been told by Warner Seebold, the doctor had some sort of coordinating role in managing whatever had happened at Camp MacArthur. Since Clark County General was the nearest hospital and might still be handling some acute cases that couldn't be dispersed, it made sense that he would spend some of his time there.

I asked, 'How did you recognize him?'

'A doctor came through the reception area where I was talking with someone from Personnel. He had on a white coat instead of a jacket, but he was wearing uniform underneath. A clerk called him to the desk and I heard his name.'

'What does he look like?'

'Forty or so, fair, medium height, thinning Army haircut, forgettable face. Slim as though he works out, but not one of your muscled types. My impression was the nurses don't like him.'

Charlie Joe was watching me. He said, 'You have something in mind?'

I did. But like all our choices, this one was risky and uncertain.

I said, 'Vipic has access to Camp MacArthur and reason to go there.'

'OK, I can buy that, but… Whoa! Are you proposing what I think you're proposing?'

'What do you think I'm proposing?'

'You want to *kidnap* him? Force him to take us there?'

'We'll never make it there on our own, but with Vipic we'd have half a chance.'

'You mean like through the roadblocks and the guards and whatever else is out on that road?'

'You have another way?'

Maria said, 'Why don't you just interrogate him? Threaten him?'

It was a good question and I treated it seriously.

'Because, if there really is a secret involving Camp MacArthur and the black patients, he'll lie about it. Why shouldn't he? How would we ever know?'

'But what makes you think there'll be anything to see at the site?'

'The heavy construction equipment. Who starts clearing a site *two days* after an earthquake?'

'They may have been searching for more survivors.'

'Did any show at Clark County after the first rush?'

'I didn't hear of any,' Maria admitted.

'No, I thought not.'

'They're hiding something, ain't they?' said Charlie Joe.

I could tell he loved the idea. I didn't know whether it was because he had courage or just comic book heroism, but I thought it was probably the latter. It didn't provide any comfort.

Pastor Judkin came bustling around us with small dancing steps as if his pointed boots pinched.

He asked, 'Y'all had enough time to find out what you was wanting to find out? Y'all want to talk dates and prices, we can do that. I can tell you our rates are very sweet.'

'We still have to decide,' Maria told him. 'But I can say that I'm very taken. May we come back tomorrow and let you know?'

Judkin recognized a brush off, but the killer smile softened the words and he mustered the politeness to say, 'Well, in that case, I look forward to seeing you folks again.'

'I'll take a brochure.'

'Right, lady, you do that.'

He moved us firmly towards the door, and once we were through, closed it behind us. He would remember us, but I doubted it would mean anything unless he was shown photographs, and I didn't see anyone had cause to flash our mugshots at a wedding chapel. And what could he say? This was one more to add to the accumulation of small risks. None of them was inherently likely to bring about disaster, yet it seemed to me that one of them was certain to, simply because they were so many. In the end this is what destroys our nerve. Not a confrontation with stark and obvious horror or the thrills and spills of popular movies, but the grinding anxiety of the trivial that we live with by the day not the moment.

We found ourselves in the parking lot with the sun at our backs and occasional cars passing along the highway, the slack traffic of a small city before the rush. I thought about cars – presumably Vipic had one. His own or one provided by the military? Probably the latter; maybe with a driver; maybe not. If he was still on duty, it would presumably be at his place of work.

'You're doing that thinking thing again, ain't you?' said Charlie Joe.

I checked my watch. Since my call at the library and Maria's at the hospital, the day had worn on. It was four o'clock. If Vipic was working a standard shift, he would finish in the next hour or two. An emergency or pressure of work might detain him later. Either way, for the moment he was still likely to be at Clark County General and identifiable by his car if it was painted the usual Army drab and carrying insignia.

I said, 'We can't take him today. It's too late to drive out to Arroyo Seco and we don't have the means to stash him overnight. Our best plan is to present ourselves under some sort of military cover, using Vipic as a front, and that means we can't use the Chevy.'

'You think the Army has given Vipic an automobile?'

'I'm counting on it. If I'm right, it's parked at the hospital. We wait until he leaves, and follow him and find out where he's staying.'

'And then what?' asked Maria. 'Are you seriously going to kidnap him from his apartment or some hotel?'

Her voice wasn't reproachful – something I could have borne because it would have given me grounds to resent her in the way that we feel justified in resenting people who tell us the truth. This was simply the voice of a woman who loved me and who spoke truth with clarity and the innocence that comes from love. She had raised the critical question.

And then what?

We kidnap Vipic. We force him to drive to Camp MacArthur and don't get killed on the way. We discover whatever it is that has happened out there: the disaster that has to be hidden. We get out with our lives.

So now we know the secret of the mystery patients.
And then what?
However I try to think this through, it ends badly.

17

The GeStaPo knew where we were.

This may or may not have been true, but it had been my working assumption since Jeb Lyman set me on the trail of the mystery patients and then walked away. As a piece of knowledge, it gave me the comfort some condemned men must feel in the face of inevitability, when the final outcome is scarcely worth thinking about and the smallest things in life become absorbing and meaningful.

In any case the most immediate threat came not from an army of Hoover's boys but from the DSD. In evaluating it I kept coming back to the same point – perhaps no more than an unjustified hope – that their forces were only a fraction of Hoover's and most of them would be dedicated to preventing other sources of leaks and, not least, to isolating the casualties of the Camp MacArthur disaster. Also – so I told myself – the DSD was organised for maintaining the Defense Department's internal security; not undertaking national manhunts. It lacked the technical skills as well as the manpower and could not call on other agencies without revealing the very secret it was trying to hide.

I chose to believe these things because, unless they were true, our plan to use Vipic to gain access to the site at Arroyo Seco was naïve and doomed to failure.

My guess about Vipic's car proved correct. It was parked on the hospital lot. He didn't have an Army driver.

The doctor finished his shift and came out of the hospital at six. His description fitted that given by Maria: a fair-haired, unremarkable man with the square set and erect carriage that comes from long service in the military. Though his name sounded Slavic, his face had the impassive bony look I associated with Norwegians from Minnesota, but I didn't take that as any guide to his character. Not a cautious man, he went straight to his car and drove off without looking around.

His route took him via a dry goods store where he made some small purchases; then to a motel on the interstate north of the city. The King of Diamonds Motor Lodge was a low rent place for budget travelers and runaway wives and I imagined Vipic stayed there because it was on the right side of town and he needed it only for occasional excursions from Chicago or wherever his current base was. Whatever the case, it was a plus. A hotel – even a cheap one – involved passage through a lobby area and most of the rooms would be on upper floors. Getting someone out of such a place against their will wouldn't have been easy.

Vipic parked and went to a row of cabins built of cinder block with wood-shingled roofs, a shaded boardwalk in front, and an ice machine standing on it. Thinking the problem over, I figured our best chance was to brace the doctor in the morning before other people were around and to take him in his cabin rather than on the open parking lot. I had him as an early riser who would want to complete his present mission and clear town as soon as possible. He would breakfast at the hospital and not at the diner by the motel. Come six-thirty, I imagined him dressed and almost ready to leave. The drive from Clark County General, ignoring the stop at the store, had taken twenty minutes, and this timetable would have him at work for seven. It seemed to me a likely scenario.

There was nothing to be done for now, so we grabbed some food and returned to our own place. Charlie Joe joined Maria and me in our room and we talked matters through, firming up the detail, and dealing with those things we had avoided in the silences that seemed to increase as the time to act approached.

I re-stated what we all knew: 'The plan is that we use

Vipic as a front to drive out to the site through the security checks. I have my DSD papers and Charlie Joe has his old Marine uniform and some ID he bought at the trailer park. He'll do the actual driving.'

I didn't say that neither of our IDs would stand up to too close a scrutiny, but there is a psychology to these things which I'd observed often enough as a foreign correspondent. If we offered up Vipic first for any check, the guard would relax and his attention would diminish once he saw the doc was good. He would in any case be careful in challenging the papers of someone who claimed to be in security. And who the hell cares about drivers? At all events, that was the theory. And the major risk with the whole scheme.

'What about me?' Maria asked.

What indeed? I'd been thinking about her role while trying to unscramble my motives which were in part practical and part emotional.

I said, 'We still need a base. I've been racking my brains about what we do with Vipic once we're finished with him. As far as I can see we've got only two choices: we have to kill him or keep him on ice until we can put some distance between us and Las Vegas. The only place we have is here; so we need to know it's secure.'

'You want to leave me behind.'

It wasn't a question.

I said, 'What's the alternative? How would we explain your presence in the car? As far as we know, there are no longer any casualties on the site. We have no call to take a nurse. Your ID is compromised and each additional person we try to put through the road checks increases the risk.'

Immediately I felt like a liar because, whatever I said, the implication that I was deliberately keeping her away from the point of maximum danger was at least part of the explanation. Yet, if I was being condescending, I felt I had no choice but to bear with the shame because the alternative of losing Maria was too terrible to contemplate.

Charlie Joe returned to his place and Maria and I turned in for the night. Despite our inner reservations at the complexity of our relationship, we made love in the tender and committed way we always tried for; but I shall say nothing of the details because they belong to her as well as me and you have no right to them.

Charlie Joe came rapping at the door at five-thirty. His Marine uniform was freshly pressed and he was hopping with excitement: full of 'Rise and shine!' I don't know if the possibility of being killed crossed his mind. Probably it did, but the pain and agony would have no real meaning for him because he would be only a spectator of the event, seeing himself as a young man sacrificed to a noble cause and crying from self-pity.

I got myself up, shaved, shook the creases from my suit and sponged off some of the stains. Maria watched and I found myself avoiding her eyes. I was caught in one of the absurd contradictions of human existence: pressing onward down a fatal road in the perverse hope that it represented the way back. I was losing Maria while trying to save her – and myself.

'If you don't mind, ma'am, I have a use for your husband,' Charlie Joe said cheerily. 'I'll be sure to have him back for dinner.' To me he said, 'Are we good to go, Harry?'

I nodded and gave Maria a parting kiss. It was dry and bereft of any indication of its possible finality, which is probably more often true than we would wish to credit. Charlie Joe and I went to the Chevy. I was carrying the same paper sack covering the stolen pistol. My companion had his own weapon tucked in his belt. I'd never seen it before.

I asked, 'Where did you get that?'

'This?' He gave me his cat-got-the-cream smile. 'This

good ol' Remington M1911? Why, it's standard Marine issue and I been carrying it in my bag all the time we been together.'

'I didn't know pistols were issued except to officers and NCO's?'

'Well, I didn't exactly say it was issued to me, but I got it all the same. Now, what say we ride into town?'

'You drive.'

'I don't mind if I do, sir.'

So we drove in the Styleline to the King of Diamonds Motor Lodge. It was a half hour to sunrise but already the horizon was tinged a biscuit red and the sky clear and purple. Traffic was light: little more than buses ferrying exhausted Mexican maids to the suburbs to make breakfast for the white kids before they went to school. I noted Vipic's car still parked outside his cabin and a few early birds at the next-door diner, sitting in the window over their plates of eggs and hash browns and staring blankly at the highway. If things went wrong, none of them looked like would-be heroes, but they would be able to identify the Chevy. One more to add to the list of small risks.

We pulled up as close to the cabin as possible to reduce the distance if we had to bundle Vipic into the car by force. I stepped up to the door, rang the bell and called out, 'Defense Security Detail!' loud enough for him to hear without disturbing the neighbors. Vipic was clearly up and about. His radio was playing an easy-listening station.

I'd remarked that Vipic wasn't instinctively cautious; maybe calling the shots made him that way. Now he opened the door without setting the chain and faced me square on, still in shirtsleeves with his tie hanging loose, in the process of knotting it. Close-up there was a determined cast to his otherwise plain face and he was obviously in shape. In one of those stupid insights that I should have had earlier, I realized that, if it came to violence, Vipic could probably take me down. But here we were and I had to follow through.

I flashed my ID. Enough of the picture so he could tell it was me. I said, 'DSD. I'd like you to accompany me, Dr. Vipic. We need your assistance on a medical matter.'

Vipic hesitated and stared at me, which was what I expected: that and maybe a few questions which I would field with a bullshit story that I was following orders and knew nothing.

Instead he launched a haymaker that floored me.

I was shaken but there was no follow up. When I collected my wits, I saw Vipic sprawled on the bed with blood leaking from his nose, and Charlie Joe Svensen pointing his pistol at him.

'You alright?' he asked me.

'What happened?'

'You made the mistake of calling him "Doctor" instead of using his Army rank. He knew you couldn't be DSD.'

I had no answer. Probability theory said we would pay for small risks if we ran enough of them, and the theory turned out to be true. This one didn't kill me only because Charlie Joe was with me. I hadn't expected to be grateful to him.

I threw Vipic a handkerchief. 'Clean yourself up.'

'You're the English guy – Bennet? – killed the agent in Washington?' He sounded cool in the way of a man who knows there's a next time.

Charlie Joe glanced at me. He'd never asked me about my ID and I'd never mentioned the killing.

I said to Vipic, 'We're taking a trip.'

'You're supposed to be in Maine. But that's the spooks for you. They told me there were confirmed sightings near the border and stood down their guys here.'

'Canada will have to wait. Get your cap and jacket.'

'Or what? I don't think you're going to shoot me. Too much noise.'

'Two of us can beat you to death. More painful, but your choice. Now put on the jacket.'

Vipic shrugged. I don't know if he saw through my cheap gumshoe act, but it didn't seem to intimidate him. The last thing I needed was a man who was courageous out of blind arrogance, but I fancied that was what I had in front of me and it made him dangerous because he had intelligence and sharp reflexes and would take any chance to turn the tables on us.

He put on his jacket and set his cap on his head just so. 'OK, where are we going?' he asked.

'To Arroyo Seco.'

He gave a dry snort. 'Figures.'

'Unless you want to tell me what's been going on there.'

'And you're going to believe what I tell you? Right.'

'Pick up the phone and call the hospital. Tell them you're sick.'

'Smart move.'

'Then do it.'

Vipic nodded and did as I asked. So far as I could tell he played it straight and I detected no concern at the other end. He replaced the phone handset. 'And what now?'

'Now we go.'

I covered the doctor with my gun while Charlie Joe checked out the parking lot and opened the car doors. I pushed Vipic into the front passenger seat and sat directly behind him. Charlie Joe took the wheel and Vipic sized him up.

'Don't think about it, doc,' I said. 'Make a grab and I'll shoot. If we crash and I die, it's no worse than what's ahead for me in any case.'

'Really?' He seemed to weigh my words against his own experience. 'Well, maybe. But I have a notion most people would rather die tomorrow than today. Comes down to it, I think you'll change your mind about shooting me while we're moving.'

'Then we'll have an interesting journey until we find out who's right.'

He gave the dry snort I'd heard before. It was a thing with him, reflecting a way of looking at the world in which he was someplace above what he saw. Maria had said the nurses didn't like him, and I believed her.

The night before, Charlie Joe had scoped the road as far as the spur from the interstate that led to Arroyo Seco, and we took it now. Though the road was unmarked, there was a Highway Patrol car laid up on a hard stand next to the roadway and a cop who noted the tags of passing vehicles but otherwise did nothing. Charlie Joe gave him a wave. Vipic had decided to stay quiet and plot his next move until he saw what we were about.

He asked, 'What do you think you're going to find at the Camp?'

I said, 'You tell me.'

'The place was hit by an earthquake a month ago. No one is making a big deal of it, but it isn't a secret. Maybe the damage is worse than the Army admitted to is all, but that wasn't my decision.'

'What sort of damage?'

'A lot of the buildings are laid flat, and those standing are dangerous. The Army isn't bound by building codes, and this is what you get.'

'Casualties?'

'Some. But none on the base. You can't bivouac in the open in Nevada, and nowhere was safe in case of aftershocks, so the place was evacuated. There's nothing to see except ruins and a handful of salvage crew.' Vipic threw a glance in my direction. 'Think on it. If there were anything secret out there, don't you think it would have been moved already? You're risking your lives on a wild goose chase.'

'And the Negros? Are they the secret that has to be moved?'

'What Negros?' As soon as he said it, Vipic changed his tack. 'OK, so there are some Negros among the casualties. The Army uses them for grunt labor; the one thing cheaper than Mexicans. It means nothing.'

I believed none of this.

The road stretched before us, two lanes of blacktop with broken desert to either side, and a scattering of scrub, creosote bushes and the occasional sentinel of a Joshua tree. High mountains rose some distance to the west but how far was hard to say in the glare and heat haze. There were more to the east, the forward slopes splintered in shades of ocher from morning shadows, and the sky was blue teetering on white and feathered with the high clouds that never bring rain.

I hadn't expected traffic, but the road wasn't empty. We had to slow to allow a convoy of five flatbeds to pass in the opposite direction. They were loaded with ditchers and bulldozers, but no ball-cranes as might have been expected if buildings were being demolished, though perhaps that phase had already passed. A few miles on and a convoy of trucks with sheeted sides passed us coming down from the Camp and the lead driver saluted us with his horn.

'Seen anything to tell you I'm wrong?' said Vipic.

I told him to shut up.

'There's traffic up there,' said Charlie Joe. He pointed to a wisp of moving dust a mile or so ahead.

'Close on it.'

'You sure about that?'

'As sure as I can be.' I asked Vipic, 'Where's the first checkpoint?'

'Five miles, more or less. You think you're going to get through it?' Another one of his snorts.

'Let's hope for all our sakes that we do.'

We closed on the line of vehicles ahead. The tail was an open-topped jeep with a heavy machine-gun mounted at the rear and a soldier smoking, unconcerned to see us. In front of him was a truck loaded with wooden cases covered in stenciling I couldn't read, and in front of that another two or three and probably a second jeep as leader.

'Keep near but don't try to pass,' I told Charlie Joe.

He gave one of his giggles that passed for a laugh and shouted over the engine noise, 'You planning on slip-streaming those boys!'

'That's the idea.'

'Well, I'll be!'

'You think you're going to escape a check?' Vipic asked.

'No. But do you want to bet on how thorough it'll be when it gets to the fifth or sixth vehicle in the line?'

'You don't know the Army.'

But I did know the Army and the mind-numbing boredom of guard duty and the indifference of conscripts to whatever they were doing. Over the last few days I'd learned that much in Life was about playing the odds, and this was as good a gamble as any of the alternatives.

Meantime the road ran on until it reached a pull-off point, where trucks could be parked to one side and searched. A few yards beyond was a line of sandbags capped with razor wire and spiked with weapons, and, blocking the roadway, a barrier with a chicane of cement slabs and oil drums behind it, backed by a further barrier and a support line of sandbags and weaponry.

A soldier flagged us to one of the search spots.

18

We parked facing a large rock, where a lizard on its shady side fixed us with a stone-eyed gaze. In the way of lizards, it seemed more motionless than the rock itself until something spooked it and it vanished as quickly as if it had never been there. We pluck signs and symbols out of the world around us because the voice of God is silent but we hope to catch his whispers. So I remember a lonely reptile on a hot chunk of desert rubble and, if I try, can find a meaning to fit my situation. But the truth is the lizard was interested only in flies. And God too, for all I know.

Two soldiers did the checks. A third cooled his sergeant's stripes in a guards' shack. A fourth manned an M60 on the sandbag line; a single man where I counted positions for six. I wasn't particularly surprised at the numbers. The War had caused a chronic manpower shortage that affected even installations like Camp MacArthur now that it was being decommissioned. I fancied there would be plenty of other men around the site to pick off intruders.

The convoy of trucks was ahead of us on the hardstand and the two guys making the checks were bantering with the drivers and slowly going over the packing cases in the back of the wagons. I calculated they would take their time over the first in line, grow bored and speed up the rest. I didn't know whether to take advantage of this and hang back until they were ready to wave us through or try to force the pace. We were in the open and the sun had burned off the cool of the day. Even at this late season the temperature here on the low ground was already in the eighties and there was no staying in the vehicles; the truck crews had dismounted, leaving the cab doors open, and they were milling around smoking and jawing. My concern was that, once we were out of the car, it would be difficult to control Vipic. We couldn't keep our hands on him and I doubted we could stop him if he made a surprise dash. My reading was this was a risk he might be prepared to run.

Charlie Joe shared my take on the situation. He said, 'I'm hotter 'n hell, Harry. What are we going to do?'

If I wasn't in the car I didn't want my ally sitting next to Vipic where it would be too easy for our hostage to get the drop on him.

'Switch places with me and keep the doc covered. I'll see if I can speed things.'

I got out of the rear seat to make way and asked Vipic for his ID. He handed over a leather pocketbook and I cast an eye over a military pass which looked OK as far as I could judge. I straightened myself and closed on the nearest of the guards, ready to try out my arrogant bastard routine. The soldier turned but, as I'd hoped, was thrown by the civilian dress. I flashed my DSD papers and, before he could take them, forced Vipic's into his hand.

I said, 'I'm escorting a doctor. There's some sort of medical emergency on the base.'

'Another idiot broke his leg on all the crap?'

My lucky guess.

'Something like that.'

'Third injury this week. Don't nobody learn?'

'Seems not.'

The soldier accompanied me to the car, peered into the front seat and compared Vipic's face against his picture. Charlie Joe volunteered his own ID which was accepted on a nod. As I'd hoped, my initial sleight of hand made the guard think he'd already checked me out and he wasn't minded to ask a DSD agent for his papers a second time.

'All in order,' he said. He waved to the sergeant at the barrier and shouted, 'OK, Joe, let 'em through!'

*

We negotiated the chicane and passed the second line. Half a mile on, Charlie Joe let out a 'Yee ha!' and Vipic gave a slow hand clap.

He said, 'Nicely done. And now I suppose you think you're in the clear.'

Which worried Charlie Joe.

'Well, we are, ain't we, Harry?'

I asked, 'Where's the main perimeter?'

'You mean we ain't there?' Charlie Joe whined.

'Another twenty miles,' said Vipic.

'Fenced?' – thinking it wasn't necessarily so. The desert itself was a formidable obstacle. If we tried an off-road approach, our car would wreck its suspension and break an axle before we got half a mile, and a man would have to be well-prepared before he made an attempt on foot. For these reasons, it was possible the Army relied on patrols to deal with outlying terrain and fenced only specific secure areas.

But this time no luck.

Vipic grinned. 'All the way – a hundred miles, give or take.'

'Single or double?'

'Double. And, if you're thinking of cutting your way through, you can shoot me now because the ground between the fences is mined.' Another cold smile. 'Still happy?'

I wasn't happy but I wasn't going to show it to a man I liked less with every minute.

There was nothing for it but to drive on and I found my mind drifting between the immediate drab vista under a shattering blue sky, the problems posed by the base perimeter fence, and the recurring image of Maria abandoned in a cheap motel to face whatever had to be faced if our cover was blown, but I thought least about

179

Maria out of the callousness that keeps despair at bay. By degrees the road climbed, we traced the edges and hollows of the mountains and the ground changed color in subtle ways but was still bare except for scrub.

The thought of finessing my way through a second security cordon filled me with dread; but the truth – which worries me now but didn't then – is that we sailed through the perimeter checks. Except that there was a double high wire fence stringing off beyond the near horizon, the layout was pretty much as at the roadblock: a guard hut, two barriers and a chicane between them; a few more soldiers and a few more guns, but the addition made little difference to the chance of getting killed. I acted out the same script as before, because it had worked and I had no better ideas. The guard doing the checks fell for the same trick with my DSD papers that I'd used on his fellow down the road. The most noticeable change was that the soldiers were wrapped in quilted jackets.

In the afflatus caused by success and the cheers from Charlie Joe once we were clear, I thought I was a smart guy, who had understood the psychology of the situation and correctly played the odds. But that was then, and this – as I write – is now; and they are a world apart from each other and a lot has happened. How far, if ever, I was the master of my fate or understood the position in which I found myself or recognized the hidden hands that helped or hindered is even now unknown to me. I grasped one end of a thread that led with twists and misdirections through the mystery at Camp MacArthur towards its solution, but whoever was at the other end remained invisible. Or maybe there was no other end – no 'who' – and things were as they seemed and I really was a smart guy.

Conspiracies are not meant to be understood.

Behind this truism is one equally banal but more existentially terrifying. We do not know if we are inside or outside the conspiracy: its actors or its victims; or if we are simply fantasists of the non-existent; and what we see with our eyes and hear with our ears does not supply an answer.

Camp MacArthur did not announce itself with any sense of drama. On the further side of the fence stretched the same expanse of reds and ochers: mostly empty desert threaded by a road streaked with feathers of wind-blown sand, and here and there a Quonset hut or low cinder block building and in the distance a complex of warehouses or industrial plant. Phone and power lines stood out in the general starkness and there were a few trucks and pieces of mobile equipment in the middle distance and a handful of crew busying about them. A hundred miles of perimeter fence were bound to enclose a whole lot of nothing and that was what I could see. In itself, the size of the area didn't trouble me – tank and artillery ranges take a lot of space – but fencing the desert on this scale in a place that was already remote and inaccessible seemed to me excessive.

'Satisfied?' asked Vipic. 'It's an army base. What are you expecting except crappy buildings and men in uniforms that don't fit?'

I scanned the near slopes for tell-tale signs of landslip and saw nothing.

'The earthquake?' I said.

'What? I'm a seismologist already? The epicenter was maybe fifteen miles further north; I never had cause to go there.'

'How many casualties?'

'Ten or a dozen – not many. It's easy to forget that it isn't the ground that swallows people up but the collapsing buildings that kill them. Here the buildings just aren't that many. The Army has left because the facilities were trashed; no other reason.'

I believed him about the normal effect of earthquakes, but he was lying about the numbers. From the scuttlebutt at Clark County General and what Maria's friends had learned, there had to be a hundred or more dead or seriously injured. This earthquake was different for some reason.

'Where are we going?' asked Charlie Joe.

'Where's the base hospital?'

'Another mile or so,' said Vipic. 'There's nothing there – there's nothing *anywhere*.'

'Down this road?'

Vipic nodded and I told Charlie Joe to drive on.

A half mile on we met a jeep heading the other way. A truck came up behind us and we let it pass. No one paid attention now we were in the magic land. Behind the truck came a bus that also passed. It carried soldiers, who gave us the finger or a dead-eyed stare. They were wearing grey coveralls of a type I didn't recognize, with hoods in the folded-back position and masks and respirators hanging loose, the nearest thing to them being a suit I'd seen on workers in chemical plants. There were persistent rumors that the U.S. Army was using gas and chemicals in its anti-insurgency campaigns. Was that what was going on at Arroyo Seco? Training in chemical warfare?

'Do you have chemical weapons stocked here?' I asked Vipic.

'What makes you think that?'

'The guys on the truck are suited-up.'

'There's a lot of hazardous stuff on site. I'm the wrong person to ask.'

'Were there chemical injuries among the casualties?' I had in mind that the earthquake could have breached tanks and pipelines.

'You're the wiseass – work things out for yourself.'

We reached an intersection where the signs had been taken down though the posts remained. Signage would have said a lot about what was happening at Camp MacArthur, and this had evidently occurred to someone else.

'Which way?' asked Charlie Joe.

'Right,' said Vipic. In that direction, the road was edged with white stones; then borders of raked gravel planted with succulents. A little further on was a military village comprising a handful of streets. I saw a general store, a diner, a place that claimed to sell women's dresses, flowers and stuff for the home; and, at right angles, what for all the world looked like family houses with graveled yards front and back. I remembered the reports of civilians on the base and guessed this was where they lived. Another street was flanked by barrack buildings that had been tricked out with curtained windows and probably housed hospital staff.

At the end of the main street we came to the hospital: a single block with a parking lot in front that was empty if you weren't bothered by the pile of junked cars bulldozed into one corner. To the left of the parking lot was a leisure area laid out for basketball with a few benches, a drinking fountain and more planted beds, except that the place had been dug out, in-filled and graded to create a low mound of sand and desert spoil, and someone had pegged it and spooled out barbed wire. An earth mover was parked up nearby. Despite the earthquake, the hospital, the shops and the other buildings in the village all looked pretty much undamaged except for one feature. Every window was blown in.

We sat for a minute in the car as I tried to figure what was wrong with this scene. Meanwhile an open truck drew up and three soldiers in fatigues sprang out. The corporal came over to the car. I wound down the window and badged him.

He snapped to attention and said, 'I don't like to ask what you're doing here, sir, but me and my men got a small job to do.'

'What's that?'

'We been detailed to clear the remaining stuff out of this place: mostly beds and things ain't worth stealing. Is that gonna be a problem for you, sir?'

'Carry on, corporal.'

I watched his back as he and his men went to the main door, which wasn't locked. They were a work detail and weren't carrying side-arms.

'You heard him,' said Vipic. 'It's sale time for whatever is left in there, and the same is true everywhere. The Army has been stripping the place naked for a month. What in God's name do you expect to find?'

'The thing you don't want me to find,' I said. 'Let's go see.'

As we got out of the car, I felt the cold, something our image of deserts does not prepare us for. Vipic, however, seemed indifferent, most likely because he was calculating the odds as he had at the two checkpoints.

I said, 'If you try to run, I'll shoot. The soldiers don't worry me. They'll report the matter but they won't start a fight with a DSD agent over something they don't understand, and in any case they're unarmed.'

'That so?'

I was tired of his contempt which was hardly justified by our roles and seemed to be just part of the man. I stared him down. I said, 'You don't seem to understand our different situations. If you play this game cautiously, you expect to survive. That's a good positive attitude that I wouldn't want to discourage, but it limits your freedom of action. For Charlie Joe and me on the other hand, it really doesn't matter. You know we're walking dead men who probably won't see out the week even if we get out alive today, which seems hardly likely. Believe me: it's a liberating place to be.'

Vipic didn't answer. When I told him to move, he walked ahead and we followed, buttoning our jackets as we went.

Charlie Joe whispered, 'You really think we're dead men, Harry?' The idea seemed to fascinate rather than frighten him because he could see his martyred corpse but could not imagine his personal extinction. He didn't wait for an answer; instead he asked, 'Where'd you learn all this psychologizing stuff? I seen you using it to read how folks behave. That's how we got through the checkpoints and now you've faked Doc Vipic good.'

I said nothing. The truth is that, back in the day when I was abusing the trust of my wives and other women, I made a lot of money playing poker and lost a lot more on the horses. This tells me that poker teaches psychology but not self-knowledge.

We entered the hospital. There was no sign of the soldiers but we could hear a clatter from the floor above. Here we were alone. A corridor ran off from the reception area with rooms either side. They were empty and the floors strewn with shattered window-glass and drifts of grit; now and then a cigarette butt or broken chair. The plaques on the doors indicated they were offices, stores or treatment rooms, but there was little to show it except some heavy-duty electrical fixtures attached to the walls.

Vipic said, 'How long d'you have? Two or three hours? The security crew are going to count everybody out and they'll come looking if they don't see you leave and unlike those bozos upstairs they will definitely be armed and dangerous. So let's say three hours, and this base is – I don't know, maybe two hundred square miles? You get where I'm coming from? Where do you go next, when you find out I'm telling the truth? How much can you hope to see?'

I ignored him and looked instead at the shards of glass underfoot and at the smooth walls of painted plaster and the anomaly that had nagged at me when we first arrived came back

I said, 'I once reported on an earthquake in Peru. In

185

buildings away from the epicenter, I remember seeing stress cracks from subsidence and ground movement. But shattered windows everywhere without cracks to the walls and floors? That I don't recall.'

'So it makes you an expert?'

'On the other hand, I was in the army during the Russian war. I saw places that had been bombed or shelled, and it can look pretty much like an earthquake if you don't know what you're looking for.'

'And?'

'In the area of the direct blast, you get fire and impact damage. Further out you still see damage caused by the pressure wave moving through the air. It isn't usually strong enough to bring down buildings because it doesn't shake the ground much. But windows? I can tell you that it smashes windows wherever you look.'

Charlie Joe said, 'I seen the same and it was puzzling me.'

I glanced at Vipic, briefly enough so that he wouldn't think I cared about any answer he came up with. I said, 'I don't think there's been an earthquake. I think we're at the outer edge of an explosion, and for some reason that's what you're hiding.'

19

'I wasn't here when it happened,' Vipic said. 'They told me it was an earthquake.'

I don't know he cared if I believed him. Since our little pep talk he'd revised his assessment of his chances and his manner was less cocksure. I thought he would bounce back, but for the moment he was biddable.

Charlie Joe said, 'I'm with you, Harry. I think there's been an explosion. What I don't get is how it has anything at all to do with all the Negros they was supposed to be having around here.'

I didn't know either.

I told Vipic, 'We'll take a look at the second floor. That's where the wards are, isn't it?'

'Uh huh. There's no elevator. The power has been out since the event.'

On the stairs, we bumped into two of the soldiers carrying a metal cot that had been dismantled so it could be moved and stacked on their truck. In the first ward, we found more sections of cot frame scattered on the floor among the glass and the corporal working with a small wrench to take another one apart. There was nothing much else to see. The ward had held about half a dozen patients. I guessed the others would be much the same. This was a small facility and serious cases had probably been flown out.

We tried the wards either side of the central corridor. There were ten in all and nothing much to choose between them. Some held cots; one was empty except for a movable screen that had lost some wheels and was canted against a wall; another had been emptied of electrical equipment and there was a wall-box with armored cable hanging out. At the end of the corridor was a door with a judas hole and a lock controlled by a numbered keypad. The door was of painted metal.

I asked, 'What's behind the door?'

'A secure ward,' said Vipic.

'You need a secure ward?'

'Most of the base garrison are kids and they can get a bit feisty. We get our share of crazies.'

'What's the code to open it?'

Vipic stepped forward and punched in a number, knowing I couldn't tell if it was the correct one. He tried the door but it stayed shut.

'They must have changed it. They do that.'

A glance told me the door wasn't going to be forced without some heavy-duty tools we didn't have to hand.

'Seen all you want to see?' said Vipic.

'What we gonna do?' asked Charlie Joe.

'Cover him,' I said and pushed the doctor aside. I keyed a number, tried the door, and failed. I keyed a second number, tried again and it opened. I glanced at Vipic and the fleeting expression on his face, which should have been surprise, looked instead like fear. It made no particular sense given that, so far, he'd been confident I would be unable to read anything into the rubbish left behind. But there it was. What did he think we might discover?

Behind me Charlie Joe said, 'How'd you do that?' He was grinning.

'This kind of lock usually works on a four-number sequence, which gives ten thousand combinations. More numbers and people forget the code and start to write it down.'

'But you got it in two!'

'Because the place is empty and no one is concerned about security any more. The only people coming here are work crews like the corporal and his men and they need a code they won't forget. Which means all the same number or a straight sequence. I tried four zeros and, when that didn't work, 1-2-3-4.'

'That is just beautiful! You are Brainiac's smarter brother!'

'Maybe. But it doesn't mean we're going to find anything.'

I pushed Vipic ahead of us into whatever lay beyond. I realized then that I hadn't initially taken in the plan of the hospital. It comprised two wings in a T shape and this was the cross piece. Somehow I'd missed it on the ground floor where I must have overlooked an entrance into a similar wing, and now I remembered we'd never seen any service areas, labs or stores.

'What the hell is this place?' whispered Charlie Joe. With the exception of a row of cubicle offices along one end-wall it was a single space. If Vipic had told the truth and this was a ward, it would have held a hundred beds.

That was a lot of crazies.

The corporal and his boys weren't needed here. Someone had done a clean sweep of any equipment and there was no obvious evidence there had ever been patients, only a couple of piles of trash. I scanned the floor for hints it might give, and saw the faint mix of shading that comes from dust, people walking and the bleaching effect of sunlight on floor-covering. There was a central strip, worn from many feet, and, either side, a grid pattern that was consistent with cots having been there. There was also what, at first appearance, looked like sets of studs fixed into the floor, two pairs to each cot space. I'd never seen anything like them and they didn't fit any image of a hospital ward I could conjure from memory. They suggested anchor points, maybe for equipment I couldn't imagine. Restraints? The raving mad are usually held in single cells and straitjackets.

I turned to Vipic. 'Are you going to explain this?'

'What for? You don't believe me.'

'Are you sticking with your story that this was just a secure ward?'

'Go fuck yourself.'

I checked one of the studs. Looked at closely, it was a small metal plate fixing a D-ring. Wear on the D-ring showed that at one time a clip of some kind had been fixed to it in order to anchor... I had no idea what.

'What's that godawful stink?' said Charlie Joe.

I'd been concentrating on interpreting the visuals but he was right: there was a smell. Whatever had caused it had been cleared, except there were stains here and there that might have been part of the explanation. It was too complex to put a single name to: a mix of animal excretions: urine, feces, blood, sweat, rot; enough to make you heave if it were stronger. What was left hung in the air like a rumor of things that cannot be said openly because they are shameful.

There was nothing left to examine except the piles of rubbish swept into the corners. I poked them over and among the broken glass and general detritus saw what looked like pieces of mattress filling. There were also some filthy rags that smelled more strongly of the peculiar stink of this place. None of it spoke to me and I noticed Vipic relaxing. Whatever had been going on in this haunted space was finished and its traces removed except for the eeriness of silence and the bars of sunlight speckled with dust. I felt that I had stumbled on an unspeakable crime, but its nature was beyond me.

'So what next?' said Vipic. Then, 'You mind if I smoke?'

'Be my guest.' I was debating whether to return to the ground floor and search the rooms we'd missed but suspected we'd find nothing.

Vipic lit a cigarette, flicking his lighter on and off like cracking knuckles. He said, 'You feel like giving up yet?'

'I'm thinking we should go closer to the epicenter of this quake you say happened here.'

The flicking stopped.

'I don't recommend that.'

'No?'

'Those buildings that weren't levelled are unsafe. Anything salvageable has been salvaged.' He was thoughtful for a moment. 'Let's say you're right and this base housed more than the Army shelling and bombing the shit out of bare rocks. There's been time to remove or bury the evidence; so what's the point?'

'I hear you. Finish the cigarette. We're going for a drive.'

We left the hospital by the way we came in. The three soldiers had loaded the truck and were locking the tailgate. I collared the corporal.

I asked, 'Did you clear the second floor of the rear wing? – the area behind the metal door?'

'Not today. Coupla weeks ago. Why?'

'What did you move? Cots like these?' – pointing to the back of the truck.

'Naw, there weren't none. Just heaps of mattresses, dirty like pigs been using 'em and no use to anyone. Risk of infection, they said. We covered 'em in gasoline and burned 'em out back.'

'Did another crew move the beds?'

'Could've but I never heard they did. Then, who talks about moving beds? I couldn't tell y'all the stuff we've hauled this last month.'

There was no going behind this answer.

We returned to the car and sat in the same places as before. I told Charlie Joe to take us back to the junction and hang a right. We were held there by a line of three troop carriers coming from the direction of the perimeter checkpoint and heading the way we wanted to go. They were loaded with men wearing the grey coveralls I'd seen earlier. Some of them were trying out masks and respirators. They could have been Martians.

We slipped behind the other vehicles and clipped along at a steady twenty.

'What do you make of the suits?' asked Charlie Joe with a note of awe in his voice. 'They got a spaceship out there?'

That brought to mind the report that the Air Force was trying out rockets in Florida. If I wanted an explanation of Arroyo Seco, it wasn't too farfetched to suspect the Army of running a parallel program out of inter-service rivalry. If one of their missiles had blown up on the starting block, it was almost certain they would hide the fact. It felt like the beginning of a solution to the mystery like my earlier suspicion that they were trialing chemical weapons. The problem was that neither accounted for the apparent scale of the incident. And neither explained the dead and injured blacks.

I scanned the landscape for signs consistent with earthquake or explosion, but to an untrained eye a desert offers few clues and I saw only rocks and mesquite bushes. The road bridged a broad, dry wash whose bed was covered in boulders. I figured it was the *arroyo seco* that gave the place its name.

Vipic grew more restless as we drove. I had him as a physically brave man, but now it seemed as if he was afflicted by a visceral fear: the kind that cannot be expressed because, like children listening to the night-time quarrels of our parents, we do not understand the cause but know only that it presages disaster and that courage will not help us. He said, 'There's another fence line ahead' – and urged: 'You need to turn around because there's no way you're going to get through that checkpoint.'

'Why's that, doc?' said Charlie Joe. 'Old Brainiac here has been doing just fine so far.'

'He means we don't have the suits,' I said.

My companion was puzzled. 'That so? What for are we needing spacesuits?'

'It's enough that you need them,' Vipic snapped. 'They won't let you through without.'

'And if we get through anyway?' I asked.

'Then you'll die.'

Which was a sobering thought. I directed Charlie Joe to pull over to the side of the road and stop.

We sat there a while – in reality probably no more than thirty seconds – watching the troop carriers open up a distance while around us the desert settled into its natural silence.

Charlie Joe spoke first. He said to Vipic, 'Those boys up there must be armed and hunting for bear if you're guaranteeing we're gonna get killed.'

I said, 'That isn't what he means.'

'No?'

'He's already told us why we die. We don't have the suits.'

'What do you mean? We die because we don't wear a spacesuit?'

'So it seems.'

In a tense voice, barely under control, Vipic said, 'We're in danger even here. For God's sake, *no one* knows the safe dosage or effects. That's what I've been trying to study, and it isn't made easier because the boundary moves with the wind. It's only a guess we're OK where we are.'

'What in hell's name is he talking about, Harry?' said Charlie Joe.

'Radiation,' I said.

'What's that?'

'Haven't you read the newspapers? A few days ago, the Japanese exploded a uranium bomb.'

'Yeah, I read that. So?'

'Well, it seems you Americans have done the same.'

'Then good for us! Let's hear it for Uncle Sam.'

I looked at Vipic and said, 'Except I don't think in your case it went according to plan. Probably the test was rushed. I'm guessing Nixon got wind of what the Japanese were up to and decided to try his wonder weapon out first so the Kennedys couldn't accuse him of leaving the country defenseless. The explanation doesn't much matter. What does is that the bomb went off, destroying the facilities here at Camp MacArthur and poisoning the whole area with radiation. Am I right, doc?'

'Well, is he?' said Charlie Joe in the strangled tone that came on when he was excited.

'I don't know. Maybe. All I did was handle the casualties. I told you the truth when I said I wasn't here when it happened.'

At least one of those statements was a lie, but I didn't know which.

'Turn the car round,' I said to Charlie Joe.

We drove back towards the village area. Charlie Joe asked, 'Are we going to die, Harry?'

'What are you worried about? They'll probably shoot us before we fall sick.'

'Is it bad, this getting sick from radiation?'

'Ask the doc.'

'Doc?'

'You won't like it,' Vipic said.

Charlie Joe nodded. After a while he said, 'I think I can face getting shot, but...' The rest was left unspoken. It was difficult for him to imagine radiation-poisoning as the fate of heroes. It sounded like one of those deaths filled with shit and screams that happen to old and sick people and the sad sacks Life abandons to chance and cruelty.

We reached the junction where the side road joined from the left. What next? Drive on towards the perimeter or take a second look at the hospital? What more did I need? I had the story and Vipic had confirmed it.

Except for the blacks.

Except for them. Always it came down to them. Everyone knows there are no blacks... But there are, and some of them had suffered and died.

I checked my watch and the position of the sun. Vipic had tried to fake us with the time; I calculated we could safely allow another couple of hours before base security got antsy and came looking for us. I directed Charlie Joe to turn off for the village and caught the look on the doc's face. He was still concerned that there was something to be found. The question was: where? We couldn't search the stores along what passed for Main Street or the houses standing on their neat little lots, and in any case what cause was there to do so? We'd been over the hospital except for the back areas on the ground, which we'd missed the first time. If we turned over the labs and stores would we find something? Would we even recognize it if we did?

We drove up to the hospital. Nothing was changed except the truck with its clear-up crew had left and the main doors were open, which was as good a sign as any that there was nothing of importance inside. The recreation area was silent, where on ordinary days, kids from the village would play or guys from the hospital would plant a few in the basketball net. Not that they could any longer because the place had been dug over and graded when they emptied the hospital of infected waste and maybe stuff contaminated by radiation.

The mound.

I'd never thought to look it over. I'd blocked it out as part of the landscape, and only now did its strangeness strike me. In hundreds of square miles of desert, why choose a spot so prominent and close to the hospital buildings?

Because it could be found again.

Because it had easy road access.

Because it was temporary and whatever was buried here was going to be moved at some future date.

I asked Charlie Joe, 'Did you notice the earth-mover on the road?'

'Uh huh.'

'Do you think you could operate it?'

'You asking a U.S. Marine? – OK, I ain't never drove one but it can't be too difficult after the other heavy stuff I've handled.'

Vipic asked, 'What are you going to do?'

'I think you know. Are you going to tell me what we'll find?'

He looked angry. 'A hole full of irradiated waste: a mess of stuff that came out of the blast zone when they brought in the casualties. There's at least two trucks they used to ferry them. They're broken up and buried there because they couldn't be used again. The guys who dug and filled it wore the suits – do you follow me? They had to wear the suits!'

'I don't believe you. Any trucks, they'd just drive them to a gully and leave them. Maybe cover them with sand and rock later. I think you're lying.'

'I'm not!'

I didn't waste any more words. We waited on Charlie Joe. I heard the machinery start up and in another minute, he'd drawn alongside.

'Last chance,' I said.

'Go to hell,' said Vipic.

I waved to Charlie Joe and shouted. 'Start trenching in the central section. Stop when you find something.'

'You got it, Harry.' He pulled on the levers and swung the machine towards the mound. It was the kind I'd often seen on road works digging cable trenches, with a simple bucket-shovel at the front end that would easily shift the loosely compacted earth. The barbed wire that had been strung around the site was no hindrance.

I glanced again at Vipic. 'Why won't you tell me what's in there?' He didn't answer. I tried to think of reasons. Not fear. Was it shame? I said, 'This affects you personally, doesn't it? What the hell have you been up to, doc?'

He shook his head. 'Everything I've done has been sanctioned by the Government of the United States.'

'Why doesn't that give me any comfort?'

'The entire program here at Arroyo Seco has been authorized by executive order of the President as well as Secretary of Defense Nixon.'

The words sounded like a mantra: the rhythm even and the tone flat.

A half dozen buckets into the dig and Charlie Joe was shouting, 'Here, Harry. I've found something! I've found …'

He'd got down from the cab and was standing on the mound kicking at something in the ground. Then he stooped and pulled, and with a yank it came free of the soil.

He cried out, 'It's a … oh, Lord Jesus! It's a…'

He didn't need to say more because I could see the object.

It was a roughly severed human arm with a manacle and length of chain at the wrist and a lock at the end of the chain that would nicely fit the D-rings on the floor of the secure ward. The owner of the arm had been black.

20

Escape and illusion work best when accompanied by distraction. Shock is a great distractor.

A corner of my mind was prepared for the sight of the pitiful remains buried at Arroyo Seco. There was a logic to the events of the last ten days or so that an insightful mind could have discerned because it was there from the beginning in the vision that called itself the American Values movement: there and veiled from us only by our hopes, our self-delusion, and by those ideals good people attributed to the American flag waved by Big A and his henchmen in the NSDAP.

Even the location of this hecatomb had a sinister allusive poetry: a basketball court in a nice clean version of small town America straight out of a Norman Rockwell painting where, until just a moment ago, mom, pop and the kids have lived the American life we all aspire to. It was not an accident, as I now realized in a moment of clarity; for it is in the nature of populist tyranny that it plays to those things that are dearest to our heart, only to exploit and desecrate them in the end. The tragedy is that we find ourselves complicit in our own degradation because we cannot escape without denying the values and history that define who we are. Our terror is existential. We become evil not from desire but because the alternative is to be insignificant victims, hardly alive at all.

As I say, a corner of my mind was prepared for what I saw. But reality is not an intellectual understanding: rather a raw confrontation with facts at a time of their choosing. I saw the severed arm in its wreath of chain and, almost in the same moment, the burned face of a black woman staring at me out of the churned earth, and I felt a jolt of horror and incomprehension: the same that had left Charlie

Joe on his knees, frozen, staring at more body parts emerging from the ground or in the loose soil of the bucket-shovel.

The only one of us who was not shocked was Doctor Vipic, who knew exactly what we were going to find. He ran for it.

'Holy shit, Harry, we're losing him!'

Charlie caught the movement from the corner of his eye and was first to react. By the time I grasped what had happened and before I could think to shoot, the doc was already half way to the front yard of the nearest house. I'd covered only a few yards when he dropped from sight.

Charlie Joe passed me, whooping and waving his gun. He reached the corner where Vipic had vanished and stopped. I caught my breath and walked over to him, and we stood a moment looking around us, like two fools who'd lost their dog. Meanwhile the sky was becoming the intense blue that presages evening and a slight breeze was stirring the desert.

'What are we gonna do, Harry?' asked Charlie Joe. He was angry at the loss of control over the situation. He waved a hand loosely at the street. 'How're just the two of us gonna find him with all the places he's got to hide?'

'We have to out-think him.'

'Right! You gonna do that Brainiac thing of yours,' he said scornfully. 'But I mean *really* do it, like you was a genius on a TV quiz show or something. So…?'

'Give me time!'

'Right…. What say we just get in the car and hit the road? Tell 'em at the checkpoint that doc is just doing his doctoring stuff?'

'The moment we leave, he'll head for the main highway. This time of day, traffic will be leaving the contaminated area. Chances are he'll flag someone down before we hit the last checkpoint and radio a warning. If we make it past the checkpoint we still have miles of road with nowhere to go except Vegas, and it's a certainty he'll get a message out before we make it that far.'

'So running ain't an option?'

'I don't think so.'

Running wasn't an option and neither was searching for Vipic. He, on the other hand, had two choices – three if he was lucky. He could try to give us the slip and make his way to the main highway. Or he could stay put and wait us out until base security came looking in a few hours' time. His third option was to find a radio or working phone somewhere in the village and alert the authorities. There was nothing I could do about option three, but I didn't rate it. Moving from building to building to find what he needed would increase Vipic's risk if we were still around. And the probability was that any communications kit had been removed or disconnected during the clearances.

There was also a fourth option but it hadn't crossed my mind.

I told Charlie Joe to get the car. He bridled at what he took to be an order. I explained, 'We've got to put ourselves between Vipic and the junction in case he tries to make a break.' More to the point, I needed to persuade the doc that we'd opted to run. If he hunkered down and sat us out, we were lost. On the other hand, leaving the scene would force him to act unless he was prepared to let us get clean away – in which case good luck with explaining that one to the DSD.

The car was parked in front of the hospital and Charlie Joe was back inside three minutes. I got in, still scanning Main Street and the nearest side street for movement.

'OK, hold it in neutral and give it plenty of gas. I want lots of noise, so the doc knows what we're about.'

Charlie Joe did what I asked, then slipped the car into gear and we cruised at low speed away from the village towards the junction, eyes still skinned for sight of Vipic but seeing nothing.

'Are we running or what?'

'Or what,' I said. 'Slow down here then head for the junction and park up.'

'Here' was a dusty spot on the road less than a mile from the village but further than Vipic could have got in the ten minutes since we lost him if he was as cautious as I hoped. As the car slowed I opened the passenger door and rolled out, hitting the ground harder than I'd have liked but suffering nothing more than scratches. Last I saw of my companion, he'd corrected the swerve when I exited the automobile, and was doing as I asked.

The only risk was he'd keep going.

For a minute, I hugged the rocks. If Vipic had been watching, I wanted him to turn his attention to other things once he was satisfied nothing out there was moving. I'd asked Charlie Joe to drop me here because it gave me clear line of sight. In the village, I would have cover but would be more likely to miss the doc when he made his move. I remained fairly sure he would make one. He was too wound up and arrogant not to, and he'd eaten a lot of humiliation since we'd picked him up. The problem was he was too smart not to have considered the game I was trying to play out.

There's a strategy in chess called *Sitzfleisch* – look it up if you need the translation. The idea is not so much actively to win as to bore the other guy into losing. It's psychologically wearing, but it helps if you know that's what you're doing. I did and Vipic didn't. In fact, he didn't even know I was out there: it was only one possibility and no more likely than the alternative, and the longer he waited the greater the risk his other option would expire. Specifically, if Charlie Joe and I really had run for it, his chances of nailing us this side of Vegas diminished the longer he waited. I thought that had to be eating him up. He needed the sight of our destruction.

And I was right.

He waited a half hour until the light was noticeably fading and the air was filled with the effect like low cloud that dusk can bring. The timing was good because twilight makes objects difficult to see, but, if that was his calculation, he hadn't taken account of the position of the sun and the low horizon, so that I caught his shape silhouetted against the sky. It was a momentary glimpse only, because shortly he dropped below the skyline to be no more than an intermediate form, half man half shadow, moving across the rocky ground and within a minute it was dark. But it was enough to give me a fix and I could hear him, the crunching of his feet, the faint breathing – the sound of a round being chambered.

That was the fourth option I hadn't considered. Somewhere in searching the houses he'd come across a weapon. If I was lucky it was one nobody had thought necessary to carry off or turn in: a cheap lady-gun kept by the bed and good for offing hubby during a night of barbiturate confusion or for junior to pop his sister. A sporting chance that Vipic would miss if he got off the first shot. Which was possible since I could no longer see him.

Maybe he could sense me. Maybe he could hear me. He was moving more slowly, but the desert carries sounds, and his were sharp and close.

Then a voice.

'You there, Harry?'

I picked up a stone and threw it, hoping to draw fire and get a bead. It clattered but nothing more.

'Nice try, Harry, but there's a world of difference between a small rock and a man walking.'

There surely is. And a world of difference between bullshit and terror. The difference being that terror is good if kept under control, but bullshit always clouds judgment. I sat on my fear the way I'd sat on a losing hand during my gambling days in the hope of bluffing my way through.

Maybe not a good example, the way I'd racked up losses, but a reminder to go out coolly if that was what it came to.

And suddenly we were three.

I don't know what it was – a coyote? – except that it made enough noise to spook my opponent. I heard Vipic whip round on his heels and saw a muzzle flash as he discharged a magazine at whatever he thought he saw. I emptied my own gun in his direction, heard a grunt, and loaded my spare ammunition before approaching closer.

I stumbled over him not five yards away. He was spread-eagled on the rocks, only faintly visible by moonlight. I don't know if he was in a state to survive and decided I didn't care.

I walked towards the junction and met Charlie Joe coming the other way. His gun was pointed at me and for a moment I thought he was edgy enough to fire it.

I said, 'You were supposed to stay with the car.'

'I heard shots. I didn't know who'd come out alive. Vipic?'

'Back there.'

'Dead?'

'Does it matter? He isn't going to be raising the alarm.'

'It matters to me,' Charlie Joe said. He brushed past me and disappeared into the shadows. A minute or so later I heard two shots. He came back but said nothing. The only sign he gave was a sly little smile.

I asked, 'Seen anyone? Base security?'

'Not yet. Guys in a jeep stopped maybe twenty minutes ago. Thought I was broken down but happy to learn I wasn't. Still, I think it's time to be heading out of Dodge. They gonna know soon enough the Cisco Kid has been in town.'

We said nothing more about Doctor Vipic but returned to the car.

I got in. Once I was settled into my seat I found I was shaking. For the second time I'd been party to killing a man and for the second time felt no moral qualms, only the physical and emotional tensions releasing themselves. I sensed again that I was becoming a different person as the course of my life turned in a second on unplanned decisions taken in crisis. It wasn't how I had previously understood the world.

We slipped into line behind trucks heading down the main highway. We passed a couple of jeeps filled with Military Police heading in the direction we'd come from. They stopped each vehicle in turn, asking for names but they weren't interested in our papers beyond a cursory glance; only in ticking off a list of those who'd come through earlier. They made no remark about Doctor Vipic's absence. I don't know why except that, if the names weren't listed by vehicle, they didn't know the doc was in our party and expected him to come through later. They checked the trunk of the car, but there was nothing in it except tools. They said zip about the shots which maybe hadn't carried as far as I'd feared. They waved us on.

We drove to Vegas by starlight following the tail of the convoy ahead until it turned onto a side road we hadn't noticed. I figured there must be a cantonment somewhere nearby that the Army had thrown up to house its clearance crews after the disaster at Arroyo Seco had destroyed or contaminated the original camp. I kept the radio on, listening for police or military traffic, but picked up nothing except small town stuff.

For half an hour or so neither of us spoke. It may have been the effect of fear or horror or, as I incline to think, an emptiness of spirit as if whatever it is that makes us human was seeking refuge in some other place and the body was merely going through its automatic responses.

Then Charlie Joe said, 'Some of those black folk was shot.'

'Shot?'

'Here.' He touched his forehead. 'I mean they was burned horrible an' all, but some of them, it wasn't burns that killed them. They was shot like you might shoot a dog that's become old and useless.' He seemed puzzled rather than distressed.

I hadn't seen any gunshot wounds, but I had no reason to disbelieve him. He'd been closer to the bodies than I had.

He said in the same voice, like a child who has seen a fairground sideshow, 'There was kids, too. Burned and shot. Kids nowhere near growed up.' He asked, 'Why did they shoot them?'

'Security,' I said, trying not to think about the children. 'There were too many to hide in the general hospital system. They picked a handful of cases and killed the rest.'

'How many do you think there was, then?'

'The ward we saw had spaces for maybe a hundred. There may have been others held somewhere else on the base.'

'That pit they dug, I reckon it coulda held a coupla hundred.'

I nodded. 'That sounds plausible.'

'And what was they there for?'

'To be experimented on by Vipic and others like him.'

'You mean for, like, diseases?'

'Radiation, I think. They want to know what dosages are fatal, what can be cured, what the long-term effects are. They plan to have a uranium bomb but they don't really know what it does.'

'It blasts the holy shit out of stuff.'

'Apart from that.'

We drove on a while longer in silence. I wondered what my companion would make of this information. At last he said, 'It don't look like there's no Negro army. I need to tell P'tit Antoine Molineaux and get the word to the boys in Oregon and other places that they got it wrong. D'you

206

ever suppose there was one?'

'There are stories that in the early days – I mean when blacks were first cleared off the land and out of the cities – many of them organised and put up a fight but they were wiped out. The government called them communist terrorists. Your friends are probably confusing themselves about ancient history.'

'My ma said there used to be millions of them. Is that right? Millions?'

'Yes.'

'Where d'you hide millions? Not at Arroyo Seco, that's for sure. And not if you had a hundred Arroyo Secos. D'you reckon there's anything to the tale that they're working for the Army, fetching and carrying to help win the war in South America?'

'Some maybe. You were there with the Marines.'

'Sure, and I saw plenty of chain gangs fixing roads and such. But millions? That's a lot of Negros – I mean like they is insects all over everywheres, so as you couldn't miss. And I never saw no women or children. What d'you know of the place I heard of somewheres where they make rubber.'

'Fordlandia – it's in Brazil.'

'Well, it can't be much, 'cause there ain't no rubber to be had except once in a while. Nobody in the country has a decent set of tires to ride on.'

I couldn't answer. Very little news came out of Fordlandia and what there was looked like stock footage of jolly black fellows playing music in front of white-painted huts, and the production figures were a fantasy.

'What do we do next?' asked Charlie Joe. He seemed to have forgotten everything we had seen.

I realized then that there had never been a 'next' in my plan – in fact not much plan at all. I had discovered the fate of the mystery patients and the secret program carried out at Arroyo Seco and I could see that these facts might be used against the Secretary of Defense in the struggle to succeed Big A in 1964 if he retired, as was rumored. Whether anyone would in fact use them I didn't know. The most obvious candidates would be the Kennedys, but if the information was known only to Hoover's GeStaPo, Jeb had suggested that the old man was capable of sitting on it and using it as a threat against a submissive Nixon. I didn't know what I wanted except I suppose I had a high-minded notion of releasing the truth to the world because I'm a newsman.

Mainly I wanted to live. And to see Maria again. And for us both to be happy in a Norman Rockwell painting of America.

These versions of 'next' were not mutually compatible.

I wasn't paying attention because a question from Charlie Joe drew me out of my thoughts.

'P'tit Antoine Molineaux, down New Orleans way, that's where we should be heading, huh?'

'Maybe. Is that where you're going?'

'I don't see there's nowheres else to go. It's only a matter of time before them DSD boys or the GeStaPo is on our tails and I don't think you being Brainiac or his smarter brother or even Aryan Man is gonna save our hides for ever.'

'I have to collect Maria from the motel.'

'No problem. I'll drive you there. We need to get out of town now – I mean now. We can grab some shut-eye on the road.'

In a flicker of moonlight breaking through a gap in the high ground, I saw the expectancy in his face. He was still pumped up with our success and the fact that he was the possessor of a secret. His invitation wasn't just to head for New Orleans. He saw us as blood brothers: Harry and Charlie Joe against the World for ever. If I accepted his invitation I might never be free of him or the obscure resentment that drove him.

I said, 'We need to travel separately.' I glanced at him to see how he took this suggestion. A flash of hurt and anger like a rejected child. I explained, 'The authorities will have us either as two men traveling together or two men and a woman. Our chances of reaching your friend are better if we split.'

He thought about this for a moment and then nodded. 'I guess you're right.' He began to give me directions as to how I would find P'tit Antoine Molineaux holed up in a Louisiana bayou and we would meet there. I repeated them, not caring much, but he kept at it until they were lodged in my memory.

The dim lights of Vegas showed on the horizon, patchy here and there because of power rationing. We found ourselves approaching a crossroads where a brace of cops in a black and white were studying two corpses hanging from a lamp at the intersection and the crew of an ambulance were trying to figure how to get them down. A small crowd had gathered from a nearby tavern and was being held back behind sawhorses by kids from the American Youth.

'Looks like someone's hung themselves a pair of fairies.' said Charlie Joe. 'Sick bastards probably had it coming to them.' He slowed to pass and took directions from one of the kids. I saw cardboard signs strung around the neck of each corpse: slick young men in their twenties; their hideous faces showing off their sharp threads and vividly lit by a spotlight on top of the cop car. I couldn't read the signs but Charlie Joe's guess was probably right. Homosexuality was illegal everywhere and punishable by death in some states. Granted that lynching was a crime, I didn't think anyone would suffer for this one.

We went on at a crawl, leaving the grotesque tableau behind us, passing people on their way to see the show and moralize that what had happened was pretty much what the Bible said should happen to sodomites. Half a mile from the motel, I asked Charlie Joe to let me out. I explained he should pick up his own things and hit the road. We shouldn't both go to my cabin in case someone we wouldn't like was waiting for us.

'Then I guess I'll see you in Louisiana,' he said. He made no mention of Maria, who didn't feature in his view of things. Instead he leaned over and gave me a hug in the stiff manner of someone unused to giving or receiving them. Then, as I got out of the car, he drove off.

I hoped I would never see him again.

I walked over to the motel, passing the office and heading for my cabin. I noticed nothing unusual among the few parked cars; no sign of people. The lights inside the cabin and above the door were both switched on.

I tapped at the door and spoke my name in a low voice. I heard the lock turning, and at the same time a figure I hadn't seen stepped up behind me and stuck a gun in my back. I didn't resist, perhaps because it was pointless; perhaps because I was tired. The door opened and I was bundled inside.

Two G-men in suits, fedoras and polished wing-tips were on their feet, interrupted in a conversation. They glanced at me indifferently. Jeb Lyman was sitting at ease in the only comfortable chair. He smiled at me like my best friend glad to see me, which is what he claimed to be after all.

There was no sign of Maria.

HOOVER PLAZA

21

There is an asymmetry in most friendships: an imbalance in intensity, a difference of interest or view of life. Occasionally I've realized I have friends I no longer even particularly like, but, after that initial moment of surprised discovery, I've carried on because old friends are in some way bound to me: markers on the journey I've taken and no more to be regretted than a myriad of other things I cannot regret without denying who I am.

I have a friend who is a secret policeman and I don't know that I ever liked him, though he could be good company and in many respects I admired him for his strange integrity and, not least, his fidelity in relationships whether towards his wife or others to whom he felt an obligation. He falls into the category of accidental friends, acquired almost in a moment of inattention or against my will, the way some people are adopted by stray cats, without any power of decision. I can say little more because that would be to pretend to an understanding I don't possess.

I asked Jeb, 'Where is Maria?'

He turned to the two agents. He said, 'Check the area, then stand down. I'll see you in the morning.' To me he said amiably, 'You don't seem surprised to see me.'

'You set me a task. I assumed that sooner or later you'd want to know how I got on.'

'How did you get on?'

'Where is Maria?'

'She's fine. My people are taking care of her. I don't know how to say that without its sounding sinister, but truthfully it isn't. She couldn't stay here or take to the road with Nixon's boys on her tail. Believe me: she's comfortable and not being mistreated in any way. I made you a promise that I wouldn't harm her, and I keep my promises.'

I examined his face for the tells poker players look for. He sounded troubled as if he feared I wouldn't believe him and wasn't convinced of his own truthfulness once he had to commit to it. A liar would have sounded sincere.

I didn't ask if I would see her again. I don't think either of us knew the answer and neither wanted to give or receive an untruth.

He poured coffee for me but as usual took only milk for himself. 'What did you discover?'

I told him briefly though I was sure he knew already. He took the news of the nuclear accident with composure. When it came to the dead Negros, his face expressed sorrow. In the face of the horror as I recounted it, neither of us spoke of the larger mystery, knowing that the answer would be still more terrible. Where had all the blacks of America gone? Instead I asked, 'What has this been all about? You must have had other people on the case.'

He nodded and smiled the engaging smile that wowed them when he was a twenty-year-old missionary stopping strangers on the streets of European cities. He said, 'It has everything to do with the source of the story and how it's released. An English reporter for *The Manchester Guardian*? It doesn't come any better.'

'You intend to make a press release?'

'About the failure of the uranium bomb? Not my call.'

'Whose, then? Hoover's? Joe Kennedy's? It has to be someone who hates Nixon enough to think this thing will be laid at his door without damaging the country.'

'Edgar's in the first place but I'm pretty sure the Kennedys know, even if they don't have proof.'

'And the President?'

A hesitation. 'As you probably suspect, Big A is largely out of the picture these days – old – sick – in his prime we wouldn't have been playing these games.'

I didn't ask about the political permutations. The Kennedys – Joe Junior, JFK and Bobby – had the intelligence, the charm and the connections; but Dick Nixon had the brutality and controlled the military through the Defense Department. Would the Army put troops in the streets if needed? Who knew? It had never been done.

And then there was J. Edgar Hoover.

Still I asked myself: what next? What did I have to do to get Maria back, extricate myself from this business and reclaim a life?

Jeb said, 'One reason I came here tonight was because I thought you might head for New Orleans.'

'Why would I do that?'

'To file your story through the British consulate. That way it couldn't be suppressed – leastways not by us. By the British Government maybe. Don't say it didn't occur to you?'

'It crossed my mind.'

'But?'

'I was sure the GeStaPo would pick me up before I got anywhere close.'

'Not the DSD? No, I suppose not: their performance hasn't been impressive so far.'

'No. At times I wondered if I was being helped.'

'Not in the way you think. The truth, if anything, is the other way round. We cover for their deficiencies without knowing it. The DSD is a parasite on the Agency's efforts. We keep society under wraps for them: they just take care of their own affairs – at which, admittedly, they're not very good. That's a point to bear in mind if Nixon ever decides to go head to head with Edgar.'

That made sense of some of my good fortune. But not of everything.

I asked, 'Who is Charlie Joe Svensen?'

'Shouldn't I be asking that question?'

'He was one of the terrorists at the Arc of Hope.'

'I don't think so. They were all killed. We have their names.'

'I found his ID – Charlie Joe Svensen's – lying on the ground with all the other stuff after they came off the bridge.' The image of that night came to mind: the great sweep of the arch under the night sky; the blazing wreckage of the car. 'I showed it to you. You recognized the name. You said it was used on dime-a-dozen fake papers.'

'I don't remember. I do recall the papers: a cheap forgery picked up in the street. We sell them ourselves if we want to keep tabs on people without their knowing.'

'You're saying there's no connection?'

'Between your guy and the incident at the Arc? No. One of the dead men may have been using the Svensen identity, but he wasn't your friend.'

'Charlie Joe isn't my friend.'

'If you say so. Either way, whoever he is, his name isn't Charlie Joe Svensen but some other John Doe. Which raises the interesting question: why did he fix on you? What was his story?'

I told Jeb what I knew: that Charlie Joe had presented himself as a former Marine and a disaffected radical hanging around with right wing conspiracy theorists and militias fighting the government in the mountain states. I recalled now that he'd said little of his early history, but silence might mean an unhappy childhood which would fit with his general alienation.

I didn't mention my opinion that Charlie Joe was someone who couldn't be controlled.

'Did you believe him?'

'I thought it was convenient, the way he turned up. But, if it was an act, it was a good one. Whoever he was working for, it wasn't the DSD.'

I explained the help Charlie Joe had given.

'So you thought he was GeStaPo?'

'Could be.'

Jeb chuckled. 'Sometimes a reputation for omnipotence doesn't do us any favors.'

'He wasn't one of yours?'

The chuckle stopped. 'Who knows? Edgar isn't above running two operations in parallel. Did your boy ever explain where the Chevy Styleline came from? Or his gun? Or the wallet full of money you say he came by in a card game?'

I'd never pressed him on any point, though we'd clocked a lot of miles in the car without being stopped by the highway patrol on the lookout for a stolen vehicle. Maybe it meant something or maybe not. That's how paranoia takes you: seeing the sinister patterns within the normal flow of chance events.

And still the unanswered question. What next?

Jeb said I must be hungry and proposed we grab a late meal at a decent restaurant in the city. He switched his conversation to easy stuff about Laura Beth and the kids. He wasn't a boastful man or a high-liver. His small talk was of the social life of his church and the unpretentious work he did with kids in the American Youth and at a homeless shelter as part of Winter Relief. I liked him for this: the innocence. I had too many issues with my past to want to talk about it and there was a balm in listening to Jeb chat unselfconsciously about the good deeds he and the other regular types in the GeStaPo did in the community, though finding the time to take part – well, you know what it's like. If he had any demons from his professional life, it seemed that he and God were square on that account.

The restaurant was mom and pop Italian with checkered tablecloths, candles in chianti bottles and pictures of the Pope on the walls. We ate spaghetti con vongole and bronzino. I drank wine and Jeb didn't. We talked a little about plans for Thanksgiving. Having no family, Maria and I intended to take a short vacation at Lake Tahoe, if circumstances allowed, such as my finding her and neither of us being dead. Jeb and Laura Beth were set to visit the folks back home in Provo, assuming he wasn't delayed by duty: a presidential visit to Texas was scheduled a week or so before because of American Patriots Day and to quieten rumors about his health; and this time of year there were always issues about weather and flights.

'A security nightmare,' Jeb said about the Texas trip. 'Nixon and the Kennedys want to show everyone that the magic dust has rubbed off on them, so they're tagging along and, since none of them trusts the others, they're bringing their own muscle. The Agency's job is to hold the ring and stop them killing each other.'

'Any chance?'

'Edgar may have hopes – I'm joking.'

God help me but the wine and the conversation relaxed me and made me think that all could end well.

'So how do things stand with me?' I asked over coffee. I couldn't bring myself to refer to the killing of the DSD agent or Vipic, which were enough to send me to the chair if anyone was so minded. 'I get to go back to my apartment?'

'Some day? Sure, why not?'

'But not now.'

'You want a medal for doing the Agency a favor? Well, maybe that too, all in good time. But we're living through a period of flux. There are forces in play and we just have to let them run.'

'And if Nixon takes over in sixty-four?'

'You'll probably need a change of address. But why look on the dark side? Until then we can provide you with cover.'

'You could get me and Maria out of the country.'

'And then?'

He meant that if I were once out of the country, the Agency would lose control of the Arroyo Seco story. There would be nothing to stop me publishing and drawing attention to the fate of the missing blacks. No assurances to the contrary were worth anything. Already I was lucky that Hoover wasn't having me killed.

Jeb leaned across the table, 'Seriously, you have a stock of goodwill in the Agency – I mean among the few of us in the know.'

'You mean...?'

He shook his head. 'For the moment, the Director doesn't need to know – can't *afford* to know.'

'Does this lead somewhere?'

'Only that you should build on your position.'

'In what way?'

'By doing what you promised Charlie Joe Svensen. Meet up with him in Louisiana like he asked. You could hardly be safer, because for sure the bozos in the DSD aren't going to chase you through the bayous.'

'And what does that do for you?'

'Let's say we have an interest in him. We'd like to know who he really is and what his intentions are.'

'You mean you want to discover if there's another faction in the Agency with its own agenda and Charlie Joe is working for them.'

'It isn't likely, but yes, we'd like an answer.'

'And which of you is working for Hoover?'

'That's a very good question,' said Jeb. 'Let me know if you find out.'

When we listen to any narrative there is a temptation to suppose the narrator knows all he claims to know, but this is just a convention. The truth is that he is as ignorant as all of us and struggles to form a view of the truthfulness of witnesses and construct a coherent story from the partial facts available to him.

Were there two factions within the GeStaPo? Jeb Lyman was careful not to say they existed, only that they were possible. Nor did he ever indicate what their separate agendas might be: whether over some point of policy or just part of a shabby power struggle. The answers to these questions are crucial to understanding what followed and yet I can only hazard a guess which may or may not be true. Or maybe there is another explanation outside the machinations of the Agency? Post the event, various conspiracy theorists have thought so, though some of them are clearly deranged.

After our meal, Jeb drove me back to the motel. He told me he'd placed a guard on the place, though I saw no one. It was a precaution but he didn't expect Nixon's boys to try anything even if they knew where I was, which wasn't certain. In the morning, he would provide me with a vehicle, new papers and money on the understanding I would take myself to the lair of P'tit Antoine Molineaux in Bayou Chaud, Louisiana, to find out whatever there was to find out.

In the end my path would take me to Hoover Plaza, a name that at that date meant nothing to me. Today it no longer stands for a place but for an encounter with the limits of my own knowledge and my capacity to understand the world. There I would discover that the truth does not always announce itself. Often it speaks in murmurs and we catch them or not. Sometimes what we hear is no more than our own fears and prejudices. Yet we turn these illusions into unquestionable certainties and surrender our reason to the men who give them voice.

22

Jeb supplied me with an Apache pick-up, a five-year-old model with rust and dings on the bodywork and dirt all over, but the engine and suspension did the business and that was enough.

'It should pass better than a sedan in the Louisiana sticks,' he said. In the cab was a cheap pasteboard valise containing cash and two changes of clothes: check shirts, jeans and workboots. My new papers said I was Harrison Stolpert from Milwaukee. My All-American Labor Union work card made me a welder last employed in Detroit. 'You get to keep the name Harry, which is safer. If anyone asks about Milwaukee say you've been there only a month and fall back on some other place you can talk about. We didn't know what job to give you that wouldn't be blown, but it's a guess there's no demand for automobile welders in the bayous, so no one likely to ask questions. OK?'

It seemed as good a cover as I was likely to get. Presumably it wouldn't be too strongly tested if Charlie Joe spoke for me.

'One last thing,' Jeb said. 'Don't count on the Agency to cover your back once you're inside. The Cajuns cause us no trouble but they're clannish and hard to penetrate.' He wrote down a number for me to memorize. 'If you get to a phone, you can report or ask for help on this number. The Louisiana field offices have an alert out for Stolpert and will pass you up the line if you fall into their hands.' He stood back to look at me as if seeing something new, then gave me a buddy hug, warmer than his usual well-mannered friendliness. Charlie Joe had done something similar and on neither occasion was I sure what it meant. He said, 'What you're doing could help this country in ways you can't imagine. And look on the bright side. Your biggest risks are probably insect bites and gumbo.'

Bayou Chaud was a backwater connected to Bayou Teche somewhere at its northern end in St. Landry parish. Or possibly not connected; it was difficult to tell from the maps of the Louisiana waterways which shifted according to the age of the map and the various public works to pump water in or out of the bayous and dredge or widen the channels or in some cases dam them. The nearest town was Port Barre, which was nowhere much and 'near' only by courtesy. There was no state highway within miles. Jeb's people had struggled to find a topographical map and the one they found made no distinction between tracks and country roads and showed nothing in the way of settlements except a scattering of French names that may have been plantations at one time or another. Charlie Joe's instructions didn't square with much I could see from the maps, but they told me that P'tit Antoine Molineaux was unlikely to be found unless he had a mind to be.

This was five days in the future when I left Vegas. I had more than sixteen hundred miles to cover, mostly across Arizona and Texas, and three hundred or so miles a day seemed a respectable score with no one to spell me at the wheel. I stayed in motor courts or fleabag hotels and ate at roadside diners or Main Street lunch counters if I happened to hit a town, and none of it was memorable. Mainly I had in mind to keep Charlie Joe ahead of me. Knowing next to nothing of him except his capacity to antagonize people, I had no idea how to approach anyone who was acquainted with him. When it came down to it, I didn't even know his real name.

I'd never had reason to visit Louisiana because they told me it was unimportant and folks did things differently there. When 'American Values' were mentioned people only pretended to go along with the idea while inwardly they were laughing. They talked strange, had sex with blacks who were probably their half-sisters, and a man who didn't take a bribe was a man you couldn't trust. But I knew these were no more than the prejudices that passed for truths in the time we were living through.

I hit Port Barre towards evening on the fifth day and found a rooming house close by Bayou Courtbleau with a spare bed, 'business being so poor with the War and all'. The owner was an elderly widow with hair in tight grey pin-curls and a printed cotton dress that had been washed and ironed too often and spoke of poverty struggling with respectability. She smiled and spoke politely, but there was bitterness behind the cheerful manner and she let slip her husband had died in an accident felling timber and her only son was killed in Nicaragua so that I felt the uncomfortable compassion one feels for people whom one does not like. She admitted that other folk were doing well enough and it was clear that behind her smiles she hated them for it with a cordial Christian hatred.

I was too tired to hunt down a restaurant and didn't want to be seen around too much. My hostess fixed me a shrimp po'boy sandwich to eat at her kitchen table, glad of company to listen to her woes. Afterwards, I went out into a mild, cloudy night and walked the streets in the hope of seeing Charlie Joe's Chevy. Half an hour exhausted what there was on offer; I caught no sign of the car and returned to the rooming house. The Widow Boudreau was glad to take coffee with me and answer any questions.

I asked about Bayou Chaud.

'Bayou Chaud?' she said with an air of distant surprise. 'Why, don't nobody talk about that place from one year to the next. There ain't nothing there. There ain't *no one* there excepting some trashy folk who don't want to work or fight. Why are you interested?'

I tapped my nose and quietly said, 'Land.'

The suggestion of a secret warmed her and she beamed. 'You're talking about timber, oil and such? I ain't never heard of none but it don't mean there's none worth having.'

I pressed her about directions, using what I'd gleaned from Charlie Joe and the topographical map. She wanted to help but had only scraps of information, most of it off the point. She told me about children murdered and women raped because they went to places they shouldn't: the stuff that scares old ladies and they relish talking about. 'I don't know what to tell,' she said to my specific question. 'I never had cause to go there and no one else I heard of except some fishermen looking to catch wide-mouth bass or some such. You're talking about driving east along Route 7 a ways and then taking a dirt road where there's an old sawmill all falling down. Further than that I can't say. Don't expect no signs.'

I got a distance for the old sawmill and it fitted more or less what Charlie Joe had told me, though he hadn't known what the ruined building was for. I tried a few more questions but got nothing useful.

I bade goodnight to the Widow Boudreau and went to my room. Outside the window a night bird was calling, but I had no name for it.

The next day was warm for the season, so the Widow told me over breakfast. The sky was a heavy mix of purples and greys splashed yellow here and there with clouds boiling on the horizon and a distant rumble of thunder. The prospect of rain troubled me when I thought of trying to navigate my way by unsurfaced roads through low-lying wetlands, but I reasoned it had to be possible if indeed there were people living along Bayou Chaud.

I quit the rooming house at nine with directions from my hostess to find the way to Route 7. A thin stream of lumber trucks and military traffic led to a two-lane concrete highway that hadn't received much in the way of upgrade since it was laid down in the twenties. I drove eastward past the last houses of respectable folks and the shotgun shacks of the rural poor with their plots of beans and squash, my eyes skinned for the abandoned sawmill; but for miles the only side roads were tracks leading to isolated oil wells and former slave cabins standing amid fields of sugar and cotton.

The flat landscape depressed me with a dreariness broken only by occasional plantations where overseers, rifles at the ready, rode their horses up and down lines of Mexican field hands stooped over the crop. Between them were long stretches of lush barrenness, a scrub of live oak and cypress saplings that had begun to cover abandoned farmland. Louisiana, like a lot of the states of the South, suffered from the contradiction at the heart of Big A's vision of a racially pure America. The labor once provided by former African slaves had to be replaced after the clearances and the only source was Hispanics, mainly Mexicans. But these could not be imported in numbers equal to the millions who had gone. Where it was tried, people asked what it had all been for: the expulsion of blacks only to replace them with strangers who were equally alien to the fears and hopes of white America. To make matters worse, the Mexicans were less productive. The Negros had known the United States to be their homeland where their ancient cultures had been smashed only to be made vibrant and new out of suffering, and they clung to their country and worked for it with a passion it did not deserve. The Mexicans were mostly prisoners of war or indentured labor. The result of the American Values movement had been a collapse of agriculture in a swathe of the South. But white people explained it otherwise and blamed the Mexicans for their inferiority and laziness, and out of perversity clung to Big A because he seemed to describe what they saw.

The sawmill was easy to miss. It stood back from the highway with a yard in front where trucks had once parked to load timber. The hardstand was broken by undergrowth and saplings masking a collection of wooden buildings overgrown by kudzu that would have been anonymous but for a board with faded lettering graced by the elaborate curlicues that marked the early years of the century as if the place had been a classy saloon or whorehouse except the words said 'Gaudet et Fils – Scierie'. To the side a dirt road ran at right angles to the main route across a coulee, then turned and was lost among the live oaks. I might have ignored it but sometime not so long ago it had been re-surfaced with crushed shells, and this told me it was still in use.

The road wound on a slight elevation between soft ground either side. The resurfacing grew patchier, sometimes crushed shells, sometimes cordwood, but care had been taken to keep it open. Side branches I could not identify from my maps or Charlie Joe's instructions forked off every mile or so, but I figured that by sticking to the main track I would find any settlement that might exist and get such news as there was of Charlie Joe or the man I took to be his mentor, P'tit Antoine Molineaux.

I had no concept of the bayous except a general one of water bordered by fetid greenness and burdened by oppressive heat. As an image it had intensity without detail because I lacked the knowledge and the language to express that detail and I assumed a uniformity that did not exist. Now, in the actual moment, I could not be sure where land ended and the bayou began among the slash pines and water oaks.

The Widow Boudreau had unintentionally led me into thinking this was an empty countryside and always had been, but it wasn't so. Either side of the dirt road I glimpsed the remains of the abandoned plantations hinted at in the maps, often no more than a thinning in the tree cover and a glimpse of a vine-covered chimney with no other sign that this was once a fine mansion. The ruins of a sugar mill were marked by rotten timbers and skeletal machinery scattered on the ground, and the site of a cotton gin was now a stand of live oaks whose branches supported the wreck of an old frame building. Though there was no sign of commercial crops, some of the land had been cleared and was being worked in small patches, but nowhere did I see any people.

I found my way through a maze of coulees and flooded pasture that at times fooled me into thinking I'd reached Bayou Chaud. The driving was slow and I had no idea how far I'd traveled when the rain came on with an intensity I wasn't used to. It overwhelmed the capacity of the Apache's wipers to clear the screen and I was frightened of losing the road which seemed to bleed into the water and vegetation at its margins.

And then I came across a tavern.

It didn't advertise itself, and might have passed for a tin-roofed shack but for the Jax sign nailed to the door next to a piece of card offering bait for sale. In front was a space for five or six cars, some benches and a barbecue pit made from the hollowed-out shell of an old refrigerator. To the side a coulee was flanked by a landing stage, and a flat-bottomed pirogue loaded with fishing gear was moored against it, though the water had the sheen of old oil spills and its share of garbage. I didn't like the spot but I pulled onto the parking lot, thinking it was a place to sit out the rain and maybe get a bite to eat and directions.

I got out of the car and was hit by the stink from the coulee and heard the chug of a motor that I guessed provided power. The rain was coming down solidly and I ran to the door. It was closed, though I could hear voices inside and a Bessie Smith number played with the tinny resonance of an original twenties recording. Except for a few underground clubs, it was the first jazz I'd heard since coming to this country and it brought back some memories

I hadn't time to reflect on.

I banged on the door. It caused the conversation to stop the way that conversations in bars don't normally stop, and that might have been a sign if I hadn't been tired and standing in the rain, spitting out mosquitoes. I called out that I was a customer wanting a drink and some food and someone came to open.

He was a giant.

'We don't normally get strangers coming t'rough here,' he said. He spoke through a fly screen, quietly, more puzzled than hostile. I'm not a short man but he could give me eight inches and he was muscled in the way of those whose bodies are shaped by hard physical labor and he dressed as men on poverty wages dress in a bib overall and collarless chambray shirt, patched from use.

A voice from the back of the room called cheerfully, 'Let the man in!'

The giant opened the fly screen. He stepped back and gave me a smile that was missing its incisors like a huge version of the goofy kid at school. At the first shock of his size, I hadn't taken in his features. He was brown-skinned, high cheek-boned, broad nosed. I put him down as Hispanic or American Indian, and the same seemed to go for the other four customers. The bartender was a stocky, barrel-chested type; otherwise like his clients except he wore a felt hat, sported a raffish moustache and smoked a cigar in a genial way. In my time, I've known a lot of bartenders and they are of a piece with their bar, giving it their own character or assuming the one that is there already; but I had no standards by which to judge a beer shack met on a dirt road in the bayous.

The bartender kept up the smile. He asked, 'Jax or bourbon? We don't run to nothing more, no.'

'Jax,' I said

I looked around the room. Bare wooden walls. Three scrubbed tables set with stools. A ceiling fan that was doing nothing to stir the smoke. An up-ended crate supporting a hand-cranked gramophone player with a small horn; the kind people took on picnics thirty years before. The Bessie Smith record was winding to its close. I could smell food.

'What do you have to eat?'

The bartender laughed with his friends, then fixed his smile on me again. 'Boudin – dirty rice. You want?' He passed me a long-necked beer.

'That sounds fine,' I said. I took the beer to one of the tables.

'You get taken bad, you go outside, yes?'

'House rules. I get it.'

My new friend liked the response. 'All right, suh! Dirty rice it is – wit' boudin.' He called the order out to someone in a room behind the bar.

A stranger who asks questions intrudes and arouses suspicion. I thought it safer to wait until unsatisfied curiosity played things my way. In five minutes the food was passed through a hatch and the bartender brought the plate to me with a shot glass of bourbon for himself. He sat across the table, lounging comfortably and watching with the amused but searching eye of a sporting man buying a fighting dog, who thinks he can master the beast however cunning it may be. And maybe he was right.

'You comfortable I sit here, suh?' he asked.

'I'm always glad to see a new face.'

'That's kind of you. They ain't something we see much of around here – new faces. Might I ax your bidness?'

'I was on my way to Bayou Chaud until the rain stopped me.'

'Uh huh? Well, you on the right road and you done right to stop, 'cause it ain't safe 'til the rain's over a coupla hours. This weather there's water on the road and the alligators get frisky.'

'I appreciate the advice.'

'Don't mention. What I don't understand is what takes you to Bayou Chaud. Ain't nothing there except a few poor folk like us, growing rice and fishing for crappie. They looked for oil but didn't discover none. The timber you can find other places where it ain't so hard to get, no.'

'I came looking for someone I know.'

'Another stranger. Hear this!' he shouted to his friends. 'We getting more visitors than New Orleans. I see I'm gonna have to tidy this place up and make it nice. Maybe t'row out some of the low-life types hanging round here, yes.'

'He isn't a stranger – the guy I'm looking for.'

That got attention. The barman looked at me acutely. 'He have a name?'

Sooner or later I'd known I would have to offer up Charlie Joe Svensen and see what reaction I got. So I spoke the words now and the bartender repeated them slowly as if disappointed.

'Don't mean not'ing.' He looked at the others. 'Charlie Joe Svensen? Mean anyt'ing to anybody?' He looked at me again. 'Don't seem like it, and I'm sure anyone hearing would've 'membered 'cause it ain't exactly a local handle.'

'Then I guess I've made a mistake, but I'll see. When the rain clears and the alligators have settled their nerves I'll carry on to Bayou Chaud and find out if anyone there can help.'

I looked at my food and pushed my fork around the plate, wondering what it was that was troubling me. I took a mouthful. 'This is tasty,' I said. And it was. But there was something wrong about it and about the other elements of the situation and I was stupid for not seeing it immediately, except that our expectations color how we interpret what we see.

Mexicans don't eat dirty rice when they cook for themselves. They don't speak in the idiom of rural

Louisiana. They don't listen to forty-year-old songs by Bessie Smith and treasure the fragile recordings so they don't break; because the words and the songs, in their joy and their sadness, are a connection to what an oppressed people has felt and achieved in a world where even the little that they have has been destroyed.

These men might pass as Hispanics and probably did when necessary in order to have survived so long. But I was as certain of one fact as I was of anything. They were Negros and determined to remain so.

23

I looked at the barman and he saw that I knew because the smile was gone. He said, 'You a bit slow today.' He slipped a .38 from his belt and pointed it at me, at the same time pushing his chair out of grab distance.

The three men at the next table broke off the game of bourée they'd been playing when I came in. They looked at me with curiosity rather than hostility. One of them took out a knife and placed it next to the cards but he didn't look as though he expected to use it.

'You may be right,' I said. 'Why did you let me in?'

'That was Armand.' The barman nodded in the direction of the giant, who didn't have a gun or a knife and wasn't playing cards but only sitting on a stool, watching as a child might watch a scene act out on television, with curiosity but without involvement. 'He also a bit slow like you.'

I said, 'My weapon is in the pickup.' An oversight on my part but carrying wasn't easy when I wasn't wearing a jacket or holster. I waited for a reaction, counted to ten and was still alive. I said, 'Can I eat my food while you figure what to do?'

'Seems I got me a cool customer,' he said.

'I don't get the impression you and your friends are hitmen for the Mob. This is probably as strange for you as it is for me.'

In the news business I'd met mass murderers, war criminals and others who were killers by choice, and they all had an inner anger and indifference to their victims these men lacked. I didn't doubt they might kill me but it would be from the necessity of desperate men under desperate circumstances, not moral emptiness or an inner compulsion. I told myself this encounter was survivable but suspected that many people had died in a similar state of optimism about the outcome of their situation.

The barman relaxed a little but kept his distance. He displayed the justified wariness his people might have when faced with any white man. He asked, 'What you really here for?'

'I told you the truth. I'm looking for Charlie Joe Svensen – except that isn't his real name, just one he goes by. I don't know what he was calling himself when he was here. We were traveling separately and he was ahead of me. I expected him to arrive first.'

'He white, too? Gotta be wit' that name. We don't get many white people in Bayou Chaud, no. How he come to be here?'

'He never explained.'

'But you sure?'

I thought over the directions Charlie Joe had given me. They may have been impossible to follow but they'd been detailed and he spoke like someone who knew what he was talking about.

'I'm sure,' I said

He'd been here and must have known Bayou Chaud was sheltering blacks who'd escaped the clearances. Why hadn't he told me? Because he was the kind who guarded information in order to exercise control and flatter his self-importance. It was the mark of men everywhere who think the exercise of power can mask their inner weakness.

I said, 'He gave me a name: P'tit Antoine Molineaux'

'Antoine!' This from the big man they called Armand. A cry of joy, the kind infants reserve for their parents, though why it should be so escaped me.

'Hush you!' snapped the barman, and to me. 'What did he tell you about Tee Antoine?'

'He seemed to regard him as a teacher – a wise man.'

'Antoine,' repeated Armand more softly but with the same ardor in his eyes. This time there was no rebuke.

'Well, y'all not so wrong,' said the barman after a moment in which he studied my words as if I'd used an expression that had never occurred to him but he found to be true. In my time, I have received such accidental insights gifted by strangers not because they understand more about the human condition but simply because they are not me. 'No, not so wrong,' he repeated. 'So tell me, what he like, your friend?'

I gave a physical description but no matter how I tried, Charlie Joe came over as nobody in a crowd of nobodies. Even as I was speaking I could tell my words were failing to register. I might have said something about his character but we don't read character the same way or politicians would never get elected, and our attempts as often as not say more about ourselves than the person we are trying to explain. Then it came to me that there was a key. Whatever name or history Charlie Joe might invent for himself there was one element his vanity would force him to include whether it was true or not.

I said, 'He told me he was in the Marine Corps. It was a big thing with him.'

The barman looked surprised for a moment and then nodded. 'It sure was,' he said, and added, 'I t'ink Tee Antoine gonna want to talk wit' you.'

An outsider coming from a liberal country and working for a liberal newspaper could easily forget that the American Values movement succeeded, despite the hatred proclaimed in its rhetoric, because millions of ordinary people listened but heard something different, believed what they wanted to believe, and so found it possible to be supporters while living a middle-class life and being good, decent human beings who practiced all the common virtues. However, for each of the President's policies and principles there a version still darker and more deluded and there were angry men who believed that Big

A and his followers had compromised a truer, more splendid vision of America's God-given mission to save mankind. They confused anarchy and a taste for violence with freedom and saw themselves as fighters for the latter; and, when the NSDAP and the GeStaPo fastened their tyranny on the country, they retreated to the mountains and formed militias to preserve the faith and train in preparation for the return of the Lord Jesus, the overthrow of the Antichrist, and the final purification of humanity through a sinless white race.

It was a fantasy of these people that Big A was a shill, fronting for the New World Order, a conspiracy of Jews, atheists and Freemasons against America, and that quite contrary to the regime's outward hostility to Negros it had spirited them away to be formed into an army that at the right moment would emerge to conquer a degenerate and effeminate country. That there was not the slightest evidence of this conspiracy was immaterial: the failure of the Administration to produce the Negros or give an adequate account of their whereabouts and condition was all the proof needed.

When I first came across Charlie Joe Svensen he recounted this story and it persuaded me that his tale of having recently spent time with the militias in the Northwest was true. On the other hand, he had conceded his mistake when confronted with evidence of the atrocity at Arroyo Seco. That was something a true believer would not have done, because it is in their nature to see facts as mere matters of opinion and contradictory arguments and compelling evidence as snares and lies propagated by malign forces to test them, so that the strength of their convictions and the intensity of their fury only increase to the extent that reality threatens to shake their faith. This irrational folly is a characteristic of human beings that fills me at times with despair because I am aware of the heroic efforts required to discover true facts that are validly grounded on evidence and logic, and that for millennia the greatest minds have worked at developing the techniques that make this possible. To throw away the fruit of this achievement out of ignorance or for the sake of cynical self-interest or to avoid confronting our neediness is to me a crime. But others might say I am merely a true believer of a different kind, though that is to misunderstand the meaning of belief.

Whatever the case, Charlie Joe had spent time with P'tit Antoine Molineaux's group of free blacks, only to leave them for the camp of their enemies and then wish to return. And in the meantime, by apparent chance, he had attached himself to my investigation into the origin of the mystery patients.

I could make no sense of this and wondered if Jeb Lyman's speculation wasn't well-founded, and Charlie Joe was a stalking horse for another faction within the GeStaPo that was in some way involved in the power struggle to succeed to the Presidency when Big A was gone. And I wondered, too, whose agenda I was helping to advance.

The barman was called Jules César Forgeron but the others called him Julie. He told me this as token of a truce between us, and I told him my name was Harry Bennet and that I was an English journalist. I had my false ID but decided that lying would not help my case. He looked over my papers and so knew of the Harrison Stolpert identity but it didn't even merit a question. Instead, to while away the time until the rain stopped, he asked about the work of a foreign correspondent and about Manchester and whether any black people lived there, and I said yes there were some but couldn't tell him how many or how things were for them.

'It the same here,' he said. 'Even before Satan and Big A got their hands on 'em, white folk knowed we was around but not'ing about us except the ideas in their own heads. It puzzles me that such a t'ing is possible but it is.'

In time the rain ceased drumming on the tin roof. Julie sent Armand to bail out the pirogue and report on the state of water in the coulee. When the big man came back he said we should go visit Tee Antoine.

We got into the boat. Armand provided the muscle power and we cast off from the landing with its smell of fish guts and sump oil, leaving the beer shack behind us. When I trailed my hand in the water, Julie snatched it out.

'What the hell you doing? You gotta be careful of cottonmouths,' he said, 'and some of them logs ain't logs. Don't they teach you that in Manchester?'

We followed a channel through cane brakes and stands of sawgrass with mosquitoes clouding above them and shallows where hyacinths and lilies grew until finally we reached the bayou. Though the rain had stopped, the live oaks and slash pines were shedding water so the surface glittered as if with a scattering of coins. The further shore was a splash of misty greens behind more sawgrass. A flock of egrets had settled on a swamp maple to wait out the rain, and in ones and twos they were returning to the water.

A few minutes of this and the sky brightened. The bayou smoothed out and shone in the way we imagine the tropics in our dreams. I was tired from the strain of travel and the fear of death, and stillness induced a torpor so that in the midst of everything I dozed and, when I woke, Julie was smiling at me with the condescension reserved for idiots.

'I guess you is easy in your conscience,' he said.

I didn't try to explain. Then it occurred to me that through everything that had happened since I arrived in Louisiana, I'd given scarcely a thought to Maria after receiving Jeb's assurance as to her safety. I tried to understand what that might mean in ways that were not too damaging to my self-esteem, but it was difficult to do. Was it the fading of love or just the mind defending itself so that the ability to act in the here and now was not burdened by problems that could not be immediately addressed? Was I a coldly indifferent person or someone experiencing a common reaction but one I had not suspected: an unadmitted callousness demanded by self-preservation, which is disguised from us by the romantic fictions that depict love as a spiritual instead of a material transaction between lonely people to save themselves from despair? I was frightened not only of losing Maria, but of being a man who could bear that loss and go on.

'We here,' announced Julie at last. He said something to Armand who began poling the pirogue towards a landing stage where a small boat with an outboard motor was moored. Behind was a break in the trees and an expanse of uncut meadow covered in St. Augustine grass dotted with pecans and persimmons and at the furthest edge an ante-bellum house that had belonged to a plantation owner in a bygone age we still idealize despite our knowledge of its cruelty. The sun had shot a bar of light through the cloud cover and in that instant the house looked white and elegant and perfect. But the moment passed and, as we approached, the light dimmed and I saw the reality of weathered cypress boards, a roof half-stripped of its covering, and a structure subsiding from the action of termites, though someone evidently cared about the place because the space in front was planted with camellias, cassias and Bourbon roses in flower.

As we moored, people appeared from the house and nearby cabins: women and children among them, many of them of mixed race, which figured if they were passing as Hispanics in the wider world. They gathered around Julie and stared at me uncertainly.

'He all right,' Julie reassured them. While Armand tied up the pirogue, he bent down to pick up any small child that approached and play the part of favorite uncle. He asked, 'Tee Antoine around? Someone tell him we got a visitor he need to see.'

They told us Tee Antoine had been sleeping, as he always did for an hour or so in the late afternoon. There was a note of affection in this explanation: the way one talks about a small indulgence granted to someone one loves. We were taken up to the house and through the porch into a grand reception room where balls might have been held in the plantation's great days before the War of Northern Aggression as some in the South still called it. The room had been cleared when the house was abandoned, but its ghosts remained: pale shapes on the walls where paintings had once hung; gilded sconces that held the stubs of candles; a lighter section of floor where an Aubusson carpet had lain. The room had been swept clean and filled with wooden cots and furniture knocked together from scraps of whatever lay to hand. It served now as a dormitory for people whose ancestors had at one time been slaves, perhaps on this very plantation. But their possession of this place was not a manifestation of justice: only of injustice of a different and more terrible kind.

Julie told the others to attend to their business while he and I spoke to Tee Antoine. He took me to what in another century had been a parlor: a tall room whose walls were decorated with the damp remains of arsenic-green wallpaper, the ceiling hung with a chandelier of cut crystal that had turned white and dusty like the eyes of a blind person. Though night hadn't fallen, the chamber was dark from the shade of live oaks that had grown up to the French window, and an oil lamp burned on the mantle of a marble fireplace carved with atlantids. In the middle of the room, a white man swathed in blankets sat in a wheel chair.

Or not a white man. His complexion was as light as mine but with a waxy pallor, the color of tallow. In this respect he might have passed as European, but his features were purest African and his hair had the unmistakable curls except that it was a deep red. He was about fifty years old.

He gave me a measured look. In the ordinary way I would have spoken, but the setting and my surprise at my host's appearance left me mute for the moment. My discomfiture didn't seem to bother him.

He said, 'Good day to you, Mr. Bennet, suh – they tell me that's your name and I'll do you the courtesy of believing it.' He waved a hand to beckon me closer where he could see me more clearly. 'Come here where you can take a look at this mongrel creature, this abominable product of racial miscegenation, this affront to American Values.' He gave a warm laugh. 'Don't worry none, I ain't gonna bite. Julie, bring Mr. Bennet a chair!'

A chair was put behind me, the wreck of a Louis Seize *fauteuil* with rubbed gilding and upholstery worn to the stuffing. I wondered what it was like to live among these relics of oppression, but I wasn't granted time to think about it. Tee Antoine brimmed with a fierce energy, both friendly and frightening, but an energy held in restraint. He carried his upper body with dignity, and I noticed that it showed neither the wasting of an illness borne since birth nor the compensatory muscles of someone injured as a young man. His disability was recent.

He seemed in no rush to talk but only looked me up and down for a minute before asking, 'What brings you here?'

'He a journalist from some city in England,' said Julie.

'That right?'

'Yes.'

'Then you in pretty close wit' the Agence – gotta be.' Tee Antoine used the French pronunciation.

I nodded. 'They check my copy. It goes with the job.'

'Well, that's an honest answer. And they know you here?'

I thought of Jeb's insistence that I should follow Charlie Joe Svensen to Bayou Chaud. He'd given no indication that the place meant anything to him, but the fact remained that he was the only reason I had come here.

I didn't answer because I wasn't sure what the true answer was. Tee Antoine watched me intently, then smiled and let it pass. He said, 'Never mind, it don't matter none. This day or some other day, they gonna find us and kill us, huh, Julie?'

'Sure, Antoine.'

'They haven't found you yet,' I said.

'Who knows? Maybe we just waiting our turn. There's a lot of killing to do before you get to a few poor colored folk living in a swamp.'

'How do you survive?'

Another smile that was both weary and authentic. 'This for your newspaper? You t'ink the *Agence* will let you print our story?'

'I don't know. Things change.'

He nodded at this truism.

Someday soon Big A would be gone and no one knew what America would be like afterwards – whether better or worse. In some way that was the point behind everything that was happening.

24

'We survive because some white folk want us to survive,' said P'tit Antoine Molineaux. 'Not all of 'em – no way, no. But some, and not always the one's you expect. Those who was our friends and didn't mind saying so got theirselves hushed up pretty quick by the Agence. Those that didn't get caught are communists and used to keeping their mouths shut. They he'p, but they few and in their hearts they don't give squat about coloreds 'cause we just part of the "proletariat" and don't got no fears or interests of our own. And then there's the rest: country folk mostly, who make no bones they got no respect for "niggas", but – and this the point – they used to having us around. We the people who pick their cotton, shine their shoes, take care of their kids, cook their dinners, clean their houses. We get to eat and drink in different places from them, sit at the back of the bus, and stoop and tip our hat if they speak to us. And we make them feel superior. A South without their darkies just don't seem natural to them – you follow? They want the Old South, not some different South that Yankee politicians have invented. And the Old South is full of people of color like us: part of the landscape, like the bayous or eating soft shell crabs and drinking a nice cool Jax all comfortable wit' your friends.'

'They give you help?' I was thinking of poor white farmers who had problems enough of their own without helping blacks for whatever reason. Part of me had prejudices against them that came from my own time and background, but the fact is that we are surprised by the goodness of people just as we are by their evil.

Tee Antoine looked thoughtful. 'Some of them,' he said. 'Not all, no. A lot of them is cheering on Big A like everyone else. But there is those will turn a blind eye and see a Mexican when they wants to, and let us work their fields or do any jobs they ain't in a mood to do. And if there are clothes they don't need or food or any other stuff that's gonna waste, they put them our way. And if the Agence comes looking for us, they get all forgetful and are pretty sure their field hands are hundred per cent Hispanic. Hell, some of them is our blood kin if you take my meaning.'

He looked at me to see if I understood him, but the understanding he looked for was not that of the mind, and that was all I could give him. Sometimes we puzzle at our bitterness when even a loved one shows sympathy towards us. The selfish truth is that we don't want others to imagine our suffering but rather to bear it instead of us and their sympathy reminds us that they don't. I think this resentment is a reasonable response because our fates are unjust, even if it is unkind to wish that injustice onto others.

Tee Antoine sighed and said, 'So wit' what they do and what we do for ourselves here, we get by.'

Julie was still in the room, listening and nodding now and again. When Tee Antoine came to a natural pause, he said, 'Mr. Bennet come here looking for a friend. Goes by the name Charlie Joe-something but it ain't what his mamma calls him. Says he was a Marine, yes.'

Tee Antoine raised an eyebrow. 'Alek?'

'I t'ink so.' Julie looked both angry and puzzled. 'Why he want to pay another visit here? If I 'member right, by the time he left he t'ought we only just come out the trees. I surprised you let him haul his hide outta here without a bullet in it.'

'He just a confused boy.'

'He a crazy person who know everyt'ing even when he dumber than a rock. Got more opinions than my mama ever had and ready to pick a fight wit' anyone who don't agree. But you have your way, Antoine.'

'He didn't call the Agence down on us.'

'No – that's true,' Julie agreed. 'Still crazy though. He wanted to go north and talk wit' a bunch up in the mountains someplace – people who t'ink they heroes like Aryan Man or one of those others you see in the comic books. From what he tell, I figure they people who'd lynch every one of us, yes.'

'He found the militias didn't live up to his expectations,' I said.

'See what I mean? You could put that boy in a room on his own and he'd come out wit' an enemy. Ain't not'ing good enough for him.'

I asked, 'What was he calling himself when he was here?'

'Alek' – said Tee Antoine – 'Alek Hidell. I can't say if it his true name.'

It meant nothing to me. Jeb had never mentioned any Alek Hidell. I asked, 'How did he find you?'

'T'rough the communists,' said Julie.

'That's right,' Tee Antoine confirmed. 'There's a group – they calls it a "cell" – in New Orleans. White men like yourself. I guess they gets money from Russia, but we ain't in a position to turn down any he'p comes our way. Alek was a communist when he come to us.'

'They only too glad to get rid of him,' said Julie.

'Mebbe. Anyhow he stay wit' us two months, then leave for the mountains six months ago. It wasn't no good to him that we was surviving. He want us to lead the revolution that's gonna overt'row Big A and this whole American Values t'ing. He say at least the militias are fighting.'

Julie said contemptuously, 'He gonna be "General Hidell" and make hisself a big name. There no end to that boy's high opinion of hisself.'

I could imagine the scenario: Charlie Joe restless and sounding off to anyone who'd listen and anyone who wouldn't. The growing feeling that people did not respect him the way he knew he should be respected: their narrow-minded ignorance. I had disliked him almost from the start though with a feeling of pity for whatever was missing in him. Two months sounded like a good stretch for him to contain his anger and outstay his welcome.

'And there was the ruckus,' said Julie. 'The fist fights wit' our boys 'cause he say they making fun of him. We got no peace the whole time he here.'

Again I wasn't surprised. I'd seen signs of Charlie Joe's propensity for violence especially when his self-image was involved. Tee Antoine, still watching me carefully, said, 'This what you expect, ain't it?' Then, 'How you come to know him?'

'I was on the road chasing a story, traveling by bus to keep a low profile. I ran into Charlie Joe – sorry, Alek – by accident, when he caught the same ride. He stuck with me – you know what he's like. He told me about someone he called P'tit Antoine Molineaux, but no details except he seemed to admire you. I was interested.'

I was careful to say nothing about Vegas or events at Arroyo Seco, but Tee Antoine noticed.

He asked, 'What story was you chasing?'

'Rumors that there was some sort of accident at an Army base near Las Vegas.'

'Uh huh. And they true?'

'Probably, but security was too tight to penetrate.'

Tee Antoine stared at me, his eyes expressive and sorrowful with knowledge I could only guess at and losses I'm not sure I could bear. He knew I wasn't being frank with him, but I didn't want to start down a road that would lead to disclosure of the crime committed against his people. I won't deny he had a right to know, but I didn't see the information as leading to anything more than a stoking up of the fear and anger that leads to bad decisions. I told myself I was doing him a favor. But I admit I also had selfish motives. As long I kept it to myself, I possessed a secret I might trade to my advantage in a situation that was otherwise outside my control, even if I didn't yet know how to use it.

Yet maybe he suspected something of the truth. He asked, 'Where do you t'ink all us colored folks is gone?'

'I don't know. What do you think?'

'When they clear us off the land and out of the cities, they say our boys gonna work for the Army: building roads and such; and the rest settled in – I t'ink it was Brazil. They was gonna grow rubber. They tol' us it a country full of people of color so we be right at home there, better than here. Some of us believed them.'

'But you didn't.'

'I can't say that. They gotta be somewhere, so maybe they in Brazil. But I pretty sure they ain't singing and dancing. No one knows. The Army load them on trucks and trains and take them away, and no news ever come back.'

Tee Antoine wasn't looking for reassurance and wouldn't have believed any I gave him. I respected him too much to try. To avoid his gaze, I looked around the room and noticed some framed photographs standing on the mantle shelf.

He said, 'If you want to stay a few days in case Alek show his face, you welcome.'

'Thank you. I'll do that. I can give you money – not a lot, but some.'

'I can't say it won't be welcome.'

I picked up a photograph and nothing was said to stop me. It was in a Victorian frame: tinplate or some other metal that wasn't silver, with molded vines dented by years of use and re-use. A family shot, the dark tones turned to sepia. Difficult to date because the people in it were too poor to follow fashion. A dozen of them stood in front of a shotgun house. Both sexes and all ages. The patriarch and matriarch center stage; arrogant or nervous young men next to them with their wives or sisters; babes in arms and small children squatting on the step. To one side, isolated through a subtle distance from her neighbor, was a woman of twenty or so, not wholly in the photograph but half-vanishing or perhaps half-emerging where the border of the picture faded. She looked out at me with expressionless truth and paid no attention to her own beauty. Read into me what you will, she said.

'They my family. You look as though you recognize someone,' Tee Antoine said.

I shook my head, but my denial was only partially true. I knew no one in the photograph. But I recognized something well enough. The courage Maria shared.

Night came on. Armand showed me a room I was to share with half a dozen of the young men. I was given a bed roll but had to sleep on the floor. The room was on the top floor under a spot where the roof had been patched; I could see the damage that rain had caused in the past.

'We eat in half an hour. Daddy say you can eat wit' us.'

'Daddy?' It came to me then that Tee Antoine was the giant's father, though it was of no great significance other than to explain his reverence and, perhaps, why Antoine got the nickname "Little".

'OK, I'll join you.'

Armand nodded but hung around a minute while he slowly made sense of the words. Meantime I laid out the bed roll.

The space until dinner gave me time to think over my situation. For the present I felt fairly safe. I believed Tee Antoine's instincts were peaceful and his plan no more complicated than to sit it out until the hatred embodied in the American Values movement exhausted itself, though I thought it more likely that the GeStaPo would find and destroy his small band of refugees before that happened.

However, I claimed no special insight into the future and they might get lucky.

My immediate concern was that things would change when Charlie Joe arrived – as I thought he would. I suspected Tee Antoine had played down the disruption he had caused and the animosity he had roused. Only someone as narcissistic as Charlie Joe could think of returning from the camp of the enemy as if he were a prophet bringing the word of the Lord and believe he could teach and lead these people. But, so far as I understood him at all, I supposed that was what he had in mind.

The evening was mild and a mist was forming over the bayou. Storm lamps were set out here and there on the grass, each with its halo of insects, and, with the sky still cloudy, it looked as if the ground itself had become the star field. A meal of bass, okra and dirty rice had been prepared and I was invited to join the others at one of the trestle tables on the broad porch, where the fly screen kept the mosquitoes away. I guessed there were thirty or so of us and Julie told me there were as many again, working as Mexicans on the nearby plantations and sleeping in cabins there. My thought was that they were so few to take on the world.

Julie had put on the role of a wary host, and had reason enough to be cautious with the stranger who had blundered into this last place of safety. He brought me a plate of food and sat beside me while I ate. He asked more questions about the life of a foreign correspondent and edged round to the subject of how I came to be with Charlie Joe Svensen. I gave the same partial answers I'd given to Tee Antoine but distracted him by agreeing that Charlie Joe was unstable and probably dangerous.

'I surprised you stay wit' him, then.'

'Journalist's instinct,' I said. An old standby answer that seems to serve, like a magician refusing to disclose the basis of his tricks. I asked, 'How long has Tee Antoine been in his wheelchair?'

Julie's expression froze, but it was sorrow not anger. 'Five years,' he said.

'How did it happen?'

'We was caught by the police – not the Agence or we not be alive. They was local boys, jus' Cajun trash no better'n us, and they pick us up in a grocery store we don't normally use, no. Hold us for two days while they figure what kind of Mexicans we are.'

'You escaped?'

Julie chuckled. 'Armand damn near tore their heads off when he and our boys come. We got clean away 'cept Tee Antoine made a bad jump from the bank into the boat. Broke his back.' He shook his head. 'Yes – broke his back. I wasn't important, me, but I got away whole. Ain't no justice, no?'

'No.'

The meal finished, a handful of the men took up instruments: trumpet, sax and an old bull fiddle with the veneers peeled back to the carcass wood; and they struck up some music to the beat of a battery of boxes and drums. They were amateurs who struggled to keep time and play true, but they had sincerity, which is something difficult to fake. I recognized numbers by Armstrong, Ellington and the other jazzmen exiled in Paris, tunes I hadn't heard since I came to America. They caused me to remember too how I used to dance with the wives I had never loved as they deserved, and with Maria, of whom the same might be said. One of the young women came over to me and asked shyly if we might step out to a slow ballad. I agreed because she was offering innocent hospitality and my griefs and regrets were not her business. So we danced languidly on the St. Augustine grass, which was still moist from the rain, and the storm lamps threw their fitful light on us as we orbited around them. Somewhere in the mists across the bayou a nutria called. And, because it was the nature of the dance, we nestled our faces on each other's shoulders and in low voices sang snatches of a love song that neither of us could recall in full.

The morning was warm and overcast and I was rested despite sleeping on the floor. We breakfasted indoors on the remains of the rice with a few slices of boudin. Then everyone went to their tasks, working the cultivated patches I'd seen among the live oaks or taking care of children and stuff about the house. I was called to Tee Antoine and found him in bed.

'Sorry you gotta see me like this,' he said. 'But I ax them to take care of the children before me. These days they treat me like a baby gotta be washed and changed by nurse. They don't have to but I let them 'cause it seem to give them comfort.'

He said he wanted to talk to me because he'd taken at face value that I was a journalist. Maybe I was and maybe I wasn't, but he'd decided to trust me, 'even though you ain't telling the whole troot about what happen in Vegas. Then again, who tells the whole troot?'

So we spent two hours while he gave me material for the article he hoped I was going to write at some point in the future for the English press that would expose the death and misery that had taken place at the time of the Resettlements: the article that was going to move the public and politicians of Europe. He appeared not to notice that I had no pen or paper for taking notes, but in any case it made no difference. The horror and chaos of the clearances had been revealed a decade before, after years when the growing oppression of the American Negros had become well known. The right-wing press had questioned the veracity of the reports and played them down, and the left-wing press had bleated ineffectually. After all, what could the Europeans do against the United States? The main concern of governments was that their countries should not be the destination for hordes of black refugees. The public supported the politicians.

We stopped when Tee Antoine sighed and waved a hand at me. 'You'd best go. I'm tired.'

'I'd like to thank you,' I said.

'I'm sure that helps,' he said, and as I was going he added, 'I expect your story will be published someday when all this storm that Big A has whipped up has come to an end. And your people will be angry and some of them will feel guilty. They will shout their fury aloud and beat their chests at their own weakness and they will say they are sorry and I do believe they will mean it. But I fear that none of my people will be alive to see their tears.'

25

I spent the morning exploring the plantation, where people in the fields smiled and waved in my direction. I had been welcomed by Tee Antoine and it seemed that was enough. There was a beguiling innocence about this place, but it did not come from naivety, rather a rational acceptance of the powerlessness of their community: an insight owed to Tee Antoine who was prepared to face whatever came with a grace and dignity that were probably religious in origin and something I could admire but not share. Serenity in the face of irresistible evil was a quality Charlie Joe would never understand; indeed, I grasped it only intellectually and could not imagine living out the ideal with inner conviction. Meantime I spoke at some length to a couple of people and gathered more material for the article I was never going to write. And as I did so, I felt like a spy obtaining the information I would use to betray them.

The day was still overcast, the live oaks and slash pines motionless in expectation, the horizon a roiling purple flickering with lightning. But there was no thunder and the storm did not come our way. I grabbed a po'boy for lunch then walked down to the water's edge and saw in the mist beyond the sawgrass and hyacinths the figure of Armand steering the pirogue with its single passenger in my direction like Charon ferrying a dead soul across the river Styx.

'Hey, you made it!' The ghostly shape squatting in the bottom of the boat was Charlie Joe. The pleasure in his voice was tainted by his usual guardedness, as if he expected to be let down and there was something hostile in my presence even though he had invited me here. And, now I think of it, there was, since in one fashion or another

I was fronting for Jeb Lyman and the GeStaPo, though I salved my conscience by telling myself I was acting as any journalist would act.

I noticed Armand's solemn expression and attributed it to his unwelcome passenger and memories of the disturbance he had caused during his last stay. Charlie Joe, however, was in a cheerful mood. He sprang out of the pirogue carrying a suitcase, grasped the hand I'd extended so he wouldn't lose his balance, and gave it the long-lost-friend shake.

He said, 'So, my directions were good, huh? You got here before me.'

'I didn't hurry. How come you didn't arrive first?'

The smile shut off. He said, 'I don't see that's anything to do with you,' then relented. 'I've been in New Orleans. Got family and business there.'

'I'd forgotten you came from New Orleans.' From what little I knew of accents I hadn't put his down to Louisiana, though I knew it was from the South.

'It's where I was born. But Ma was always the restless kind, and when I was a kid we lived a good spell in Texas and even stayed a while with my brother in New York. People are always telling me they can't place exactly where I'm from on account I done so much traveling when I was young.'

'And your business? You said you had business.'

He looked sideways at me. 'So I did. But it's mine, not yours, and I'll thank you kindly to keep your nose out of it.'

Within a couple of minutes, we had gone from friends meeting to sullen acquiescence in each other's company. I suppose I was as much responsible for this as Charlie Joe, but his fickle moods had a way of driving these situations. He picked up his suitcase and trudged with me towards the house. We ran into Julie on the porch. He was dressed in a bib overall ready to go to the fields, and made no attempt to hide his displeasure at the sight of his visitor.

'I'm surprised you show your face here,' he said.

Charlie Joe beamed at him, 'Don't say you ain't pleased to see me, Mr. Forgeron, sir. Is that any way to treat someone who's been spying out the lie of the land and the forces of the enemy and come back to tell y'all the things he has learned?'

'That what you been doing?'

'It surely is.' Charlie Joe looked around the older man towards the door. 'Ain't you gonna show me to my room?'

'What room? You can bunk wit' Mr.Bennet.'

Charlie Joe's face fell. In his eyes something was going wrong that he hadn't looked for. He asked, 'When can I see P'tit Antoine?'

'Tee Antoine sleeping. When he wake, I'll tell him you here. Mebbe he see you and mebbe he won't. It ain't my bidness, no.'

I took Charlie Joe to the room I shared with the other men. He threw his case on the floor and turned on me with an angry look in his eyes as though I were the cause of whatever had distressed him, but his voice was cool and controlled.

'Look at the state of this place! There ain't nothing changed the whole time I been away. Problem with these people, Harry, is they got no get-up-and-go, no initiative. Ain't one of them would have done what I done and gone out in the world to look see what's there.'

The room was fine. The occupants kept it tidy. The 'problem' with these people was poverty and persecution, but I didn't correct him.

I pointed out, 'If they'd done what you did, the idiots in the militias would have killed them.' But he wasn't listening. He was following his own train of thought and I had the impression he was practicing a speech he hoped to make to Tee Antoine. He held a belief in his powers of persuasion that experience should have told him was unjustified but didn't.

'If there's gonna be a revolution you need a handle on the forces against you. Find out who your friends are and get the lowdown on your enemies. I been taking all the risks and picking up valuable intelligence that anyone with a few smarts and the courage to use them would act on.'

'I thought the mountain boys were a bunch of losers with no time for blacks. Isn't the Army winning its campaign against them? That's what you told me. I don't see them as a threat to Tee Antoine's people, or likely to give them any help.'

'You ain't been there. You don't understand nothing. It's all a question of the objective conditions for revolution being there. The opinions of individuals don't matter 'cause they got what they call "false consciousness" that don't allow them to see beyond their noses. Those white boys are natural class allies of poor oppressed Negros even if everyone's too dumb to recognize it. But you need someone who can see into the heart of the situation and bring people together.'

This was half-digested Marxist claptrap, but I understood well enough that Charlie Joe saw himself as the man to bring the parties together despite his talent for making people dislike him. I didn't have time for this and he wasn't someone to be persuaded out of his fantasies.

I changed the subject. 'Where's your car?'

'Other side of the bayou, by Julie's beer joint.'

'Why not this side?'

''Cause there ain't no road – not all the way. The bridges across a coupla coulees was washed out in a storm a few years ago and ain't been repaired. It works out good. No one bothers this place 'cause no one can get here – not easy anyway. Everything comes in or out in the pirogue or that little biddy motor boat they got but don't use much so's to save on gas.'

I had other questions, such as what Charlie Joe hoped

to achieve here beyond the high-flown nonsense he had just spouted. Did he seriously think he was going to train the young men of Bayou Chaud to fight like marines then take them off to make war in Oregon or Montana? Did he expect Tee Antoine's people to place their trust in someone who had just spent six months with a gang of racist fanatics and end-of-the-world fantasists? I decided there was no point in asking. No doubt he would tell me sometime, since he seemed to regard me as his ally.

I left him to make his bed and wait for Tee Antoine to summon him. I went outside and sat on the porch looking at the distant lightning and tasting the scent of decay hanging over the bayou and the eerie stillness. Whatever happened next, I didn't see us staying here long, no matter what Charlie Joe's plans might be. In any case I wanted to leave because the longer I remained the more likely I was to draw Jeb Lyman and the Agency here. If Jeb's interest was only in Charlie Joe, then it was better we move on and away from people I'd grown to like and admire.

I must have dozed a while because the light had changed and evening was coming on. There was noise inside the house, banging and raised voices, and Armand came out looking tearful and confused.

He said in a defiant voice, 'I'm gonna lay me some trot lines, catch me some fish! That's what I'm gonna do!' He stared at me as though I was going to stop him, then rushed off towards the landing stage.

Julie came out next, glanced in my direction, and asked heatedly, 'Where'd that fool boy go?'

'To lay some trot lines and fish.'

'What the hell has fishing got to do with anything?' His voice lowered and he sighed. 'I guess that poor soul don't understand nothing, just storming out for no cause. Still, I don't s'pose fishing will do him no harm, no.'

He didn't wait for an answer but went back into the house and a minute later I heard his voice shouting among the others. I decided it wasn't my fight and went down to the landing stage to keep an eye on Armand. I found him sitting in the pirogue, squeezing a few notes out of a small concertina and mumbling a song, the fish forgotten.

I sat next to him and let him alone for a while, then asked, 'What happened?'

He kept playing but said in a low painful voice, 'It that Alek – allus causing trouble. Making everyone mad wit' him.'

'What did he say?'

'That we can't stay here. That we all gotta follow him. He say we got no fishin'. But that ain't true. We got all the fishin' a body could need.'

'He said you have no fishing?'

'No fishin' – hah! They say I stupid but I know more than him. Don't no one catch wide mouth bass like me, no.'

This made no sense until it came to me that Charlie Joe had said that Tee Antoine had no 'vision'. Armand had misheard or misunderstood; I doubt the word meant much to him and I saw no purpose in explaining. The mistake was funny in the sad way that life's cruel absurdities touch us but I didn't like to see the big man upset. Even though I knew him, I was surprised that Charlie Joe had outstayed his welcome quite so quickly.

The argument inside fell quiet and the man himself came out of the house in a state of quiet fury. He paced up and down the boardwalk under the porch with the jerky strut angry people use who talk to themselves. He saw me and moved to come over. I met him half way so Armand wouldn't have to hear whatever he had to say.

He began punching the air. 'What is it with these people? Goddamn morons! Don't they see they just walking dead men if they stay here doing nothing about their situation? They got no appreciation – no gratitude! The risks I ran with those mountain folk. The sacrifices I

258

made. The studying I done so's to figure out the way forward – I'm talking Karl Marx, thc laws of history, even Hegel hisself! Ain't no one understands what's going on in this country and what needs to be done about it better than me. They should be begging me to help them!'

I saw then that he was almost in tears. For different reasons his incomprehension was as great as Armand's. But his response was anger not puzzlement.

I didn't know where things were heading.

Rain came on with darkness. Tables were set up on the porch and in the house and we sat there, closed in our little box of light with water drumming on the roof and forming a curtain against the world beyond.

Tee Antoine stayed indoors, swathed in shawls, sharing his table with Julie, Armand and others I did not know. Charlie Joe by his own choice was banished to the porch, and by association I was banished with him. The musicians had set up there, but tonight the music seemed flat and discordant and there was no dancing.

We spoke little but hunched over our bowls and afterwards looked out into darkness, and this suited me because Charlie Joe's conversation was the same tedious mix of grievances and great thoughts.

At length he said with the curious formality he sometimes assumed, 'I guess I owe you an apology, Mr. Bennet, sir.'

'Why is that?'

He waved a hand. 'For all this. I had P'tit Antoine as a wise person, which I think is what I was explaining to you. I thought that, while I was away pursuing my researches, folks here would ponder on the lessons I'd taught them and that things would be different when I came back. I see now that I was sorely mistook. That old man is too set in his ways and these Negros are all a bunch of spiritless creatures who won't do nothing 'less he tell them to. There ain't nothing to hope from Julie. I know things about him' – he glanced at me. 'I won't say nothing more. But I gotta leave this place.'

'Where will you go?'

'Texas. Last I heard, my Ma and my wife was living in Fort Worth.'

'You have a wife?' Then I recalled he'd mentioned her but I'd struggled to imagine the woman who would marry someone so self-absorbed and so put the thought aside.

'Mercedes,' he said, adding in a monotone, 'I loved her because it's in my nature to love with all my heart. But it turns out I was just her ticket out of Mexico.'

'Then why are you going back to her?'

''Cause she's carrying my child – maybe had it already. And I'm not a person to run away from his responsibilities. In any case, I'm pretty much out of money and need to get myself a roof and a job.'

'What kind of job?'

'I know a thing or two about photography. Maybe I'll become a reporter like you.' He glanced at me with momentary hopefulness. 'Maybe your newspaper will give a job to a soldier who knows his way about the world? There's lots of things I could do if only my Ma hadn't denied me an education on account of her moving all the time so I could never settle into steady schooling.'

This was the nearest Charlie Joe came to giving me an insight into the life that lay behind his opinions. If he had been less abrasive I might have been more sympathetic, but it was in his nature to turn sympathy away with a scowl or a crass remark. In the end, he was too fixed on his fantasies of glory to be more than a drifter forever wondering why the world did not admire him.

Or so I thought. But my own preconceptions had allowed me to capture only a part of the truth. What I have just written is fine as far as it goes; which is to say as a generality that describes some of the ineffectual misfits who make up humanity's numbers. Indeed, I had gone even further in my conversation with Julie and agreed with him that Charlie Joe might be dangerous, though what I had in mind was the small-time sociopaths who stick up gas stations for chump change, leaving bodies on the floor, only to be in turn gunned down by the police in parking lots and rooming houses.

What I had ignored was that the mediocre ranks of the criminally reckless and borderline insane contain outliers who possess cunning and a certain courage that lift them above the average. And, too, there are the effects of pure chance.

Sometimes a million-to-one event will occur. Our mistake is to forget that the world offers billions of opportunities for such events to happen.

We sat on the porch while the rain eased off and moths flapped against the screen. Charlie Joe spoke no more of his personal circumstances but carried on expounding his complaints and the great ideas he had come by from studying what he called 'the Book of Life'. I ignored him and sat absorbed in thought, trying to make sense of my own situation.

We were like this a while, when Charlie Joe suddenly stood up and announced, 'I ain't putting up with this. This just ain't right. If I don't receive proper respect, I ain't one to hang around while fools laugh at me.'

'We'll leave in the morning,' I said.

'The hell with that! I'm leaving now, this very minute!'

He got up to go inside the house. I put a hand on his shoulder and he turned ready to hit me, but I got in first and said, 'Calm down, for God's sake. It's night. We're in a place the wrong side of the bayou, and the road is just a track that's likely deep in mud from the rain. I'm with you for leaving, but we have to do it tomorrow.'

For a moment, I thought I had him, but after a flicker of

hesitation my opposition only added to his anger and self-will. He shook my hand off. He said, 'You stay or come with me. Don't make no difference except it'll show who my true friends are.'

I didn't answer and I didn't follow.

He went to the house and a few minutes later I heard him arguing with Julie. Then Charlie Joe burst through the door with Julie on his tail while those of us on the porch stood and watched how this would play out.

Julie shouted, 'Goddamn it! Go then! You t'ink I care if you kills yourself? We didn't ax you to come here, no. We don't need your damn fool crazy notions.' He looked behind him to a figure out of sight and called, 'Armand, gas up the boat so's Alek can take hisself somewhere his stink don't trouble us none.' And to me, 'You still welcome, Mr. Bennet. Leastways 'til it light and you can go safely.'

I checked Charlie Joe to see if he remained intent on leaving this instant. He had quietened down and was biting his lip as if he was still capable of doubt. But he said, 'I'm gonna pick up my bag. You coming, Harry?'

There was a plea in his voice, but I would have ignored it except for one thing. If I lost him I didn't know how Jeb Lyman would take it; and I had no other plan to recover Maria.

'I'll go with him,' I said to Julie.

I went to the room and collected my possessions. Charlie Joe brushed past me without a word. I followed and found Julie holding the main door of the house open. The two men passed each other in silence.

Armand was coming from the landing stage, holding a lamp in one hand and a gasoline can in the other. He murmured, 'I done gassed up the boat. Keys is there.'

Charlie Joe ignored him but I said, 'Thank you,' and shook his hand, actions that seemed so inadequate I felt almost inclined to regret them.

'You coming?' said Charlie Joe.

'I'm with you,' I said and repeated my thanks and took the proffered lamp. I trailed Charlie Joe down to the boat, where another lamp burned, and we threw our stuff into the back. I took the passenger seat, supposing my companion knew the lie of the bayou better than I did.

He got in the boat, stuck the key in the ignition and turned on the spotlight that was mounted on the prow for night-fishing. His manner had cooled and I speculated he was having second thoughts. His hand was hesitating before firing up the engine.

'We can still go back,' I said. 'Leave in the morning.'

'The hell with that.'

'What then?'

'I ain't a quitter.'

'Who said you were?'

He stared at me but the glare of the lamp and the light and shade cast across his face prevented me from reading his expression. But when he spoke there was a coldness and a hurt in his voice I hadn't heard before.

He said, 'I ain't leaving like this. It just ain't right.' His hand was still on the key and for a minute or so he did nothing. Then without another word he got out of the boat. 'You stay here, Harry. Me and Julie gotta have a few last words.' He walked off towards the house, a silhouette against the lights on the porch, and I waited with the fearful certainty that something would happen and it would be bad.

I don't know exactly what I expected: another argument – a fight. We fear the worst, though most times we do not experience its full measure or it would crush us. Yet sometimes we do. And sometimes we underestimate what it may be.

There was no argument. Charlie Joe stepped into the house and almost at once I heard the pop-pop of pistol

263

shots before he reappeared on the porch and began running back towards the boat. Behind him there was uproar, the night filtered out the noise and I caught only isolated voices calling like distressed parents summoning their lost children. Then the young men emerged, maybe half a dozen of them, and one had had the wit to bring a gun which he fired after the fleeing figure though to no purpose because the target was escaping into darkness. The others set off in pursuit.

Charlie Joe had maybe fifteen seconds' lead and he was fit enough to hold it. He reached the boat and looked back long enough to loose a couple of shots that gave the others cause to hesitate. Then he let slip the mooring rope and turned the key in the ignition.

And I? What was I doing?

The answer is: nothing. In the real world, events sometimes happen so quickly they overpower our capacity to react in time and they continue to unfold while we are still struggling to understand what is already past and beyond our power to remedy. Charlie Joe was in the boat and armed and we were leaving the landing stage for the mists of the bayou and it was too late for me to undo whatever he had done.

I looked back as more people were coming out of the house and giving pointless chase. I saw Armand. He was standing on the landing stage with his arms outstretched like Christ crucified.

I heard him cry, 'Julie!' as if his heart would break.

26

'You shot Julie? Is that what you've done? You shot Julie?'

I can't explain the lack of emotion in my voice except that there are events so appalling that in retrospect we struggle to understand our own reaction. Why was I not distraught? Not furious? Perhaps it is an error to suppose that what we see and how we truly feel are synchronized. But afterwards we are left to wonder which of our responses was authentic; which manufactured by how we are supposed to feel?

Charlie Joe said, 'This isn't the time.' He spoke in his Southern drawl with the precision of someone who is all fired up but keeping himself under control. 'It isn't – believe me, sir. Those boys on the bank are as like to shoot you as me, and I need to watch what I'm doing 'cause the last thing we need is to hit a goddamn alligator in the dark.'

He was right on both counts. The men behind us had laid hands on more guns and were firing wildly in our direction, and two of them had untied the pirogue though there was no chance of their catching us unless something happened to stop the boat. I knew nothing of the habits of alligators, but there was plenty in the way of mud banks, driftwood and weeds that could ruin our chances, and even with the spotlight we could see only ten or so yards clearly.

The desire to escape danger is instinctive, and for the moment it was all I could think of. Safety lay in the pickup truck, but on my first trip across the bayou I'd dozed through most of the journey, so I had little sense of how long it would take to reach the beer shack where I'd left it and didn't know if it would still be there.

We turned the head of a mud promontory thick with sawgrass, and the dots of light marking the plantation went out one by one. Charlie Joe cut back the engine to reduce the risk of collision or grounding and we puttered along, fleeing for our lives at two miles an hour. But I was wrong about our advantage over the pirogue. Under these conditions when it was crewed by men who knew the water intimately, they had an edge. Though we had a good distance over them when I spotted their lanterns, they were making an angle to our course, not directly following.

'What the hell they doing?' Charlie Joe asked. I couldn't see his face but the calmness had left his voice. It rose in pitch, and I was reminded that he was little more than an adolescent playing an older role only because his disturbed self-image demanded it.

I said, 'The pirogue draws less water than we do and there's no propeller to snag the weeds. They think they can take a short cut and reach the other side first. We'll have to take a risk. Open her up.'

He did as I asked but we still couldn't make more than five miles an hour. Maybe it was enough – maybe not. The spotlight skimmed the top of a surface mist that hid any obstacles. A few times I heard a thud and felt the nudge of a drifting tree branch, and once there was a scrape below the hull and for a few seconds we slowed – but only for a few. Meanwhile the pirogue was on a parallel course that didn't lag much behind ours.

Charlie Joe said, 'You got your gun, Harry? Looks like we may need it.'

'It's in the glove compartment of my pickup' – assuming Julie had left it there after our first encounter.

'I got only one in the chamber and one in the magazine. Ain't enough. I need to reload. Take the wheel.'

'We can't lose time on the change-over. Give me the gun and your spare shells.'

He paused. 'You're right. We can't afford to lose time.'

266

He didn't pass me the gun or the spare shells. Perhaps he feared I would use them on him and he may have been right though I was still in flight mode, running on adrenalin. Afterwards… well, afterwards I wondered if I shouldn't have tried to kill Charlie Joe Svensen. But I have never reached a conclusion that doesn't depend on foreknowledge of what he was truly capable of, and whether what came of his actions was good or evil.

The beer shack floated out of the mist and live oaks as a grey shape behind swags of Spanish moss. There was a breathless stillness, no sound except the call of a nutria and no sign of the pirogue or its crew, though it would be a small thing to douse the lanterns and crouch low so they were invisible until we were in their gunsights. But this was just natural apprehension and the truth was that for the moment we were ahead in the race and had reached the landing stage first.

I spotted Charlie Joe's Chevy parked next to my truck. I said, 'We'll take the pickup. It'll hold the road better.'

It would also give me possession of a gun, I hoped.

'Whatever you say, Harry,' he said and headed for the passenger door.

I turned the key in the engine, fearing it would be dead from the damp air. In the nervous rush, I came close to flooding the carburetor before, on the sixth attempt, it started. While I was doing this, Charlie Joe dug into the glove compartment and came out with my pistol.

'Hey, y'all going up in the world! A Makarov PM, no less. Heard of them but never seen one before.'

'Souvenir of the Russian war' – the story Jeb had given me to account for a weapon that couldn't be traced to the U.S. government after it became clear I'd have to lose the gun I'd taken from the DSD agent – the one I'd used to shoot Vipic.

'I forgot you was a war hero.'

'Just an office boy, nothing more.'

Charlie Joe grinned. 'If you say so, Harry.' Then: 'Shit! They're here!'

I looked and he was right; the pirogue was already at the landing stage. We had to fight or move. And – whatever armchair heroes say – aside from ambush, gunfights are a crap shoot and running is almost always safer. I pressed my foot on the accelerator and let slip the clutch; and at the same time Charlie Joe swung out of the passenger door and put his last two bullets into the Chevy in the hope of disabling it. Then with a jerk we were away into the night with the engine roaring and the mud sucking at our wheels.

Cunning not speed is the key to escapes unless you happen to be an antelope. Speed is what leaves teenage boys dead in pile-ups on the highway. I knew from the outward trip that, on this road and in this light, if I let the engine rip we would go into a corner slide the first time I hit an unseen bend and it would all be over – and that was if we didn't hit a rock or a pothole and smash the suspension first. The same cautious lesson had served us well when we crossed the bayou without incident. But this time Charlie Joe didn't get it.

He whined, 'What you doing, Harry? You're driving like my Aunt Flo!'

'Save it and reload your gun. Keep an eye behind us.'

For the moment, my main fear was that we would wreck the pickup, and I wasn't convinced we'd put the Chevy out of action. Sure enough, we'd been on the road for ten minutes and I was just starting to relax when Charlie Joe shouted, 'God damn! They found us! Put your foot down; we can't be doing more than ten miles an hour!'

'Keep calm,' I told him. 'We can't outrun them, but they're not going to pass us – not on this road.'

'They can shoot at us.'

'Well good luck with that. Let them put as many slugs in the tailgate as they like, a couple of ours in their engine will finish them. Hold your nerve. Their best hope is to run us off the road; so, if they get too close, fire a couple of shots to make them keep their distance.'

Some of this was from experience in the world's more desperate corners. Most of it was bullshit from watching movies. My instinct said the most important thing was to concentrate on the road. In comparison, random bullets from a revolver or pistol were no more than a distraction unless we were unlucky.

A shotgun was different.

We were following the line of a coulee when I heard the blast and the shock nearly drove me into the water. The pellets clattered against the rear glass; but for the moment the distance was too great and the glass held. Charlie Joe wound down the window and gave return fire before dropping back into his seat.

'No use – the truck bed and the tailgate are stopping me getting a clear line of sight. I'm shooting at air.'

'Keep trying. If they get close enough, they'll blow the tires out with that thing.'

'I told you… Holy shit!'

A second blast. Another rattle of pellets. Charlie Joe returned fire again but the mirror told me he was having no effect; the driver of the Chevy didn't budge an inch from his course.

'Any nearer and we're cooked.'

'Maybe,' I said.

It all depended on whether I was the 'lucky explorer'.

An old newshand once told me a story. This was in a bar in Mogadishu and I was much younger; but I never forgot it because it was the first time I'd met with the lazy style of American folk-telling and the first time I drank bourbon whiskey.

He said that an explorer was crossing a barren African plain when he found himself face to face with a man-eating lion. So he looked around for a way to escape. He figured he could run but he knew the lion would be faster. Or he could hide behind a rock but the fact was there were no rocks. Or he could climb a tree but damn it if there weren't no trees. So what did he do?

I didn't know.

'He climbed a tree.'

'But,' I said with all the puzzlement of a young man, 'there are no trees.'

My friend nodded.

'You may be right,' he said, 'But you see, son: when you're an explorer about to be eaten by a lion, there has to be a tree.'

I like this story because it's a celebration of human courage and ingenuity in adversity. But despite our desire that it might be otherwise, it's also untrue. As the old hand said, 'Sometimes you find the tree and sometimes you don't. And sometimes you have no idea what it was you just climbed. Still, belief in that tree is a comfort if you're in the habit of meeting lions.'

The driver of the Chevy knew what he was doing. He closed the gap between us to where he reckoned his partner could shoot out the pickup's tires, and, whenever I braked to throw him off, his reflexes were sharp enough to avoid a collision that was more likely to damage him than me.

What he didn't take into calculation was that, by hanging so close to my tail, he was blind to anything on the road.

The Chevy flipped.

I did nothing cause this – leastways nothing deliberate. It's a guess I jinked to avoid a pothole and that he didn't see it in time. But was there in fact a pothole? A fallen branch? Who knows? It was night and someone was shooting at me and I saw nothing but a few yards in front of the truck and was living only in the instant. The last pothole – the last branch – was history as remote as that of ancient Rome.

The Chevy flipped and careened off a live oak. It rolled and burst into flame. I saw the flash in the mirror, and heard the explosion of the gas tank and the sound of men screaming, though I don't see how the last was possible. The chase was over and yet for a minute or two Charlie Joe and I drove on as if nothing had happened; our bodies still tense; our guts still churning. Finally I let the pickup drift to a halt and put my head in my hands and shook and cried a while. Charlie Joe remained silent but for his breathing and the muttering of a holy-roller prayer he may have heard at a revival meeting when he was a child. I do not know what was on his mind.

These days I feel grief when I think of the men who died trying to save themselves and their families and keep the little they had at Bayou Chaud, men whom a short time before I'd been ready to admire. On the night, however, I was in a state of shock and relief from a mortal peril. And that, not shame or regret, was the only reason I was crying.

May I be forgiven for this, but I was glad I'd killed them.

We arrived at Port Barre in dead of night, too late to check in a hotel or rooming house and in any case too wild-looking to do so safely. I parked in a side-road a little way out of town where we were unlikely to be spotted by a prowl car, and we slept in the cab as best we could until morning came, disturbed only by the calls of night birds and raccoons rooting in garbage cans.

We ate breakfast at a diner. A busload of soldiers – kids of eighteen – were putting away eggs and pancakes before heading for garrison duty in Mexico or wherever. In Europe they would be working on a factory line, assembling refrigerators and cars and dancing with their girlfriends at weekends, but these boys were from the plains of the Mid-West. Behind all their joshing, they had a strange piety that came from a sincere belief in the values for which they were fighting; a sense of their God-given mission. It was one of the things that caused their Christian parents to support the unending war: because, if nothing else, it gave purpose to their children's lives; and massacres of strangers in distant countries were more innocent and more easily ignored than sexual encounters in drive-in cinemas with the daughters of their neighbors.

I caught these boys sneaking glances at Charlie Joe and it caused me to ask him, 'Why aren't you still in the Marines?'

He put down his fork and assumed his earnest manner. 'I told you, sir. I received an honorable discharge. I remember telling you that most particularly.'

'You did. But you didn't give me the reasons.'

'They had a good three years of my life.'

'I don't doubt it. Even so…'

'You would probably misunderestimate me if I told you.'

'I was in the army myself.'

'So you tell me. In an office – the one where they teach you to get around high security and kill people if I seen what I seen.'

I didn't repeat the question because I didn't want to play to his sense of self-importance. I ordered more coffee and, while it came, went to the washroom to freshen up. When I returned, the soldiers were gone; I saw them forming up on the parking lot to be counted off before they boarded the bus. In their absence, Charlie Joe had relaxed.

He said, 'I didn't want to be overlistened, but now they're gone it's OK. Not everyone would understand about my honorable discharge even if I was to produce the paper which I got here in my bag.' He paused and looked at me for what was probably only seconds but seemed longer. 'Seeing as we are friends I'll tell you the truth because I know you recognize that a person who has served three years doing things you wouldn't want to talk to your momma about can say he has done enough for his country and still keep his self-respect if he decides that his mission in life is somewhere else. The fact is I got myself a medical discharge.'

'A medical discharge?'

'What I said. I told them that the things I'd seen and done was too much for a body to stand and my poor brain couldn't handle the strain. Lord knows, there was plenty of those who couldn't take it. I was fooling them of course. I seen some horrible stuff but I ain't crazy. Still, if they thought I was, it wasn't for me to tell them they was wrong.'

He grinned in the guilty way of children and I could only guess what he had gone through. Yet, though I felt an abstract pity for him, I liked him no more after his confession than before. For that matter, I wasn't certain it was true: at least not so far as the unspoken horrors were concerned. Among my contemporaries I had met many who had been damaged by war yet not gone mad, and something was subtly off in the way Charlie Joe presented himself. The men I knew did not boast of their suffering or their own cleverness. They kept their silence, lay awake at night next to their sleeping wives, and never spoke of the war to their sons even when they asked.

I asked, 'Did you kill Julie?'

I don't know what he was expecting: praise, perhaps, for pulling the wool over the eyes of the authorities? My change of subject shocked him.

He snapped, 'What are you bothered with Julie for? You hardly knew him.'

'Did you kill him?

'Who the hell knows? You think I stuck around to find out?'

'Why? What was it about?'

'The man disrespected me: acted like my knowledge and my opinions wasn't worth nothing after everything I done and the risks I took. I offered them leadership! They should have been pleased I treated their raggedy-assed outfit seriously. How many white folks you think pretend like they was worth something? None 'cept me, that's how many.'

This was fantasy, but he wasn't finished. And what he had to say shook me.

'You think he was a saint? Hah! That man was nothing but a spy for the GeStaPo! Selling his own just so's he and P'tit Antoine and a few like them can live quiet at Bayou Chaud.'

'I don't believe you. Who told you?'

'I got my sources.'

'Where? You mean some crazies in the militias said so before they threw you out? Or do you have a direct line to the GeStaPo?'

This time he froze as though I had slapped his face.

'Everyone talks to the GeStaPo,' said Charlie Joe Svensen. 'How long you been in this country that you don't know that?'

And he was right, of course. Everyone does.

27

'So what happens next? I mean, what are you going to do? I'm set on heading for Dallas 'cause I been away a while and ought to do my duty by Mercedes. Only problem is I don't have no wheels.'

Charlie Joe eyed me cautiously. I might have told him he could steal another car or however he'd come by the Chevy. Instead I said, 'You could take the Greyhound. I can give you the fare.'

'I was thinking that, since you don't seem to have anything particular to do, we might drive there together. Give you a chance to see places that as a journalist it may be you ain't seen. You could meet my family: Mercedes – my mother if she's still in town. Us being friends is what I'm saying.'

This was the second time he'd referred to me as his friend. I didn't know what his notion of friendship was. After the event, everyone said he'd been a lonely child whose exaggerated opinion of himself and sensitivity to slights made it difficult for him to establish relationships with other kids so that his capacity for true friendship was damaged. But after the event we are all wise, and what was once seen as normal becomes abnormal and the unpredictable finds an explanation that makes it inevitable. What was clear was that he wanted me to be his friend and that he understood me so poorly he thought it was possible. I wasn't his friend – not then or ever. But I was sorry for his loneliness and anger, and this may explain why I didn't make more of the death of Julie or think about any further havoc he might cause.

Sometimes pity is a vice.

I asked, 'How far is Dallas?'

'Three fifty – four hundred miles maybe. We could do

it in a day if we take spells driving and don't stop. Two days is easy. What do you say?'

'I'll think about it.'

I didn't have any other plan. I still didn't know how to get Maria back and free myself of this situation. I was second-guessing Jeb Lyman's interest in Charlie Joe, assuming he had an interest other than in getting me out of the way until things cooled down. In the scheme of things, did a detour to Dallas for a few days matter?

'I need to buy a change of clothes,' I said. 'You could probably do with the same.'

'Thank you. I'll pay you back as soon as I get a job. You may trust me on this, sir. I hold it important to be honorable in the matter of debts and suchlike.'

'Sure.'

We found a store that sold clothes, mostly workwear. We bought what we needed for three or four days and, in my case, dumped the old stuff once I'd persuaded the store owner to let me change on the premises.

On the sidewalk as we left, I told Charlie Joe, 'OK, I'll take you to Dallas. But after that, it's over. Is that understood? I have a life to get back to.'

'Understood,' he said. Though I was doing him a favor, he sounded touchy as if I was about to cheat him.

I gassed-up the truck and checked the oil, the tires and radiator, and by late morning we were on Route 71 heading north and west out of the bayou country. Charlie Joe kept sullen silence, but that was all right; I had problems of my own to think about. When he did speak, it was a rehash of things he had said before, ideas he claimed to have got from his reading of Proudhon, Marx and Nietzsche ; even Spengler's *The Decline of the West* which Big A sometimes quoted in his speeches. On the other hand, I'd once seen him struggle to read a newspaper. I suspected he got his 'philosophy', as he called it, from listening to people who at some time or another had impressed him until, as was inevitable, he quarreled with them because they hadn't given him his due regard.

As we neared Shreveport, we picked up snatches of country and western music from the Louisiana Hayride program, which lifted the mood and set us humming like buddies going fishing so that, seeing his fresh young face, I could almost persuade myself I liked him and everything else was a misunderstanding. But the moment passed as moments do. We checked in a cheap motel on the south side, a rundown place that suffered from the wartime shortage of construction materials so that things that got broken were never properly fixed. It was used as a hot bed hotel by hookers and a stopover by long distance truckers who didn't care for anything except a bed, a meal and cold beers, and those same things were fine with us. I had no trouble presenting the new ID Jeb had given me but the clerk was unhappy with Charlie Joe's age.

He grumbled, 'You look as though you should be in the Army. You on furlough or something?'

'I got me an honorable discharge.'

'Uh huh? And there are papers to prove that?'

Charlie Joe took an envelope out of his kitbag and extracted some official-looking sheets bearing his photograph and a discharge certificate. I couldn't say if they were genuine, but they bore the name Alek James Hidell, the same that he had used at Bayou Chaud.

At breakfast Charlie Joe took himself off to the payphone by the check-in desk.

'I gotta call one of Mercedes' friends. Tell her we'll be there tonight.'

'Why a friend?'

'We been moving around – finding a place we can afford and keeping up the rent ain't easy. I don't know for sure where Mercedes is living.'

'You've been away for months and you don't even

know where she lives?'

He rounded on me. 'You criticizing me? Come out and say it if that's what you mean. You think it's easy having to go places, trying to make up for the education you didn't get 'cause your mother never had no taste for settling? I tell you I done wonders with my life considering the disadvantages I've had which I didn't deserve. There's no end to the things I know that a person in my position ain't supposed to know.'

'Calm down. I'm not criticizing you.'

'Damn right.'

Later he tried to mend fences by confiding in me. He said 'They tell me they found me a job. Start any time I like.'

'That's good. What is it?'

'I don't know exactly. Something in management maybe. There's a warehouse in the city holds stuff that doctors and hospitals buy: beds, gurneys, all kinds of fancy equipment. Probably it's old folks and Mexicans doing the grunt work. I guess they need someone to take it in hand.'

I didn't see anyone hiring Charlie Joe in a manager's role sight-unseen, but it wasn't my business to correct him and any comment would only spark off another complaint about how hard-done-by he was. The prospect of a job and a reunion with his wife did nothing for his spirits and he began pressing me to get on the road as though I had been holding him back. It was the last thing I had in mind.

So we took Route 80, heading west towards Mineola, making the best time we could, concentrating on the road not the scenery. To pass the hours, I asked a few questions about my companion's wife.

'Mercedes – that's a Spanish name.'

He glared at me. 'Are you trying to make something out of it? 'Cause I don't take kindly to slurs against her good name or on account of her origins.'

'You're forgetting Maria,' I pointed out.

'All right then. Just so's things are understood between us.'

'And Mercedes? How did you two meet?'

'In Mexico. I stayed on and worked there a while after I was given my discharge. It's a benighted place and I thought it could do with some American get-up-and-go.' He shook his head. 'But the fact is they don't recognize it when it's put in front of them.'

'And that's where you married?' I was thinking of the racial purity laws but didn't want to put the question directly. The fact was that an American citizen couldn't just bring a Mexican wife into the country, and any children would be classed as half-breeds.

'I know what you driving at,' he said, 'but it ain't that. Mercedes is like Maria: what they call a "Privileged Hispanic", meaning her folks are European since way back and she counts as white.'

I knew what he meant and that as like as not her papers were forgeries, which was mostly the case as we were both aware. Privileged Hispanics lived in dread of the time when the GeStaPo would turn its attention to them.

I asked, 'You have children?'

'I got a daughter and may have a second for all I know, if she drops it early.' He laughed bitterly. 'You try to drag yourself up by your own efforts, but Fate drags you down again. There ain't no fairness in it. Not that I ain't gonna do my duty as a husband and a father.'

'I'm sure things will get better,' I said. But neither of us believed this to be true.

Dallas was not a city I knew well. I was no different from most foreign correspondents in relying on agency stories heavily censored by the regime. Apart from oil it was most famous as the place where, back in the twenties, Big A found an audience and the American Values movement first got traction. In those days its message was mainly about old-time religion and traditional masculinity, something the Texas oil magnates subscribed to even while they were whoring and robbing their way to a fortune. The racial element came in more strongly ten years later when the NSDAP absorbed the Klan and its leaders went to the chair for treason. A leftover from the times was American Patriots Day, commemorating the death of some party thugs in an attempted coup against the state governor back in 1923. It was celebrated in November, a little before Thanksgiving and sometimes the President traveled to Dallas and made a speech to prove he was still alive and in control. I recalled Jeb Lyman telling me that this was one of those years. I had no plans to be there.

We reached town towards evening and hit traffic heading for the suburbs. Our goal was Irving, a place on the west side which didn't consider itself part of Dallas but was. Charlie Joe didn't claim to know the area well and we cruised the streets a while before we found West 5th Street and a modest white single storey frame house of the kind teachers, clerks and other decent folk might live in.

'So who are we seeing?' I asked.

Charlie Joe had been cagey. I had a feeling this entire business of seeing his wife and child again was a defeat in his eyes as it might be for a deserter returned home from a war on which he had set out with a conviction of his own courage.

He said, 'Place belongs to one of Mercedes's friends, name of Ruth. Don't be fooled by her none. She's learned nice manners but she's one of those undermining women a man can never do enough for.'

He rang the bell. A neat, pretty woman with short dark hair answered the door. I put her age at about thirty.

'Alek.'

'Ruth.'

'And your friend?'

'Harry Bennet. You gonna let us in?'

Ruth – I didn't get her last name – didn't answer directly. She turned around and called out, '*Mercedes, tu marido está aquí!*' I heard the sound of small children and one of them came to the door and haunted behind his mother's skirt the way that infants do with strangers.

Charlie Joe pushed his way inside. Another woman appeared: this one dark, attractive, closer to her husband in age and heavily pregnant. Seeing him, her face assumed a doll-like stillness and she muttered something in Spanish. Charlie Joe gave her a perfunctory kiss and a hug. A toddler emerged from another room and he picked her up and swung her with something that looked like pleasure, all the while crooning, 'Is my little Junie glad to see her poppa?'

Ruth gave me the look reserved for people who don't fit. She said, 'Take a seat. I can offer you coffee or a soda.'

'Not for me.'

'Alek? You want coffee or a soda?'

'Nothing. I want to talk with Mercedes.' He took her arms firmly, turned her round and ushered her through a door into the next room.

My host and I faced each other like two people on an unfortunate date. Raised voices came through the door. Ruth said calmly, 'He can't stay here, Mr. Bennet. They fight all the time and he beats her. There's nothing she can do to make him happy because the truth is I don't think he wants to be happy. He'd have to give up too many other things that are important to him, though don't ask me what they are, for I'm sure I don't know. Does that make sense?'

I nodded.

'You heard me speak to her in Spanish? We talk English between us when he isn't here, but Alek doesn't want her to learn it because it means he can't control her. What kind of man does that?'

281

'I don't know.'

'No, I don't either. How did you meet him?'

'I was traveling. We met on the road.' To avoid explanations I said, 'Alek will tell you more if you want to know. I'll be going shortly.'

The door to the other room opened and Charlie Joe came through. He wasn't pleased but I'd seen him angrier.

Ruth said, 'I was telling Mr. Bennet that I don't want you staying here. Space is tight and I have to think of the children. I've been looking through the newspaper for rooms to rent and, when you said you'd be arriving today, I took the liberty of calling one. It's in Oak Cliff. You don't have to take it if you don't like it. And the job…'

'Mercedes told me about the job.'

'My friend Mae Randall's brother, Buell, works there. I can't say it's permanent, but if you make a good impression…'

'It's for chumps, but it'll do until I get on my feet again.'

'I'll leave you to talk,' I said. And to Charlie Joe, 'This is it, Alek. It's been interesting to meet you, but this is as far as it goes.'

I went to the truck. The leafy street was quiet, the sky clear, the air balmy; and after the tense atmosphere of the house I experienced one of those passing moments when it seems everything is going to get better. Then, in the cab, I found that Charlie Joe – or Alek, or whoever he was – had left his bag.

I picked it up and was returning to the house when he came out. Seeing his wife and child had done nothing for his temper.

He snapped, 'I need you to take me to Oak Cliff.'

'I told you this was the end.'

'What d'you mean, "the end"? You heard that bitch!

She wants me out of the house. You gotta take me to Oak Cliff.'

'I don't "gotta" do anything.'

'I don't get you. What kind of friend are you?'

He meant it. He really didn't understand.

We stood in silence probably for no more than a second or two, but it was enough because I saw in him – or thought I did – the misjudgments that mark the life of every young man and which we get over or don't. Mine had lasted into my thirties and had cost me two wives, and I felt I owed him something not for himself but in return for the help that other people had given me. I was wrong because I had misread Charlie Joe as badly as he had misread me. Yet the deaths of Vipic and Julie should have told me that he had reached a point beyond the kindness any other person could offer.

I said, 'OK, get in the cab'

'I thank you, sir. I knowed I could count on you, and I apologize if I didn't treat you polite. Thing is they're holding this room for the one night, and I don't want to lose it 'cause it's just two miles from the warehouse where I expect to be working.'

'Fine.' I could skip the explanations. I gathered Oak Cliff was not far from the center of the city, and after I'd dropped my passenger off I should be able to find a room at one of the hotels. The drive from Irving was a half hour, so that at worst I would be clear of him inside the hour.

And that is much as it played out. Ruth had booked the last room in a sprawling single-storey rooming house in North Beckley Street run by a Mrs. Johnson. Eight dollars a week for a box wide enough to touch both walls if you stretched your arms, but Charlie Joe didn't seem to care. He'd been raised in poverty and I'd noticed that he instinctively bought whatever was cheapest and didn't expect more, even if I was paying. This time I remembered to unload his bag.

That night I found a room at the Adolphus in Commerce Street, which cost more than I cared to pay but I used the GeStaPo's money Jeb had given me. In my working clothes, I looked like someone fresh from the farm but the hotel was OK with that when my ID checked out. In the morning, with breakfast inside me, I decided that my mission was at an end and I would call Jeb and ask him to bring me in. My hope was that somehow he had squared things with Nixon's people.

When I set out for Bayou Chaud, Jeb had given me contact numbers for the New Orleans office. No one in Dallas was expecting me and a call out of the blue promised complications. I had Jeb's direct line in Washington and I asked the long-distance operator to put me through. I got a tone I didn't recognize.

She said, 'It seems there's a problem with the number you gave me.'

I asked her to try the Agency's general number, and this time I got an answer. A bright voice said, 'General State Police. Which service do you require?'

'FBI.'

'Hold the line please.'

Another woman came on. 'Do you have a particular person you wish to contact or an enquiry I can help you with?'

I gave her Jeb's direct line.

She came back a moment later. 'I'm afraid, sir, that number's been disconnected.'

'Disconnected? What does that mean?'

'I can't say, sir. The party you wish to speak to may have left the Agency. Can you give me his name? And can you tell me who I'm speaking to?'

There was nothing in her tone of voice to give me concern. And it may be that the whirrs and clicks on the line signified no more than a worn-out telephone system because the Army took all the new equipment. On the other hand, I might have every reason to be worried.

I put the phone down and made ready to leave in a hurry.

28

I couldn't contact Jeb Lyman and didn't know what that meant. In the febrile atmosphere of the Kennedy– Nixon power struggle and Hoover's maneuvering to preserve his position, individuals were expendable. Jeb – if I believed him – had been digging into the secret of Arroyo Seco and protecting me against DSD reprisals, both of which exposed him to a possibly fatal miscalculation.

Or it could be he had just moved office. How was I to know? The only thing I could be certain of was that I needed to get out of the hotel.

I had to assume my current location hadn't been logged or I would have been picked up when I checked in the Adolphus. But I also knew the GeStaPo had the means to track the call I'd made to Washington. The telephone directory told me there was an FBI office no more than a couple of blocks away along Commerce Street. How long before they put a snatch squad together? I thought I was probably good for half an hour while the facts went up for a decision and the necessary calls were made. But it was no more than a guess.

My suitcase and its contents were worth nothing; I decided to dump them. I still had money. What I lacked was transport. The pickup was on the hotel lot but the front desk had its details even if the GeStaPo didn't, which meant I could count on no more than twenty miles before the Highway Patrol stopped me on an APB. My best option was the first train out of Union Terminal which was close by and where papers were only spot-checked for deserters and illegals. The odds were I wouldn't be noticed unless the station was flooded with agents, which was unlikely in the time available. The destination of the train and what I was going to do afterwards were for the moment immaterial.

I collected the cash, my gun and the spare set of papers I'd got from the scoot box not so many days ago, then put on my jacket and slipped out of the room to catch the elevator. I was mid-way across the lobby to the main door when a man in a cheap suit broke away from the desk and placed himself in front of me.

'Mr. Stolpert,' he said in an outwardly friendly voice while placing a hand firmly on my forearm, 'I'd like a word with you.'

One thing I hadn't taken into account in my calculations was that the Adolphus had a house detective.

His name was Herbie Grauman. He was fat, middle-aged and not looking for trouble though able to handle it. He said. 'You and I should have a quiet conversation, Mr. Stolpert, and if everything is copacetic then no harm done, we stay friends, and the hotel may run to a free dinner.'

I was caught off balance and didn't bother with the innocent protests. Instead I said, 'I'm carrying a gun.' I had no intention of using it. Once a firefight started, it wouldn't be just Grauman on the other side and the overwhelming odds were that I'd get killed.

Grauman nodded. 'Then I'll kindly ask you to hand it over.'

I let him take me through a door marked 'private' that led to a small room in the service area, where bellhops and front desk clerks went to smoke in the corridor outside. There was a table with a couple of chairs, and a telephone and the usual stuff on the table. Grauman indicated one of the chairs and lit himself a cigarette, offering me one.

'You don't? You should try. Luckies are recommended by doctors. But suit yourself. You know why you're here.'

'No.'

'Seriously? Then how can I put it? Do you know what this hotel costs?'

'I paid in advance.'

'You're missing my point.' Grauman reached into his pocket and pulled my ID, the one I'd left at the desk for the overnight police check, the same one Jeb had provided. He read out, '"Harrison Stolpert – welder – from Milwaukee". That you?'

'Yes.'

'Uh huh – well, you sure dress like a welder from Milwaukee.'

'So we're both agreed.'

'I repeat my question. Do you know what this hotel costs? This *five star* hotel?'

I knew then what it cost.

'You were maybe thinking this was a cheap flophouse that a guy on the road looking for work might stay at? Fine, if that's the way you want to play it, Mr. Stolpert. Please empty your pockets.'

I took out my cash and papers and placed them on the desk. Grauman stared at the papers, poking them with his pen so he could read them. He sucked his teeth.

'Well, Mr. Whoever-you-are, I think we got ourselves a problem, and not one I can solve.' He reached for the phone and made a call to the front desk. 'This is Herbie. Tell Dave he won his bet on Stolpert. But first get on to the FBI and ask them to send some guys round. I got a fish for them. And tell them this: he's English, though he's faking it like he's not.'

He looked at me and smiled. 'Nice try. But a welder? At the Adolphus? Sheesh!'

It took twenty minutes for two G-men to arrive. One remained in the room while Grauman took the other outside to brief him. When they came back the agent looked me over and said, 'Herbie tells me you've behaved yourself. Is that how you intend to carry on?'

'Yes,' I said.

He nodded, then stepped towards me and gave me a punch in the guts that doubled me up and sent me slamming into the wall.

'I can't resist it when I'm offered a free shot,' he said and he and his friend laughed.

I was pulled to my feet, cuffed and frogmarched out of the hotel. They bundled me into a car for the short drive to the Agency's office. There I was pushed into a cell and left for an hour while they did their paperwork and tried to figure what it was they had hold of. There was no mention of a call from Washington, which I supposed was a good sign but unlikely to last.

At the end of the hour one of the original pair came in with a new player, aged forty or so, in a well-cut brown suit with a chalk stripe and a Party badge pinned to a lapel. He gave his name as Special Agent Fiorello.

'So who are you?' he asked, 'Since you're obviously not Stolpert – nor, I'm guessing, the other guy whose papers you're carrying.'

'My name is Harry Bennet. I'm an English journalist.'

The name didn't register with him. The journalist credentials didn't impress.

I said, 'Can I ask you to phone the Washington bureau and speak to Special Agent Jubal Lyman? He can vouch for me, and, if I've done anything wrong, he'll take the necessary measures.'

I'd switched from fearing Jeb was dead to counting on his being alive. This wasn't because the odds had changed but because the exposure of my two fake identities had left me with no option but to disclose my real one. For good or ill my fate was being determined as part of a game played at the national level and I had to get myself out of the hands of the Dallas area office. The alternative was a set of violent interrogations going nowhere. If I was going to be killed, at least let it be by people who knew why they were doing it and maybe feared what cards I might hold though

I wasn't sure I held any.

Fiorello was evidently a cautious man. He told his colleague to keep an eye on me and give me cigarettes, food, coffee and comfort breaks if it seemed I needed them. He left and I didn't see him for an hour. When he came back, he told me I was being taken to Washington. He was under orders to do so personally.

It was still only noon. I was cuffed and driven the six miles to Love Field, where we checked at airport security and completed the paperwork before I was taken to an area where they kept light aircraft.

Fiorello was an old-fashioned secret policeman who revealed nothing, even if it was good news. He didn't speak about Jeb Lyman. Instead he sat quietly and read a pocket New Testament the whole journey. I mention this simply as a fact and not as a general criticism of Christians. Many were opposed to the President. On the other hand, many felt that the right to bear arms, hate homosexuals and oppress women were enshrined in religion and to be protected at all costs. In a shrewd insight, Big A had realized it was not practical to abrogate the Second Amendment; and that it was also unnecessary. To defeat freedom, he did not need to take guns out of the hands of his fellow Americans: only to exploit their fear of change and of the differences between people so that their weapons were always enlisted in his support against a mythical Other. The threat to his rule was not a mass uprising by god-fearing, liberty-loving patriots – even if they were armed to the teeth – but a conspiracy among his henchmen or the delusions of a fanatic sitting at this very moment somewhere in the loneliness of his bedroom, whose actions represented nobody but himself and whose concept of freedom was mere insanity.

By evening I was in Washington in a cell in the Hoover Building, though I didn't know this for certain because I'd been taken from the plane in a closed wagon. I consoled myself that at least I hadn't been handed over to the DSD. Fiorello left and I never saw him again. Instead I was alone with a clean bed, a toilet, and food pushed through a flap in the door. The corridor was tiled and through the night I heard the echo of feet, the mutter of voices and the occasional cry or scream that was too remote to be truly frightening. In the morning, I was given breakfast and afterwards a razor, soap and a towel and told to freshen up. These are not the courtesies normally extended to someone about to be tortured.

Two agents came to collect me. They took me to a fancy suite on an upper floor. To my surprise, I caught a glimpse of Hoover himself: a short, plump character with a mincing walk who might have passed for a vaudeville comedian but for his manner and reputation. He was deep in conversation with his number one boy and presumed lover, Clyde Tolson, in an office full of secretaries and filing cabinets. I was turned away and taken to a suite at the other end of the corridor. The outer door bore a plaque labelled 'Deputy Director', and below it was space for another marked by four screw holes where the last occupant's name had been removed. My escort knocked and we were admitted into a secretary's office much like Hoover's only smaller, with the stock portrait of the President set between the usual pair of national flags and, either side, a vase of artificial flowers. There was also a framed copy of the citation that went with Big A's Nobel Peace Prize. The committee, with a stunning lack of irony, had awarded it to him in the fifties for brokering a ceasefire in a war in which he was not involved.

A young woman who had the severe beauty that attracts men to nurses volunteered to see if the Deputy Director was free to see me. He was. I was shown alone into his room, and there, behind the desk, looking immaculately groomed as always was Jeb Lyman.

I suppose I was expecting this but all the same I said, 'You're Deputy Director of the GeStaPo?'

'Alas, only of the FBI – and one of several at that. Don't be fooled by the office. It's only temporary until they find a cupboard for me. On these occasions, everyone moves and for a month no one knows where anyone is, but life still goes on.'

He came from behind the desk and pumped my hand vigorously. His delight seemed genuine even if disconcerting, like a preacher welcoming a convert.

He asked, 'Are you OK? You weren't mistreated?'

'They were a little unsociable, but nothing to complain about. Not like whoever was screaming in one of the cells.'

'Damn it, they put you in a cell? I told them to find a hotel. I gather you tried to call me on my old number?'

'Yes.'

'That's another thing: I specifically asked them not to disconnect it; but, I tell you, office services and the finance department are laws to themselves. I swear, if our enemies are right and what we're running is a police state, we've got to sharpen up our act.'

'And the screaming?'

Jeb paused for a second. 'Yeah – that's another thing we've got to do something about. It's cruel and – inefficient. But changes take time and these days the men who forged the revolution have grown old and set in their ways.'

'So who's going to change things? Nixon or Joe Kennedy Junior?'

'Good question. We'll talk about it later after your coffee.'

Coffee came. We settled into comfortable chairs in a corner beneath a Remington painting of the Old West that was probably original. With all that had happened since we had last met it seemed strange to ask about Mary Beth and the kids, and the old folks in Provo where Jeb planned on spending Thanksgiving, but that's what I did; and Jeb answered with the enthusiasm I expected: that of someone who was at heart a family man.

'And you?' he asked as if we were going to talk about golf. 'How did you get on with Charlie Joe Svensen and Bayou Chaud?'

'His name is Alek Hidell – Charlie Joe's name. He has a wife and a daughter and the wife is pregnant. When I last saw him a couple of days ago, he'd taken a room in Dallas but I wouldn't count on his staying there.'

'And Bayou Chaud?'

'Some Cajuns are squatting in an old plantation and earning a hard living growing vegetables for the pot and hiring themselves out as labor.'

'You don't think they're of interest to the Agency?'

'Which?'

'Take your pick.'

'Neither. Alek Hidell is an unstable drifter who was probably released from the Marines because of mental health problems. The Cajuns may include some undocumented Mexicans, but they're not looking to cause trouble.'

I hoped Jeb would buy both stories. I had no desire to bring grief on Charlie Joe because any attempt to get justice for the shooting of Julie would bring the GeStaPo down on Tee Antoine's people, who deserved better than I could ever give them.

For now, he seemed uninterested. He said he'd get one of his men to take more details – addresses in Dallas and so forth. It confirmed my opinion that the whole episode in Louisiana was just a distraction to get me safely out of the way while things developed in Washington.

I asked, 'How is Maria?'

He looked hurt. 'I'm sorry. I should have been more sensitive. You must have been anxious. She's fine, trust me – I get daily reports. She misses you and asks after you. I've told her you've been on a mission, but not a dangerous one.'

'And do I get to see her again?'

Our future – mine and Maria's – was bound up with politics, as it had been since that fateful night at the Freedmen's, and I found myself trusting in the friendship and integrity of a secret policeman who was fully aware of what the GeStaPo was capable. In retrospect and thinking of Jeb, I find it difficult to consider good and evil as choices between opposites: rather that we do things in ignorance and classify them afterwards and are often surprised by our accidental immorality. This isn't true of everyone, but of most of us, I think.

'I've been looking for leverage,' Jeb said. 'Something to trade for Dick Nixon's acquiescence in the loss of one of his people. Personally, he doesn't care, of course, but he has to be seen defending his team – unless it's worth his while to do otherwise. And I think I'm almost there.'

'You came up with something?'

'I did – with your help.'

I didn't know what help I'd given beyond killing a DSD agent and discovering the disaster at Arroyo Seco, neither of which was likely to earn Nixon's gratitude.

'Did you know,' Jeb said in a measured tone with more than a hint of irony, 'that the test of the uranium bomb was a success?'

'You mean apart from blowing up Camp MacArthur and killing more than a few American soldiers?'

'Dickie had his doubts too. But he has a problem. He can't simply stay quiet and bury what happened. It isn't just that facts have an inconvenient habit of leaking out. The Japanese bomb test is a game changer. Silence isn't an option. He has to come up with a positive counter that shows we're ahead.'

'And you've given him one?'

'In outline. And I've offered him the Agency's co-operation in making sure his account sticks.'

'You're going to help Nixon peddle a lie?'

'No. That's the beautiful thing. We're going to tell the truth – or most of it. You see, the test was a success, but Dickie is too paranoid and the idiots in Defense too busy running for cover to see the bigger picture.' He laughed. 'You see, the fact is we really *are* ahead of the Japanese.'

'You'll have to run that one by me again.'

Jeb shook his head. 'I have to tell you, it puzzles me that I'm the only one seems to have seen this, yet when I explain it, everyone says I'm right.'

I found out then why Jeb Lyman was a Deputy Director of the FBI.

He said, 'What blinds people, Harry, is that they keep looking at the bomb itself – as if that's all there is. And on that score the Japanese have us beat. They did a nice clean test, while we blew the hell out of a patch of desert, destroyed a billion dollars-worth of installations and killed a bunch of people.'

'So I heard.'

'As you say. But even then, the disaster isn't as big as everyone makes out, once you see through the chaos. What people forget is that the damn thing went Bang! It worked! We demonstrated that we could produce weapons-grade uranium in large enough quantities and bring it together to create a critical mass and cause an explosion – and that fact isn't lost on the Japanese, who, you can be sure, have their sources. The disaster at Arroyo Seco was caused by second-order events: problems with the equipment or the procedures for setting up and triggering the bomb. They don't know yet what those problems were, but they're getting there. It may amount to nothing more than a fifty-cent electrical switch, who knows? Whatever the explanation, it's fixable in a few months, tops. We have another test site at Los Alamos in New Mexico.'

'OK, let's say you're right. That still leaves America behind Japan,' I pointed out.

'*If* you think only about the bomb itself. But that's the mistake. The bomb is only one part of a two-part system. The other is the means of delivering it to the target. And that's where we have the Japanese licked.'

'I don't see.'

'No, guess not. You've heard of the rocket program?'

'I've seen the press releases. There's a site someplace in Florida.'

'Cape Canaveral.'

'I understood it was for a moon-landing program.' I'm not sure I ever believed this.

'In twenty years, maybe. Its main purpose is as a long-range delivery vehicle for the uranium bomb, and according to the latest reports it's ready to go. If the President wants to, he can hit the Japanese home islands.'

'Once he has a working bomb – all right, in a few months. Meantime what are the Japanese doing?'

'Panicking. The problem is that they're victims of their obsession with China, where they can build landing strips close to the forward lines of their armies. The result is their research effort has been on developing short and medium range bombers to destroy cities within a few hundred miles' range. At a stretch, they could mount a plane on a carrier and bomb Pearl Harbor maybe, but that's it. They've never needed a rocket program and they don't have one worth spit. Opinions differ between two and five years to get where we are today – two years, in my view, but it scarcely matters. The crucial point is that, *as a result of the success at Arroyo Seco*, we are on the brink of a complete nuclear weapons delivery system. And that is what Dickie has to boast about!'

'Which leaves Maria and me where, exactly?'

29

I was given a car and a driver and taken to my apartment.

'Maria will be there,' Jeb said.

As he promised, his story about the 'success' of the test of the uranium bomb at Arroyo Seco made sense, and I could see it might earn a measure of gratitude and co-operation from Nixon, assuming these were things of which he was capable. Even so, the Secretary of Defense owed me nothing and I could imagine him puzzling over Jeb's interest in saving my life. Friendship seemed a frankly inadequate explanation.

'I offered him two things by way of a trade,' Jeb said. 'I told him you'd write a puff piece for the international press as a scoop from an eye-witness at Arroyo Seco. If you accept what I just told you about the test result and the advances we've made in rocketry, that shouldn't be too difficult.'

'Nixon could give the same story to any other journalist.'

'And I gave him a guarantee that you'd keep quiet about – the other matter.'

The 'other matter'. The thing we do not talk about because we dare not think about our complicity even if it is merely silence. The atrocities committed by Vipic against God alone knew how many blacks in the name of research into the effects of radiation on human beings. Other than those directly involved, only Maria, Charlie Joe and I were witnesses. From Nixon's point of view there was another solution to that problem.

I said, 'He'd take my word for it? That doesn't sound like the man I know.'

'I agree he isn't the most trusting type, but I told a white lie. I said you'd written the story up and distributed copies for publication in case you didn't regularly report to your office; and that no amount of torture could guarantee we had all the names out of you.'

'He believed you?'

'Wrong question – who cares what he believes? It doesn't matter. He'd never know if he was safe, and removing that uncertainty has a value. To be honest, Dickie could survive this scandal; your story is uncorroborated and people have suspected worse things about him. On the other hand, the price of silence is a small one: your life. One dead DSD agent just isn't that important. So the end result is he bought the deal. You get to go home to Maria.'

I knew that Maria was safe and I would see her again. It would be easy to say that the morality of suppressing the full story of Arroyo Seco troubled me, but the truth is it did not – at least not for this reason. I could not sacrifice the safety of the living to justice for the dead, and, if I was among those to be saved, it did not seem an unforgiveable act of selfishness. I was not a hero at any time and never sought to be.

Jeb had the tact to leave his office and let me use his phone. I called my apartment and Maria answered. And, for a moment – nothing: a silence too layered with meaning and emotion to be understood.

Then: 'It's me,' I said.

'Harry.'

'Are you all right?'

'Yes.'

'Have you been treated well?'

'Yes.'

I paused a while, then added, 'I love you.'

'I know,' she said. But it sounded as if she didn't.

In my experience people who meet every day can find in the passage of that day enough to talk about for hours.

People who have not seen each other for forty years will dispose of decades of their life-story in fifteen minutes. The short time that Maria and I had been apart seemed like a sundering of lives and – for now at least – there was nothing to be said about the interval when we had been apart because it was incommunicable.

We exchanged a few more words to no great effect, and then I accepted Jeb's proffered lift to the apartment, wondering who I was going to find there. Maria met me at the door. She was wearing something she rarely wore: one of the colorful dresses sold in Mexican stores, the kind women buy that are flaunted at home in the glamour of a full-length cheval glass in a bedroom filled with the other small illusions of our lives, but never in the real world because no occasion can capture the magic of imagination. She was barefoot and had braided her hair and did not look like a 'Privileged Hispanic'. I could smell refried beans and chicken cooked in a certain way, and see a bottle of wine on a table and hear guitar music on the radio. I could smell her scent and brush the dry texture of her lips. I could feel the softening flesh of a middle-aged woman holding me with tenderness.

Was this enough to save us?

We made love but, for now, said nothing about the things that had happened to two other people.

Next day I went to the office and put through a call to Manchester. The people there wanted to know what the hell had been going on; why I hadn't been filing reports and was incommunicado with no explanation. They calmed down when I told them I was going to wire an eyewitness report of the testing of a uranium bomb: a test that was both disastrous and successful; and that with it they would get an opinion piece on Japanese-American relations.

I spent two days keeping my promise, which involved

more time clearing my script through the local censors than actually writing it. As a badge of honor my work was even syndicated in the American newspapers; I was, after all, the only man who'd been on the spot. I fought off all enquiries as to how this had come about.

Meantime two G-men worked shifts outside my apartment in case the DSD decided to ignore Nixon, and Maria and I tried tentatively to explore what had happened to us.

Apart from the glorification of American military power after the recent bomb test, two stories dominated what remained of October. The first was the climax of an action by the army against militia groups in the Northwest states. The particular emphasis was on the penetration of these organizations by GeStaPo agents, and the message was unsubtle: 'We know what you are doing and you can't make a move without our catching you.' It didn't interest me except that Alek Hidell, alias Charlie Joe Svensen, had recently spent time with the militiamen and got out before the crackdown. I assumed it was coincidence.

The second story was political gossip. Mostly it did the rounds of diplomatic parties and the salons of Republican, Democratic and NSDAP grandees, but different coded versions appeared in newspapers controlled by the Kennedy and Nixon factions.

In the past, it had been forbidden to speculate about the President's retirement, but recently it had been made generally known in a low-key way that, after thirty-two years in power, Big A would not stand in the 1964 election. Admittedly he'd be seventy-five years old, but age doesn't usually stop dictators from carrying on. The best-informed guess – the one that most of us in the foreign press corps subscribed to – was that the Old Man had grown senile but was still fronting the Administration because the Vice President, Joe Kennedy Senior, had been laid low by a stroke, and neither Nixon nor Joe Junior yet felt in a position to make his move.

That autumn's speculation and rumor came directly out of the advertised success of the uranium bomb test. It gave Nixon a platform to claim that the defense of the country was safe in his hands and, more specifically, that the new wonder weapon would result in final victory in the South-American wars.

'Which is bullshit,' Jeb Lyman said when we next lunched together. 'We developed the bomb because we knew the Japs were developing one. And the Japs developed theirs because they knew we were developing ours. If you want an example of pure insanity you need look no further. As for using it in Brazil or Venezuela, you can forget it, because we're fighting a guerrilla war against hundreds of local bands, all of them on the move. You may as well bomb fog. Dickie knows that as well as anyone else.'

'So why did you feed him the line that the test at Arroyo Seco was a success? You must have known it would boost his standing.'

'His people would have worked it out sooner or later. It seemed wiser to get in first and gain the credit.'

'How are the Kennedys taking it?'

'Which one? The father no longer counts. They say Joe Junior is philosophical. JFK is taking his lead from Bobby. And Bobby is incandescent!' Jeb snorted into his glass of milk.

'I don't know why you're laughing. I thought you were on the side of the Kennedys?'

Jeb put down his glass and gave me the blue-eyed gaze of the man who knows that Jesus is his savior. He said, 'You're mistaken, Harry. My position is four square with that of the Agency. And the Agency's position is to defend American Values and whoever supports them.'

'You mean whoever J. Edgar Hoover supports. And who is that?'

'You tell me.'

But he and I both knew that Hoover was putting his weight behind Richard Nixon. My mission to Arroyo Seco had been to gain something he could use as leverage with his favored candidate. But why me instead of the Agency's own people? That had always been a puzzle and I'd never accepted Jeb's explanation that it was to shelter the Agency from Nixon in the event its spy was caught. Tricky Dicky was too suspicious to fall for such a ploy even if the Kennedys weren't. Now the answer came to me.

Joe Kennedy Junior was Attorney General and Hoover's nominal superior. Given that Edgar intended to betray him by supporting his enemy, he wanted as far as possible to prevent any leak to the Kennedy camp. I was still the deniable cut-out. The patsy if it all went wrong.

So we went into November with weather in the low fifties and pleasant enough for walking. Between straight news stories mostly tailored from the daily White House press briefings, I produced general articles for the weekend editions in which I tried to convey something of life in Big A's America, and opinion pieces based on scuttlebutt from various social and diplomatic receptions and the occasional guarded conversation with artists and intellectuals.

It was research for the general articles that in the early days took me around the country, mostly by train. I went to the industrial cities where, even after nearly thirty years, workers still credited the President with the economic recovery after the Great Depression and acquiesced in the smashing of the labor unions and the poor factory conditions. In the farming states, I visited small towns with little more than a grain silo and a general store, and saw how, to affirm their allegiance to the spirit that had made America great, many women had abandoned makeup and taken to wearing bonnets and long prairie dresses like their ancestors who had settled these territories in the last century.

I learned from chatting at lunch counters and visiting homes and rural Baptist churches that, in the fifties, sparked by the losses in the War, a hellfire revival had swept through the Plains, led by women and appealing to their sisters who found themselves widowed and in poverty with their children and wanted an explanation why this should be so. They were polite and modest and angry. Their culture told them that they got what they worked for. How could it be that they had worked for this?

The preachers told them to pray and to have faith in the goodness of the Almighty and His chosen instrument, the American Values movement. Those who did not and voiced their opinions disappeared into remote camps and lost their kids. But, frankly, they were few, for how was it possible for good folks not to believe in American Values?

In my newspaper articles I insisted on this: that most of the American people were trying to act with decency and goodwill. There lay the pity.

It was general research for a political piece that took me to a black-tie reception at the Cuban embassy for a festival that was celebrated there and nowhere else. Cuba was one of the few Latin-American states with which the U.S. was on good terms, because its dictator, Fulgencio Batista, was fighting a communist insurgency and Big A was supporting him. The embassy was in a ponderous building of white stone at 16th Street Northwest in the Adams Morgan neighborhood, a modest section of the city mostly settled by Hispanics and heavily policed by the GeStaPo.

Maria wasn't with me; even in better times she never came to these events. She found the other women over-groomed, vacuous and cunning, and the men smooth and deceitful. They found her lacking in sophistication and style and uncomfortably earnest when she talked about poor people. This evening she was working a late shift at the Freedmen's. I suppose we were each trying to rebuild the life we used to have and find our way back to whatever we had been to each other.

The Cubans weren't important and their receptions were mainly occasions for single men with dubious girlfriends to get loaded on excellent rum. I recognized Bob Hardacre, the head of the British consular section, whose wife didn't conform to Maria's stereotype but was a pleasant woman with a Home Counties suburban manner and an interest in children and tennis. Tonight she was at home babysitting and watching television. Seeing a friendly face he came over to me.

'You hoping to pick up a story?'

'My wife is working this evening – a nurse.' Maria wasn't my wife but usually the explanation wasn't worth the effort. 'And you?'

'Everyone above my pay grade is sick, but I'm told I'm not.'

'Do we have any interest in Cuba that I don't know of?'

'Not that I heard. The place is strictly the Americans' affair. That said, Batista is our kind of dictator. If the communist fellow – Castro? – overthrew him, we'd probably be a little miffed. Washington, on the other hand, would have apoplexy. They might be tempted to give their new uranium bomb an outing – much good it would do them in my opinion.'

We changed subject.

I said, 'I'm thinking of returning to the UK. I was wondering about the status of my wife.'

'From that, I take it she isn't British. American?'

'Mexican – Privileged Hispanic.'

'Oh, one of those. Got a piccy?'

I reached into my wallet and produced the shot used for her papers. Bob studied it before handing it back.

'She's a little – what's the word? – *tanned* for someone

with however many generations of European blood a Privy is supposed to have. You don't mind my saying so, do you?'

'No.'

'It isn't that we have a color bar or anything of that sort.'

'I don't suppose so.'

'It's just that we suspect that one of these days the Yanks are going to give their Hispanics a good spring-cleaning, and HMG doesn't want boatloads of the beggars tipping up on our shores and pushing up the unemployment figures; so they've placed a block now, while the weather's fine.'

'And Privileged Hispanics?'

'Dear boy, you don't think that wheeze fools anybody, do you? It just suits the Americans to pretend to believe in all those "Certificates of Racial Purity" and whatnot until the GeStaPo can give them a good seeing-to. The only thing saving Hispanics – Privileged or otherwise – is the labor shortage while the war lasts. Good luck to 'em, I say. But don't expect any help from HMG. Sorry if it's not the answer you were looking for. I say, is that Jack Kennedy just come in?'

I turned and saw a handsome man with a slim, elegant wife; both of them well-known from the celebrity section of the local press. I'd interviewed JFK once and he came over as the liberal face of the regime.

Bob said, 'I wouldn't have thought this was his sort of "do", but I suppose it'll help his big brother's chances of the succession if he hobnobs with scribblers and diplomatic riffraff. Nixon wisely stays away. He looks too much like Dracula Prince of Darkness to make a good impression.'

The news about Maria's status in the event we married only confirmed what I feared. British disapproval of American policy had always been tinged with a degree of pragmatic hypocrisy and I wasn't surprised that they wouldn't take in the people Big A persecuted, even if married to a British citizen. Bob Hardacre and I had nothing else to say to each other, and I'd just noticed that Jeb Lyman was here and chatting with JFK. It seemed to be a serious conversation because they left the room and returned five minutes later. I helped myself to another rum cocktail and waited until they were finished.

'You still talk to the Kennedys?' I said when Jeb came over to me.

'Whatever Edgar may be planning, he approves of our talking to everyone. Unlike Joe Junior, who hangs around the Hoover Building, I don't get much chance to speak with Jack. And, to be frank, it's taken my promotion to make me worth his notice.'

'What were you discussing?'

'Smalltalk. Dallas – American Patriots Day. It may look like overkill if the whole Kennedy clan turns out and on the other side there's only Dick Nixon on his lonesome. Jack isn't sure he'll go. How do you think the international press will read it if he doesn't show?'

'JFK isn't the candidate. I don't think they'll care.'

'Some people think he would make a better president than Joe Junior. Rumors are he'd make a real effort to negotiate an end to the war and soften some of the rough edges of American Values. What do you think?'

I looked across to the man. A six-piece band had set up on a small stage at one end of the room and a handsome mulatto was crooning *Bésame mucho*. Kennedy, with his easy sense of style, took hold of his wife; and the rest of the guests stood back while they danced a bolero with romantic closeness, then applauded.

I turned to Jeb and said, 'How many politicians could get away with that? In answer to your question, it depends what the country wants and what it's prepared to sacrifice. The war is unwinnable by either side. JFK has the glamour to wind it down without too much loss of face and he could clean up America's international image – which, God knows, it could do with.'

'Fix the roads and bridges, huh?' Jeb was referring to the grim shabbiness one saw everywhere: the result of a policy that tried to combine decades of warfare with low taxes.

'Fix the roads and bridges. End the torture and disappearances.'

'Roads would be a good start.'

'Sure.'

While we were speaking, the Kennedys had made their presence felt and then abruptly left. The band had shifted to mood music.

'I can never leave America,' I said for no reason except that it occurred to me that Jeb really was my friend; and who else could I tell? 'Not if I want to take Maria with me. Not if I don't want to live in – Bolivia?' I waited. 'Nothing to say?'

'I would have told you that if you'd asked me. I can always find you a job.'

For a minute or two we didn't speak but cast our eyes around the uninteresting crowd in the room. Then Jeb said, 'You should join the press pack for American Patriots Day.'

'Go to Dallas? Why? American Patriots Day is a strictly American event: a chance for the Party blowhards to sleep with whores and talk the same BS as every previous year. Foreign correspondents stay away, and not because no one wants them there. Why should I go?'

'Because I'm trying to help you.'

'Really? I'm going to get a scoop that no one has the slightest notion about?'

'Uh huh.'

'Like what?'

'This isn't the place.' Jeb turned and headed for one of

the doors, leaving me to follow. We exited the reception room by a corridor with Jeb opening each door and apologizing to the occupants. Finally he found one that led into a service area. It wasn't empty but the staff were busy carrying trays of canapés and replacement ashtrays and spared us no more than a glance.

'So what is this about?' I asked.

And Jeb told me.

He said, 'Whatever you may think of it, American Patriots Day is important to the President. Dallas is where everything really got started for him. This year things are different. We've never had an event where Big A's retirement is on everyone's agenda.'

'He's going to make an announcement?'

'Yes.'

'And?'

'Richard Nixon is going to be the next President of the United States.'

I let out a breath. So that's how it was. And – what do you know? – I'd predicted it. Tricky Dicky for Prez! Huzzah!

I said, 'That's why you were talking to Jack Kennedy.'

30

I applied for a pass to attend American Patriots Day as part of the press contingent. It came back the same afternoon without any questions, even though I was the first foreign correspondent to attend the event as far as I knew. I added my photographer, Dave Kowalczyk, who had covered the Arc of Hope terrorist story, and he too was approved. There would be plenty of syndicated pictures from the local agencies, but if the occasion was going to be the momentous event Jeb had promised, I wanted my own shots to seal the scoop.

While I was at this I booked transport and a hotel. Unsurprisingly the Adolphus and all the other classy places in Dallas were full, though I'd been told the President would be staying at the Hotel Texas in Fort Worth. I wanted a room with access to international phone lines, for which the hotel required a GeStaPo permit, and the nearest I could find was in Grapevine. What I couldn't do was give any advance notice to Manchester that a scoop was on the way without betraying Jeb's confidence and landing me in a heap of trouble.

Like the rest of the media I'd been given the President's itinerary. Most of it was either off limits or uninteresting. I didn't want to listen to him open a school of aerospace medicine in San Antonio or give a speech at the Rice Hotel in Houston to honor some Congressman I never heard of. The tip from Jeb was for a luncheon the following day at the Texas Trade Mart when he was going to deliver his bombshell.

So while Big A carried out what looked like a punishing schedule, I took the train to Dallas since, like most people, my status didn't run to a seat on a plane. The journey wasn't one I looked forward to with any relish. It meant sweating in a hot carriage filled with teenage soldiers, wives, girlfriends and traveling salesmen: the same crowd I'd seen on the journey to Chicago in what seemed like another life: an image Americans would retain to old age as a memory of the war years along with the music of Elvis Presley, who had served in Nicaragua and was a patriotic icon. I distracted myself by working on an article about American art during the Depression, one that I took with me from hotel to hotel whenever I traveled, and wrote at leisure because I didn't expect it to be published. That and sleep, and dreaming to the harmonica music soldiers played to while away their boredom, and the crooning of mothers to tired children. Dave on the other hand was one of those people who seem able to sit and wait for days without doing anything. I can't speculate what was going through his mind. He denied anything was.

Dallas was hung with flags, and every billboard commemorated the 40th Anniversary of the events of 1923 with images of square-jawed figures bearing arms and striding to the Future, the kind authoritarian movements seem to like. Four decades later, a failed coup had become a milestone in the Progress of Humanity instead of a shabby street fight with a few guns thrown in and a handful of dead thugs who became martyrs. We had problems finding a local train. The platforms were jammed with Hispanics: whole families, including kids, carrying bedrolls and cooking pots. The single men were mostly indentured factory hands, chained-up in a filthy mess of food scraps and latrine buckets in one of the migrant labor pens found at every large station. The area was surrounded by a cordon of old men and college kids from the National Guard, and the usual welcoming-party of G-men mingled in the crowd checking papers while looking bored and stressed. When we finally found a cab and got underway, I noticed the buses too seemed packed with Mexicans. I asked the driver, a Texas good ol' boy with a lot of drinking muscle, about them.

'Your question shows you ain't from here,' he said. 'Nice accent, though.'

'So what's the answer?'

'Same thing this time ever' year. The National Guard clear the whole downtown area of Spics and all along the route to Love Field, and truck 'em out to camps. Same in Fort Worth near the President's hotel. They spend a coupla nights in tents and then they truck 'em back. Don't ask me why they don't just resettle 'em once and for all in Brazil or wherever, like they done with the niggers. I don't see no difference between 'em.'

I asked Dave to take some shots, but I didn't expect to be able to use them.

'I saw that,' said the cabbie, 'but I go blind for a five spot.'

I gave him a dollar.

Though I used Dave Kowalczyk as my photographer when needed, it was just business and we weren't friends. That night we ate dinner in a Greek restaurant and found we had nothing to talk about, so we called it early and retired to our rooms. I tried to put a long-distance call through to Maria but the operator told me there was a backlog and she would call me back when she could give me a line. She never did, and I spent the evening writing about the painter, Grant Wood.

This was on Thursday.

The following day the President was to deliver a breakfast speech to the Chamber of Commerce at his hotel in Fort Worth. I'd been given an advance copy and it was about the happier time that was to come now that the wars in Brazil and Venezuela were close to being won and the insurgencies in Mexico and Central America were under control – which was much the same story as for the previous two decades. After breakfast, he was to board Air Force One at Carswell Air Force Base for the short hop to Love Field. My plan was to be there when he arrived, which was fixed for eleven, and then join the press bus in the motorcade to the downtown area.

Despite talk over the years about upgrading its capacity for passenger traffic, Love Field, like most airfields of the South, was mainly used by the military as a jumping off point for Mexico. A small, single story terminal was reserved for civilians. Our route there wasn't the one the President would take into the city, so Dave and I missed the crowds reported on the radio, and arrived not long after ten. We used the time to clear security, find the press bus for later, and shake hands with the journalists from the *Dallas Morning News* and *Times Herald* who were wondering what the hell I was doing there. A platoon of Guardsmen duly showed up and led us out onto the tarmac to the area allocated for us to take our pictures without getting in the way of the TV crews. All of this was as expected.

In the event the President was late at close to 11.40. Then two planes came flying in: converted twin-engined Boeings with the noses painted red and the presidential insignia on the fuselage. The second would normally carry the Vice President but Joe Senior was too sick to travel much after his stroke and today it carried two of his sons, though we didn't yet know which ones. Air Force One rolled to its spot close by us and powered down.

All the while we waited in the tension between anticipation and boredom.

Big A had never married. There was talk of a mistress but she never appeared in public and didn't have a name. Part of the old man's mystique was that he was not as others: that he lived an ascetic life wholly dedicated to his people, and that, if they suffered, he suffered more because it was he who had to bear the responsibility for the hard decisions such as sending American boys to war. In recent times, he had become more reclusive. Because of the burdens of his office, they said.

It was impossible to live in America for a period of years as I had without being affected by this carefully crafted image. Unless I took care to examine my own attitudes, I found myself adopting the same justification that others used to explain away the sins they did not want to acknowledge. The crimes of the regime could not be laid at the door of the President. Rather they were committed by his henchmen, who kept him in the dark while claiming to carry out his orders. It was a fiction that allowed people to balance loyalty with a degree of dissent, and if they recognized their own dishonesty they kept it to themselves.

And now here he was in the open doorway of the plane, wearing a pale grey suit; and his trademark toothbrush moustache and the lock of hair hanging over his forehead were a youthful black, though I guessed they were dyed. He took a step forward so he could be seen clearly, and waved to the National Guardsmen, Secret Service agents and media types, though the TV news reports would patch in some stock footage that wouldn't show how thin the reception committee was. Waving done with, he posed in his characteristic way with his hands resting in front of him, one lying flat over the other, an image of quiet and noble authority. I thought I detected a slight Parkinson's tremble, but may have been projecting the rumors of his growing senility. Then the photo opportunity was over and he was whisked to his car, a blue Lincoln convertible.

In contrast with this staged scene, Air Force Two decanted its passengers like fractious businessmen competing for the same deal. They ignored the press except once in a while somebody noticed he was being filmed, straightened himself, and tried out a hokey smile. I spotted Jeb Lyman, who was expected, and JFK, who wasn't since Jeb had said he was thinking of staying in Washington. Instead, in deference to Nixon, the Kennedys had left Bobby behind so as not to appear to crowd him. Joe Junior and Nixon were walking together with stiff formality – and not thinking warm thoughts, I fancied. Their entourages of well-built men in suits brought up the rear.

'No Hoover,' said Dave as we headed for the bus.

'You thought he'd be here?'

'He always is – or used to be. They even named a place in town after him. He was an Old Fighter and this is the 40th anniversary after all. Don't you know nothing?'

'Old Fighter' was the term used for Big A's comrades of 1923, most of them long dead. Back then, Hoover must have been in his late twenties, still with his bones to make. Against the odds, he had seen there was something in the nascent American Values movement, which goes some way to explaining why he was head of the GeStaPo.

'I guess he's sick,' Dave said, though there had been no rumors in a business full of rumors.

'You think so?' I wasn't so sure. If Jeb was right, Hoover was about to pull off the biggest coup of his career and fix the succession for Nixon. It seemed inconceivable he would miss Big A's announcement, scheduled in the next couple of hours.

But maybe he'd come on ahead in order to shake up the Dallas field office.

Or maybe he had other plans I didn't know of.

I wasn't alone in being puzzled. Hoover's absence that day became one of the loose ends that people would theorize about in the years ahead when they tried to make sense of what was about to happen.

The presidential motorcade comprised a white Mercury mostly filled with chiefs from the local cops, the

President's Lincoln with a motorcycle escort, and a slew of other cars, mainly Chevy Impalas, with the Secret Service back-up, the Mayor and other local bigwigs. The press bus followed last of all, after the TV crews and a couple of carloads of Congressmen and other VIPs. I mention this order because the subject has been gone over in detail in various books to see whether it had any significance. As far as I know, it didn't except that for most of the time the Lincoln was blocked from my view or that of anyone in the press bus by the vehicles ahead of us, and at the critical moment we saw nothing at all.

The other thing that has exercised both serious analysis and wild speculation is the seating arrangement in the President's car. There were three banks of seats. The front was occupied by the driver, an agent called Greer, and next to him Roy Kellerman, the Assistant Special Agent-in Charge. Behind them, on the pull-down seats were Nixon and Kennedy, both facing towards the front. Lastly, on the honor seats, sat the President and Governor Connally of Texas.

After the event, some said that Jeb Lyman, as a Deputy Director, should have been in the Kellerman spot instead of schmoozing with Mrs Connally in the Mayor's car, and on this basis, they claim he had wind of things. Others allege that the seating order was not that originally planned and that Nixon, not Connally, should have been placed next to the President as heir apparent, but the arrangement was changed. Who made the change depends upon which conspiracy theory you support. The significance of the seating plan is that – if it was changed – then it may have led to confusion and the eventual outcome may not have been what was intended.

As far as I was concerned, everything looked fine.

On a clear road, Love Field is no more than forty-five minutes from the Texas Trade Mart, even allowing a slowish speed to give the crowds their money's worth and two halts to hand out donations to nuns. I wasn't alert to every turn of the route because, frankly, it wasn't of interest: just a clear Texas sky and a mass of people who gave every sign of loving their President. I was tired from early rising and dozed and might have grabbed a few winks if it hadn't been for the cheering outside and the arguments inside about why the Dodgers had creamed the Yankees in the World Series, and whether Mickey Mantle should hang up his bat.

At last Dave nudged me. 'We're almost there. This is Main Street.'

I looked out on the same old big city sight. Office buildings. More crowds. More flags and a billboard with a picture of Big A in a Stetson on a rearing horse, and below it an honor-guard of American Youth and a kids' band playing *Texas, Our Texas*. Dave took some pictures, saw that I noticed, and shrugged.

'It makes you proud,' I said.

He grinned.

So we drove down Main Street; a fantasy Germanic castle in red sandstone on our left. 'The Old Court House,' said Dave, as if I cared. Another band outside: veterans this time, in uniforms with caps and medals on show, and in front of them a bunch in wheelchairs with empty sleeves or pant legs folded, pressed and neatly stitched where limbs should be, and next to them a women's choir, dressed in blouses and Western hats and skirts, holding up banners in favor of Family, Home and Moral Decency and singing the line '*Texas, dear Texas! From tyrant grip now free*' with no sense of irony.

I said, 'Wake me up when we get there.'

On to a junction, where Main Street continued but there was no through road because of the railroad or the freeway or something, and so the circus parade had to take a right into Houston Street at a junction with a wide area of grass and trees bisected by Main Street. This was Hoover Plaza, Dave told me. Named after the Old Fighter himself by a grateful President. Because of the turn, it was now on our left and, as we approached the next corner into Elm Street, two stand-alone buildings faced us on the further side of the junction. The nearer one was the Texas Medical Supply Warehouse, but I learned this only later because there was no sign I could see and, in any case, I had no reason to pay attention. It was just a square block in red brick or stone with a yellow Hertz board on the roof and a clock saying it was approaching 12.30.

There is a painting – by one of the Breughels, I think – at the Musée des Beaux Arts in Paris. It shows Icarus as a small figure falling out of the sky on his melting waxen wings. In the foreground a sailing ship plies its trade and a peasant ploughs his field, and no one anticipates the event or pays it attention or is in a position to describe accurately what happened. Of course, on this day in Dallas plenty of people were looking at the presidential motorcade, but whether they were seeing is a different matter, and what they were prepared for was a triumphal parade and not what actually happened. The proof is I was there and saw nothing. And the thousands of people for the most part also saw nothing because their view was blocked by the people in front, or because they were talking to their neighbor or stooping to pick up a child or lighting a cigarette or…. Most were simply not close to the President's car. It had already passed them and they were looking at the Mayor or the VIPs, or some poor souls were peering at the press bus and wondering if we were important.

Afterwards people made a lot of claims. Journalists made a lot of claims. But as far as I can recall we were still making the turn from Main into Houston as the lead car and the Lincoln were at the junction with Elm and opposite the Texas Medical Supply Warehouse. Yet I may be mistaken because we are talking of a single instant in a moving series of instants that did not cease because one of them proved to be of historical significance. For certain, the key footage of the event didn't come from the TV camera crews, who at best were filming the scene from the rear, but from some guy named Zapruder who owned a rinky-dink home movie camera. And my viewpoint was behind even the TV cars.

All I can say is what I heard. Three shots.

Other people said there were more.

31

Everyone on board the bus heard the shots and we all knew them for what they were because men of our age had fought in wars and were not prone to panic. After the weary cries of 'Goddamn!' and 'Fuck!', the thought going through everyone's mind was: 'Do I stay on the bus or get off? Where is the story happening?' Call it wrong and you might miss the biggest scoop of your career. Yet it wasn't clear what the story was. To me it seemed probable that someone had fired at the President. But I was English and this was Texas, where kids rob gas stations, Bubba loads his semi-automatic and goes on a spree, and National Guardsmen are he-men who get antsy with their weapons. Statistically, an attempt on the President's life was the least likely explanation.

The bus had come to a halt. Someone said in a calm voice, 'Jeff, go see what'n hell's happening.'

A fat guy in shirt sleeves, suspenders and a loud silk tie laughed and said, 'I guess some cracker has had hisself a bellyful and is celebrating.'

'More likely one of those morons in uniform has dropped his fucking carbine.'

But outside the window an incoherent roar of voices reminded me of a storm blowing through trees, and the crowd, like a shoal of fish, began to move. I told Dave, 'Stay here and take what pictures you can. I'm going to find out what's going on' – and slipped off the bus.

Immediately I was caught up in the mill of people. Groups of them were taking the lead from whoever looked like he knew what he was doing, but since he didn't, they were moving in all directions, except that the National Guard were pushing back anyone who tried to cross the roadway though there was no obvious reason to do this and it would make sense to let people escape the area of danger.

There was no going back to the bus. After the brief halt, the motorcade had set off again and was picking up speed. My guess was the President's driver had put his foot down in order to get Big A away. Whatever the case, I couldn't see the Lincoln and had no exact notion of what had happened or if anyone had been hurt.

Pressed back by the guardsmen, most of the spectators were fleeing towards the County Records and the Criminal Court Buildings which overlooked the plaza. I grabbed a stocky type who seemed to have kept his nerve and asked, 'What's happened?' He shook me off and pointed vaguely at the junction of Elm and Houston. 'Some sonofabitch has took a shot at the President.'

'Did it hit him?'

'Who knows? He didn't exactly stick around.'

I let the man go and headed for the junction, thinking the President's car had to be in Elm Street when the shots were fired, which made it the likeliest spot for witnesses. Several times I heard people in high emotion say, 'They've killed the President!' but when I stopped them no one could confirm the fact. I still wasn't convinced it was so. Hitting a moving target, even one in a slow vehicle, is tricky, and I didn't rate the chance of success as better than fifty per cent. This wasn't an assassination story.

Not yet.

I shouted out so anyone near could hear: 'Who knows where the shot came from?'

Several people pointed vaguely. Other's shouted, 'There! There!' but I could make no sense of where was meant. A neat young woman in a pretty dress and a hat, who looked as if she wanted to show off her figure to the President, spotted my badge.

'Are you a journalist?'

'I am, ma'am.'

322

She smiled as though I was going to take her picture and make her famous, then indicated a spot high on the Texas Medical Supply Warehouse and said, 'It was from there. That window there, just below the top floor. I could see a rifle sticking out and a colored man behind it.'

Disturbed pigeons were circling overhead in a glitteringly clear sky. I looked at the window and it was open but nothing else. I doubted the young woman saw 'a colored man' or anyone beyond a vague shape. She spelled out her name but I straightaway forgot it. I headed in the direction she pointed. I saw some police who seemed to be going the same way.

I didn't make the connection between Alek Hidell, alias Charlie Joe Svensen, and the Texas Medical Supply Warehouse. I knew he had a job shifting boxes at some place in the city, but though the name had been mentioned it held no significance and I'd never seen the building before.

Three or four minutes had gone by since the shots. The snatches of voices overheard in the hubbub indicated a growing certainty that someone had been hit; some of those speaking had to be actual witnesses. Still it wasn't clear who the target was. Most people said the President, but that may have been supposition not fact. I also heard Kennedy and Nixon. No one knew if they were talking about a wound or a fatality.

The authorities weren't prepared for this. Ordinary traffic was still passing along Elm Street. The National Guard were holding back people for no reason except something to do. The crowd was growing quieter as it became clear there were no more shots. A few people were singing hymns and waving American Values placards and the national flag.

I saw Charlie Joe.

He was coming out of the front door of the warehouse,

walking faster than normal pace but not running. He wore a shirt and slacks: stuff from Kmart that a man in a low-paying job might wear. I called out to him, but he couldn't hear me over the general noise, and my attempt to cross Elm Street was blocked by the guardsmen and the traffic. He was heading away from the scene as if none of it concerned him. And that was the point of interest.

Yet still the insistent reporter's question: *Where was the story?* I could feel it slipping away from me. More and more it seemed likely the President or someone else in his entourage had been shot and any action was at one of the Dallas hospitals or the mortuary. In which case I'd missed the bus in the most literal sense. The only choices open to me were to stick it out in Hoover Plaza in the hope the police were going to catch the shooter and meantime pick up a couple of interviews from the spectators; alternatively to follow Charlie Joe Svensen on a hunch.

What decided me was that, underlying the tears and the shouting, were two basic reactions. People either decided the situation was too dangerous and got away as quickly as they could; or they took a view it was safe and stayed around to see what was happening and have something to tell their grandchildren. Except Charlie Joe did neither of these things. He didn't look at the disturbance all about him or spare a backward glance at the building from which the shots had most probably come – the place where he'd been only a minute before. Neither did he show any sign of being afraid; he was walking calmly and determinedly and looking ahead without regard for any danger behind him. My memories came back of his violent edginess, which, God knows, I'd witnessed in his willingness to finish off Vipic, and the bloodshed at Bayou Chaud. If there had been a crazed shooter in the Texas Medical Supply Warehouse, Charlie Joe had to be a prime candidate.

But in the time it took me to work this out he was out

of sight somewhere along Elm Street and had maybe turned a corner because I couldn't see him.

Think it through!

What were his options? If he intended to flee immediately, his quickest route was by train out of Union Station, but he wasn't going in that direction. His wife and daughter – though he had two kids by now, I guessed – were at her friend's house in Irving. Would he go there? He'd been willing to abandon them in the past when his moods moved him, and, if he was a would-be assassin trying to escape, he wouldn't get far with his family in tow. Logic said he'd tell himself they were better off without him, and in his self-centered way he'd believe this amounted to taking care of them.

What did that leave? I recalled then that he wasn't carrying a bag or case: no clothes; no toiletries. Not necessary if he had money, but I knew Charlie Joe was thrifty. His third choice was to return to his rooming house for his stuff – assuming he was staying at the same place, which I didn't know.

The problem was I couldn't remember the address. I'd had no reason to.

I set off along Elm in the direction I'd seen him go. I scanned the cross-streets in case he'd taken one but didn't see him. All the while I scoured my memory but the only thing I could come up with was the general area, Oak Cliff.

Incredible though it was, traffic was still flowing, and that gave me a chance because a cab dropped off a fare and I snagged it while the passenger was still sorting change. I told the driver, 'Oak Cliff.'

'Whatever you say.' He let me aboard and pulled away then asked. 'You got any notion what's going on? The radio just cut short the report on the President's visit. They put on *Back to the Bible* – like I want to listen to that shit when I'm working.'

'Some sort of accident, I think.' I didn't want to spook him in case … I had no idea what.

'Where in Oak Cliff?'

'Just take me to the general area. The address'll come to me or I'll recognize it.'

'Whatever you say, it's your money.'

It was a short trip, a matter of minutes before we passed under the freeway and found ourselves in a set of numbered streets, but it wasn't a numbered street I was looking for.

'Give me some names – something "Avenue".'

'You think I'm a map?'

'Cut the jokes.'

'OK – lemme see. North Bishop – North Maddison – North Zang – North Bishop, which I've said – don't get me confused – North Maddison – North Beckley…'

'North Beckley – take me there.'

'Like the man said.'

We made a turn and a minute later the driver said, 'North Beckley. Which way?'

'Go right.' I didn't know, but the street broadened to the left to become wider than I remembered. 'Slow down, I need to look at the houses.'

He slowed and almost immediately the scene looked familiar, though most of the streets hereabout were probably lined with the same kind of low painted frame house with a small front yard covered with lawn and hedging. Then I recognized – or thought I did – a porch under a broad semi-circular arch and a red shingled roof. As sure as I could be, this was the place.

I stopped the cab, paid it off and asked the driver to wait. He said 'Sure', took his money and drove off all the same; probably because he doubted the next fare would cover his waiting time, or he didn't like the English. I went up to the door and rang the bell. A comfortable woman with a round face and short wavy hair answered.

'Excuse me, ma'am. Does Mr. Charlie Joe Svensen live here?'

She looked at me as if I was a doorstep salesman. 'Never heard of him.'

'Alek Hidell?'

'Which is it?'

'Hidell.'

She looked me over cautiously, then said, 'He was here not more than five minutes ago. Breezed in and breezed out in an almighty hurry. He done something?'

'Not that I know of. Which way did he go?'

She pointed left.

'Thank you, ma'am.'

She nodded. 'Nice accent.' She closed the door.

There comes a point of stress when we begin to act reflexively. To speak of our intentions is misleading, though afterwards we may construct a narrative to explain our behavior because we regard ourselves as rational beings. I think that Charlie Joe had reached this point and that, beyond a vague desire to escape, he no longer had a plan after he left the rooming house in North Beckley Avenue. Not least, I suspect a part of him wanted to be caught: not because he felt a sense of guilt but because, of all the dismal versions of the future that were open to him, his arrest and trial offered the most drama, the most glory; and he probably saw himself as a Clarence Darrow figure, his eloquence moving his audience to tears of indignation at the injustices he had suffered.

I headed south along Beckley, checking the side streets as I'd done before. At a junction to my left, I saw ahead of me a man in a beige jacket keeping up a brisk pace I recognized, though at the distance and among the parked cars I couldn't be sure it was Charlie Joe. I broke into a trot, but lost my quarry when he crossed the street and took a right. The street sign told me it was Patton Avenue but it meant nothing and when I turned the corner there was no sign of him.

I halted there: not certain I was following Charlie Joe, or where he was, or what to do. And always the same question: *Is this the story?*

Then there was a series of shots. I couldn't count them but it sounded like a magazine being emptied.

Nothing I could see accounted for the shots but they were close enough to come from one of the streets off Patton. I checked the first I came to and saw a parked prowl car but no sign of a police officer. Half a block away was a taxi and a man I took to be the driver sheltering behind it. Elsewhere people simply stood in shock or crying. I saw no sign of the shooter.

I felt for my own gun, recent events having put me in the habit of carrying, but I didn't draw it because I wanted to avoid making the situation worse, which in most instances is what a gun does. I approached the prowl car and saw a pair of uniformed legs stretched out on the pavement; then a torso, then a whole body, and beside it a man helping himself to the officer's sidearm – in self-defense or to catch the killer, I thought.

A woman shouted, 'He went that way!' and pointed at one of the houses. 'Through the yard – through the yard!' I nodded and followed her direction across a strip of St. Augustine grass, weaving through hedges and picket fencing until I came out on Patton again. I saw a man loping away from me and turning at the end of the block into a road signed Jefferson Avenue. I recognized the beige jacket and was fairly certain it was Charlie Joe. I gave chase.

I reached the junction and scanned a street of low rent businesses serving people on a budget. A salesman was placing price tickets on vehicles in a car lot. A shoe store called Hardy's advertised unmissable bargain loafers and Western boots. Charlie Joe was standing in the doorway of the shoe store, strangely motionless, while police cars howled past, heading for East Tenth Street where the shooting had happened.

Fifty yards on, a cinema occupied the middle of a block. Its vertical neon sign jutted out from a faded stucco façade of a vaguely Spanish style. *Cry of Battle* was showing in a double bill with *War is Hell*. The posters said Audie Murphy, a decorated hero from the fighting in Colombia, was in one of them.

Charlie Joe broke his trance and dashed into the cinema before I could stop him. At least one other person seemed to be taking an interest and I shouted out to call the police. When I reached the small foyer of the Texas Theater there was no one except a woman at the ticket desk and a male concession clerk.

I asked, 'Has someone just bought a ticket? A young guy – early twenties.'

'I didn't see no one,' said the concession clerk.

'I saw him come in,' I said. 'I think he may have shot a cop just a few streets away.'

'There was someone,' said the woman, 'but he didn't buy a ticket. You sure you didn't see him, Butch?'

'I didn't see him.'

They may not have seen him slip into the auditorium but Charlie Joe had to be there. I drew my gun and pushed open the nearest door. The guy I'd seen in the street was on my heels, and I asked him to take a position by one of the emergency exits. He was smart enough to tell Butch the concession clerk to watch the other.

So the three of us entered the auditorium, where a thin audience sat still in darkness, while the only violence played itself out on the screen. My two companions headed for the lights over the side doors. I walked down the left-hand aisle, peering along each row for sight of

Charlie Joe, conscious that, if he had reloaded after shooting dead the police officer, he had little to lose by killing me and making an escape by one of the emergency exits.

But I recognized no one. The flickering images on the screen and the low background lighting made even the sex of the spectators hard to tell, and anyone in the center of a row could slide to the floor and be effectively invisible. Yet he had to be here – he *had* to.

I shouted out, 'Butch, turn up the house lights! I'll cover the door.'

Where were the damned cops?

'I'm on it!'

He passed me as he headed for the switch box for the theatre electrics. I took his place at the exit. I called out, 'Charlie Joe – you here?'

A voice from a spot only a few rows away said quietly, 'Harry? Is that you, Harry? What have you come here for?' The tone was even but it wrapped up an existential puzzlement and sadness that haunt me still. A figure in the shadows rose. The house lights went on. Alex Hidell, alias Charlie Joe Svensen, stood before me, a nice-looking young man in cheap clothes, whose inner darkness would not be suspected from his appearance.

In that instant, I pointed my gun at him, meaning to put an end to this whole pitiful business and gain a measure of justice for the death of Julie and the other innocent blacks.

But beside me a cold steady voice said, 'Drop the gun, you murdering sonofabitch, or I'll blow your goddamn head off.'

32

They say everyone remembers where they were when they heard of Kennedy's assassination. I was in the Texas Theater, a small cinema in Dallas, and a cop was threatening to kill me. In the event, he didn't. Butch, the concession clerk, told him he'd got the wrong man and he believed him. A minute later Alek Hidell was arrested. He smiled as if he was happy, and then or later – I forget which – he said he was innocent: just a patsy.

That's more or less what I recall, but memory is a nuanced thing. We add color and drama. We elide events so that two incidents close together in time become connected. We borrow details told to us by other people and shape things to accord with our prejudices. We create comprehensible stories out of partial facts.

I can tell you a story about the Kennedy assassination. But I can't tell you what happened or why. At least, not for certain.

When the officer threatened to kill me, I dropped my gun and raised my arms.

Butch shouted, 'You've got the wrong guy! It's that one – that one!' – pointing at Charlie Joe, who had turned away and was scuttling along the row of seats. But the place was filling with cops and he could play tag with them only so long before they grabbed him, brought him to the ground and cuffed him. It was when he was dragged to his feet that he gave his eerie smile and – I think – said that he was innocent and a patsy.

All the same we were also cuffed – me, Butch and the third guy – so that when we emerged blinking into the sharp blue daylight at what looked like a cops' convention, the police, mourning one of their own, were prepared to throw in a few more corpses at no extra charge until it was explained that there was only one suspect and the rest of us were witnesses.

We were put in separate cars and driven to the local precinct house. I'd hoped to be taken to the FBI area office in Commerce Street, where I could have played my Deputy Director card. The name Jeb Lyman would mean nothing to the City boys.

I was booked as a material witness, placed in a cell for an hour then taken to an interview room, where two plain-clothes detectives – one big, one small, and both overweight, ugly and dressed in cheap suits – were sitting behind a desk flicking through my wallet and sniffing my gun which had never been fired.

I said, 'Shouldn't you be handing me on to the FBI?'

'Right – like that's going to happen,' said Big, and his companion grinned. I realized then that, whatever Charlie Joe might have done, at this stage my involvement was only in relation to the shooting of the officer in Oak Cliff, which was a matter for the Texas authorities not the Feds. Jeb might not even be informed that I'd been picked up. The Dallas cops could hold me as long as they liked, and might do so rather than release me then try to get me back from Washington.

There was another problem. Charlie Joe had said my name when I confronted him in the cinema. Butch may have been in a position to hear. Maybe he did: maybe he didn't. Either way, Charlie Joe knew I'd been on the point of putting a bullet in him. If Butch didn't name me, it was certain that under interrogation by the GeStaPo Charlie Joe would sooner or later give me up. Once that happened, Jeb wouldn't be able to protect me. He would have too much explaining of his own to do.

I had to get out of this place, and didn't know how.

I stuck to the simplest story, which was true as far as it

went. I hadn't witnessed the shooting of officer Tippit but a woman at the scene had pointed me in the direction of the killer's escape. I'd followed and caught up with Alek Hidell at the Texas Theater. I couldn't swear of my own knowledge that he was the man the police wanted but it seemed likely. The other witnesses ought to be able to confirm this.

The interrogation was a short session. Ten minutes to get my basic story then I was placed in a corridor, sharing a bench with people I didn't know. All of them were innocent and all of them were terrified because innocence didn't matter. There was maybe a dozen of us, and the precinct didn't have resources to process that number of witnesses. It explained why I wasn't asked the question to which I didn't have an answer. When the story of a lifetime was unfolding in downtown Dallas, what was a journalist doing in Oak Cliff?

A woman on the bench looked at me. She said, 'You're the man who chased the murderer.'

'It was you who told me where he'd gone?'

She nodded.

She looked a sympathetic person. I said, 'Could you explain that when they talk to you? I didn't see the shooting. I just chased a guy.'

She thought that over and nodded again. A few minutes later she was called off the bench to the interrogation room. I don't know what she told them.

At the end of another hour a uniformed sergeant, one of the large comfortable types that seem a Texan specialty, came along checking names. When I gave mine, he said, 'Call for you.'

'A call?'

'Uh huh.'

He took me to an office and passed me the phone, then sat at a desk doing nothing much.

A voice said, 'Hi, Harry.'

'Jeb?'

'The same.'

'What's going on? How did you find me?'

'We got a call from the City police.'

'Why would they do that? The murder of a local cop is a local matter.'

'It is. But you aren't. Thank your stars you're a foreign correspondent, which makes anything that happens to you a State Department problem. The protocol is the police inform the FBI, and we inform State.'

'So what happens?'

'They'll release you. They don't need you to make a case against Hidell. Go to your hotel and get out of town first thing tomorrow.'

I checked on the sergeant.

'This is a call from the FBI,' I said.

'I know. You got important friends. A De-pu-ty Di-rec-tor.'

'Can I have some privacy?'

He thought about this, then got to his feet and shuffled out of the room.

I asked Jeb, 'What about Alek Hidell? Do you have him?'

If so, we were in control of what he might say.

'Not yet. The Dallas cops are still holding out that this is a case for the City. The DA is a blowhard and they have an order from a local judge who sees good publicity in a show-trial. I don't have authority to overrule them, and Edgar – who does – isn't here.'

'Where is he?'

'Washington. Sick and not talking to anyone. Look, this isn't the time. Get to your hotel then out of town.'

'Hidell –'

'– is a problem that's going to be solved.'

The police called me a cab and I returned to my hotel. On

334

the way, I tried to make sense of what Jeb had told me. The FBI, the state police and the city cops were all divisions of the General State Police, the internal security empire Hoover had created in the thirties. Jeb had made clear to me that his promotion to Deputy Director covered only the FBI, which was why he couldn't take the Hidell case off the City authorities. Equally it meant that, in Hoover's absence, when it came to a crisis there was no co-ordination on the ground between the various branches of the GeStaPo.

That didn't alter the fact that Jeb was Washington's senior man on the spot. If Hoover's 'sickness' was the political kind, I wondered: had he known that an attempt would be made on the President, and set Jeb up to take the fall?

It was six in the evening by the time I reached my room – five and a half hours since the shooting. I switched on the TV and ran through the channels but the networks and the local stations had all pulled their news programmes 'for technical reasons' and were showing the same Mickey Rooney film of teenage kids dancing in a barn. I picked up the phone and tried the international operator. I was told the service wasn't available. Evidently the situation was fluid, no one was sure who was in control, and there was no agreed story to put out.

There was a rap on the door. Dave Kowalczyk complete with camera, looking tired and smelling of beer.

I asked, 'What do you have?'

He threw the camera onto a chair and stretched out on my bed.

'Bupkis – two rolls with nothing but the rear end of a Lincoln and a bunch of G-men looking like they want to kill someone or throw up.' He glanced at me. 'You know it was Kennedy got killed?'

'Yes.' I'd overheard the police talking about it.

'Nixon was shot, too.'

'Nixon?'

'That's rumor, not fact, but the source is pretty good. They're not saying how serious. In fact, officially they haven't even admitted to Kennedy, but there are too many witnesses and you don't get better from having your brains spread out over the upholstery of a limo.'

'Where was he taken?'

'Parkland Hospital. You can't get near it. There's a National Guard cordon around the place and the Secret Service are thicker than flies on shit. What about you? Did you get a story? There must have been witnesses in Hoover Plaza and I hear they got the assassin.'

'The story…' I thought it over for a moment and shook my head. I came near to getting killed but I didn't have a story – not one I could use. In theory I could make something out of my part in the slaying of Officer Tippit and the arrest of Alek Hidell, but I would run into the same difficulty I'd avoided when questioned by the police: I would have to explain what I was doing in the neighborhood.

However, the lack of a story was the least of my problems; the core of which was Hidell himself. As long as he was alive and talking, people who couldn't give an innocent account of their relationship with him were in danger; and in my case it was particularly acute. Through me, a connection could be made from Hidell to Jeb Lyman by anyone who had Jeb in their sights.

It occurred to me then that it would make sense for Jeb to have me taken out.

But I told myself he was my friend and wouldn't do that.

The international and long distance telephone services were down but the local wasn't. I made a call to check trains to Washington the following day, but it was too late to make a booking. I told Dave he could return with me, or

336

he might care to stay on and grab any shots that came his way in which case I would take anything of interest. He said he would think about it.

I made some more calls from the business cards I'd picked up from the boys on the bus. They were strange conversations, part cold shock at what had happened and part whoop-de-do excitement. The story was still developing; no one knew when or what they would be publishing because no guidelines had come down from the Federal News Bureau, but everyone was collecting material and feeling like real journalists. Because of censorship the notion of a political scoop wasn't really in their book, but they liked the idea of being the first in the know.

Ray Bamburg of the *Dallas Times Herald* thought he had something when he told me, 'They've made an arrest out in Oak Cliff. The name hasn't been released.'

'Alek Hidell,' I said.

'Is that straight? How do you know?'

'FBI source.' I let that sink in then asked, 'Do you know where they'll hold him?'

'The Municipal Building. He's there already.'

'Not the County Jail?'

'Maybe tomorrow. It's a question of space – not for prisoners but for detectives, the DA and the whole circus; more swinging dicks than you'll see in a lifetime. The media are all there so that when the word comes from Washington there'll be the biggest splash since McKinley got his.'

I was asking questions out of habit. There was nothing I could do with the information. Then Ray Bamburg said, 'My guess is they'll put the guy on show tomorrow and tell us who takes the rap: the blacks, the Hispanics, the fairies, or those bearded guys up in the hills, whoever. Maybe all of the above. You going to be there?'

'Could be,' I said. But that wasn't the plan; not if there

was an early train. Were they going to let Charlie Joe speak?

'You should show,' Ray said. 'My cop pal who gave me the tip says this – Hidell? – likes all the attention he's getting. There's every chance he'll be naming names.'

Meanwhile Dave had gone to sleep on my bed and Mickey Rooney had got the girl. The TV was flickering with an image of the President. It looked like he was in the White House press room; they must have flown him straight back after the assassination. I examined the picture closely. The black hair and moustache sat oddly on the drawn face like the stage make-up of an actor long past his time. The characteristic clasped hands hid any sign of tremor. The shift of his eyes and the uncertain pacing of his words said he was reading from a cue-board. Senile? Somewhere along that road, I thought. I turned the TV off. The speech was anodyne, directed at reassuring the populace that Big A was unharmed and his God-given mission to restore American Values would continue. No details were given of the assassination beyond confirmation that Kennedy was dead and Nixon injured. No one was blamed beyond vague enemies of the American people. My guess was they would have difficulty accepting that Charlie Joe might have acted on his own. Their mind-set naturally inclined towards conspiracies by devilish forces. In the event, I was wrong – but that was later.

I woke Dave and packed him off to his room and went to sleep myself. The following morning was another sharp, clean day. Dave said he'd decided to return to Washington, but when I told him I'd had word the Dallas DA was likely to parade the assassin to the press today, he changed his mind.

After breakfast, I took a cab to Union Station. I had a ticket but no reservation. They told me that, because of people leaving the city after American Patriots Day, they were operating a fully reserved service and could offer me nothing until the evening. I had hours to spare and had to make up my mind what to do with them. After taking coffee and reading the newspaper, which made no mention of the assassination but had a big piece on the President, my first inclination was to go to Hoover Plaza. The events of the previous day had happened too quickly for me to pick up more than a sketchy picture of the area, and I had an idea I might be able to write an atmospheric mood piece and maybe interview ordinary people, some of whom would almost certainly have been there when the shots were fired. Then I realized the place would be wrapped up tight by the GeStaPo because that's what always happens after this kind of event, and that, if I tried to interview anyone, I would certainly get stopped and my papers checked. I didn't want to fall into police hands a second time.

The choice was between watching a movie and scoping out the Municipal Building, which I didn't know but had to be close by. The first was the prudent choice but I picked the second. I reasoned that I wouldn't stand out in a crowd of journalists and TV crew, and that no one would take it amiss if I asked a few questions. It was also possible I'd catch a glimpse of Charlie Joe and hear anything he had to say. In some ways that was safer than wandering about, not knowing if he'd denounced me to his interrogators as an accomplice. At least I would be prepared.

The check-out at the lunch counter gave me directions to South Harwood Street, which was near Commerce and Main. Part of it was fenced off and a crowd was milling outside a handsome Beaux Arts building, jockeying for position so as to be close if the DA chose to wheel his man out. Part of me marveled. This wasn't the usual way the regime handled news; but if Kennedy, Nixon and Hoover were all out of action and the President was losing his grip, who was minding the store?

I flashed my press pass at a National Guardsman, who wouldn't know the difference from a soap coupon, and gained entry inside the fence. In the crush, I couldn't see Dave Kowalzyk anywhere, but Ray Bamburg spotted me and his belly came wading in my direction with Ray close behind.

'Have you ever seen anything like it?' he boomed with delight. 'Who's in control? The story is the city cops, the state cops, the FBI, the DSD and the Secret Service are like cats in a sack over who owns this thing. They say Hoover is sick – I even heard dead – which would explain. Any truth in it?'

'I hear he's sick.'

'Your FBI contact?'

'Yes.'

'Jeez!'

I wasn't sure even Hoover could deal with this. The DSD reported to the Secretary of Defense and the Secret Service to the President, and neither to the GeStaPo. I recalled Jeb telling me at one of our talks before this thing blew up, that Hoover was minded to give the DSD and Secret Service their head in managing security on American Patriots Day. Again I wondered if he'd expected something and was setting up scapegoats.

'Hey!' Ray was pointing at the fence towards the front and side of the media pen. I could hardly hear his voice over the roar. 'You want a looky-see?' He was already carving a path with his gut. I was swept along. I could see above the heads that the pack had broken through the fence line and were streaming towards the side and rear of the building, and the National Guard, not sure what their job was, had pulled back.

I didn't know why or where I was going. Probably few of us did. I was squeezed up against Ray Bamburg and, arms sweeping, he was swimming through anyone who got

340

in his way.

I shouted as loud as I could, 'What the hell is going on?'

Ray shouted back, 'Who except Jesus knows? There's a garage entrance back there – nothing else I can think of.'

Someone yelled, 'They're trying to sneak him out to County – the killer!'

'Sonofabitch!' said Ray.

The County Jail was only a few blocks away but they would have to drive him there. Everyone knew the garage was the best chance of getting a picture.

There wasn't much choice but to go with the crowd, and in Ray's wake I was drawn along towards the ramp and the garage entrance, and, once inside, the mob of reporters and camera men started heading for the doors leading to the corridors and rooms of the Municipal Building. There was an insane excitement drawn partly from the chaos of the moment and partly from the feeling that for once we were doing the job we'd aspired to do.

And then there was a shot.

I wasn't close enough to see who fired or who was hit.

Only later did I discover that a local club owner, a nobody called Jack Rubenstein, had shot and killed Alek Hidell, the assassin of Joseph Kennedy Junior.

33

Conspiracies are not meant to be understood.

The Kennedy assassination may have been the result of a conspiracy or maybe not. The Warren Commission said Alek Hidell was a narcissistic sociopath who acted alone and his intended victim was probably the President. The exiled liberals in London and Paris disagreed because they wanted to believe the regime of American Values was corrupt to its core. The right-wing cranks disagreed because they are by nature paranoid. In the end everyone found enough material to build a case that fitted their preconceptions. And no one knew the answer.

I don't know the answer either.

I didn't stick around after the shooting at the Dallas Municipal Building. I treated Jeb Lyman's earlier advice to get out of town as a warning that I was in danger. I was associated with the suspected assassin and now he had been killed. For all I knew I was also a target; it depended on whether the Secretary for Defense had been seriously injured or suffered nothing more than a scratch, which nobody could confirm. On the face of things, with Joe Kennedy Junior dead, Nixon's faction had a clear field and, despite any promises he might have made to enlist Hoover's support, I could see no good reason why he should keep the DSD off my case – especially if he had a guilty conscience and loose ends to tie up.

I spent the rest of the day holed up in a bar, waiting for the evening train. There was an air of excitement about the place and little conversation except about the killings. A couple of G-men, recognizable by their pretend-casual clothes in a blue-collar hangout, kept an ear open for any overt sedition but generally let the customers shoot their mouths off. In any case people knew the rules and were too smart to start denouncing the government. In this respect dictatorships are mostly self-policing.

This was where I picked up the name of Charlie Joe's killer. A big man in a red plaid shirt with a masonry hammer and a construction worker's helmet hanging from his belt came in. He had the red face and excited manner of someone who'd had a few already and announced to anyone who'd listen, 'Y'all hear who shot the murderin' s.o.b. who popped Joe Kennedy's boy? Only Jack Rubenstein is all!'

Unimpressed, someone asked, 'Who in hell is Jack Rubenstein?'

'Y'all ain't heard of him? Where y'all been livin'? He's the little faggot owns the Carousel Club.'

'I don't go to no Carousel Club.'

'Your old lady must love you.'

'She does. You saying the Mob is involved?'

'I'm sayin'…' The big man spotted the two GeStaPo agents. 'I ain't sayin' nothin'. Y'all gotta make your own minds up what it means, is what.' He ordered a beer and took it to a table where there were more construction crew, and the atmosphere went quiet for a while. I knew why. Since the Italian, Jewish and Irish gangs had been broken by Hoover in the thirties, the 'Mob' was a code word for the politicians who had taken over the rackets. In the name of American Values, Joe Junior, as Attorney General, had been driving a clean-up campaign in those states where the governors favored Nixon and in the course of it had made a lot of enemies. Later this was to develop into a fully-fledged theory that the assassination was payback, and that Rubenstein was a cut-out between Alek Hidell and those behind the plot. But that was in the future when there was money to be made out of theorizing and writing books.

In the here and now, someone asked, 'Who heard the shots?'

A few murmurs.

'How many? I counted three but I've been told there was four maybe five.'

This seemed a safer topic and everyone had an opinion. Most said three but the count went as high as nine. This was where I first heard about 'the grassy slope', a subject that has found its way into the literature. A fat guy who looked as though he couldn't get out of his seat said wheezily, 'I was standing on the corner of Elm near the Medical Supply Warehouse –'

A laugh and, 'Al, you ain't *stood* nowhere these past twenty years.'

'– near the Medical Supply Warehouse, and there's no way a shooter could have put three aimed shots into the President's car. On the other hand, I could see 'long the street and there's a slope with a fence on top and – I think it's a parking lot behind.'

'I know it.'

'Well, I think that's where a whole posse of gunmen could have set theirselves up and got clean away afterwards.'

Everyone agreed this was possible.

It was in this bar that I picked up the bones of the various conspiracy theories that became popular later. The detail was added by genuine and bogus witnesses and self-appointed experts, and by the time everyone had straightened out their stories and remembered the things they'd forgotten to mention years before and the charlatans and conmen had added their ten cents, the general public had no idea of the true facts. Not that it stopped them from holding an opinion.

I left the bar for the station and collected my bag from its locker. I caught my train, which was scheduled to arrive in Washington early the following morning. I'd like to say it was a comfortable ride, but there were no comfortable rides during the war years and I passed the hours to the sound of children wailing, draftees horsing around, and salesmen bullshitting like on every other long journey.

The only difference was that this time I was arrested.

It happened as I was crossing the main station concourse. Four men broke out of the crowd and picked me up as neatly as could be, with nothing more than a polite, 'We'd be grateful if you would come with us, sir.' They had the youth, the trim build and the buzz cuts I'd come to associate with the DSD. I was groggy from sleeplessness and tenser than I'd realized, which accounted for a feeling that was close to relief because here, at last, events would be taken out of my hands, even if it looked like I was going to be killed.

I was in their hands for two days. I don't know I'd have survived a third. In the event, I was spared and moved to a private room in Walter Reed with a guard on the door and medics who took care of my injuries without asking how I came by them. Jeb Lyman appeared on the fifth day.

'They told me you were fit to receive visitors,' he said. He looked glowing with his improbable Hollywood good looks.

'I was hoping for Maria.'

'You obviously haven't seen a mirror.'

Jeb had brought flowers from Laura Beth. He called a nurse for water to put them in.

He asked me, 'Have you confessed to anything I should know about?'

'No.'

'In the circumstances you'd be forgiven.'

'No.'

'Really? Well, there you go. More heroic than you make out, huh? What did you say you did during the Russian war?'

'I was a clerk at Divisional HQ. I ordered rations and toilet rolls and ran a betting syndicate.'

'Right – that's what we turned up on our background checks when you applied for a visa.' He looked for a chair, smiled and sat down. 'Still, you know how it is. We also came across a character called Henry Benoit – similar age and appearance – who was in British Special Forces. Some of our people wanted to make a connection.'

'I'm not Henry Benoit. He wouldn't have been grabbed by four kids from DSD.'

'That was my answer too. It doesn't matter.'

That was all for the first visit but he returned the next day. He told me he'd spoken with Maria and she was OK and would come to see me.

We spoke about the assassination and what followed.

'I want your take on Alek Hidell,' he said. 'There's going to be a Commission headed by Chief Justice Warren.'

'When?'

'As soon as we can tell Earl what his findings are going to be.'

'That figures.'

I gave him what I could, still keeping back what had happened at Bayou Chaud. His only comment was, 'Where do you think Hidell came by the Chevy Styleline that no one seemed to be looking for? Or his pistol? Or the wallet full of money?'

'Except for the gun, he said he won them in a card game.'

'You think that really happened?'

I didn't answer.

Jeb nodded. He said it was enough and he'd be back if he needed more. He told me the intention was to keep me out of the picture. He didn't need to say why.

We turned to other things. I asked how he had managed to find me and get me out of the hands of the Department of Defense.

'It turns out Nixon's injuries are serious. There's talk of

permanent paralysis, but they won't be sure for a few months. He hasn't resigned, but everyone expects it; and in the meantime, Defense are treading water. No one wants to make enemies at this time. We got a phone call.'

So now I knew why I was alive.

Before the next visit, I had nothing better to do than work out possible permutations behind the events at Hoover Plaza. If Charlie Joe hadn't acted alone – which I didn't discount – and Joe Kennedy Junior was all along the intended target, the obvious mastermind behind the set-up was Richard Nixon who stood to gain a clear run at the succession. I put this to Jeb.

'The only problem is that getting shot himself doesn't exactly square with that theory,' I said.

Jeb laughed in his easy way and agreed, 'Yeah, it does sound rather dumb.' Then, 'Have you heard the story that the seating arrangements in the Lincoln were changed?'

'No. Is it true?'

'We're checking. The allegation is that Nixon was supposed to sit next to Big A but switched with the Governor. If the shots came from someone placed on the grassy slope alongside Elm, Joe Junior and Connally would have shielded Nixon from the direct line of fire.'

'It's a theory – but a big risk for Nixon. Even with a safer seat, a miss or a through-shot might have hit him anyway.'

'Sometimes you have to take risks.' Jeb checked his watch. 'I have to go. Laura Beth will drop in on Maria and tell her you're doing OK.'

'Thanks.'

'It's nothing.' He rose and the folds of his expensive suit dropped out.

'You're going up in the world,' I said. He looked embarrassed, but not too much.

'The Land of Opportunity – all part of American

348

Values. And, while I remember, you heard that Hoover was sick?'

'Uh huh.'

'Yes – well he died. Heart or something.'

That's what Jeb Lyman told me and it remains the official account. J. Edgar Hoover, Director of the General State Police, after a lifetime of service to American Values, died quietly in his sleep from a long-standing heart condition. He was given a state funeral with a parade along Pennsylvania Avenue past the building that bears his name and through the Triumphal Arch celebrating the victories that have never come. He lies buried in Arlington National Cemetery.

However, there is a different version of Hoover's death that operatives in the security and intelligence fields share among themselves in Washington's bars when they've had a few drinks and feel like living dangerously. So far it hasn't appeared on the conspiracy circuit.

They say that on the Monday of Assassination Week and fully eight days before the death was reported, an FBI team from Salt Lake City flew into the capital and holed up in a cheap hotel on the Alexandria side of the Potomac without reporting to the Agency's head office. The evening of the following day, they gained entry to Hoover's house at 4936 Thirtieth Place NW, discovered the Director and Tolson in bed together, and shot them both. Afterwards they removed the bodies and cleaned the place up. Finding him absent on Wednesday morning, Hoover's staff assumed that, as planned, he had flown to Dallas for American Patriots Day, but there was a call to the Dallas bureau to the effect that Hoover was sick and wouldn't be coming. The person who made it has never been identified.

Advocates of this story say that the corpses of Hoover and Tolson were disposed of in the woods of North

Virginia and that a box of rocks was buried at Arlington. No one has ever opened up the tomb to find out.

No mention was made of Clyde Tolson after these events – not even to say he died or retired.

Was there a conspiracy? Who knows? I've lost track of the number of solutions proposed for the alleged mystery of the Kennedy assassination. If Alek Hidell hadn't been murdered by Jack Rubenstein, it's possible the fuss would have died down, but the fact is he was murdered and in a way that from the point of view of timing and drama was near perfect. To many the coincidence seems too improbable to be ascribed to chance: the dramatis personae a pair of nobodies too insignificant to bear the weight of the tragedy.

If there is no conspiracy, the assassination of Kennedy is without meaning, a casual death like a road accident or an old man expiring in a nursing home. If there is no conspiracy, History is the working out of impersonal processes and random events, and human fate has no shape or purpose. If there is no conspiracy, there is no God.

The investigators have been thorough if not always accurate. They have gone over Alek Hidell's career as a Marine and uncovered his alias as Charlie Joe Svensen. They have also made the connection between that name and the 'Charlie Joe Svensen' whose papers were picked up among the car wreckage at the Arc of Hope, but whose body was never found. They reject the story that the false identity was being used by one of those who died at the scene and say instead that the GeStaPo are shielding one of their own: that Hidell/Svensen was an FBI agent used to penetrate the Washington terrorist cell and also the militias in the Northwest and who knows what else?

Support for this version of events is found in the detail of Hidell's last days, when he seems to have gone on an otherwise inexplicable journey, wandering from Oregon by an indirect route to Las Vegas, then to New Orleans, and then off the face of the earth until he appeared in Dallas. For all or part of that time he was in the company of a man aged forty or so, who may have been Canadian or Australian or English, and who went under various identities. This man has been named by at least one investigator as Henry Benoit, said to be a former soldier and gun for hire. It is said, based on witness testimony, that he was present under an alias at both the assassination of Kennedy and the shooting of Alek Hidell. The most vociferous defenders of Hidell's innocence maintain that Benoit was in fact responsible for both killings, but his role has been covered up by the politicians behind the conspiracy.

I can't say if Henry Benoit exists or not. But – as I told Jeb Lyman – I am not him.

If there was a conspiracy, there is a Latin tag that may lead to the conspirators.

Cui bono? Who benefits?

Nixon received a bullet to the spine that left him a paraplegic. He resigned his position as Secretary of Defense and died twelve months later without taking further part in public affairs. The vacancy at Defense was taken by Joe Kennedy Junior's younger brother, JFK, and Bobby stepped into the position of Attorney General. The youngest brother, Teddy, became his deputy.

In December 1963, Big A announced that he wouldn't stand for the Presidency in 1964. As usual, the parties put forward candidates – a Texan called Johnson for the Democrats and an Arizonan called Goldwater for the Republicans – and as usual the NSDAP brokered a unity candidate who was duly adopted. The Old Man died a year into his retirement, when they tell me his mind was all but gone. After the ballyhoo of a state funeral and the unveiling of his monument, his memory vanished and he became a face on a banknote along with all the other presidents who are little more than the fictions we tell about our history. In public, Big A is neither praised nor condemned. He has become the abusive father whose actions cannot be admitted because we feel our own guilt: our inadequacy as moral human beings able to recognize evil and willing to fight it.

John Fitzgerald Kennedy became thirty-third President of the United States with Bobby as his VP. His victory was helped by my friend, Jubal Nephi Lyman, who was promoted to Director of the General State Police.

After JFK's election, I was made head of the Federal News Bureau on condition that I became an American citizen.

It is a curse of humanity that we value symbols more than the reality they are supposed to represent. We worship Jesus, who preached to the poor, but we despise the poor for their idle fecklessness. Every politician, journalist, religious huckster and charlatan knows he must manipulate our symbols if he wants to lead us by the nose.

Big A appropriated American Values and turned them to his purpose. He owned the words so they had no meaning except the one he gave them; and though he is gone they still survive because we have too much invested in them. As his successors, our job has not been to do away with American Values but to redefine them so that, after the darkness of decades, they represent our aspirations not our fears. But don't mistake me. We are not good men. We are too compromised for that. Our small claim to virtue is only that we are better than those who came before us, even though we were complicit in their crimes – indeed it is our complicity that equips us for the task because we are changing the thing we helped create.

Slowly the wars in Central and South America are coming to an end. In most places ceasefires are in effect and the soldiers have been brought home. Where we can, we leave behind sympathetic governments, but as often as not they collapse within months and others take up the burden of finding remedies to the chaos and destruction. It is a ragged peace marked by bitterness, suspicion and civil strife, but it is peace of a sort.

The prisons and labor camps have been largely emptied except for regular felons. The inmates have gone home to make the best of their broken lives. Indentured labor has been ended; chain gangs are no longer seen in the countryside and labor pens have vanished from our railroad and bus stations. The Supreme Court reversed its earlier judgment and discovered that the system is contrary to the Thirteenth Amendment – the one about slavery – and always was.

All the changes are partial and imperfect; marked by failures as well as successes. Homosexuality is still illegal because it is plainly contrary to Leviticus 18:22 and a bunch of other texts, or so they tell me. On the other hand, most years the lynchings are in single figures. Tee Antoine's people have vanished from Bayou Chaud. I can find no trace of them and fear the worst.

Among our successes, jazz is now permitted, but tastes have moved on and no one listens to it much. Most books are freely available and, if you know where to look, you can buy those about the famous conspiracy to assassinate Kennedy – even the ones naming Henry Benoit as the killer. Censorship is in place, but I like to think I administer it with a light touch through the Federal News Bureau.

Why is there still censorship? For that matter, why are the political parties still tightly controlled, and why is the GeStaPo still in business even if milder than it used to be? The answer to those questions lies in the way our revolution in American Values has come about – the story of this book, in fact. The fear of those who lead it is that, if people were told in full what was done by us in their name, they would tear us apart rather than admit the terrible truth.

We did only what, in the unexamined corners of their hearts, they secretly wanted – provided that they did not have to do it themselves.

I was released from Walter Reed. Maria met me and we took the bus home because, like most Americans in the cities, we did not have a car. We hadn't terminated the lease and so we moved back into our apartment. We still live there, despite my promotion and my fancy connections, because Maria remains a nurse and you don't give up a rent-controlled apartment in Washington.

We married but our age meant we never had children. I have kids in England; Maria once had a son but he died. We have a lot of free time when she is not working shifts, and we go dancing at a few clubs where they play swing music and people who like the fashions of the wartime years pretend to the youth they lost because of the conflict.

I haven't asked her what she knows or believes about my role and that of Charlie Joe Svensen who was apparently called Alek Hidell. I don't know if I would tell the truth or lies, or even if the truth would be believed. For her part, she is a woman and for this reason never expects a man to tell the whole truth, even if he is the man she loves.

In the end, we all of us live by compromise. Love makes this possible.

It is a principle of American Values that everyone has a second chance. All it takes is effort. But this isn't so. We may seek to remedy the evils we have done, but they remain as scars on our history that we carry for ever, and nothing is made wholly new. We cannot return to innocence.

Everyone knows there are no blacks in America, where

once there were millions. It was the mystery that confronted me when I became involved in the events that I've described. In time, I was able to put the question to Jeb Lyman and he asked me, as a friend, if I really wanted to know the answer. I said that I did, and he told me. It was an answer filled with horror, and some of that horror lay in the fact that I had already known what he would tell me. You know it too.

Everyone knows that there are no blacks in America.

And they are never coming back.

Readers' Notes

I did not write *American Values* with Donald Trump in mind. Rather I came up with the idea 20 years ago and began writing when his presidential success was inconceivable. Indeed, even now my focus is not on the President/Dictator – called 'Big A' in the text – but on the compromises people are forced to make in order to live under a dictatorship, and the problems of succession following a period of tyranny – think of Russia after the fall of the USSR, Iraq after Saddam Hussein, Libya after Gadhafi. However, if you think I show any degree of prescience, it isn't for the first time. Three of my previous books – *The Hitler Diaries*, *Farewell to Russia* and *Anti-Soviet Activities* – have all to some degree come true. I could make extravagant claims but in fact I put it down to coincidence, though admittedly an odd one. It explains the *Sunday Telegraph*'s (presumably ironic) comment that I am 'the author journalists read for their next scoop'.

The location of the action in the United States should not be understood as a sign of hostility towards America. It is simply a fact that plots have to be set somewhere, and only the United States offered a large enough canvas for the theme. I do not think that America is especially vulnerable to the installation of a populist dictator. History shows that it survived the likes of Huey Long in the 1930s, and there are reasons to suppose its institutions are robust enough to curtail Trump's worst instincts, though not without damage.

In the same vein, I do not wish to attack American values more than those of any other country. I find them absurd in their pretensions, but not uniquely so. 'British values' are equally ridiculous, and probably the same holds for those of every nation that has a history long enough to form a myth about itself. The British Empire was not created out of 'a civilizing mission'. Britain did not stand alone and was not the major player in the defeat of Nazi Germany, though its performance was creditable enough. On their face such national 'values' have a use in motivating populations to positive action. But as often as not they are captured by demagogues, who use their alleged 'defense' as grounds for extreme measures both internally and in foreign affairs, and it is this perversion of values that interests me.

I chose 'American Values' as the name of Big A's ideology because Nazism comes with very specific German associations. We can imagine the latter as an *imposed* system, as in *The Man in the High Castle*, but black-uniformed SS troopers goose-stepping down Pennsylvania Avenue are not something that would emerge naturally from American culture and for that reason not credible. What we must bear in mind, however, is that Nazism expresses dictatorship only in a historically specific form suited to Germany in the 1930s and it is a distraction to focus on its outward trappings in order to convince ourselves that 'it couldn't happen here'. Nazism seduced a large section of German society, and the same thing, dressed up in American flim-flam, could work in the United States – or, indeed, in Britain. I have tried to describe it in a believable form.

We tend to think of Adolf Hitler as almost supernaturally evil. This is partly because the Nazis presented themselves with much of the symbolism of a death cult. In reality the scale of his human rights abuses, even including the Holocaust, was probably lower than that of both Stalin and Mao, if only because his activities were cut short. Most of the deaths associated with his regime arose from warfare.

He fell not because he was a monster – though he was – but because there was no living with him: he attacked those who were to bring him down and gave them no choice. It is a terrible thought, but, if he had confined himself to Germany, he could probably have massacred its Jews with impunity.

Hitler could have survived to old age, and in *American Values* he does. This is because his aggression is confined to the Americas without intruding into the spheres of the only Powers who might have destroyed him. Indeed – and this is a chilling thought – a Power that *could* have brought the United States down does not exist either in the present or in my fictitious world. The identification of Big A with Hitler highlights this point, that the latter's downfall was dependent on historical context.

Turning to technical aspects, you may notice that, on three critical occasions, I lead Readers to a certain point and then leave them to draw their own conclusions. Specifically: 'Big A' is never named as Adolf Hitler though all the indicators of his identity are given; and similarly, Charlie Joe Svensen/Alek Hidell fulfils the role of Lee Harvey Oswald but Readers are left to infer that they are the same person. Finally, the ultimate fate of African-Americans – though known to the Narrator – is never expressly stated to the Reader. This reticence is intentional. Here are the reasons.

Concerning Big A, I use his identification with Hitler to draw attention to the effect of cultural and historical factors on his career as I've tried to explain above. However, once that identity is established, I do not want it to act as a distraction – a constant reminder that this story is fiction – which would be the case if it were always at the forefront of the Reader's mind. So my object is to pull off a delicate artistic trick: to remind Readers of Hitler for the purpose of the book's subtext, only to make them forget him for the purpose of the unfolding narrative.

In the case of Charlie Joe Svensen / Oswald, the reasons are different. While the Big A / Hitler identification is made clear from the book's opening, that between Charlie Joe Svensen and Lee Harvey Oswald is far less upfront. Except for those Readers who know that Alek Hidell was an alias actually used by Oswald, it will not become apparent until well into the second part of the book as the focus begins to shift to Dallas. The explanation of this difference is that the Hitler disclosure is essential to establish the basic background i.e. to tell Readers at the outset that the action takes place in a fascist state. In contrast, the Kennedy assassination is not background: it is an event occurring as part of the plot, and a key revelation that is intended to surprise Readers. Accordingly, the object of my writing is to set down all the evidence necessary to make the Svensen / Oswald identity plausible, while withholding the final revelation until it has the maximum dramatic effect.

That leaves the matter of the fate of African-Americans. Here the reasons for my reticence are partly artistic and partly ethical. The artistic reason is simple. Silence keeps readers in suspense and allows them to speculate. Often horror lies more in what we imagine than what is said – only you can decide. My ethical reservation stems from the difference between fiction and life. In *American Values* the genocide of America's people of color is implied but never explicitly stated and other explanations are possible. This 'solution' to the mystery hints at the Holocaust but no more, and I have made no attempt to call on images of the fate of Jewish people in a real tragedy in order to exploit them to illustrate a fictitious one. It is a question of showing decent respect.

Readers may notice that *American Values* puts two superficially unrelated alternative histories together:

namely a fascist America and a new take on the Kennedy assassination. Structurally they are joined by making the assassination serve as the key event in effecting the transition to the world after Big A's dictatorship, but the connection is an artifice, not inherent in the material. So why both?

Framing the narrative and coloring its interpretation is the repeated statement: *Conspiracies are not meant to be understood*. Here there are two: namely the struggle between the Nixon and Kennedy factions over the presidential succession, and the assassination of Kennedy. I say 'two' because, though these storylines appear connected, it could be that the assassination is not the result of a conspiracy to succeed Big A but a fortuitous action by a lone sociopath: nothing more than a coincidence. The Narrator tells Readers that he does not know the answer.

This is another instance of reticence on my part, intended to engage your imagination to fill in the blank with your own conclusion. It won't be easy. Whether you opt for the conspiracy or the lone gunman theory, you will find it difficult to reconcile all the facts or make either solution wholly convincing. There will always be stray details that do not seem to fit. This uncertainty reflects that surrounding the actual Kennedy assassination: the numerous conspiracy theories and the doubtful state of much of the evidence. My personal belief – not that it should affect yours – is that Oswald acted alone and there was no conspiracy. But what is more significant and of interest to me, is that the conspiracy theories are myriad and contradictory. They cannot all be true. What conclusion are we to draw from this?

American Values is full of instances of the capacity of human beings to hold irrational views of the world to cope with inner anxieties. Examples are the belief of Big A's supporters in his paranoid racist ideology, and that of his opponents in the militias with their fantasy of a secret black army kept in reserve by the New World Order. Most of all it is evident in the incoherent thinking of Charlie Joe Svensen. In the real world, Oswald claimed to be a communist, but I doubt that communism was a significant contributor to his behavior. The indicators are that it was no more than a way of framing his alienation, and, if he were alive today, I could easily imagine his joining an Islamic jihad. For this reason, in my fictitious world, I have no problem in giving Charlie Joe different beliefs to the historical Oswald. To put the point more generally, I think that irrational thinking as a coping strategy in a mystifying world explains most conspiracy theories including the 9/11 tragedy and the Moon Landing. This forms the unifying theme linking all the plotlines of the present book.

Finally I wish to thank, in no particular order, those who have helped me and kept faith with my writing: Mark and Adrienne Turner, 'Toots' Eveleigh, Sue Webb, and Miranda Ingram.

Jim Williams

June 2017

If you enjoyed reading *American Values* then please share your reflections with others by posting a review online.

Connect with Jim Williams and Marble City Publishing

http://www.jimwilliamsbooks.com/

http://www.marblecitypublishing.com

Join Marble City's list for updates on new releases by Jim Williams at http://eepurl.com/vek5L or scan the QR code below:

Follow on Twitter:

http://twitter.com/MarbleCityPub

Other Marble City releases by Jim Williams

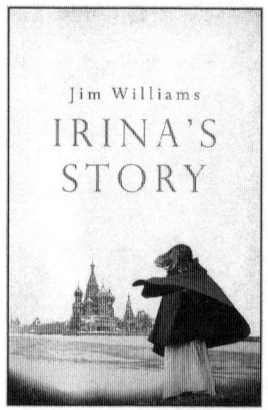

At the age of 90, Irina Uspenskaya is the last surviving witness of these events. In her Moscow apartment, while her young relative Slavochka and his friends in "the International Syndicate" aspire to become successful drug dealers, Irina collects the letters and diaries of her parents' generation and sets down the tale of what happened to them all.

In turn she describes the doomed marriage of her father Nikolai and her mother Xenia, who love but never understand each other; her idealistic aunt Adalia, who marries the sinister Grodsky; her disreputable uncle Alexander and his feisty wife Tatiana. These and a host of other colourful characters populate the story and we see their world through their eyes and understand it through their thoughts and writings.

Our guide, Irina is wry, funny, insightful and humane. Born with a disability, she views events through detached yet sympathetic eyes and reflects on her own history and her unrequited love for a boy she met as a little girl and the family and children she will never have.

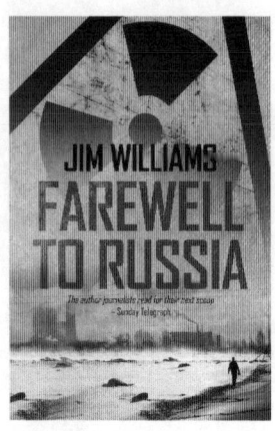

The unthinkable has happened at the Soviet nuclear plant at Sokolskoye. An accident of such terrifying proportions, of such catastrophic ecological and political consequence that a curtain of silence is drawn ominously over the incident. Major Pyotr Kirov of the KGB is appointed to extract the truth from the treacherous minefield of misinformation and intrigue and to obtain from the West the technology essential to prevent further damage. But the vital equipment is under strict trade embargo….

And in London, George Twist, head of a company which manufactures the technology, is on the verge of bankruptcy and desperate to win the illegal contract. Can he deliver on time? Will he survive a frantic smuggling operation across the frozen wastes of Finland? Can he wrong-foot the authorities … and his own conscience? Is it possible to say farewell to Russia?

Farewell to Russia is the first of Jim Williams's astonishingly prophetic novels about the decline and fall of the Soviet Union.

For Colonel Pyotr Andreevitch Kirov there is only one inescapable truth in modern Russia – if the old order does not change, it is impossible to bury the past.

When Kirov's routine investigation into black market antibiotics is linked to the former head of the KGB – and Kirov himself is put under investigation by his own men – the course for collision is set.

As the old and new factions in the Soviet machine grapple for power, the stock in trade is the hardest currency known to the Socialist Republic … murder. Will Mikhail Gorbachev share the same fate?

Anti-Soviet Activities is the second of Jim Williams's astonishingly prophetic novels about the decline and fall of the Soviet Union.

A stunning literary prophecy! The international bestseller that caused a sensation when it was published 9 months before the famous Hitler Diaries forgery scandal.

A French aristocrat and his mistress are murdered. A mysterious businessman offers the Fuehrer's diaries to a new York publishing house. Are they a hoax or a record of terrifying truth? A controversial historian and his beautiful assistant are commissioned to find out the answer following a trail that draws them into a terrifying web of conspiracy and slaughter as competing forces fight to publish or suppress Hitler's account of the War and of secret negotiations with his enemies.

But are the Diaries genuine or just a plot to destabilise contemporary politics? A shattering revision of history whose revelation must be prevented at all costs: or a fake, just a sinister manoeuvre in the Cold War?

If the Hitler Diaries are authentic, then who left the bunker alive?

A disillusioned soldier looks for love. An exiled Emperor fears assassination. Agatha Christie takes a holiday. And George Bernard Shaw learns to tango.

In the aftermath of World War I, Michael Pinfold a disillusioned ex-soldier tries to rescue his failing family wine business on the island of Madeira. In a villa in the hills the exiled Austrian Emperor lives in fear of assassination by Hungarian killers, while in Reid's Hotel, a well-known lady crime novelist is stranded on her way to South Africa and George Bernard Shaw whiles away his days corresponding with his friends, writing a one act play and learning to tango with the hotel manager's spouse.

A stranger, Robinson, is found murdered and Michael finds himself manipulated into investigating the crime by his sinister best friend, Johnny Cardozo, the local police chief, with whose wife he is pursuing an arid love affair; manipulated, too, by Father Flaherty, a priest with dubious political interests, and by his own eccentric parent, who claims to have been part of a comedy duo that once entertained the Kaiser with Jewish jokes. Will Michael find love? Will the Emperor escape his would-be killers? Will any of the characters learn the true meaning of the tango?

The poet Shelley wasn't murdered. This book tells you whodunit.

A group of glamorous English socialites spend the summer of 1930 holidaying on the Italian Riviera where the poet Shelley died in a sailing accident in 1822. To pass the time, they tell amusing stories, much as Shelley, Byron and their friends had done a century earlier. For their theme they choose the death of Shelley and the stories progress towards a solution to the "murder mystery". Yet is that truly what the stories are about? Or, despite their witty surface, are they a code for dark and dangerous secrets hidden behind an urbane façade?

Guy Parrot, a naive young doctor, finds himself falling in love with the beautiful and enigmatic Julia, the truth of whose past flickers between the lines of the stories, tantalising both Guy and the Reader. Guy discovers that truth, and its terrible reality leads to two murders and the destruction of his happiness and sanity.

In 1945, in the aftermath of war, Guy returns to Italy with the army and is given an opportunity to re-examine the events of fifteen years before. This time will he understand what happened and finally redeem himself?

"A skilful exercise, bizarre and dangerous in a lineage that includes Fowles' *The Magus*."

Guardian

You get to be a lot of people when you are a vampire.

Meet old Harry Haze: war criminal, Jewish stand-up comedian, friend of Marcel Proust and J. Edgar Hoover. John Harper encounters him while spending the summer in the South of France with his mistress Lucy, and is entranced by Harry's stories of his fabulous past. Then Lucy disappears without explanation and both John and Harry fall under suspicion.

Yet how are we to know the truth when it is hidden in the labyrinth of Harry's bizarre memories and John's guilt at abandoning his wife? Nothing in this story is certain. Is Lucy dead? Is Harry a harmless old druggie or really a vampire? Deep inside his humorous tales is the suppressed memory of a night of sheer horror. And it is possible that one of the two men is an insane killer.

Summer 1941. France is occupied by the Germans but the United States is not at war. Four glamorous young Americans find themselves whiling away the hot days in the boredom of a small Riviera town, while in a half-abandoned mansion nearby, Teresa and Katerina Malipiero, a mother and daughter, wait for Señor Malipiero to complete his business in the Reich and take them home to Argentina.

The plight of the women attracts the sympathy of 'Lucky' Tom Rensselaer and he is seduced by the beauty of Katerina. Tom has perfect faith in their innocence, yet they cannot explain why a sinister Spaniard has been murdered in their home and why Tom must help them dispose of the body without informing the police.

Watching over events is Pat Byrne, a young Irish writer. Twenty years later, when Tom has been reduced from the most handsome, admired and talented man of his generation to a derelict alcoholic, Pat sets out to discover the facts of that fateful summer: the secrets that were hidden and the lies that were told. It is a shocking truth: a tale of murder unpunished and a good man destroyed by those who loved him most.

MEET two unusual detectives. Ludovico – a young man who has had his testicles cut off for the sake of opera. And Monsieur Arouet – a fraudster, or just possibly the philosopher Voltaire.

VISIT the setting. Carnival time in mid-18th century Venice, a city of winter mists, and the season of masquerade and decadence.

ENCOUNTER a Venetian underworld of pimps, harlots, gamblers, forgers and charlatans.

BEWARE of a mysterious coterie of aristocrats, Jesuits, Freemasons and magicians.

DISCOVER a murder: that of the nobleman, Sgr Alessandro Molin, found swinging from a bridge with his innards hanging out and a message in code from his killer.

Scherzo is a murder mystery of sparkling vivacity and an historical novel of stunning originality told with a wit and style highly praised by critics and nominated for the Booker Prize.

Janet Bretherton, a widow at 60, suspected of her husband's murder and involvement in the fraud which brought his company down, exiles herself to Puybrun, a small village in a picturesque corner of south-west France, where she nurses her grief and tries to rebuild her shattered world. She meets six other Englishwomen who live the expatriate life. Earthy has fled from a hippy camp in a damp corner of Wales. Carol claims to have slept with every man in the world called Dave. Belle has a husband, Charlie, who may or may not be real because no one has ever seen him. Joy is married to the appalling Arnold. And Veronica and Poppy try to discover the basis for the love they have for each other. The women form a group in which they take turns to teach each other the lessons life has taught them. At the same time, they grow more confident and gradually reveal the secrets of their pasts.

When Janet finds she has attracted the attention of Leon, thirty years younger than she is, yet seems to find her still sexually desirable as he invites her to go dancing with him, she asks herself: What are his real motives? And does she care? In the end, the process of discovery reveals a terrible secret which forces the women to decide how much they love each other: how far they can rely upon each other … even when the question is one of murder.

In the pretty Devonshire town of Dartcross an elderly lady diarist struggles with her memory to write a history of her colourful past, her hateful cat and her murderous husband. At the same time, Janet Bretherton and her friend Belle try to discover a purpose to their retirement. Is it enough to discuss the latest novels in their readers' group, go to the theatre or attend a séance? Perhaps, instead, they should try to solve the mystery of the dead Polish man whose body is found by the river?

The Demented Lady Detectives' Club is both a whodunit and a funny yet poignant account of a group of women growing old and seeking love and meaning in both the past and the present. The unnamed lady diarist finally faces up to the horror she has buried in her memory and the love she has lost. And Janet has to deal with the tender feelings she is still capable of evoking in a man who is twenty years her junior.

Lord T'ien Huang controls the universe through poetry, telepathy and the violence of his insane Angels. His subjects consider him to be God. Emperor of a universe ruled by the Ch'ang, immortal but not invulnerable, his interest is aroused by Sebastian, a novice monk on the remote and wasted planet of Lu, who can see and speak to God. Should he destroy the boy or toy with him?

Sebastian is rescued from the Lord T'ien Huang's avenging Angels by Mapmaker, an ancient Old Before the Fall with a forgotten history of betrayal, and they journey to the snowbound north. They are accompanied by Velikka Magdasdottir, a girl belonging to the Hengstmijster tribe of warrior herdswomen who maintain a veiled harem of husbands.

In the frozen wastes they encounter the remains of the Ingitkuk who rebelled against the Ch'ang in antiquity and lost their witch princess, She Whom the Reindeer Love. Mapmaker knew her when she died half a millennium ago as Her Breath Is Of Jasmine.

Will Mapmaker lead Sebastian, the Hengstmijster and the Ingitkuk to their doom against the Ch'ang? Can Sebastian master his own powers? How will they survive against the Angel Michael, thawed and frozen more times than he can recall, with his power to destroy humanity by the billion?